THE COMPLEAT ANGLER

IZAAK WALTON (1593–1683), angler and biographer, was born in Stafford, the son of an alehouse-keeper and his wife. He attended grammar school in Stafford and then became a linen draper and garment-maker in London. Walton's long life was marked by wide reading, an unwavering devotion to the Church of England, and a remarkable talent for friendship. Already known in literary circles by the age of twenty, Walton was a parishioner and later the biographer of John Donne, and he would go on to write the *Lives* of other notable Anglicans, including George Herbert and Richard Hooker. The Civil Wars and Interregnum tested Walton's ideals: he participated in a royalist conspiracy after the battle of Worcester, and in *The Compleat Angler* (first published in 1653), Walton expressed his political and religious allegiances while exploring humanity's relationship to the natural world. After the Restoration, Walton joined the household of his friend George Morley, who became the bishop of Worcester and then the bishop of Winchester. Walton was buried in Winchester Cathedral, where he is now commemorated by a stained-glass window in the Fishermen's Chapel.

CHARLES COTTON (1630–87), country gentleman, poet and translator, was born at Beresford Hall, Staffordshire, by the River Dove, where he built a fishing house for himself and Walton. Cotton's many works include *The Wonders of the Peake* (a topographical poem), *Scarronides* (a popular burlesque of Virgil) and his highly regarded translation of Montaigne's *Essays*. In 1676, at Walton's invitation, he wrote the second part to *The Compleat Angler*.

MARJORIE SWANN, Professor of English at Hendrix College, Arkansas, grew up fishing for perch and pike on St Joseph Island, Ontario. She subsequently earned degrees at Queen's University and Oxford. She is the author of *Curiosities and Texts: The Culture of Collecting in Early Modern England* (2001) and is now writing a book about Walton's *Angler* and its post-seventeenth-century afterlives.

OXFORD WORLD'S CLASSICS

For over 100 years Oxford World's Classics have brought readers closer to the world's great literature. Now with over 700 titles—from the 4,000-year-old myths of Mesopotamia to the twentieth century's greatest novels—the series makes available lesser-known as well as celebrated writing.

The pocket-sized hardbacks of the early years contained introductions by Virginia Woolf, T. S. Eliot, Graham Greene, and other literary figures which enriched the experience of reading. Today the series is recognized for its fine scholarship and reliability in texts that span world literature, drama and poetry, religion, philosophy, and politics. Each edition includes perceptive commentary and essential background information to meet the changing needs of readers.

OXFORD WORLD'S CLASSICS

IZAAK WALTON AND
CHARLES COTTON

The Compleat Angler

Edited with an Introduction and Notes by
MARJORIE SWANN

OXFORD
UNIVERSITY PRESS

OXFORD
UNIVERSITY PRESS

Great Clarendon Street, Oxford, OX2 6DP,
United Kingdom

Oxford University Press is a department of the University of Oxford.
It furthers the University's objective of excellence in research, scholarship,
and education by publishing worldwide. Oxford is a registered trade mark of
Oxford University Press in the UK and in certain other countries

Editorial material © Marjorie Swann 2014

The moral rights of the author have been asserted

First published 2014
First published as an Oxford World's Classics paperback 2016
Impression: 7

Published in the United States of America by Oxford University Press
198 Madison Avenue, New York, NY 10016, United States of America

British Library Cataloguing in Publication Data
Data available

Library of Congress Control Number: 2015941612

ISBN 978–0–19–874546–4

Printed and bound in Great Britain by Clays Ltd, Elcograf S.p.A.

CONTENTS

INTRODUCTION

IF you want to curl up with a good book on 'a rainy evening', says Izaak Walton, look no further (p. 7). For more than three and a half centuries, readers from all walks of life around the globe have responded to this gentle invitation in astonishing numbers. The most famous work in the literature of sport, *The Compleat Angler* ranks second only to the King James Bible as the most frequently reprinted book in the English language.[1] Ever since it first appeared in 1653, Walton's book has been remarkably popular. Walton published a total of five editions of the *Angler* during his lifetime, and by the time the last version was printed in 1676, he had greatly expanded the work, adding not only material about fishing, but also more poems and amusing anecdotes to increase the book's provision of *'innocent, harmless mirth'* (p. 5). For the fifth and final edition, Walton enlisted the aid of his good friend and angling companion, Charles Cotton, who wrote a pioneering fly-fishing treatise as Part II of *The Compleat Angler*, a work that is now regarded as a classic in its own right.[2] Several months before Walton celebrated his ninetieth birthday, the poet Thomas Flatman described him as a 'Happy Old Man, whose worth all mankind knows',[3] and the success of *The Compleat Angler* was an important source of Walton's widespread esteem.

Walton was neither the first nor the last writer in early modern England to publish a book about angling. He himself borrowed extensively from other fishing manuals,[4] and the genre has continued to flourish long after Walton's death. Yet Walton has achieved a unique stature as an angling writer. Since the first posthumous

---

[1] David Novarr, rev. of *The Compleat Angler 1653–1676* by Izaak Walton, ed. Jonquil Bevan, *Modern Language Review*, 80 (1985), 122.

[2] 'Its instructions remain to this day the best ever penned for fishing the clear and narrow waters of the upper Dove' (Gerald G. P. Heywood, *Charles Cotton and His River* (Manchester, 1928), 9).

[3] Thomas Flatman, 'To my worthy friend Mr. Isaac Walton', in *Thealma and Clearchus*, by John Chalkhill, ed. Izaak Walton (London, 1683), A4ʳ.

[4] See Jonquil Bevan's detailed analysis of Walton's borrowings from other angling treatises in her introduction to *The Compleat Angler 1653–1676*, by Izaak Walton, ed. Bevan (Oxford, 1983), 15–24.

version of the *Angler* was issued in 1750, the text has been almost constantly in print. The readership of Walton's beloved book has spanned generations, oceans, and cultures, and the hundreds of editions of *The Compleat Angler* published over the years include translations into French, Danish, Norwegian, Dutch, Chinese, German, Finnish, Spanish, Korean, Swedish, and Japanese. Enthusiasm for *The Compleat Angler* has always been grass roots: unlike the works of Shakespeare, whose ongoing cultural survival has been ensured by their place in school and university curricula, Walton's book has been embraced by a strictly voluntary readership. As Walton intended, the *Angler* offers something for everyone. Thanks to his voracious reading and love of literature, Walton's book is not only a 'compleat' guide for fishermen: it is also an anthology of verse penned by the likes of Christopher Marlowe, John Donne, and George Herbert, as well as a treasure trove of the wisdom of writers ranging from Pliny to Montaigne. Today, Izaak Walton is regarded as the patron saint of recreational fishermen and outdoors enthusiasts, but as historian Richard C. Hoffmann observes, Walton is also 'the only writer on fishing whose name even non-anglers recognize'.[5] As it has done since 1653, *The Compleat Angler* continues to engage a great diversity of readers because it offers a uniquely accessible and compelling vision of human existence.

The Compleat Angler tells what is, on the face of it, a simple story: two urbanites take a break from work and go on a fishing trip. But for Izaak Walton in 1653, nothing was simple. Walton places a fictionalized version of himself at the centre of his narrative, and Walton's own experience of the English civil wars and their aftermath decisively shapes his book. The civil wars which convulsed England from 1640 to 1651 pitted different concepts of political and religious order against each other. The entire population suffered from the violence and upheaval of these years, but for supporters of the king and the Established Church like Walton, the results were catastrophic. On 30 January 1649, King Charles I was executed—murdered by his own people. Shortly after the regicide, the monarchy and the House of Lords were abolished, and on 19 May 1649, England became a commonwealth. Just weeks before *The Compleat Angler* was published in the spring of 1653, Oliver Cromwell, soon to be named Lord

---

[5] Richard C. Hoffmann, *Fishers' Craft and Lettered Art: Tracts on Fishing from the End of the Middle Ages* (Toronto, 1997), 25 n. 13.

Protector, eradicated the final vestige of England's pre-war system of government when he dissolved the last remnant of the Long Parliament. In tandem with the escalation of this political crisis, religious reformers—Puritans—who believed that the Church of England was insufficiently Protestant sought to purge it of popishness. Thus by the time Charles I mounted the scaffold at Whitehall, the archbishop of Canterbury, William Laud, had been executed for treason, the episcopal Church had been dismantled, a quarter of all ministers had been ejected from their livings, the Book of Common Prayer had been abolished, and celebrations of traditional holidays—including Christmas—had been banned.[6] The human cost of this political and religious turmoil was staggering: 180,000 people (3 per cent of the population) died during the civil wars—a far higher death-rate than England would suffer during either of the world wars of the twentieth century—and tens of thousands of men were left wounded or maimed.[7]

Walton had actively—indeed, daringly—supported the royalist cause in its bleakest moments. Cromwell and his troops had crushed the Scottish army led by Charles II in a matter of hours at Worcester on 3 September 1651. As the 21-year-old king fled for his life, he entrusted his Lesser George—a medal which symbolized Charles's leadership of the Order of the Garter—to one of his attendants, Colonel Thomas Blague. Blague took shelter at the home of royalist sympathizers near Stafford, where he hid the king's George 'under a heap of dust and chips'.[8] After Blague was captured and imprisoned in the Tower of London, the fate of Charles's powerfully symbolic medal depended solely on the courage and resourcefulness of a network of Staffordshire royalists. The medal was retrieved from its hiding place and passed to Robert Milward, who was 'then a Prisoner to the Parliament, in the Garrison of *Stafford*'.[9] Milward needed a trustworthy courier with nerves of steel who could first pocket the king's George under the noses of the soldiers at Stafford and then deliver it to Colonel Blague in the Tower of London.

[6] John Morrill, *The Nature of the English Revolution* (London and New York, 1993), 14–18.

[7] Ian Gentles, *The English Revolution and the Wars in the Three Kingdoms, 1638–1652* (Harlow, 2007), 436–7.

[8] Robert Plot, *The Natural History of Stafford-shire* (London, 1686), 311.

[9] Elias Ashmole, *The Institution, Laws & Ceremonies of the Most Noble Order of the Garter* (London, 1672), 228.

Milward enlisted a man unlikely to arouse any suspicion: a 58-year-old linen draper and sempster,[10] born and raised in Stafford, who had lived in London for decades. And so, during the nadir of the royalist cause in the autumn of 1651, Izaak Walton quietly spirited the king's Lesser George out of his garrisoned home town of Stafford and carried it to the imprisoned Colonel Blague in London. After he had received the medal from Walton, Blague escaped from the Tower, secured passage to France, and personally returned the George to Charles II. Facing prison or the gallows if his treachery had been discovered,[11] Walton had put his life on the line as a royalist agent.

Walton's audacious participation in the nightmare of England's civil wars came on the heels of a long period of personal grief. Walton's first wife, Rachel Floud, had died in 1640, several weeks after giving birth to the couple's seventh child, Anne. All of the Waltons' previous six children—including their first-born, a son named Izaak—predeceased their mother, and baby Anne later died just a couple of months short of her second birthday. In 1647, Walton married his second wife, Anne Ken; their first and third children, a daughter and a son, would survive to adulthood, but their second child—born in 1650 and given his father's name—died after only four months of life. So when he published *The Compleat Angler* in the spring of 1653, the foundations of Izaak Walton's identity—as a royalist, an Anglican, a husband and a father—had been profoundly shaken. Walton's story of vacationing fishermen thus embodies his artistic response to trauma, a search for meaning and hope in the wake of terrible anguish. Born of national tragedy and personal sorrow, *The Compleat Angler* presents Walton's deeply felt response to a universal question: How should we live? As a survivor of war and heartbreak, Walton turned to the natural world for his answer to this question and in the process created one of the most important, formative environmental texts in the English language.[12]

---

[10] A draper and sempster both sold cloth and sewed garments.

[11] Geoffrey Smith, *Royalist Agents, Conspirators and Spies* (Farnham, Surrey, and Burlington, VT, 2011), 6–7.

[12] Lawrence Buell coins the term 'environmental text' in *The Environmental Imagination: Thoreau, Nature Writing, and the Formation of American Culture* (Cambridge, MA, 1995), 7–8.

The Brotherhood of the Angle

The Compleat Angler depicts the education of a novice fisherman by an experienced angler, with the countryside north of London serving as the men's outdoor classroom. As the book opens, three strangers—Piscator (Fisherman), Venator (Hunter), and Auceps (Falconer)[13]—meet as they travel north from Tottenham through the valley of the River Lea towards Ware in Hertfordshire. Auceps soon goes his own way, but as the remaining two men walk along, Piscator (Walton's alter ego in the text) praises the virtues of angling so persuasively that Venator asks the older man to teach him how to become an angler. Over the course of several days, Piscator obligingly gives Venator a series of tutorials about the appearance and behaviour of English freshwater fish, as well as techniques for catching them; in between lessons, the two men enjoy their rustic surroundings. At night, Venator and Piscator lodge at an alehouse where they meet up with another pair of fishermen, sing songs, eat fish, and wash down their catch of the day with plentiful beer. As the two men return to Tottenham High Cross at the end of their time together, Venator proclaims himself an enthusiastic new member of the 'Brotherhood of the Angle' over which Piscator presides.

The Compleat Angler is, in part, a manual of instruction, but Walton goes far beyond discussions of bait and tackle to demonstrate how people can transform their shared experiences of the natural world into new structures of social bonds. Yet neither the society Walton creates nor the vision of nature he presents in *The Compleat Angler* is simple. Walton draws on a long and multifaceted tradition to portray Piscator and his followers as covert royalist Anglicans whose piety encodes a subversive criticism of the condition of the English church and state in the 1650s. The very title of Walton's book would have carried a veiled political charge in 1653: as Douglas Bush notes, 'It would hardly have strained seventeenth-century etymology to identify "angler" and "Anglican",'[14] and Walton deliberately encourages this identification. Early in the book, Piscator reminds his companions that when Christ was recruiting his twelve apostles, he 'chose four

---

[13] In the first edition of 1653, there are only two characters at the beginning of Walton's narrative, Piscator and Viator (Traveller).

[14] Douglas Bush, *English Literature in the Earlier Seventeenth Century, 1600–1660* (2nd edn., Oxford, 1962), 239. Steven N. Zwicker analyses the political charge of Walton's text in 'Hunting and Angling: *The Compleat Angler* and *The First Anniversary*', in his *Lines of Authority: Politics and English Literary Culture, 1649–1689* (Ithaca, NY, 1993), 60–89, 222–8.

that were simple Fisher-men' because 'he found that the hearts of such men by nature were fitted for contemplation and quietnesse; men of mild, and sweet, and peaceable spirits, as indeed most Anglers are' (p. 37). Walton's evocation of the fishermen-apostles of the ancient Church continues when Piscator is joined at the alehouse by another angler named Peter, and at the very end of the book, Venator alludes to the apostolic succession when he invokes 'the blessing of St. *Peters* Master' (p. 165). The connection Walton makes between angling and Anglicans also draws on the history of the Church's relationship to field sports: canon law, Piscator observes, had long forbidden clergy to hunt, 'as being a turbulent, toilsom, perplexing Recreation', but allowed them to fish, 'as being a harmless Recreation' (p. 39). This tradition of angling clergy gained new relevance during the Interregnum when dispossessed Anglican churchmen—including friends of Walton—occupied their enforced leisure by fishing.[15] Walton builds on these associations by creating within his book a pantheon of exemplars of Anglican piety who are also fishermen: the Elizabethan churchman Alexander Nowell, dean of St Paul's, 'was as dear a lover, and constant practicer of Angling, as any Age can produce' (p. 39); Sir Henry Wotton, provost of Eton College, 'was also a most dear lover, and a frequent practiser of the art of angling' (p. 40); and Venator concludes that George Herbert must have been a fisherman 'because he had a spirit suitable to Anglers' (p. 82). Before he published the first edition of *The Compleat Angler*, Walton had written biographies of both John Donne and Sir Henry Wotton, and he would later publish lives of Richard Hooker, George Herbert, and Robert Sanderson as well: like his biographies of notable Anglicans, Walton's creation of a group of angling/Anglican worthies in *The Compleat Angler* was designed to forge an enduring 'religious identity' for his beleaguered Church.[16]

Walton's celebration of angling as a communal—and community-building—activity departs radically from earlier depictions of the

[15] B. D. Greenslade, '*The Compleat Angler* and the Sequestered Clergy', *Review of English Studies*, NS 5/20 (1954), 361–6.

[16] I am extending to *The Compleat Angler* Judith Maltby's analysis of Walton as 'the Inventor of Anglicanism' ('Suffering and Surviving: The Civil Wars, the Commonwealth and the Formation of "Anglicanism", 1642–1660', in Christopher Durston and Maltby (eds.), *Religion in Revolutionary England* (Manchester, 2006), 174). On Walton as a biographer, see Jessica Martin, *Walton's 'Lives': Conformist Commemorations and the Rise of Biography* (Oxford, 2001).

social dynamics of the sport. Previous writers had portrayed angling as a solitary endeavour that was conducive to contemplation and prayer precisely because the angler was alone with his thoughts. One of Walton's most important sources, William Samuel's *The Arte of Angling*, promotes this time-honoured view of the angler as an isolated figure. Although Walton, following Samuel, casts his book as a dialogue between teacher-and-pupil anglers, Walton's characterization of his protagonist, likewise named 'Piscator' in *The Arte of Angling*, departs strikingly from his source. Unlike Walton's sociable and loquacious master-angler, Samuel's Piscator is an acerbic loner who believes that angling 'is most meetest for a solitary man' and misanthropically forbids stream-side conversation not because the sound of human voices might scare fish, but because it might attract 'some bungler, idle person, or jester'.[17] Walton, by stark contrast, depicts angling as an inherently gregarious activity. This dynamic of sociability likewise informs the structure of Walton's book: not only does Piscator quote from many sources as he discusses the history and practice of angling, but he often designates the authors he quotes as his personal acquaintances. *The Compleat Angler* thus functions as an anthology not only of texts but of friends, a brotherhood of the angle in both structure and content.

This strong impulse towards inclusiveness also extends to Walton's readers. As an author, Walton solicitously tries to please us. Piscator is always apologetically alert to the danger that his enthusiasm for his subject might make him long-winded, and Walton deliberately ranges far beyond the boundaries of the genre of the how-to manual in order to provide his reader with poems, songs, illustrations, amusing tales, and other diversions from the nitty-gritty of angling techniques. In his opening remarks to the reader, Walton candidly advises that '*he that likes not the book should like the excellent picture of the* Trout, *and some of the other fish*' (p. 5): you have to love a writer who invites you to ignore his words and look at the pictures instead. But there are limits to Walton's authorial empathy. By promoting crowd-pleasing merriment, Walton deliberately defies the Puritans' prohibitions against communal holiday pastimes, and he characterizes any reader who might

---

[17] *The Arte of Angling, 1577*, ed. Gerald Eades Bentley, introd. Carl Otto v. Keinbusch, notes by Henry L. Savage (Princeton, 1956), 31, 17. Thomas P. Harrison has identified the author of *The Arte of Angling* as William Samuel, a Huntingtonshire vicar ('The Author of "The Arte of Angling, 1577"', *Notes and Queries* 7 (1960), 373–6).

be offended by his book's merriment as '*a severe, sowre-complexion'd man*' who cannot be '*a competent judge*' of Walton's work (p. 5).[18] Walton aims to please a wide audience, but he draws the line at killjoys.

The place of women in *The Compleat Angler* is also problematic. Although there are a few female characters in Walton's narrative—the hostess of the alehouse at which Piscator lodges, and the milkmaid and her mother who sing for the anglers—women seem irrelevant to the Brotherhood of the Angle. In this way, Walton again diverges significantly from the model of human relationships which he found in William Samuel's *The Arte of Angling*. While Walton leaves intact the interchange between Piscator and his angler-pupil that is central to Samuel's text, Walton completely erases the character of Piscator's wife, Cisley, who appears prominently in Samuel's book. And the suggestion that sensible men admire fish rather than women appears more than once in *The Compleat Angler*: Piscator declares that the markings of trout and salmon 'give them such an addition of natural beauty, as I think, was never given to any woman by the Artificial Paint or Patches in which they so much pride themselves in this Age' (p. 97), and Thomas Weaver declares in a prefatory poem,

> His fate's foretold, who fondly places
> His bliss in womans soft embraces.
> All pleasures, but the Angler's, bring
> I'th' tail repentance like a sting. (p. 12)

The nineteenth-century English playwright Charles Dance apparently found the gender dynamics of *The Compleat Angler* unsatisfactory, and he accordingly revised the plot of Walton's book. In his 1839 drama *Izaak Walton*, Dance refashions *The Compleat Angler* into a boy-gets-girl narrative: Venator—who becomes, in Dance's revision, the rural persona of a London law student named Arthur Graham—ventures into the countryside and takes angling lessons from Walton solely as part of a scheme to win the hand of Walton's attractive female ward, Anne Evelyn (a character who exists in neither the *Angler* nor Walton's biography).[19] In Dance's rewriting of Walton's text, the Brotherhood of the Angle functions solely as a cover for

---

[18] Gregory M. Colón Semenza, 'The Danger of "Innocent, harmless mirth": Walton's *Compleat Angler* in the Interregnum', in his *Sport, Politics, and Literature in the English Renaissance* (Newark, DE, 2003), 139–57, 207–10.

[19] Charles Dance, *Izaak Walton: A Drama in Four Parts* (1839; Far Hills, NJ, 2000).

heterosexual matchmaking—a far cry from the female-free existence of Walton's original characters.

Two components of Walton's book are fundamental to the unique identity of *The Compleat Angler*: the relationship between Piscator and his protégé, and the relationship between the anglers and the natural world. Dance's play, in changing the dynamics of the former and simplifying the latter, helps us to appreciate more clearly both the distinctiveness and the complexity of the original text. In Dance's rewriting of *The Compleat Angler*, the countryside along the banks of the River Lea becomes a place where Londoners can adopt rustic identities and pursue love affairs frustrated by the social norms of the city. Dance thus underlines the kinship between Walton's *Angler* and the genre of comedy: in comedy, characters leave their workaday surroundings, enter a green world, and then return to their urban milieu with their relationships transformed by their experiences in a natural setting.[20] Yet in depicting Hertfordshire as a stereotypical green world of comic reconciliation and renewal, Dance's play loses much of the distinctive richness of Walton's portrayal of the environment.

The Compleat Angler *and the Environment*

Walton's characters perceive the natural world in multiple ways. In his revision of *The Compleat Angler*, Charles Dance drew on one important component of Walton's environmental vision: the pastoral mode. Since classical antiquity, urban writers have used pastoral—the depiction of the lives of shepherds—to idealize and celebrate rural life. The shepherds of pastoral typically lead a simple, leisurely existence in a countryside that meets their needs without the tillage and sweat of agriculture; pastoral thus depicts men dwelling in peace with one another and the natural world.[21] Some writers tweaked the conventions of pastoral by substituting anglers for shepherds, and Walton positions his book within this revised version of the mode, at one point quoting from the poetry of Phineas Fletcher, whom Walton hails as 'an excellent Divine, and an excellent Angler, and the Author

---

[20] Northrop Frye provides a classic analysis of this pattern in *Anatomy of Criticism: Four Essays* (1957; Princeton, 1973), 182–3.

[21] For a discussion of these qualities of pastoral and how they have been problematized in both literature and scholarship, see Terry Gifford, *Pastoral* (New York, 1999), esp. 1–12.

of excellent piscatory Eclogues' (p. 136). At times, Walton's anglers clearly perceive their lifestyle and surroundings through the lens of pastoral: 'No life, my honest Scholar, no life so happy and so pleasant, as the life of a well governed *Angler*; for when the *Lawyer* is swallowed up with business, and the *States-man* is preventing or contriving plots, then we sit on *Cowslip-banks*, hear the birds sing, and possess our selves in as much quietness as these silent silver streams, which we now see glide so quietly by us' (p. 83). But Walton's details in such passages—the cowslips, birds, and silver streams—are conventional and generalized. As W. J. Keith astutely observes, 'We certainly receive the effect of an English landscape, but is it not localized. The stretch of the river Lea between Ware and Waltham will never become known as "Walton's Country" since he is at pains to recreate not *a* countryside but *the* countryside.'[22]

As Charles Dance's play indicates, Walton's pastoral landscape description was seized upon with great enthusiasm by nineteenth-century readers of *The Compleat Angler*. Charles Lamb gushed about the 'delightful innocence and healthfulness' of Walton's rural 'scenes', and Wordsworth found Walton's 'cow-slip bank' and 'fresh meads' to be '[f]airer than life itself'; William Hazlitt simply called Walton's book 'the best pastoral in the language'.[23] Yet the first readers of *The Compleat Angler* would have found the timeless beauty of Walton's forays into pastoral complicated by the contemporary resonances of the mode. As Walton's anglers take shelter under a sycamore tree during a shower of rain, Piscator is reminded of the herdsmen Tityrus and Meliboeus who sought cover under a 'broad *Beech-tree*' in Virgil's first Eclogue (p. 83): in Virgil's poem, Meliboeus has been evicted from his farm during a time of war, making him a precursor of the many English royalists who found themselves homeless in the 1650s after either fleeing into foreign exile or suffering the confiscation of their estates by Parliament.[24] And the balmy climate and natural plenitude inherent to pastoral description would have seemed like wishful thinking during the Interregnum, for

---

[22] W. J. Keith, *The Rural Tradition: A Study of the Non-Fiction Prose Writers of the English Countryside* (Toronto, 1974), 32.

[23] *The Letters of Charles Lamb*, ed. Alfred Ainger (London, 1900), ii. 23; 'Written upon a Blank Leaf in "The Compleat Angler"', in *William Wordsworth: The Poems*, ed. John O. Hayden (New Haven, 1981), ii. 398; *The Collected Works of William Hazlitt*, ed. A. R. Waller and Arnold Glover (London, 1902), i. 56.

[24] Annabel Patterson, *Pastoral and Ideology, Virgil to Valéry* (Oxford, 1988), 151, 171.

England had experienced a prolonged agricultural crisis between 1646 and 1651, 'when disastrous weather conditions had ruined harvests and spread sickness among livestock'.[25] So Walton's excursions into the pastoral mode would have appeared bittersweet to the first readers of *The Compleat Angler*, reminding them just how much distance existed between such literary idealization and the lived reality—political and environmental—of England in the middle of the seventeenth century.

Walton's sustained attention to natural history likewise challenges the idealized vision of the pastoral mode. Knowledge of particular ecosystems is fundamental to angling: the successful angler must understand what species of fish inhabit a specific locale and what kinds of prey these fish are likely to seek, all the while taking into account such variables as topography, time of day, weather, and season. Unlike the shepherd of pastoral who inhabits a beautiful, unchanging natural world, the angler must cope with a multifarious environment in continual flux. In his opening remarks to his reader, Walton notes that '*the observations of the* nature *and* breeding, *and* seasons, *and* catching of Fish' make up '*the more useful part of this* Discourse' (pp. 5–6): as a manual of instruction, *The Compleat Angler* often abandons the idyllic generalities of pastoral and presents instead detailed observations about the appearance, behaviour, and habitat of myriad creatures. Most obviously, *The Compleat Angler* is full of information about (and pictures of) fish: after providing an illustration of a barbel, for example, Walton specifies techniques for catching this 'lusty and cunning' fish that will craftily 'nibble and suck off your worm close to the hook, and yet avoid the letting the hook come into his mouth' (p. 128). But Walton also spends a significant portion of his work describing animals that can be used as bait. When Piscator lectures Venator about fishing techniques, he reveals a natural world filled with a dizzying array of fauna, and grasshoppers, frogs, snails, worms, flies, and maggots regularly swarm across Walton's pages. 'You are to know,' Piscator advises Venator at one point, 'that there are so many sorts of Flies as there be of Fruits: I will name you but some of them, as the *dun-flie*, the *stone-flie*, the *red-flie*, the *moor-flie*, the *tawny-flie*, the *shell-flie*, the *cloudy*, or *blackish-flie*, the *flag-flie*, the

[25] Joan Thirsk, 'Plough and Pen: Agricultural Writers in the Seventeenth Century', in T. H. Aston et al. (eds.), *Social Relations and Ideas: Essays in Honour of R. H. Hilton* (Cambridge, 1983), 308–9.

vine-flie: there be of *flies*, *Caterpillars*, and *Canker-flies*, and *Bear-flies*, and indeed too many either for me to name or for you to remember' (p. 72). This astonishing plenitude of creatures exists because the English countryside encompasses so much diversity of geography and vegetation. Piscator notes that worms 'for colour and shape alter even as the ground out of which they are got, as the *marsh-worm*, the *tag-tail*, the *stag-worm*, the *dock-worm*, the *oak-worm*, the *gilt-tayle*, the *twachel* or *lob-worm* . . . and too many to name, even as many sorts, as some think there be of several hearbs or shrubs, or of several kinds of birds in the air' (p. 69). Walton thus promotes a keen appreciation of what we would now term *ecology*, that is, the relationships among living creatures and their environment. But Piscator's understanding of ecology usually has a practical application: the successful angler is a sharp-eyed opportunist who can analyse and adapt to highly localized and variable environmental conditions. In order to create an artificial fly that will catch fish, Piscator advises, a talented angler 'may walk by the River and mark what flies fall on the water that day, and catch one of them, if he see the *Trouts* leap at a fly of that kind' (p. 79). This combination of ecological expertise and pragmatism also leads Walton's anglers to appreciate—and exploit—features of the environment antithetical to pastoral idealization, such as Piscator's detailed and very useful knowledge of manure: a type of worm called a 'brandling', Piscator tells us, 'is usually found in an old dunghil, or some very rotten place near to it: but most usually in Cow-dung, or hogs-dung, rather than horse-dung, which is somewhat too hot and dry for that worm' (p. 69). Walton's painstaking descriptions of ecosystems that abound with both fish and faeces complicate, even contradict, the pastoral vision of flowers and silver streams found elsewhere in *The Compleat Angler*.

Walton's fascination with natural history can modulate into different environmental keys. On the one hand, Piscator's emphasis on the practical application of such knowledge sometimes places *The Compleat Angler* within the georgic mode, which is characterized by the realistic—and often didactic—portrayal of the sweaty, difficult tasks involved in raising crops and livestock. Indeed, during his discussion of techniques for catching roach and dace, Piscator explains how Venator can create his very own maggot-farm by burying the flyblown carcass of a cat (p. 143). Yet at other times, Piscator's appreciation for natural history leads him instead towards natural theology, the concept that one may understand God by studying the natural world which he has created. At such moments, Piscator regards invertebrates not as fish-bait to be harvested but instead as objects of spiritual reflection: 'what a work it were in a Discourse but to run over those very many *flies*, *worms* and little living creatures with which the Sun and Summer adorn and beautifie the River banks and Meadows; both for the recreation and contemplation of us Anglers' (p. 72). Natural theology combines memorably with both the pastoral mode and echoes of Scripture in Venator's beautiful concluding speech: 'So when I would beget *content*, and increase confidence in the *Power*, and *Wisdom*, and *Providence* of Almighty God, I will walk the *Meadows* by some gliding stream, and there contemplate the *Lillies* that take no care, and those very many other various little living *creatures*, that are not only created but fed (man knows not how) by the goodness of the God of *Nature*, and therefore trust in him' (p. 165).[26] Walton's 'God of *Nature*', as this passage implies, can create things that defy human understanding, and Walton's focus on natural history thus often leads him into the territory of *wonder*.[27] Wonderful knowledge is extravagantly impractical: it has no purpose other than to allow us to appreciate God's ongoing role as the Creator of surprises in the natural world. In one passage, Piscator provides Venator with information germane to angling: a type of caddis worm (the larva of a caddis fly) called a '*Cock-spur*' is 'a choice bait'. But Piscator leaves practicality far behind to revel in his delighted astonishment at the home-building techniques of this remarkable insect: 'the case or house in which this [caddis worm] dwells is made of small husks, and gravel, and slime, most curiously made of these, even so as to be wondred at, but not to be made by man no more than a *Kingfishers* nest can, which is made of little Fishes bones, and have such a Geometrical inter-weaving and connexion, as the like is not to be done by the art of man' (p. 145). Piscator's love of 'wonderful' natural history also leads him to share accounts of such oddities as carp with frogs stuck to their heads, pike-killing tadpoles, and a huge stuffed eel on display at a Westminster coffee house (pp. 107, 125). As Walton's

---

[26] Walton's reference to 'the *Lillies* that take no care' evokes Matthew 6:28 and Luke 12:27.

[27] I have analysed Walton's enthusiasm for wonder-filled natural history in '*The Compleat Angler* and the Early Modern Culture of Collecting', *English Literary Renaissance*, 37 (2007), 100–17.

characters contemplate their world through the lens of natural theology, they see God's providential handiwork in all creatures—the beautiful, the diminutive, and the marvellous alike.

Yet at other times, Walton's anglers regard the animals around them with clinical detachment. Piscator does not practise catch-and-release fishing, and although he describes how to angle with artificial flies and pastes made from bread, Piscator himself always uses live bait during his vacation in Hertfordshire. When he discusses how to capture fish, Piscator uses the verb 'kill' as a synonym for 'catch', and he provides detailed instructions for vivisecting frogs, worms, insects, and minnows by carefully skewering them onto hooks for use as live (but, of course, dying) bait. Thus as Venator's education proceeds, Walton provides a series of matter-of-fact descriptions of the deaths of living creatures. Lord Byron was repulsed by the treatment of animals in *The Compleat Angler*, and he yearned to give Walton a taste of his own medicine: 'The quaint, old, cruel coxcomb, in his gullet | Should have a hook, and a small trout to pull it.'[28] In his notes to this passage from *Don Juan*, Byron elaborated, 'It would have taught him humanity at least. This sentimental savage, whom it is a mode to quote (amongst the novelists) to show their sympathy for innocent sports and old songs, teaches how to sew up frogs, and break their legs by way of experiment, in addition to the art of angling, the cruellest, the coldest, and the stupidest of pretended sports. . . . No angler can be a good man.'[29] There is death among the cowslips in Walton's world, and whether or not we share Byron's response to this paradox, *The Compleat Angler* forces us to grapple with the ethical implications of field sports.

Walton's attitude towards the non-human inhabitants of the countryside takes on yet another layer of complexity early in *The Compleat Angler*. Before Venator begins his angling tutorials with Piscator, the two men join a group of hunters who track down and kill an otter and most of her pups. Many twenty-first-century readers will find disturbing not only the destruction of animals now protected and beloved, but also Piscator's bloodthirsty response to this violence: 'God keep you all, Gentlemen, and send you meet this day with another Bitch-Otter, and kill her merrily, and all her young ones too' (p. 45). Yet Piscator's hatred of otters is rooted in his concern for

---

[28] George Gordon Noël Byron, *Byron's Don Juan: A Variorum Edition*, ed. Truman Guy Steffan and Willis W. Pratt (2nd edn., Austin, 1971), iii. 407.

[29] *Byron's Don Juan*, iv. 259.

wildlife conservation: Piscator champions the enforcement of '*Fence months*' (the breeding season when fishing is prohibited), criticizes officials who allow undersized fish to be sold, and regards the destruction of fish-predators like otters as a necessary protective measure (p. 46). In twentieth-century America, Walton's advocacy of environmental stewardship inspired the genesis of the Izaak Walton League, a mass-membership conservation organization that was especially influential from the early 1920s until the Second World War. The Izaak Walton League promoted what was at the time a cutting-edge vision of conservation focused broadly on ecosystems, and the group was crucial in forcing Congress to protect endangered watersheds by creating federal nature preserves. Izaak Walton the otter-hater thus became a progenitor of the modern American conservation movement, a 'Defender of Woods, Waters and Wild Life'.[30]

In *The Compleat Angler*, Walton depicts conservation as an important element of food-production. Without wildlife management, Piscator warns, fish stocks will decline and members of the Brotherhood of the Angle will be 'forced to eat flesh' (p. 46). Nearly all the fish Piscator and Venator catch during the course of Walton's narrative end up eaten, and the anglers' evenings of conviviality are structured around their consumption of fish. The centrality of food in Walton's book is indicated even by its subtitle, 'The Contemplative Man's Recreation', since in the seventeenth century the word 'recreation' could refer to a refreshing meal as well as an enjoyable pastime.[31] The modern British poet Tony Williams wittily captures *The Compleat Angler*'s emphasis on victuals when he imagines Walton interacting with a freshly caught fish: 'He fondles the side of a trout, whose eye | stares back in alarm with the sternness of food | before it is eaten. . . .'[32] There is certainly a political element to Walton's relentless focus on eating fish: the observance of days when meat should not be consumed, known as 'fish days', was part of the Anglican tradition rejected by the Puritans, and Piscator explicitly decries 'the casting off

[30] This quotation is the motto of the Izaak Walton League as found on the title page of the organization's magazine, *Outdoor America*, 2/3 (Oct. 1923). On the history of the Izaak Walton League, see Stephen Fox, *John Muir and His Legacy: The American Conservation Movement* (Boston, 1981), 159–72.

[31] *Oxford English Dictionary*, s.v. 'recreation'.

[32] Tony Williams, 'Izaak Walton's Flight', *The Corner of Arundel Lane and Charles Street* (2009; London, 2010), 67.

of Lent and other Fish-daies' (p. 27).[33] But Piscator and his followers also display a connoisseur's apolitical love of fresh, well-prepared fish. In an era before refrigeration, fish was highly perishable, and most Londoners, lacking the purpose-built fish ponds found on many rural estates, would have had little choice but to eat salted or dried fish, which was not considered delectable.[34] Walton's close friend and self-proclaimed angling 'son', Charles Cotton, declared that 'a Trout especially, if he is not eaten within four, or five hours after he be taken, is worth nothing' (p. 215): to enjoy fish at its best, a seventeenth-century English foodie needed to dine waterside. Thus during their days of fishing together, Piscator and Venator become locavores, and Piscator proves himself a superior angler not only by catching fish for his friends, but also by providing recipes that make their catch of the day highly palatable; indeed, the influential American chef James Beard included Walton's recipe for roasted pike in one of his cook-books.[35] An attraction of the alehouse at which the anglers lodge is the training in fish-cookery that Piscator has given the hostess on previous visits, and after a meal of trout prepared to Piscator's gourmet stand-ards, Peter declares that Venator is 'happy to be Scholar to such a Master; a Master that knows as much both of the nature and breeding of fish as any man: and can also tell him as well how to catch and cook them, from the *Minnow* to the *Salmon*, as any that I ever met withall' (p. 63). To the delight of his followers, Piscator has transformed their Hertfordshire alehouse into a seventeenth-century gastropub.

'My most Worthy FATHER and FRIEND'

Izaak Walton published his fifth and final edition of *The Compleat Angler* in 1676. In late February or early March of that year, about six months before his eighty-third birthday, Walton asked Charles Cotton to write 'Directions for the taking of a Trout' to accompany the new edition, giving Cotton 'but a little more than ten days time' to 'scribble' his text (p. 169). It is signal proof of Cotton's regard for Walton that he fulfilled this request

---

[33] From the Tudor period until the Interregnum, the observation of multiple 'fish days' each week, in addition to periods of fasting prescribed by the Church, had been used to promote ocean fisheries and thus the English navy (Joan Thirsk, *Food in Early Modern England: Phases, Fads, Fashions 1500–1760* (London and New York, 2006), 159–60).

[34] Charles L. Cutting, *Fish Saving: A History of Fish Processing from Ancient to Modern Times* (New York, 1956), 26–7.

[35] James Beard, *James Beard's New Fish Cookery* (1954; Boston, 1976), 329–30.

on such short notice and a testimony to the depth of his knowledge and
clarity of style that anglers still regard Cotton's 'Instructions how to
angle for a TROUT or GRAYLING in a clear Stream' (p. 167), the
first specialized account of fly fishing ever written, as one of the pre-
eminent works on its subject.[36] In many ways, Cotton and Walton made
an unlikely pair. Despite their shared roots in Staffordshire, they had
followed very different paths in life, since Cotton spent most of his time
as a country gentleman at his family's seat in the valley of the River
Dove on the Derbyshire–Staffordshire border; and Walton, who had
also known Cotton's father, was thirty-seven years older than the squire
of Beresford Hall. While Cotton, like Walton, supported the royalist
cause, the two men had disparate sensibilities: whereas Walton, through
Piscator, condemned 'lascivious jests' as the products of a 'corrupt
nature' (p. 47), Cotton was best known for his off-colour burlesque
poetry.[37] Even as anglers, the two differed in approach: Walton primarily used live bait such as worms, Cotton was mainly a fly fisherman.[38]
Yet Cotton warmly addresses Walton as 'My most Worthy | FATHER
and FRIEND' and humbly asks that in publishing his treatise on fly
fishing, the elderly tradesman will *'permit me to attend you in publick,
who in private, have ever been, am, and ever resolve to be* | Sir, | Your
most affectionate | Son and Servant' (p. 169); in reply, Walton desig-
nates Cotton as *'my most Honoured Friend'* and describes himself as
'Your most affectionate | *Father and Friend'* (p. 223).

Cotton deliberately structures his discussion of fly fishing as an
extension of Walton's book. Cotton frames his sequel as a dialogue
between two travellers, Piscator Junior—Cotton's persona in the
text—and Viator, who is 'the very Man decipher'd in [Walton's]
Book under the name of *Venator*' (p. 174). As Viator passes through
Derbyshire on his way to Lancashire, he encounters Piscator Junior.
The two men chat and discover that they both love not only fishing,
but also the same master-angler, Izaak Walton himself. As soon as he
realizes that Viator is a fellow 'Brother of the Angle', Piscator Junior
persuades Viator to revise his travel plans and stay with him at
Beresford Hall for a couple of days, during which time Piscator

[36] John McDonald, *The Origins of Angling* (Garden City, NY, 1963), 24.

[37] Paul Hartle, 'Charles Cotton', *Oxford Dictionary of National Biography*.

[38] We see in the divergent angling practices of Walton and Cotton the beginnings
of what would later become a cultural divide between bait fishing and fly fishing; the
latter is now widely regarded as more sporting and socially elite than the former (Charles
F. Waterman, *A History of Angling* (Tulsa, OK, 1981), 10, 38).

Junior provides 'some instructions how to Angle for a Trout in a clear River, that my Father *Walton* himself will not disapprove' (p. 174). Although Cotton's work pays homage to Walton and his book, Cotton's depiction of the natural world also adds a new element to Walton's multifaceted portrayal of the environment. Rather than the conventionally bucolic countryside of Walton's work, Cotton portrays his beloved River Dove and the rugged landscape of the Peak District in particularized detail, and he acknowledges that his vast knowledge of fly fishing springs from his lifelong immersion in this unique environment, 'the recreation of angling in very clear Rivers . . . and the manner of Angling here with us by reason of that exceeding clearness, being something different from the method commonly us'd in others' (p. 185).[39] Cotton's treatise thus celebrates regionalism, and his evocation of place brings Dove Dale to life for his reader.

Despite their differences, this seventeenth-century odd couple—Izaak Walton, the elderly linen-draper who fishes with minnows and maggots, and Charles Cotton, the genteel fly-fisherman—had become devoted friends. In 1674, to honour their relationship, Cotton built on the grounds of his estate beside the River Dove a fishing cottage, and in his sequel to *The Compleat Angler*, Piscator Junior proudly shows it off to Viator, pointing out that 'over the door of which you will see the two first Letters of my Father *Walton's* name and mine twisted in *Cypher*' (p. 175). Piscator Junior reports to Viator that Walton saw this calligraphic embrace 'cut in the stone before it was set up; but never in the posture it now stands: for the house was but building when he was last here, and not rais'd so high as the Arch of the dore, and I am afraid he will not see it yet; for he has lately writ me word he doubts his coming down this Summer, which I do assure you was the worst news he could possibly have sent me' (p. 184). We do not know if Walton was ever able to make the journey back to Beresford to see the fishing house in its completed state, but as he prepared the final edition of his book for publication, he had the cipher replicated on the title page of Cotton's Part II of *The Compleat Angler* (p. 167). Like the fishing house with the engraved lintel over the door—which still stands to this day 'in a kind of *Peninsula* . . . with

---

[39] Cotton's patterns for artificial flies, now more than 300 years old, are still used by anglers on the River Dove (J. N. Watson, *Angling with the Fly: Flies and Anglers of Derbyshire and Staffordshire* (Yeadon, West Yorkshire, 2008), 3).

a delicate clear River about it' (p. 184)—the men's intertwined initials function in Cotton's book as a lapidary monument to an enduring friendship.

How should we live? Charles Cotton's partnership with Walton provides one example of how the values and behaviour depicted in *The Compleat Angler* might shape real life. Cotton's heartfelt portrayal of himself as Walton's adopted 'son' has decisively framed Walton's posthumous reputation, with subsequent generations of admirers styling themselves as the offspring of 'Father Walton', and through his book, Izaak Walton continues his recruitment drive for new followers hundreds of years after his death. In *The Compleat Angler*, Walton explores how a sustaining (and sustainable) human society might be generated neither within frameworks of religion and polity that can be destroyed by war, nor within the confines of the biologically fragile family unit. Walton turns instead to the environment and seeks to forge relationships among otherwise disparate people who come to be bound together—with each other and with him—by their mutual love of a beautiful yet complex and challenging natural world. When we have 'a rainy evening to read this following Discourse', Walton hopes we will take 'pleasure *or* profit' from his book, where we will find *'flowers and showers and stomachs and meat and content and leasure to go a fishing'* (pp. 7, 5, 160).[40]

---

[40] Thanks to Judith Luna and William M. Tsutsui for their helpful comments on earlier versions of this essay.

NOTE ON THE TEXT

IZAAK WALTON'S *The Compleat Angler* was first published in May 1653. In this version of the text, Piscator initially meets only a character named Viator, who becomes his pupil. When Walton published a new edition of the *Angler* in 1655, Viator was renamed 'Venator', Auceps joined the travellers, and Walton added eight additional chapters to his book. Walton continued to expand the work in the third edition of 1661, which was reissued in 1664; the fourth edition of 1668 was not revised. The fifth edition of *The Compleat Angler*, which appeared in 1676, was the final version published in Walton's lifetime. Walton again revised the text and asked his friend, Charles Cotton, to contribute a discussion of fly fishing which became *The Compleat Angler*, Part II. An edition of Robert Venables's *The Experienc'd Angler* was published along with Walton's and Cotton's texts under the title *The Universal Angler*: each of Walton's, Cotton's, and Venables's works had its own title page, and book-buyers could purchase and bind any or all of the texts as they pleased.

The text of this new edition is based on the 1676 edition of Walton's *The Compleat Angler* and Cotton's *The Compleat Angler*, Part II (Wing [2nd edn.] / W666 and Wing [2nd edn.] / C6381). I have also consulted the version of the 1676 text of Walton's *Angler* found in Jonquil Bevan's magisterial Clarendon Press edition.[1] In the texts of both Walton and Cotton presented here, the authors' original spelling and punctuation have largely been retained, but typographical errors have been silently corrected, long 's' and 'vv' (w) have been modernized, quotations have been consistently presented in italics, brackets within brackets have been converted to commas, and punctuation marks appearing before the second bracket have been placed after it. An anonymous 'Short Discourse . . . Touching the Lawes of Angling', first added as a postscript to the 1661 edition of *The Compleat Angler*, has been omitted.

---

[1] Dr Bevan's edition of Walton's *Angler* includes an apparatus that shows how the 1676 text differs from the previous four editions of Walton's book, and her introduction analyses in detail the publication history of Walton's work (*The Compleat Angler, 1653–1676*, by Izaak Walton, ed. Jonquil Bevan (Oxford, 1983)).

Explanatory notes are indicated in the text with an asterisk. Cues for inset notes (where they appear in the original) are given as superscript numbers. Angling terms which recur in the texts are defined in a Glossary that is prefaced by a brief description of the fishing tackle used by Walton and Cotton. Four maps of the countryside traversed by the anglers in the narratives of Walton and Cotton are also included. The maps are taken from Izaak Walton and Charles Cotton, *The Compleat Angler*, ed. Richard Le Gallienne, illus. Edmund H. New (London, 1897), and are reproduced, together with the concluding advertisement, courtesy of the Lilly Library, Indiana University, Bloomington, Indiana.

SELECT BIBLIOGRAPHY

Bibliography

Coigney, Rodolphe L., *Izaak Walton: A New Bibliography, 1653–1987* (New York, 1989).

Biographies

Hartle, Paul, 'Charles Cotton', *Oxford Dictionary of National Biography* (Oxford, 2004–12).

Martin, Jessica, 'Izaak Walton', *Oxford Dictionary of National Biography* (Oxford, 2004–12).

Editions of The Compleat Angler

The Complete Angler, by Izaak Walton and Charles Cotton, ed. Sir Nicholas Harris Nicolas (London, 1875).

The Complete Angler, by Izaak Walton and Charles Cotton, 2 vols., ed. J. E. Harting (London, 1893).

The Compleat Angler, by Izaak Walton and Charles Cotton, introd. A. B. Gough, notes by T. Balston (Oxford, 1915).

The Compleat Angler, 1653–1676, by Izaak Walton, ed. Jonquil Bevan (Oxford, 1983).

Critical Studies: Books

Bevan, Jonquil, *Izaak Walton's 'The Compleat Angler': The Art of Recreation* (New York, 1988).

Bottrall, Margaret, *Izaak Walton* (London, 1955).

Cooper, John R., *The Art of 'The Compleat Angler'* (Durham, NC, 1968).

Heywood, Gerald G. P., *Charles Cotton and His River* (Manchester, 1928).

Stanwood, P. G., *Izaak Walton* (New York, 1998).

Critical Studies: Articles and Chapters in Books

Adrian, John M., 'Izaak Walton, Lucy Hutchinson, and the Experience of Civil War', in *Local Negotiations of English Nationhood, 1570–1680* (Basingstoke and New York, 2011), 120–53, 206–12.

Anselment, Raymond A., 'Robert Boyle, Izaak Walton, and the Art of Angling', *Prose Studies*, 30 (2008), 124–41.

Camé, Jean-François, and Charles F. Sadowski, 'Attitudes towards Money in Izaak Walton's *The Complete Angler*', *Cahiers Élisabéthains*, 9 (1976), 41–54.

Greenslade, B. D., '*The Compleat Angler* and the Sequestered Clergy', *Review of English Studies*, NS 5/20 (1954), 361–6.

Keith, W. J., 'Izaak Walton', in *The Rural Tradition: A Study of the Non-Fiction Prose Writers of the English Countryside* (Toronto, 1974), 25–37.

Losocco, Paula, 'Royalist Reclamation of Psalmic Song in 1650s England', *Renaissance Quarterly*, 64 (2011), 500–43.

Low, Anthony, 'The Compleat Angler's "Baite"; or, The Subverter Subverted', *John Donne Journal*, 4 (1985), 1–12.

McIlhaney, Anne E., 'Pastoral Community and the Hooks of Memory: The Mnemonic Landscape of Izaak Walton's *Compleat Angler* (1653)', *Renaissance Papers 2002* (Rochester, NY, and Woodbridge, 2002), 1–16.

McRae, Andrew, 'The Pleasures of the Land in Restoration England: The Social Politics of *The Compleat Angler*', in Roze Hentschell and Kathy Lavezzo (eds.), *Essays in Memory of Richard Helgerson: Laureations* (Newark, DE, and Lanham, MD, 2012), 163–79.

Nardo, Anna K., '"A Recreation of a Recreation": Reading *The Compleat Angler*', *South Atlantic Quarterly*, 79 (1980), 302–11.

Oliver, H. J., 'The Composition and Revisions of *The Compleat Angler*', *Modern Language Review*, 42 (1947), 295–313.

Radcliffe, David Hill, '"Study to be quiet": Genre and Politics in Izaak Walton's *Compleat Angler*', *English Literary Renaissance*, 22 (1992), 95–111.

Semenza, Gregory M. Colón, 'The Danger of "Innocent, harmless mirth": Walton's *Compleat Angler* in the Interregnum', in Semenza, *Sport, Politics, and Literature in the English Renaissance* (Newark, DE, 2003), 139–57, 207–10.

Smith, Nicholas D., 'Angling Literature 1653–1800: Friendship, Socialization and the "Fishing Career"', *Aethlon: The Journal of Sport Literature*, 19 (2001), 109–24.

——'The Early American Reception of Izaak Walton's *The Compleat Angler*', *Symbiosis: A Journal of Anglo-American Literary Relations*, 7 (2003), 222–40.

Smith, Nigel, 'Oliver Cromwell's Angler', *Seventeenth Century*, 8 (1993), 51–65.

Swann, Marjorie, '*The Compleat Angler* and the Early Modern Culture of Collecting', *English Literary Renaissance*, 37 (2007), 100–17.

Tranter, Kirsten, 'By the Rivers of Babylon: Biblical Allusion and the Politics of Pastoral in Izaak Walton's *The Compleat Angler*', in Philippa Kelly and L. E. Semler (eds.), *Word and Self Estranged in English Texts, 1550–1660* (Farnham, Surrey, and Burlington, VT, 2010), 195–204.

Zwicker, Steven N., 'Hunting and Angling: *The Compleat Angler* and *The First Anniversary*', in Zwicker, *Lines of Authority: Politics and English Literary Culture, 1649–1689* (Ithaca, NY, 1993), 60–89, 222–8.

Environmental History and Ecocriticism

Glacken, Clarence J., 'Early Modern Times', in *Traces on the Rhodian Shore: Nature and Culture in Western Thought from Ancient Times to the End of the Eighteenth Century* (Berkeley, Los Angeles, and London, 1967), 355–497.

Hiltner, Ken, 'Early Modern Ecology', in Michael Hattaway (ed.), *A New Companion to English Renaissance Literature and Culture* (Malden, MA, 2010), 555–68.

—— *What Else Is Pastoral?: Renaissance Literature and the Environment* (Ithaca, NY, 2011).

Thomas, Keith, *Man and the Natural World: Changing Attitudes in England, 1500–1800* (London, 1983).

History of Angling

Billett, Michael, 'Angling', in *A History of English Country Sports* (London, 1994), 185–202.

Herd, Andrew, 'The Seventeenth Century', in *The History of Fly Fishing*, vol. i (Ellesmere, 2011), 73–117.

McCully, C. B., *Fly-Fishing: A Book of Words* (Manchester, 1992).

Trench, Charles Chenevix, 'The Renaissance of Angling', in *A History of Angling* (Chicago, 1974), 27–59.

Natural History

Chinery, Michael, *Collins Complete Guide to British Insects* (London, 2005).

Goddard, John, *John Goddard's Waterside Guide* (2nd edn., repr. Machynlleth, 2010).

Stace, Clive A., *New Flora of the British Isles* (3rd edn., Cambridge, 2010).

Svensson, Lars, et al., *Birds of Europe* (2nd edn., Princeton and Oxford, 2009).

Wheeler, Alwyne, *The Fishes of the British Isles and North-West Europe* (East Lansing, 1969).

General Studies of History and Literature

Bucholz, Robert, and Newton Key, *Early Modern England, 1485–1714: A Narrative History* (2nd edn., Chichester and Malden, MA, 2009).

Clark, Peter, *The English Alehouse: A Social History, 1200–1830* (Harlow and New York, 1983).

Gentles, Ian, *The English Revolution and the Wars in the Three Kingdoms, 1638–1652* (Harlow, 2007).

Keeble, N. H. (ed.), *The Cambridge Companion to Writing of the English Revolution* (Cambridge, 2001).

Miner, Earl, *The Cavalier Mode from Jonson to Cotton* (Princeton, 1971).

Morrill, John, *The Nature of the English Revolution* (London and New York, 1993).

Smith, Nigel, *Literature and Revolution in England, 1640–1660* (New Haven and London, 1994).

Thirsk, Joan, *Food in Early Modern England: Phases, Fads, Fashions, 1500–1760* (London and New York, 2006).

A CHRONOLOGY OF IZAAK WALTON
AND CHARLES COTTON

Life	*Historical and Cultural Context*
1593 Walton born in Stafford to Gervase (a 'tippler' or alehouse-keeper) and his wife, Anne; baptized 21 Sept.	
1597 Walton's father dies; his mother remarries eighteen months later.	
1603	Elizabeth I dies. James VI of Scotland ascends the English throne as James I.
1611 After attending grammar school in Stafford, Walton is apprenticed to his brother-in-law, Thomas Grinsell (a linen draper), in London.	Authorized Version of the Bible published. Aemilia Lanyer, *Salve Deus Rex Judaeorum*
1613 Samuel Page dedicates his narrative poem, *The Love of Amos and Laura*, to Walton.	Princess Elizabeth, daughter of James I, marries the Elector Palatine.
1616	William Shakespeare dies. Ben Jonson publishes his *Works*.
1618 Walton becomes a freeman of the Ironmongers' Company, the guild under which Walton practises his trade as a linen draper and sempster (garment-maker).	James I publishes the 'Book of Sports', sanctioning Sunday recreations.
1620	Pilgrims (nonconforming Puritans) sail to New England on the *Mayflower*.
1622	Michael Drayton, *Poly-Olbion* (begun in 1612) Henry Peacham, *The Compleat Gentleman*
1623 Walton's mother dies in Stafford.	First Folio of Shakespeare's works is published.
1624	John Donne becomes vicar of Walton's London parish, St Dunstan-in-the-West.
1625	James I dies. Charles I succeeds to the throne.
1626 Walton marries Rachel Floud. Seven children are born from 1627 to 1640, all of whom die by 1642.	

	Life	*Historical and Cultural Context*
1627		Sir Francis Bacon, *New Atlantis* and *Sylva Sylvarum*
1629		Charles I dissolves Parliament, begins personal rule (until 1640).
1630	Charles Cotton born at Beresford Hall, Staffordshire (28 Apr.), the only child of Charles and Olive (*née* Stanhope).	
1633	Walton contributes an elegy to the first edition of Donne's poems.	Charles I publishes the second issue of the 'Book of Sports'. George Herbert, *The Temple*
1639	Walton's friend, Sir Henry Wotton, dies.	
1640	Walton's *Life* prefixed to Donne's *LXXX Sermons*. Rachel Walton dies (22 Aug.).	Long Parliament meets.
1642		Civil Wars begin. Parliament closes theatres. First edition of Thomas Browne, *Religio Medici* (unauthorized)
1644		John Milton, *Areopagitica*
1645		William Laud, archbishop of Canterbury, is executed (10 Jan.). Parliament prohibits the Prayer Book.
1646		Charles I surrenders to the Scots. Episcopacy abolished.
1647	Walton marries Anne Ken (23 Apr.). Cotton's mother, Olive, petitions for alimony from her estranged husband.	First folio edition of Francis Beaumont and John Fletcher, *Comedies and Tragedies*
1648	Walton's daughter Anne is born (dies 1715).	Robert Herrick, *Hesperides*
1649	Cotton contributes an elegy on Henry, Lord Hastings, to *Lachrymae Musarum*.	'Rump' of the Long Parliament's House of Commons assumes authority. Charles I is executed (30 Jan.). The monarchy is abolished and England becomes a commonwealth.
1650	Walton's son Izaak is born (dies four months later).	Anne Bradstreet, *The Tenth Muse Lately Sprung Up in America* (unauthorized)
1651	After the battle of Worcester, Walton is entrusted with the garter jewel of King Charles II, which he delivers to Col. Blague in London. Walton's son, yet again named Izaak, is born on 7 Sept. in London (becomes a Church of England	Charles II attempts to invade but is defeated at the battle of Worcester (3 Sep.). Thomas Hobbes, *Leviathan*

	Life	*Historical and Cultural Context*
	clergyman, dies 1719). Walton's *Life of Sir Henry Wotton* is published in *Reliquiae Wottonianae*, which Walton edited.	
1652	Cotton's mother dies.	
1653	Walton publishes *The Compleat Angler* (May).	Oliver Cromwell expels the Rump, creates the Barebones Parliament (July–Dec.). Cromwell becomes Lord Protector under a written constitution (Instrument of Government). Margaret Cavendish, *Poems and Fancies* (first edition) and *Philosophical Fancies*
1655	Walton publishes *The Compleat Angler*, second revised edition.	
1656	Cotton marries his cousin, Isabella Hutchinson. Of nine children, one son and four daughters survive infancy.	James Harrington, *Oceana* William Dugdale, *The Antiquities of Warwickshire*
1658	Cotton's father dies.	Oliver Cromwell dies; his son, Richard, succeeds him as Protector.
1659	Cotton's elegy on Richard Lovelace printed with *Lucasta*.	
1660	Walton becomes the steward of George Morley, the newly consecrated bishop of Worcester. Cotton becomes a revenue commissioner for Derbyshire and Staffordshire.	Charles II restored. Royal Society founded. Theatres reopen. Samuel Pepys begins to write his *Diary*.
1661	Walton's pastoral eclogue praising the king is published as a dedicatory poem in Alexander Brome's *Songs and Other Poems*. Walton provides a commendatory poem for the fourth edition of Christopher Harvey's *The Synagogue*. Walton publishes *The Compleat Angler*, third revised edition.	
1662	Walton's second wife, Anne, dies in Worcester. George Morley becomes bishop of Winchester, and Walton moves with him.	Church of England restored.
1664	Cotton publishes *Scarronides* (a burlesque of the first book of Virgil's *Aeneid*) and his translation of Guillaume du Vair's *Morall Philosophy of the Stoicks*.	John Evelyn, *Sylva, or A Discourse of Forest-Trees* Katherine Philips, *Poems*
1665	Walton publishes *The Life of Mr. Richard Hooker*. Cotton publishes a continu-	Great Plague (last major outbreak of bubonic plague) kills

Life	*Historical and Cultural Context*
ation of *Scarronides* (a burlesque of Book 4 of Virgil's *Aeneid*). Cotton becomes a magistrate.	15 per cent of London's population.

	Life	*Historical and Cultural Context*
1666		Great Fire of London (2–5 Sept.)
1667	Cotton becomes a captain in the regiment of his cousin, Lord Chesterfield; the regiment is soon disbanded.	Milton, *Paradise Lost* Thomas Sprat, *The History of the Royal Society*
1668	Walton publishes *The Compleat Angler*, fourth edition (unrevised).	John Dryden becomes Poet Laureate.
1669	Cotton's wife, Isabella, dies.	
1670	Walton publishes *The Life of Mr. George Herbert* and a collected edition of the *Lives* of Donne, Wotton, Hooker, and Herbert. Cotton travels to Ireland, but the fall of the Duke of Ormonde, the Lord Lieutenant of Ireland, prevents him from taking up military service. Cotton publishes his translation of Guillaume Girard's *The History of the Life of the Duke of Espernon*.	Aphra Behn, *The Forced Marriage*
1671	Cotton publishes his translation of Corneille's *Horace*.	Game Act restricts sporting rights to those with freehold income of at least £100 per year. Milton, *Paradise Regained* and *Samson Agonistes*
1673	Cotton completes 'To my Old, and most Worthy Friend, Mr. Izaak Walton, on his Life of Dr. Donne, &c.' (17 Jan.), which Walton includes in the 1675 edition of his *Lives*.	
1674	Cotton weds Mary, dowager countess of Ardglass (no children by this marriage). Cotton builds his fishing house; he publishes his translation of the *Commentaries* of Blaise de Lasseran-Massencôme, seigneur de Montluc.	*The Compleat Gamester* and *The Fair One of Tunis*, both attributed to Cotton, are published.
1675	Walton publishes a second edition of the collected *Lives* (revised). Cotton publishes *The Planters Manual* (a translation of a French treatise) and a burlesque of Lucian, *The Scoffer Scoft*.	
1676	Walton's *The Compleat Angler*, fifth edition (revised) and Cotton's Part II, are published as *The Universal Angler*.	
1678	Walton publishes *The Life of Dr. Sanderson*.	John Bunyan, *The Pilgrim's Progress*

	Life	*Historical and Cultural Context*
1680	Walton anonymously publishes *Love and Truth* (a religious polemic).	
1681	Cotton sells Beresford Hall, but continues to reside there. Cotton publishes *The Wonders of the Peake*.	Dryden, *Absalom and Achitophel* Andrew Marvell, *Miscellaneous Poems*
1683	Walton edits and publishes the pastoral narrative poem *Thealma and Clearchas* by John Chalkhill (d. 1642). Walton dies in Winchester on 15 Dec.; buried in Winchester Cathedral.	The Great Frost (winter of 1683–4), an unusually long and severe period of freezing weather.
1685	Cotton publishes his translation of Montaigne's *Essays*.	Charles II dies. James II succeeds to the throne.
1687	Cotton dies in London (13 Feb.); buried in St James's Piccadilly.	Sir Isaac Newton, *Principia Mathematica*
1688		Glorious Revolution: William of Orange (Charles I's grandson) invades, James II flees to France.
1689	Cotton's *Poems on Several Occasions* is published.	William III (of Orange) and his wife, Mary II (James II's daughter), succeed.
1694	Cotton's translation of the *Memoirs of the Sieur de Pontis* is published.	Mary II dies.

MAPS

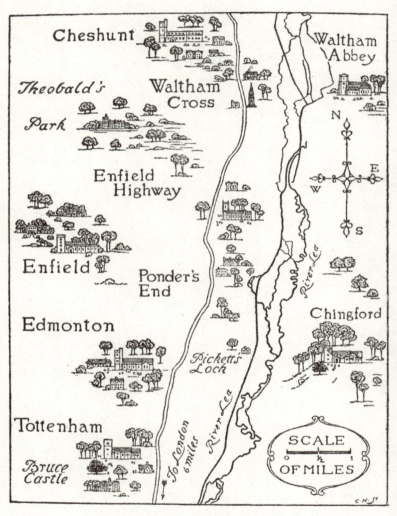

MAP I. TOTTENHAM TO WALTHAM CROSS

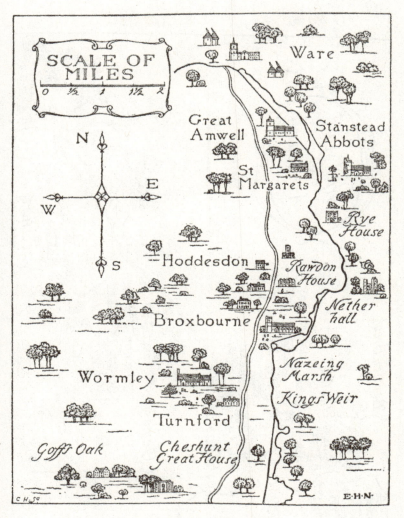

MAP 2. CHESHUNT TO WARE

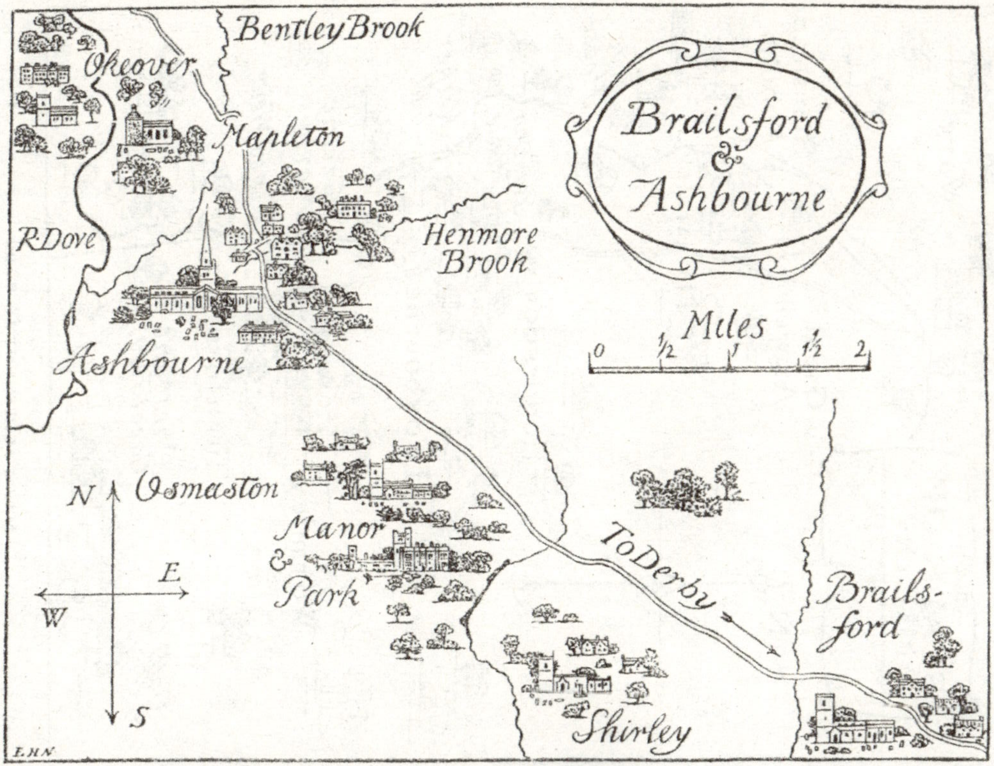

MAP 3. BRAILSFORD AND ASHBOURNE

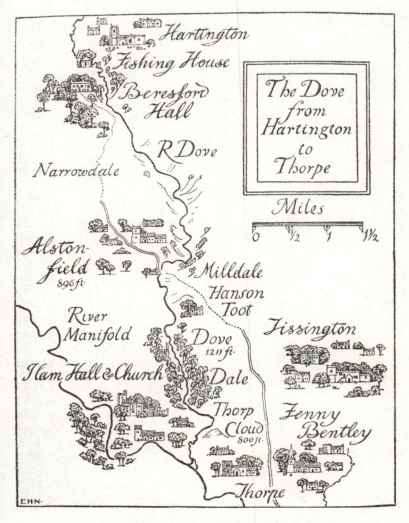

MAP 4. THE RIVER DOVE FROM HARTINGTON TO THORPE

The first part.

The Compleat Angler or. the Contemplative man's Recreation.

PART. I.
BEING A
DISCOURSE
OF
Rivers, Fish-ponds, Fish and Fishing.

Written by *IZAAK WALTON.*

The Fifth Edition much corrected and enlarged.

LONDON,
Printed for *Richard Marriott.* 1676.

FACSIMILE OF THE TITLE PAGE TO THE FIFTH EDITION OF PART I, 1676

SIR,

I HAVE made so ill use of your former favours, as by them to be encouraged to intreat that they may be enlarged to the *Patronage* and *protection* of this Book; and I have put on a modest confidence, that I shall not be deny'd, because it is a Discourse of *Fish* and *Fishing*, which you know so well, and both love and practise so much.

You are assured (though there be ignorant men of another belief) that *Angling* is an *Art*; and you know that *Art* better than others; and that this is truth is demonstrated by the fruits of that pleasant labour which you enjoy when you purpose to give rest to your mind, and devest your self of your more serious business, and (which is often) dedicate a day or two to this *Recreation*.

At which time if *common Anglers* should attend you, and be eye witnesses of the success, not of your *fortune* but your *skill*, it would doubtless beget in them an emulation to be like you, and that emulation might beget an industrious diligence to be so; but I know it is not attainable by common capacities. And there be now many men of great *wisdom*, *learning* and *experience* which love and practise this *Art*, that know I speak the truth.

Sir, This pleasant curiosity* of Fish and Fishing, (of which you are so great a Master) has been thought worthy the *Pens* and *Practises* of divers in other Nations, that have been reputed men of great *Learning* and *Wisdom*, and amongst those of this Nation, I remember Sir *Henry Wotton** (a dear lover of this Art) has told me that his intentions were to write a Discourse of the Art, and in praise of *Angling*, and doubtless he had done so, if death had not prevented him; the remembrance of which hath often made me sorry, for if he had lived to do it, then the unlearned *Angler* had seen some better Treatise of this Art, a Treatise that might have prov'd worthy his perusal, which (though some have undertaken) I could never yet see in English.

But mine may be thought as *weak*, and as *unworthy* of common view; and I do here freely confess, that I should rather excuse my self, than censure others, my own Discourse being liable to so many exceptions; against which you (Sir) might make this one, *That it can contribute nothing to your Knowledge.* And lest a longer Epistle may diminish your pleasure, I shall make this no longer than to add this following Truth, *That I am really,*

SIR,

Your most affectionate Friend,
and most humble Servant,
Iz. Wa.

To all Readers of this Discourse,
but especially to the honest
ANGLER.

I think fit to tell thee these following truths, That I did neither under-take, *nor* write, *nor* publish, *and much less* own, *this Discourse to please my self: and having been too easily drawn to do all to please others, as I propos'd not the gaining of credit by this undertaking, so I would not willingly lose any part of that to which I had a just title before I begun it, and do therefore desire and hope, if I deserve not commendations, yet, I may obtain pardon.*

And though this Discourse may be liable to some Exceptions, yet I cannot doubt but that most Readers may receive so much pleasure *or* profit *by it, as may make it worthy the time of their perusal, if they be not too grave or too busie men. And this is all the confidence that I can put on concerning the merit of what is here offered to their consideration and censure; and if the last prove too severe, as I have a liberty, so I am resolv'd to use it and neglect all sowre Censures.*

And I wish the Reader *also to take notice, that in writing of it I have made my self a* recreation *of a* recreation; *and that it might prove so to him, and not read* dull *and* tediously, *I have in several places mixt (not any scurrility, but) some innocent, harmless mirth; of which, if thou be a severe, sowre-complexion'd* man, then I here disallow thee to be a competent judge; for* Divines *say,* There are offences given, and offences not given but taken.

And I am the willinger to justifie the pleasant part of it, because though it is known I can be serious at seasonable times, yet the whole discourse is, or rather was, a picture of my own disposition, especially in such days and times as I have laid aside business, and gone a fishing with honest Nat. *and* R. Roe;* *but they are gone, and with them most of my pleasant hours, even as a shadow, that passeth away, and returns not.*

And next let me add this, that he that likes not the book should like the excellent picture* of the Trout, *and some of the other fish; which I may take a liberty to commend, because they concern not my self.*

Next let me tell the Reader, *that in that which is the more useful part of this* Discourse, *that is to say, the observations of the* nature *and* breeding, *and* seasons, *and* catching of Fish, *I am not so simple as not to know, that a captious Reader may find exceptions against something said of some of these; and therefore I must entreat him to consider, that experience teaches us to know, that several Countries alter the time, and I think almost the manner, of fishes breeding, but doubtless of their being in season; as may appear by three Rivers in* Monmouthshire, *namely* Severn, Wie, *and* Usk, *where* Cambden* (Brit. f. 633.) *observes, that in the River* Wie, Salmon *are in season from* Sept. *to* April, *and we are certain, that in* Thames *and* Trent, *and in most other Rivers they be in season the six hotter months.*

Now for the Art of catching fish, *that is to say, how to make a man that was none, to be an Angler by a book? he that undertakes it shall undertake a harder task, than Mr.* Hales (*a most valiant and excellent Fencer*) *who in a printed book called,* A private School of Defence* *undertook to teach that art or science, and was laugh'd at for his labour. Not but that many useful things might be learnt by that book, but he was laugh'd at, because that art was not to be taught by words, but practice: and so must Angling. And note also, that in this Discourse I do not undertake to say all that is known, or may be said of it, but I undertake to acquaint the Reader with many things that are not usually known to every Angler; and I shall leave gleanings and observations enough to be made out of the experience of all that love and practise this recreation, to which I shall encourage them. For* Angling *may be said to be so much like the* Mathematicks, *that it can ne'r be fully learnt; at least not so fully, but that there will still be more new experiments left for the tryal of other men that succeed us.*

But I think all that love this game may here learn something that may be worth their money, if they be not poor and needy men; and in case they be, I then wish them to forbear to buy it; for I write not to get money, but for pleasure, and this Discourse boasts of no more; for I hate to promise much, and deceive the Reader.

And however it proves to him, yet I am sure I have found a high content in the search and conference of what is here offer'd to the Readers view and censure: I wish him as much in the perusal of it, and so I might here take my leave, but will stay a little and tell him, that whereas it is said by many, that in flye-fishing for a Trout, *the Angler must observe his* 12 *several flies for the twelve months of the year; I say, he that follows that rule, shall be as sure to catch fish, and, be as wise, as he that makes* Hay *by the fair days in an* Almanack, *and no surer; for those very flies that use to*

appear about and on the water in one month of the year, may the follow-
ing year come almost a month sooner or later; as the same year proves
colder or hotter; and yet in the following Discourse I have set down the
twelve flies that are in reputation with many Anglers, and they may serve
to give him some observations concerning them. And he may note that
there are in Wales *and other Countries, peculiar* flies, *proper to the par-*
ticular place or Country; and doubtless, unless a man makes a flie to coun-
terfeit that very flie in that place, he is like to lose his labour, or much of
it: But for the generality, three or four flies *neat and rightly made, and*
not too big, serve for a Trout *in most Rivers all the Summer. And for*
Winter flie-fishing *it is as useful as an Almanack out of date. And of these*
(because as no man is born an artist, so no man is born an Angler) I
thought fit to give thee this notice.

When I have told the Reader, that in this fifth Impression* there are
many enlargements, gathered both by my own observation, and the com-
munication with friends, I shall stay him no longer than to wish him a
rainy evening to read this following Discourse; *and that (if he be an*
honest Angler) the East wind may never blow when he goes a Fishing.

I. W.

To my dear Brother Mr Izaak Walton, *upon his* Compleat Angler.

ERASMUS in his learned Colloquies*
Has mixt some toys, that by varieties
He might entice all Readers: for in him
Each *child* may wade, or tallest *giant* swim.
And such is this Discourse: there's none so low,
Or highly learn'd, to whom hence may not flow
Pleasure and information: both which are
Taught us with so much art, that I might swear
Safely, the choicest Critick cannot tell,
Whether your matchless judgment most excell
In *Angling* or its *praise*: where commendation
First charms, then makes an *art* a *recreation*.
    'Twas so to me: who *saw* the chearful *Spring*
Pictur'd in every *meadow*, heard *birds* sing
Sonnets in every *grove*, saw *fishes* play
In the cool *crystal streams*, like *lambs* in *May*:
And they may play, till *Anglers* read this *book*;
But after, 'tis a wise *fish* 'scapes a *hook*.

Jo. Floud,* Mr. of Arts.

To the Reader of the *Compleat Angler*.

FIRST mark the Title well; my Friend that gave it
Has made it good; this book deserves to have it.
For he that views it with judicious looks,
Shall find it full of *art, baits, lines* and *hooks*.
    The *world* the *river* is, both you and I,
And all mankind are either *fish* or *fry*:
If we pretend to reason, first or last
His baits will tempt us, and his hooks hold fast.
Pleasure or profit, either prose or rhime,
If not at first, will doubtless take's in time.
    Here sits in secret blest *Theology*,
Waited upon by grave *Philosophy*,

Both *natural* and *moral, History*
Deck'd and adorn'd with flowers of *Poetry*,
The matter and expression striving which
Shall most excell in worth, yet not seem rich:
There is no danger in his *baits*, that *hook*
Will prove the safest, that is surest took.

    Nor are we caught alone, but (which is best)
We shall be wholesom, and be toothsom drest:
Drest to be fed, not to be fed upon;
And danger of a surfeit here is none.
The solid food of serious Contemplation
Is sauc'd here with such harmless recreation,
That an *ingenuous* and *religious* mind
Cannot inquire for more than it may find
Ready at once prepar'd, either t' excite
Or satisfie a curious appetite.

    More praise is due; for 'tis both positive
And truth, which once was interrogative,
And utter'd by the Poet then in jest,
    *Et piscatorem piscis amare potest.**

             *Ch. Harvie,** Mr. of Arts.

To my dear Friend, *Mr.* Iz. Walton, *in praise of Angling, which we both love.*

    Down by this smooth streams wandring side,
    Adorn'd & perfum'd with the pride
    Of *Flora's** Wardrobe, where the shrill
    Aerial Quire express their skill,
    First in alternate melody,
    And then in Chorus all agree.
    Whilst the charm'd fish, as extasi'd
    With sounds, to his own throat deni'd,
    Scorns his dull Element, and springs
    I'th' air, as if his Fins were wings.

      Tis here that pleasures sweet and high
    Prostrate to our embraces lye.
    Such as to Body, Soul or Fame

Create no sickness, sin or shame.
Roses not fenc'd with pricks grow here,
No sting to th' Hony-bag is near.
But (what's perhaps their prejudice)
They difficulty want and price.

An obvious Rod, a twist of hair,
With hook hid in an insect, are
Engines of sport, would fit the wish
O'th' Epicure and fill his dish.

In this clear stream let fall a *Grub*,
And straight take up a *Dace* or *Chub*.
Ith' mud your worm provokes a *Snig*,*
Which being fast, if it prove big
The *Gotham** folly will be found
Discreet, e're ta'ne she must be drown'd.
The *Tench* (Physician of the Brook)*
In yon dead hole expects your hook,
Which having first your pastime been,
Serves then for meat or medicine.
Ambush'd behind that root doth stay
A *Pike*, to catch and be a prey.
The treacherous Quill in this slow stream
Betrays the hunger of a *Bream*.
And at that nimbler Ford, (no doubt)
Your false flie cheats a speckled *Trout*.

When you these creatures wisely chuse
To practise on, which to your use
Owe their creation, and when
Fish from your arts do rescue men;
To plot, delude, and circumvent,
Ensnare and spoil, is innocent.
Here by these crystal streams you may
Preserve a Conscience clear as they;
And when by sullen thoughts you find
Your harassed, not busied, mind
In sable melancholy clad,
Distemper'd, serious, turning sad;
Hence fetch your cure, cast in your bait,
All anxious thoughts and cares will straight

Fly with such speed, they'l seem to be
Possest with the *Hydrophobie.**
The waters calmness in your breast,
And smoothness on your brow shall rest.

   Away with sports of charge and noise,
And give me cheap and silent joys,
Such as *Actaeons** game pursue,
Their fate oft makes the Tale seem true.
The sick or sullen *Hawk* to day
Flyes not; to morrow, quite away.
Patience and Purse to Cards and Dice
Too oft are made a sacrifice:
The Daughters dower, th' inheritance
O'th' son, depend on one mad chance.
The harms and mischiefs which th'abuse
Of wine doth every day produce,
Make good the Doctrine of the *Turks*,
That in each grape a devil lurks.
And by yon fading sapless tree,
Bout which the *Ivy* twin'd you see,
His fate's foretold, who fondly places
His bliss in womans soft embraces.
All pleasures, but the Anglers, bring
I'th' tail repentance like a sting.

   Then on these banks let me sit down,
Free from the toilsom Sword and Gown,
And pity those that do affect
To conquer Nations and protect.
My Reed affords such true content,
Delights so sweet and innocent,
As seldom fall unto the lot
Of Scepters, though they'r *justly got*.

1649.   *Tho. Weaver,** Mr. of Arts.

To the Readers of my most ingenuous Friends Book,
The Compleat Angler.

HE that both knew and writ the lives of men,
Such as were once, but must not be agen:
Witness his matchless *Donne* and *Wotton*,* by
Whose aid he could their speculations try:
He that convers'd with *Angels*, such as were
Ouldsworth and *Featly*,* each a shining star
Shewing the way to *Bethlem*; each a Saint;
(Compar'd to whom our *Zelots* now but paint)
He that our pious and learn'd *Morley** knew,
And from him suck'd *wit* and *devotion* too:
He that from these such excellencies fetch'd,
That *He* could tell how high and far they reach'd;
What learning this, what graces th'other had;
And in what several dress each soul was clad.

Reader, this *HE*, this *Fisherman* comes forth,
And in these Fishers weeds would shroud his worth.
Now his mute Harp is on a Willow hung,
With which when finely toucht, and fitly strung,
He could friends passions for these times allay;
Or chain his fellow-*Anglers* from their prey.
But now the musick of his pen is still,
And he sits by a brook watching a quill:
Where with a fixt eye, and a ready hand,
He studies first to hook, and then to land
Some *Trout*, or *Pearch*, or *Pike*; and having done,
Sits on a Bank, and tells how this was won,
And that escap'd his hook; which with a wile
Did eat the bait, and Fisherman beguile.
Thus whilst some vex they from their lands are thrown,*
He joys to think the waters are his own,
And like the *Dutch*, he gladly can agree
To live at peace now,* and have *fishing* free.

April 3. 1650.   *Edv. Powel*, Mr. of Arts.*

To my dear Brother, Mr. Iz. Walton *on his* Compleat Angler.

THIS Book is so like you, and you like it,
For harmless Mirth, Expression, Art & Wit,
That I protest ingenuously 'tis true,
I love this Mirth, Art, Wit, the Book and You.

Rob. Floud,* C.

Clarissimo amicissimoq; Fratri, Domino *Isaaco Walton*, Artis Piscatoriae peritissimo.

UNICUS est Medicus reliquorum piscis, & istis
Fas quibus est Medicum tangere, certa salus.
Hic typus est Salvatoris mirandus Jesu,
[b]*Litera mysterium quaelibet hujus habet.*
Hunc cupio, hunc capias (bone frater Arundinis) ἰχθὺν;
[q]*Solveret hic pro me debita, teque Deo.*
Piscis is est, & piscator (mihi credito) qualem
Vel piscatorem piscis amare velit.*

Henry Bayley,* Artium Magister.

[b]	Ἰχθὺς	Piscis.
	Ι Ἰησοῦς	Jesus.
	χ Χριστὸς	Christus.
	θ Θεοῦ	Dei.
	υ Υἱὸς	Filius.
	ς Σωτὴρ	Salvator.

[q] Mat. 17. 27. the last words of the Chapter.

Ad Virum optimum, & Piscatorem peritissimum, *Isaacum Waltonum*.

MAGISTER artis docte Piscatoriae,
Waltone *salve, magne dux arundinis,*
Seu tu reductâ valle solus ambulas,
Praeterfluentes interim observans aquas,
Seu fortè puri stans in amnis margine,

Sive in tenaci gramine & ripâ sedens,
Fallis peritâ squameum pecus manu;
O te beatum! qui procul negotiis,
Foriq; & urbis pulvere & strepitu carens,
Extraq; turbam, ad lenè manantes aquas
Vagos honestâ fraude pisces decipis.
Dum caetera ergo paenè gens mortalium
Aut retia invicem sibi & technas struunt,
Donis, ut hamo, aut divites captant senes,
Gregi natantûm tu interim nectis dolos,
Voracem inescas advenam hamo lucium,
Avidamvè percam parvulo alburno capis,
Aut verme ruffo, musculâ aut truttam levi,
Cautumvè cyprinum, & ferè indocilem capi
Calamoq; linoq; (ars at hunc superat tua)
Medicamvè tincam, gobium aut escâ trahis,
Gratum palato gobium, parvum licet,
Praedamvè, non aeque salubrem barbulum,
Etsi ampliorem, & mystace insignem gravi.
Hae sunt tibi artes, dum annus & tempus sinunt,
Et nulla transit absq; linea dies.
Nec sola praxis, sed theoria & tibi
Nota artis hujus; unde tu simul bonus
Piscator, idem & scriptor; & calami potens
Utriusq; necdum & ictus, & tamen sapis.
Ut hamiotam nempe tironem instruas!
Stylo eleganti scribis en Halieutica
Oppianus alter, artis & methodum tuae, &
Praecepta promis rite piscatoria,
Varias & escas piscium, indolem, & genus.
Nec tradere artem sat putas piscariam,
(Virtutis est & haec tamen quaedam Schola
Patientiamq; & temperantiam docet)
Documenta quin majora das, & regulas
Sublimioris artis, & perennia
Monimenta morum, vitae & exempla optima;
Dum tu profundum scribis Hookerum, *& pium*
Donnum *ac disertum, sanctum &* Herbertum, *sacrum*
Vatem; hos videmus nam penicillo tuo

Graphicè, & peritâ, Isace, *depictos manu.*
Post fata factos hosce per te Virbios
O quae voluptas est legere in scriptis tuis!
Sic tu libris nos, lineis pisces capis,
Musisq; litterisq; dum incumbis, licet
*Intentus hamo, interq; piscandum studes.**

Aliud ad *Isaacum Waltonum*, virum & Piscatorem optimum.

Isace, *Macte hâc arte piscatoriâ;*
Hâc arte Petrus *Principi censum dedit;*
Hâc arte Princeps nec Petro *multò prior,*
Tranquillus ille, teste Tranquillo, Pater
Patriae, solebat recreare se lubens
Augustus, hamo instructus ac arundine.
Tu nunc, Amice, proximum clari es decus
Post Caesarem hami, gentis ac Halieuticae:
Euge O Professor artis haud ingloriae,
Doctor Cathedrae, perlegens Piscariam!
Nae tu Magister, & ego discipulus tuus,
(Nam candidatum & me ferunt arundinis)
Socium hac in arte nobilem Nacti sumus.
Quid amplius, Waltone, *nam dici potest?*
Ipse *hamiota Dominus en orbis fuit!**

Jaco. Dup. D.D.*

THE
COMPLEAT ANGLER,

OR,

The Contemplative
MAN'S RECREATION.

PART I.

CHAP. I.

A Conference betwixt an Angler, *a* Faulkner, *and a* Hunter, *each
commending his Recreation.*

> PISCATOR.
> VENATOR.
> AUCEPS.*

PISC. You are well overtaken, Gentlemen, a good morning to you
both; I have stretched my legs up *Tottenham-hill* to overtake you,
hoping your business may occasion you towards *Ware* whether* I am
going this fine, fresh *May* morning.

Venat. Sir, I for my part shall almost answer your hopes, for my
purpose is to drink my mornings draught at the *Thatcht House* in
*Hodsden,** and I think not to rest till I come thither, where I have
appointed a friend or two to meet me: but for this Gentleman that you
see with me, I know not how far he intends his journey; he came so
lately into my company, that I have scarce had time to ask him the
question.

Auceps. Sir, I shall by your favour bear you company as far as
*Theobalds,** and there leave you, for then I turn up to a friends house
who mews a Hawk* for me, which I now long to see.

Venat. Sir, we are all so happy as to have a fine, fresh, cool morning,
and I hope we shall each be the happier in the others company. And
Gentlemen, that I may not lose yours, I shall either abate or amend

my pace to enjoy it; knowing that (as the Italians say) *Good company in a Journey makes the way to seem the shorter.**

Auceps. It may do so Sir, with the help of good discourse, which methinks we may promise from you that both look and speak so chearfully: and for my part I promise you, as an invitation to it, that I will be as free and openhearted, as discretion will allow me to be with strangers.

Ven. And Sir, I promise the like.

Pisc. I am right glad to hear your answers, and in confidence you speak the truth, I shall put on a boldness to ask you Sir, Whether business or pleasure caused you to be so early up, and walk so fast, for this other Gentleman hath declared he is going to see a Hawk, that a friend mews for him.

Ven. Sir mine is a mixture of both, a little business and more pleasure, for I intend this day to do all my business, and then bestow another day or two in hunting the *Otter*, which a friend that I go to meet, tells me, is much pleasanter than any other chase whatsoever; howsoever I mean to try it; for to morrow morning we shall meet a pack of Otter dogs* of *noble Mr Sadlers** upon *Amwell hill,** who will be there so early, that they intend to prevent* the Sun-rising.

Pisc. Sir, my fortune has answered my desires, and my purpose is to bestow a day or two in helping to destroy some of those villanous vermin,* for I hate them perfectly, because they love fish so well, or rather, because they destroy so much; indeed so much, that in my judgment all men that keep *Otter-dogs* ought to have pensions from the King to encourage them to destroy the very breed of those base *Otters*, they do so much mischief.

Ven. But what say you to the Foxes of the Nation, would not you as willingly have them destroyed? for doubtless they do as much mischief as *Otters* do.

Pisc. Oh Sir, if they do, it is not so much to me and my fraternity as those base Vermine the *Otters* do.

Auc. Why Sir, I pray, of what Fraternity are you, that you are so angry with the poor *Otters*?

Pisc. I am (Sir) a brother of the *Angle*, and therefore an enemy to the *Otter*: for you are to note, that we Anglers all love one another, and therefore do I hate the *Otter* both for my own and for their sakes who are of my brotherhood.

Ven. And I am a lover of Hounds; I have followed many a pack of dogs many a mile, and heard many merry huntsmen make sport and scoff at Anglers.

Auc. And I profess my self a Faulkner, and have heard many grave, serious men pity them, 'tis such a heavy, contemptible, dull recreation.

Pisc. You know Gentlemen, 'tis an easie thing to scoff at any Art or Recreation; a little *wit* mixt with ill nature, confidence and *malice* will do it; but though they often venture boldly, yet they are often caught even in their own trap, according to that of *Lucian*,* the father of the family of Scoffers.

> Lucian *well skill'd in scoffing, this hath writ,*
> *Friend, that's your folly which you think your wit:*
> *This you vent oft, void both of wit and fear,*
> *Meaning another, when, your self you jeer.*

If to this you add what *Solomon* says of Scoffers,* that they are an abomination to mankind, let him that thinks fit scoff on, and be a Scoffer still, but I account them enemies to me, and to all that love vertue and Angling.

And for you that have heard many grave serious men pity Anglers; let me tell you Sir, there be many men that are by others taken to be serious and grave men, which we contemn and pity. Men that are taken to be grave, because Nature hath made them of a sowre complexion, money-getting-men, men that spend all their time first in getting, and next in anxious care to keep it; men that are condemned to be rich, and then always busie or discontented: for these poor-rich-men, we Anglers pity them perfectly, and stand in no need to borrow their thoughts to think our selves so happy. No, no, Sir, we enjoy a contentedness above the reach of such dispositions, and as the learned and ingenuous *Mountagne*[1]* sayes like himself freely, [1]*in Apol. for Ra. Sebeud* *When my Cat and I entertain each other with mutual apish tricks (as playing with a garter) who knows but that I make my Cat more sport than she makes me? Shall I conclude her to be simple, that has her time to begin or refuse to play as freely as I my self have? Nay, who knowes but that it is a defect of my not understanding her language (for doubtless Cats talk and reason with one another) that we agree no better: and who knows but that she pitties me for being no wiser than to play with her, and laughs and censures my follie for making sport for her when we two play together?*

Thus freely speaks *Mountaigne* concerning Cats, and I hope I may take as great a liberty to blame any man, and laugh at him too let him be never so grave, that hath not heard what Anglers can say in the justification of their Art and Recreation; which I may again tell you is so full of pleasure, that we need not borrow their thoughts to think our selves happy.

Venat. Sir, you have almost amazed me, for though I am no scoffer, yet I have (I pray let me speak it without offence) always looked upon Anglers as more patient and more simple men, than I fear I shall find you to be.

Pisc. Sir, I hope you will not judge my earnestness to be impatience: and for my *simplicity*, if by that you mean a harmlesness, or that simplicity which was usually found in the primitive Christians, who were (as most Anglers are) quiet men, and followers of peace; men that were so simply-wise, as not to sell their Consciences to buy riches, and with them vexation and a fear to die. If you mean such simple men as lived in those times when there were fewer Lawyers; when men might have had a Lordship safely conveyed to them in a piece of Parchment no bigger than your hand, (though several sheets will not do it safely in this wiser age) I say Sir, if you take us Anglers to be such simple men as I have spoke of, then my self and those of my profession will be glad to be so understood: But if by simplicity you meant to express a general defect in those that profess and practise the excellent Art of Angling, I hope in time to disabuse you, and make the contrary appear so evidently, that if you will but have patience to hear me, I shall remove all the Anticipations that discourse, or time, or prejudice have possess'd you with against that laudable and ancient art; for I know it is worthy the *knowledge* and *practise* of a wise man.

But (Gentlemen) though I be able to do this, I am not so unmannerly as to ingross all the discourse to my self; and therefore, you two having declared your selves, the one to be a lover of *Hawks*, the other of *Hounds*, I shall be most glad to hear what you can say in the commendation of that recreation which each of you love and practise; and having heard what you can say, I shall be glad to exercise your attention with what I can say concerning my own Recreation & Art of Angling, and by this means, we shall make the way to seem the shorter: and if you like my motion, I would have Mr. *Faulkner* to begin.

Auc. Your motion is consented to with all my heart, and to testifie*
it, I will begin as you have desired me.

And first, for the Element that I use* to trade in, which is the Air,
an Element of more worth than weight, an Element that doubtless
exceeds both the Earth and Water; for though I sometimes deal in
both, yet the Air is most properly mine, I and my Hawks use that
most, and it yields us most recreation; it stops not the high soaring of
my noble generous *Falcon*; in it she ascends to such an height, as the
dull eyes of beasts and fish are not able to reach to; their bodies are too
gross for such high elevations: in the Air my troops of Hawks soar up
on high, and when they are lost in the sight of men, then they attend
upon and converse with the gods, therefore I think my *Eagle* is so
justly styled, *Joves servant in Ordinary**: and that very *Falcon*, that I
am now going to see deserves no meaner a title, for she usually in her
flight endangers her self, (like the son of *Daedalus*)* to have her wings
scorch'd by the Suns heat, she flyes so near it, but her mettle makes
her careless of danger, for she then heeds nothing, but makes her
nimble Pinions cut the fluid air, and so makes her high way over the
steepest mountains and deepest rivers, and in her glorious carere*
looks with contempt upon those high Steeples and magnificent
Palaces which we adore and wonder at; from which height I can make
her to descend by a word from my mouth (which she both knows and
obeys) to accept of meat from my hand, to own me for her Master, to
go home with me, and be willing the next day to afford me the like
recreation.

And more; this Element of Air which I profess to trade in, the
worth of it is such, and it is of such necessity, that no creature whatsoever, not only those numerous creatures that feed on the face of the
Earth, but those various creatures that have their dwelling within the
waters, every creature that hath life in its nostrils stands in need of
my Element. The Waters cannot preserve the Fish without Air, witness the not breaking of Ice* in an extream Frost; the reason is, for
that if the inspiring and expiring Organ of any animal be stopt, it
suddenly yields to Nature, and dies. Thus necessary is Air to the
existence both of Fish and Beasts, nay, even to Man himself; that Air
or breath of life with which God at first inspired Mankind, he, if he
wants it, dies presently,* becomes a sad object to all that loved and
beheld him, and in an instant turns to putrefaction.

Nay more, the very birds of the air (those that be not Hawks) are both so many, and so useful and pleasant to mankind, that I must not let them pass without some observations: They both feed and refresh him; feed him with their choice bodies, and refresh him with their Heavenly voices. I will not undertake to mention the several kinds of Fowl by which this is done; and his curious palate pleased by day, and which with their very excrements* afford him a soft lodging at night. These I will pass by, but not those little nimble Musicians of the air, that warble forth their curious* Ditties, with which Nature hath furnished them to the shame of Art.

At first the *Lark*,* when she means to rejoyce; to chear her self and those that hear her, she then quits the earth, and sings as she ascends higher into the air, and having ended her Heavenly imployment, grows then mute and sad to think she must descend to the dull earth, which she would not touch but for necessity.

How do the *Black-bird* and *Thrassel** with their melodious voices bid welcome to the chearful Spring, and in their fixed Months warble forth such ditties as no art or instrument can reach to?

Nay, the smaller birds also do the like in their particular seasons, as namely the *Leverock*, the *Tit-lark*, the little *Linnet*, and the honest *Robin*, that loves mankind both alive and dead.*

But the *Nightingale* (another of my Airy Creatures) breaths such sweet loud musick out of her little instrumental throat, that it might make mankind to think Miracles are not ceased. He that at midnight (when the very labourer sleeps securely) should hear (as I have very often) the clear airs, the sweet descants, the natural rising and falling, the doubling and redoubling of her voice, might well be lifted above earth, and say; Lord, what Musick hast thou provided for the Saints in Heaven, when thou affordest bad men such musick on Earth!

And this makes me the less to wonder at the many *Aviaries* in *Italy*, or at the great charge of *Varro* his *Aviarie*,* the ruines of which are yet to be seen in *Rome*, and is still so famous there, that it is reckoned for one of those Notables which men of forraign Nations either record, or lay up in their memories when they return from travel.

This for the birds of pleasure, of which very much more might be said. My next shall be of Birds of Political use; I think 'tis not to be doubted that Swallows have been taught to carry Letters betwixt two Armies. But 'tis certain that when the Turks besieged *Malta* or *Rhodes** (I now remember not which 'twas) *Pigeons* are then related to carry and recarry Letters. And Mr. *G. Sandis* in his Travels* (*fol.* 269.)

relates it to be done betwixt *Aleppo* and *Babylon*. But if that be disbelieved, 'tis not to be doubted that the *Dove* was sent out of the Ark by
Noah,* to give him notice of Land, when to him all appeared to be Sea;
and the *Dove* proved a faithful and comfortable messenger. And for
the Sacrifices of the Law,* a pair of *Turtle Doves* or young *Pigeons* were
as well accepted as costly *Bulls* and *Rams*. And when God would feed
the Prophet *Elijah*,* (1 *King.* 17.) after a kind of miraculous manner he
did it by *Ravens*, who brought him meat morning and evening. Lastly,
the Holy Ghost when he descended visibly upon our Saviour, did it
by assuming the shape of a *Dove*.* And, to conclude this part of my
discourse, pray remember these wonders were done by birds of the
Air, the Element in which they and I take so much pleasure.

There is also a little contemptible winged Creature (an Inhabitant
of my Aerial Element) namely, the laborious *Bee*, of whose *Prudence*,
Policy and regular Government of their own Commonwealth* I
might say much, as also of their several kinds, and how useful their
honey and wax is both for meat and Medicines to mankind; but I will
leave them to their sweet labour, without the least disturbance,
believing them to be all very busie at this very time amongst the herbs
and flowers that we see nature puts forth this *May* morning.

And now to return to my Hawks from whom I have made too long
a digression; you are to note, that they are usually distinguished into
two kinds; namely, the long-winged and the short-winged Hawk*: of
the first kind, there be chiefly in use amongst us in this Nation,

> The *Gerfalcon* and *Jerkin*.*
> The *Falcon* and *Tassel-gentel*.
> The *Laner* and *Laneret*.
> The *Bockerel* and *Bockeret*.
> The *Saker* and *Sacaret*.
> The *Marlin* and *Jack Marlin*.
> The *Hobby* and *Jack*.
> There is the *Stelletto** of *Spain*.
> The *Bloud* red *Rook* from *Turky*.*
> The *Waskite* from *Virginia*.*

And there is of short-winged Hawks

> The *Eagle* and *Iron*.*
> The *Goshawk* and *Tarcel*.*
> The *Sparhawk* and *Musket*.*
> The French *Pye* of two sorts.*

These are reckoned Hawks of note and worth, but we have also of an inferiour rank,

The *Stanyel*, the *Ringtail*.*
The *Raven*, the *Buzzard*.
The forked *Kite*, the bald *Buzzard*.*
The *Hen-driver*,* and others that I forbear to name.

Gentlemen, If I should enlarge my discourse to the observation of the *Eires*, the *Brancher*, the *Ramish Hawk*, the *Haggard*, and the two sorts of *Lentners*,* and then treat of their several *Ayries*, their *Mewings*, rare order of casting,* and the renovation of their *Feathers*; their reclaiming,* dyeting, and then come to their rare stories of practice; I say, if I should enter into these, and many other observations that I could make, it would be much, very much pleasure to me: but lest I should break the rules of Civility with you, by taking up more than the proportion of time allotted to me, I will here break off, and entreat you Mr. *Venator*, to say what you are able in the commendation of Hunting, to which you are so much affected, and if time will serve, I will beg your favour for a further enlargement of some of those several heads of which I have spoken. But no more at present.

Venat. Well Sir, and I will now take my turn, and will first begin with a commendation of the earth, as you have done most excellently of the Air, the Earth being that Element upon which I drive my pleasant, wholsom, hungry trade. The Earth is a solid, setled Element; an Element most universally beneficial both to man and beast: to men who have their several Recreations upon it, as Horse-races, Hunting, sweet smells, pleasant walks. The Earth feeds man, and all those several beasts that both feed him, and afford him recreation: What pleasure doth man take in hunting the stately *Stag*, the generous *Buck*,* the *Wild Boar*, the cunning *Otter*, the crafty *Fox*, and the fearful *Hare?* And if I may descend to a lower Game, what pleasure is it sometimes with Gins to betray the very vermine of the earth? as namely, the *Fichat*, the *Fulimart*, the *Ferret*, the *Pole-cat*, the *Mould-warp*,* and the like creatures that live upon the face, and within the bowels of the earth. How doth the earth bring forth *herbs, flowers* and *fruits*, both for *physick* and the *pleasure* of mankind? and above all, to me at least, the fruitful *Vine*, of which, when I drink moderately, it clears my brain, chears my heart, and sharpens my wit. How could *Cleopatra* have feasted *Mark Antony* with eight Wild Boars roasted whole at one Supper,* and other meat suitable, if the earth had not been a bountiful mother? But to pass by the mighty *Elephant*, which the earth breeds and nourisheth, and descend to the least of creatures, how doth the earth afford us a doctrinal example in the little *Pismire*,* who in the Summer provides and lays up her Winter provision, and teaches man to do the like? The earth feeds and carries those horses that carry us. If I would be prodigal of my time and your patience, what might not I say in commendations of the earth? That puts limits to the proud and raging *Sea*, and by that means preserves both man and beast that it destroys them not, as we see it daily doth those that venture upon the Sea, and are there ship-wrackt, drowned, and left to feed Haddocks; when we that are so wise as to keep our selves on *earth*, *walk*, and *talk*, and *live*, and *eat*, and *drink*, and go a *hunting*: of which recreation I will say a little, and then leave Mr. *Piscator* to the commendation of Angling.

Hunting is a game for Princes and noble persons; it hath been highly prized in all Ages; it was one of the qualifications that *Xenophon** bestowed on his *Cyrus*, that he was a Hunter of wild beasts. Hunting trains up the younger Nobility to the use of manly exercises in their riper age. What more manly exercise than *hunting the Wild Bore*, the *Stag*, the *Buck*, the *Fox* or the *Hare?* How doth it preserve health, and increase strength and activity?

And for the Dogs that we use, who can commend their excellency to that height which they deserve? How perfect is the Hound at *smelling*, who never leaves or forsakes his first scent, but follows it through so many changes and varieties of other scents, even over, and in the water, and into the earth? What musick doth a pack of Dogs then make to any man, whose heart and ears are so happy as to be set to the tune of such instruments? How will a right *Greyhound* fix his eye on the best *Buck* in a *herd*, single him out, and follow him, and him only through a whole herd of Rascal game,* and still know and then kill him? For my Hounds I know the language of them, and they know the language and meaning of one another as perfectly as we know the voices of those with whom we discourse daily.

I might enlarge my self in the commendation of *Hunting*, and of the noble Hound especially, as also of the docibleness of *dogs* in general; and I might make many observations of Land-creatures, that for composition, order, figure and constitution, approach nearest to the compleatness and understanding of man; especially of those creatures which *Moses* in the Law permitted to the Jews,* (which have cloven

Hoofs and chew the Cud) which I shall forbear to name, because I will not be so uncivil to Mr. *Piscator*, as not to allow him a time for the commendation of *Angling*, which he calls an Art; but doubtless 'tis an easie one: and Mr. *Auceps*, I doubt we shall hear a watry discourse of it, but I hope 'twill not be a long one.

Auc. And I hope so too, though I fear it will.

Pisc. Gentlemen; let not prejudice prepossess you. I confess my discourse is like to prove suitable to my Recreation, *calm* and *quiet*; we seldom take the name of God into our mouths, but it is either to praise him or pray to him; if others use it vainly in the midst of their recreations, so vainly as if they meant to conjure, I must tell you, it is neither our fault nor our custom;* we protest against it. But, pray remember I accuse no body; for as I would not make a *watry* discourse, so I would not put too much *vinegar* into it; nor would I raise the reputation of my own Art by the diminution or ruine of anothers. And so much for the Prologue to what I mean to say.

And now for the *Water*, the Element that I trade in. The *water* is the eldest daughter of the Creation, the Element upon which the Spirit of God did first move,* the Element which God commanded to bring forth living creatures abundantly;* and without which those that inhabit the Land, even all creatures that have breath in their nostrils must suddenly return to putrefaction. *Moses* the great Lawgiver and chief Philosopher, skilled in all the learning of the Egyptians,* who was called the friend of God,* and knew the mind of the Almighty, names this Element the first in the Creation; this is the Element upon which the Spirit of God did first move, and is the chief Ingredient in the Creation: many Philosophers* have made it to comprehend all the other Elements, and most allow it the chiefest in the mixtion of all living creatures.

There be that profess to believe that all bodies are made of *water*, and may be reduced back again to water only: they endeavour to demonstrate it thus,

Take a *Willow* (or any like speedy growing plant) newly rooted in a box or barrel full of earth, weigh them altogether exactly when the tree begins to grow, and then weigh all together after the tree is increased from its first rooting to weigh an hundred pound weight more than when it was first rooted and weighed; and you shall find this augment of the tree to be without the diminution of one dram weight of the earth. Hence they infer this increase of wood to be from water of rain, or from dew, and not to be from any other Element. And they affirm, they can reduce this wood back again to water;* and they affirm also the same may be done in any *animal* or *vegetable*. And this I take to be a fair testimony of the excellency of my Element of Water.

The *Water* is more productive than the *Earth*. Nay, the earth hath no fruitfulness without showers or dews; for all the *herbs*, and *flowers*, and *fruit* are produced and thrive by the water; and the very Minerals are fed by streams that run under ground, whose natural course carries them to the tops of many high mountains, as we see by several springs breaking forth on the tops of the highest hills; and this is also witnessed by the daily trial and testimony of several Miners.

Nay, the increase* of those creatures that are bred and fed in the water, are not only more and more miraculous, but more advantagious to man, not only for the lengthning of his life, but for the preventing of sickness; for 'tis observed by the most learned Physicians, that the casting off of Lent* and other Fish-daies, (which hath not only given the Lie to so many learned, pious, wise Founders of Colledges, for which we should be ashamed) hath doubtless been the chief cause of those many putrid, shaking, intermitting Agues, unto which this Nation of ours is now more subject than those wiser Countries that feed on Herbs, Sallets, and plenty of Fish; of which it is observed in Story,* that the greatest part of the world now do. And it may be fit to remember that *Moses* (*Lev.* 11.9. *Deut.* 14.9.) appointed Fish to be the chief diet* for the best Common-wealth that ever yet was.

And it is observable not only that there are *fish*, (as namely the *Whale*)* three times as big as the mighty Elephant, that is so fierce in battel; but that the mightiest Feasts have been of Fish. The *Romans** in the height of their glory have made Fish the mistress of all their entertainments; they have had Musick to usher in their *Sturgeons, Lampreys*, and *Mullets*, which they would purchase at rates rather to be wondred at than believed. He that shall view the Writings of *Macrobius* or *Varro*, may be confirmed and informed of this, and of the incredible value of their Fish, and fish-ponds.

But, Gentlemen, I have almost lost my self, which I confess I may easily do in this Philosophical Discourse; I met with most of it very lately (and I hope happily) in a conference with a most learned Physician, Dr. *Wharton*,* a dear Friend; that loves both me and my Art of Angling. But however I will wade no deeper in these mysterious Arguments, but pass to such Observations as I can manage with more pleasure, and less fear of running into error. But I must not yet forsake the Waters, by whose help we have so many known advantages.

And first (to pass by the miraculous cures of our known *Baths*) how advantagious is the *Sea* for our daily Traffique; without which we could not now subsist? How does it not only furnish us with food and Physick for the bodies, but with such Observations for the mind as ingenious persons would not want?

How ignorant had we been of the beauty of *Florence*, of the *Monuments, Urns*, and *Rarities* that yet remain in, and near unto old and new *Rome*, (so many as it is said will take up a years time to view, and afford to each of them but a convenient consideration); and therefore it is not to be wondred at, that so learned and devout a Father as St. *Jerome*,* after his wish to have seen Christ in the flesh, and to have heard St. *Paul* preach, makes his third wish, to *have seen Rome in her glory*; and that glory is not yet all lost, for what pleasure is it to see the Monuments of *Livy*, the choicest of the Historians: of *Tully*,* the best of Orators; and to see the Bay-trees that now grow out of the very Tomb of *Virgil*? These to any that love Learning must be pleasing. But what pleasure is it to a devout Christian to see there the humble house in which St. *Paul* was content to dwell; and to view the many rich *Statues* that are there made in honour of his memory? nay, to see the very place in which St. *Peter* and he lie buried together? These are in and near to *Rome*.* And how much more doth it please the pious curiosity of a Christian to see that place on which the blessed Saviour of the world was pleased to humble himself, and to take our nature upon him, and to converse with men: to see Mount *Sion, Jerusalem*, and the very Sepulchre of our Lord Jesus? How may it beget and heighten the zeal of a Christian to see the Devotions that are daily paid to him at that place? Gentlemen, lest I forget my self I will stop here, and remember you, that but for my Element of water the Inhabitants of this poor Island must remain ignorant that such things ever were, or that any of them have yet a being.

Gentlemen, I might both enlarge and lose my self in such like Arguments; I might tell you that Almighty God is said to have spoken to a *Fish*,* but never to a *Beast*; that he hath made a *Whale* a Ship* to carry and set his Prophet *Jonah* safe on the appointed shore. Of these I might speak, but I must in manners break off, for I see *Theobalds* house.* I cry you mercy for being so long, and thank you for your patience.

Auceps. Sir, my pardon is easily granted you: I except against*
nothing that you have said; nevertheless, I must part with you at this
Park-wall,* for which I am very sorry; but I assure you Mr. *Piscator*,
I now part with you full of good thoughts, not only of your self, but
your Recreation. And so Gentlemen, God keep you both.

Pisc. Well, now Mr. *Venator* you shall neither want time nor my
attention to hear you enlarge your Discourse concerning Hunting.

Venat. Not I Sir, I remember you said that *Angling* it self was of
great Antiquity, and a perfect Art, and an Art not easily attained to;
and you have so won upon me in your former discourse, that I am
very desirous to hear what you can say further concerning those
particulars.

Pisc. Sir, I did say so, and I doubt not but if you and I did converse
together but a few hours, to leave you possest with the same high and
happy thoughts that now possess me of it; not only of the Antiquity
of *Angling*, but that it deserves commendations, and that it is an Art,
and an Art worthy the knowledg and practise of a wise man.

Venat. Pray Sir, speak of them what you think fit, for we have yet
five miles to the *Thatcht-House*, during which walk, I dare promise
you, my patience, and diligent attention shall not be wanting. And if
you shall make that to appear which you have undertaken, first, that
it is an Art, and an Art worth the learning, I shall beg that I may
attend you a day or two a fishing, and that I may become your Scholar,
and be instructed in the Art it self which you so much magnifie.

Pisc. O Sir, doubt not but that *Angling* is an Art; is it not an Art to
deceive a *Trout* with an artificial Flie? a *Trout*! that is more sharp
sighted than any Hawk you have nam'd,* and more watchful and
timorous than your high mettled *Marlin* is bold? and yet, I doubt not
to catch a brace or two to morrow, for a friends breakfast: doubt not
therefore, Sir, but that *Angling* is an Art, and an Art worth your
learning: the Question is rather, whether you be capable of learning
it? for *Angling* is somewhat like *Poetry*, men are to be born so:*
I mean, with inclinations to it, though both may be heightned by
discourse and practice, but he that hopes to be a good *Angler* must not
only bring an inquiring, searching, observing wit;* but he must bring
a large measure of hope and patience, and a love and propensity to the
Art it self; but having once got and practis'd it, then doubt not but
Angling will prove to be so pleasant, that it will prove to be like
Vertue, *a reward to it self*.*

Venat. Sir, I am now become so full of expectation that I long much to have you proceed; and in the order that you propose.

Pisc. Then first, for the *antiquity* of *Angling,** of which I shall not say much, but onely this; Some say it is as ancient as *Deucalions* Flood: others that *Belus,** who was the first Inventer of Godly and vertuous Recreations, was the first Inventer of *Angling*: and some others say (for former times have had their disquisitions about the Antiquity of it) that *Seth,** one of the Sons of *Adam*, taught it to his Sons, and that by them it was derived to posterity: others say, that he left it engraven on those pillars which he erected, and trusted to preserve the knowledge of the *Mathematicks, Musick*, and the rest of that precious knowledge, and those useful Arts which by Gods appointment or allowance and his noble industry were thereby preserved from perishing in *Noahs* flood.

These, Sir, have been the opinions of several men, that have possibly endeavored to make *Angling* more ancient than is needful, or may well be warranted; but for my part, I shall content my self in telling you that Angling is much more ancient than the Incarnation of our Saviour; for in the Prophet *Amos* mention is made of *fish-hooks*; and in the Book of *Job* (which was long before the days of *Amos*, for that book is said to be writ by *Moses*) mention is made also of fish-hooks,** which must imply Anglers in those times.

But, my worthy friend, as I would rather prove my self a *Gentleman* by being *learned* and *humble, valiant*, and *inoffensive, vertuous*, and *communicable,** than by any fond ostentation of riches, or wanting those vertues my self, boast that these were in my Ancestors (and yet I grant that where a noble and ancient descent and such merits meet in any man, it is a double dignification of that person): So if this Antiquity of *Angling*, (which for my part I have not forced), shall like an ancient family, be either an honour or an ornament to this vertuous Art which I profess to love and practice, I shall be the gladder that I made an accidental mention of the antiquity of it; of which I shall say no more but proceed to that just commendation which I think it deserves.

And for that I shall tell you, that in ancient times a debate hath risen, (and it remains yet unresolved) Whether the happiness of man in this world doth consist more in *Contemplation* or *action?*

Concerning which some have endeavoured to maintain their opinion of the first, by saying, *That the nearer we Mortals come to God by way of imitation, the more happy we are*. And they say, *That God enjoys himself only by a contemplation of his own infinitenesse, Eternity, Power and Goodness*, and the like. And upon this ground many Cloysteral men of great learning and devotion prefer *Contemplation* before *Action*. And many of the fathers seem to approve this opinion, as may appear in their Commentaries upon the words of our Saviour to *Martha, Luke* 10. 41, 42.

And on the contrary, there want not men of equal authority and credit, that prefer *action* to be the more excellent, as namely *experiments in Physick, and the application of it, both for the ease and prolongation of mans life*; by which each man is enabled to act and do good to others; either to serve his Countrey, or do good to particular persons; and they say also, *That action is Doctrinal, and teaches both art and vertue, and is a maintainer of humane society*, and for these, and other like reasons to be preferred before *contemplation*.

Concerning which two opinions I shall forbear to add a third by declaring my own, and rest my self contented in telling you (my very worthy friend) that both these meet together, and do most properly belong to the most *honest, ingenuous, quiet*, and *harmless* art of *Angling*.

And first, I shall tell you what some have observed, (and I have found it to be a real truth) that the very sitting by the Rivers side is not only the quietest and fittest place for *contemplation*, but will invite an Angler to it: and this seems to be maintained by the learned *Pet. du Moulin*,* who (in his Discourse of the fulfilling of Prophesies) observes, that when God intended to reveal any future events or high notions to his Prophets, he then carried them either to the *Desarts* or the *Sea-shore*, that having so separated them from amidst the press of *people* and *business*, and the cares of the world, he might settle their minds in a quiet repose, and there make them fit for Revelation.

And this seems also to be intimated by the Children of *Israel*, (*Psal.* 137.) who having in a sad condition banished all mirth and musick from their pensive hearts, and having hung up their then mute Harps upon the Willow-trees growing by the Rivers of *Babylon*, sate down upon those banks bemoaning the ruines of *Sion*, and contemplating their own sad condition.

And an ingenuous *Spaniard** says, *That Rivers and the Inhabitants of the watry Element were made for wise men to contemplate, and fools to pass by without consideration*. And though I will not rank my self in the number of the first, yet give me leave to free my self from the last, by offering to you a short contemplation, first of *Rivers*, and then of *Fish*; concerning which I doubt not but to give you many observations that will appear very considerable: I am sure they have appeared so to me, and made many an hour pass away more pleasantly, as I have sate quietly on a flowry Bank by a calm River, and contemplated what I shall now relate to you.

And first concerning Rivers; there be so many wonders reported and written of them, and of the several Creatures that be bred and live in them; and, those by Authors of so good credit, that we need not to deny them an historical Faith.

As namely of a River in *Epirus*, that puts out any lighted Torch, and kindles any Torch that was not lighted. Some Waters being drank cause madness, some drunkenness, and some laughter to death. The River *Selarus* in a few hours turns a rod or wand to stone: and our *Cambden* mentions the like in *England*, and the like in *Lochmere* in *Ireland*. There is also a River in *Arabia*, of which all the sheep that drink thereof have their wool turned into a Vermilion colour. And one of no less credit than *Aristotle*,* tells us of a merry River, (the River *Elusina*) that dances at the noise of musick, for with musick it bubbles, dances and grows sandy, and so continues till the musick ceases, but then it presently returns to its wonted calmness and clearness. And *Cambden* tells us of a Well near to *Kerby* in *Westmoreland*, that ebbs and flows several times every day: and he tells us of a River in *Surry* (it is called *Mole*)* that after it has run several miles, being opposed by hills, finds or makes it self a way under ground, and breaks out again so far off, that the Inhabitants thereabout boast, (as the *Spaniards* do of their River *Anus*)* that they feed divers flocks of sheep upon a Bridge. And lastly, for I would not tire your patience, one of no less authority than *Josephus** that learned Jew, tells us of a River in *Judea*, that runs swiftly all the six days of the week, and stands still and rests all their *Sabbath*.

But I will lay aside my Discourse of Rivers and tell you some things of the Monsters, or Fish, call them what you will, that they breed and feed in them. *Pliny* the Philosopher* says, (in the third Chapter of his ninth Book) that in the *Indian Sea*, the fish call'd the *Balaena* or *Whirle-Pool** is so long and broad, as to take up more in length and bredth than two Acres of ground, and of other fish of two hundred cubits long; and that in the River *Ganges*, there be Eeles of thirty foot long. He says there, that these Monsters appear in that Sea only, when the tempestuous winds oppose the Torrents of Waters falling from the Rocks into it, and so turning what lay at the bottom to be seen on the waters top. And he says, that the people of *Cadara* (an Island near this place)* make the Timber for their houses of those Fish-bones. He there tells us, that there are sometimes a thousand of these great Eeles found wrapt, or interwoven together. He tells us there, that it appears that Dolphins love musick, and will come, when call'd for, by some men or boys, that know and use to feed them, and that they can swim as swift as an Arrow can be shot out of a Bow, and much of this is spoken concerning the *Dolphin*, and other Fish, as may be found also in learned Dr.*Casaubons* Discourse of Credulity, and Incredulity,* printed by him about the year 1670.

I know, we Islanders are averse to the belief of these wonders: but, there be so many strange Creatures to be now seen (many collected by *John Tredescant*, and others added by my friend *Elias Ashmole** Esq; who now keeps them carefully and methodically at his house near to *Lambeth* near *London*) as may get some belief of some of the other wonders I mentioned. I will tell you some of the wonders that you may now see, and not till then believe, unless you think fit.

You may there see the *Hog-fish*, the *Dog-fish*, the *Dolphin*, the *Cony-Fish*,* the *Parrot-fish*, the *Shark*, the *Poyson-fish*,* *sword-fish*, and not only other incredible fish! but you may there see the *Salamander*, several sorts of *Barnacles*, of *Solan Geese*,* the *bird* of *Paradise*, such sorts of *Snakes*, and such *birds-nests*, and of so various forms, and so wonderfully made, as may beget wonder and amusement in any beholder: and so many hundreds of other rarities in that Collection, as will make the other wonders I spake of, the less incredible; for, you may note, that the waters are natures store-house, in which she locks up her wonders.

But, Sir, lest this Discourse may seem tedious, I shall now give it a sweet conclusion out of that holy Poet Mr. *George Herbert** his Divine Contemplation on Gods Providence.

> *Lord, who hath praise enough, nay, who hath any?*
> *None can express thy works, but he that knows them;*
> *And none can know thy works, they are so many,*
> *And so compleat, but only he that ows* them.*
>
> *We all acknowledg both thy power and love*
> *To be exact, transcendent and divine;*
> *Who dost so strangely and so sweetly move,*
> *Whilst all things have their end, yet none but thine.*

> *Wherefore, most sacred Spirit, I here present*
> *For me, and all my fellows, praise to thee;*
> *And just it is that I should pay the rent,*
> *Because the benefit accrues to me.*

And as concerning Fish in that Psalm, (*Psal.* 104.) wherein for
height of Poetry and Wonders the Prophet *David* seems even to exceed
himself, how doth he there express himself in choice Metaphors, even
to the amazement of a contemplative Reader, concerning the *Sea*, the
Rivers, and the *Fish* therein contained? And the great Naturalist *Pliny*
says,* *That Natures great and wonderful power is more demonstrated in the*
Sea than on the Land. And this may appear by the numerous and various Creatures inhabiting both in and about that Element; as to the
Readers of *Gesner*,* *Rondeletius*,* *Pliny, Ausonius*,* *Aristotle*, and others,
Dubartas in may be demonstrated. But I will sweeten this Discourse
the fifth day. also out of a Contemplation in Divine *Dubartas*,* who says,

> *God quickned in the sea and in the rivers,*
> *So many Fishes of so many features,*
> *That in the waters we may see all creatures,*
> *Even all that on the earth are to be found,*
> *As if the world were in deep waters drown'd.*
> *For seas (as well as skies) have Sun, Moon, Stars;*
> *(As well as air) Swallows, Rooks, and Stares;**
> *(As well as earth) Vines, Roses, Nettles, Melons,*
> *Mushroms, Pinks, Gilliflowers, and many millions*
> *Of other plants, more rare, more strange than these,*
> *As very fishes living in the seas:*
> *As also Rams, Calves, Horses, Hares and Hogs,*
> *Wolves, Urchins,* Lions, Elephants and Dogs;*
> *Yea men and Maids, and which I most admire,*
> *The mitred Bishop, and the cowled Fryer.**
> *Of which, Examples but a few years since,*
> *Were shewn the* Norway *and* Polonian* *Prince.*

These seem to be wonders, but have had so many confirmations
from men of learning and credit, that you need not doubt them;
nor are the number, nor the various shapes of fishes, more strange or
more fit for *contemplation*, than their different natures, inclinations
and actions; concerning which I shall beg your patient ear a little
longer.

The *Cuttle-fish* will cast a long gut out of her throat, which (like as an Angler doth his line) she sendeth forth and pulleth in again at her pleasure, according as she sees some little fish come near to her; and the *Cuttle-fish* (being then hid in the gravel) lets the Mount. Essays, and smaller fish nibble and bite the end of it, at which others affirm this. time she by little and little draws the smaller fish so near to her, that she may leap upon her, and then catches and devours her: and for this reason some have called this fish the *Sea-Angler*.*

And there is a fish called a *Hermit*,* that at a certain age gets into a dead fishes shell, and like a Hermite dwells there alone, studying the wind and weather, and so turns her shell, that she makes it defend her from the injuries that they would bring upon her.

There is also a fish called by *Ælian* (in his 9. book of Living Creatures, Chap. 16.) the *Adonis*,* or Darling of the Sea; so called, because it is a loving and innocent fish, a fish that hurts nothing that hath life, and is at peace with all the numerous Inhabitants of that vast watry Element: and truly I think most Anglers are so disposed to most of mankind.

And there are also lustful and chast fishes, of which I shall give you examples.

And first, what *Dubartas* sayes of a fish called the *Sargus*;* which (because none can expresse it better than he does) I shall give you in his own words, supposing it shall not have the less credit for being Verse, for he hath gathered this, and other observations out of Authors that have been great and industrious searchers into the secrets of Nature.

> *The Adult'rous* Sargus *doth not only change*
> *Wives every day in the deep streams, but (strange)*
> *As if the hony of Sea-love delight*
> *Could not suffice his ranging appetite,*
> *Goes courting she-Goats on the grassie shore,*
> *Horning their husbands** that had horns before.*

And the same Author writes concerning the *Cantharus*,* that which you shall also hear in his own words.

> *But contrary, the constant* Cantharus
> *Is ever constant to his faithful Spouse,*
> *In nuptial duties spending his chaste life,*
> *Never loves any but his own dear Wife.*

Sir, but a little longer, and I have done.

Venat. Sir, take what liberty you think fit, for your discourse seems to be Musick, and charms me to an attention.

Pisc. Why then Sir, I will take a little liberty to tell, or rather to remember you what is said of *Turtle-Doves*; First, That they silently plight their troth and marry; and that then, the Surviver scorns (as the *Thracian women** are said to do) to out-live his or her mate, and this is taken for a truth, and if the surviver shall ever couple with another, then not only the living, but the dead, (be it either the He or the she) is denyed the *name* and *honour* of a true *Turtle-dove*.

And to parallel this Land-Rarity, and teach mankind moral faithfulness, and to condemn those that talk of Religion, and yet come short of the moral faith of fish and fowl; Men that violate the Law affirmed by Saint *Paul* (*Rom.* 2. 14, 15.) to be writ in their hearts, (and which he says, shall at the last day condemn and leave them without excuse), I pray hearken to what *Dubartas* sings, (for the hearing of such conjugal faithfulness, will be Musick to all chast ears) and therefore I pray harken to what *Dubartas* sings of the *Mullet*.

Dubartas fifth day.

> *But for chast love the* Mullet *hath no peer;*
> *For, if the Fisher hath surpriz'd her pheer,*
> *As mad with wo, to shore she followeth,*
> *Prest to consort him both in life and death.**

On the contrary, What shall I say of the *House-Cock,** which treads any Hen, and then (contrary to the *Swan*, the *Partridge* and *Pigeon*) takes no care to hatch, to feed or to cherish his own brood, but is senseless though they perish.

And 'tis considerable, that the Hen (which because she also takes any *Cock*, expects it not) who is sure the Chickens be her own, hath by a moral impression her care and affection to her own Brood more than doubled, even to such a height, that our Saviour in expressing his love to *Jerusalem* (*Mat.* 23. 37.) quotes her for an example of tender affection; as his Father had done *Job* for a pattern of patience.*

And to parallel this *Cock*, there be divers fishes that cast their Spawn on flags or stones, and then leave it uncovered, and exposed to become a prey, and be devoured by Vermine or other fishes: but other fishes (as namely the *Barbel*) take such care for the preservation of their seed, that (unlike to the *Cock* or the *Cuckoe*) they mutually labour (both the Spawner and the Melter)* to cover their Spawn with sand, or watch it, or hide it in some secret place unfrequented by Vermine or by any Fish but themselves.

Sir, these Examples may, to you and others, seem strange; but they are testified some by *Aristotle*, some by *Pliny*, some by *Gesner*, and by many others of credit, and are believed and known by divers, both of wisdom and experience, to be a Truth; and indeed are (as I said at the beginning) fit for the contemplation of a most serious and a most pious man. And doubtless this made the Prophet *David* say, *They that occupy themselves in deep waters see the wonderful works of God*:* indeed such wonders and pleasures too as the land affords not.

And that they be fit for the contemplation of the most prudent, and pious, and peaceable men, seems to be testifyed by the practise of so many devout and contemplative men, as the *Patriarchs* and *Prophets* of old; and of the *Apostles* of our Saviour in our latter times; of which twelve, we are sure he chose four that were simple Fisher-men, whom he inspired and sent to publish his blessed Will to the *Gentiles, and inspir'd them also with a power to speak all languages,* and by their powerful Eloquence to beget faith in the unbelieving Jews: and themselves to suffer for that Saviour whom their fore fathers and they had Crucified, and, in their sufferings, to preach freedom from the incumbrances of the Law, and a new way to everlasting life*: this was the imployment of these happy Fishermen. Concerning which choice, some have made these Observations.

First that he never reproved these for their Imployment or Calling, as he did the *Scribes* and the *Mony-changers*.* And secondly, he found that the hearts of such men by nature were fitted for contemplation and quietnesse; men of mild, and sweet, and peaceable spirits, as indeed most Anglers are: these men our blessed Saviour, (who is observed to love to plant grace in good natures) though indeed nothing be too hard for him, yet these men he chose to call from their irreprovable imployment of Fishing, and gave them grace to be his Disciples, and to follow him and doe wonders, I say four of twelve.

And it is observable, that it was our Saviours will, that these our four Fishermen should have a priority of nomination in the Catalogue of his twelve Apostles,* (*Mat.* 10.) as namely first St. *Peter*, St. *Andrew*, St. *James* and St. *John*, and then the rest in their order.

And it is yet more observable, that when our blessed Saviour went up into the Mount, when he left the rest of his Disciples, and chose only three to bear him company at his *Transfiguration*,* that those

three were all Fishermen. And it is to be believed, that all the other
Apostles, after they betook themselves to follow Christ, betook themselves to be Fishermen too; for it is certain that the greater number of
them were found together Fishing by Jesus after his Resurrection, as
it is recorded in the 21. Chapter of St. *Johns* Gospel.

And since I have your promise to hear me with patience, I will take
a liberty to look back upon an observation that hath been made by an
ingenuous and learned man,* who observes that God hath been pleased
to allow those, whom he himself hath appointed to write his holy Will
in holy writ, yet, to express his Will in such Metaphors as their former
affections or practice had inclined them to; and he brings *Solomon* for
an example, who before his conversion was remarkably carnally-
amorous; and after by Gods appointment wrote that spiritual Dialogue
or holy amorous Love-song (the *Canticles*) betwixt God and his Church;
(in which he sayes his beloved had *Eyes like the fish-pools of Heshbon*). *

And if this hold in reason (as I see none to the contrary), then it
may be probably concluded, that *Moses* (who, I told you before, writ
the Book of *Job*) and the Prophet *Amos*, who was a Shepherd,* were
both Anglers; for you shall in all the Old Testament find Fish-hooks,*
I think but twice mentioned, namely, by meek *Moses* the friend of
God,* and by the humble Prophet *Amos*.

Concerning which last, namely the Prophet *Amos*, I shall make but
this Observation, That he that shall read the *humble, lowly, plain style* of
that *Prophet*, and compare it with the *high, glorious, eloquent style* of the
Prophet *Isaiah* (though they be both equally true) may easily believe
Amos to be, not only a Shepherd, but a good-natur'd, plain *Fisher-man*.

Which I do the rather believe by comparing the affectionate,
loving, lowly, humble Epistles of S. *Peter*, S. *James* and S. *John*,
whom we know were all Fishers, with the glorious language and high
Metaphors of S. *Paul*, who we may believe was not.

And for the lawfulness of Fishing it may very well be maintained
by our Saviours bidding* St. *Peter* cast his hook into the water and
catch a Fish, for mony to pay Tribute to *Caesar*. And let me tell you,
that Angling is of high esteem, and of much use in other Nations. He
that reads the Voyages of *Ferdinand Mendez Pinto*, shall find, that
there he declares to have found a King and several Priests a Fishing.*

And he that reads *Plutarch*, shall find, that Angling was not contemptible in the days of *Mark Antony* and *Cleopatra*, and that they in the
midst of their wonderful glory used Angling as a principal recreation.*

And let me tell you, that in the Scripture, Angling is always taken in the best sense, and that though hunting may be sometimes so taken, yet it is but seldom to be so understood. And let me add this more, he that views the ancient Ecclesiastical Canons,* shall find *Hunting* to be forbidden to *Church-men*, as being a turbulent, toilsom, perplexing Recreation; and shall find *Angling* allowed to *Clergy-men*, as being a harmless Recreation, a recreation that invites them to *contemplation* and *quietness*.

I might here enlarge my self by telling you, what commendations our learned *Perkins*＊ bestowes on Angling: and how dear a lover, and great a practiser of it our learned Doctor *Whitaker*＊ was, as indeed many others of great learning have been. But I will content my self with two memorable men, that lived near to our own time, whom I also take to have been ornaments to the Art of Angling.

The first is Doctor *Nowel*＊ sometimes[1] Dean of the Cathedral Church of St. *Pauls* in *London*, where his Monument stands yet undefaced,* a man that in the Reformation of Queen *Elizabeth* ¹⁵⁵⁰· (not that of *Henry the VIII*.) was so noted for his meek spirit, deep learning, prudence and piety, that the then Parliament and Convocation* both, chose, enjoyned and trusted him to be the man to make a Catechism for publick use, such a one as should stand as a rule for faith and manners to their posterity. And the good old man (though he was very learned, yet knowing that God leads us not to Heaven by many nor by hard questions) like an honest Angler, made that *good, plain, unperplext* Catechism which is printed with our good old Service Book.* I say, this good man was as dear a lover, and constant practicer of Angling, as any Age can produce; and his custom was to spend besides his fixt hours of prayer, (those hours which by command of the Church were enjoyned the Clergy, and voluntarily dedicated to devotion by many Primitive Christians): I say, besides those hours, this good man was observed to spend a tenth part of his time in Angling; and also (for I have conversed with those which have conversed with him) to bestow a tenth part of his Revenue, and usually all his fish, amongst the poor that inhabited near to those Rivers in which it was caught: saying often, *That charity gave life to Religion*: and at his return to his House would praise God he had spent that day free from worldly trouble; both harmlesly, and in a recreation that became a Church-man. And this good man was well content, if not desirous, that posterity should know he was an Angler, as may appear by his Picture, now to be seen, and carefully kept in *Brasennose Colledge* (to

which he was a liberal Benefactor) in which Picture he is drawn lean-
ing on a Desk with his Bible before him, and, on one hand of him his
lines, hooks, and other *tackling* lying in a round; and on his other hand
are his Angle-rods of several sorts: and by them this is written, *That
he died* 13. *Feb.* 1601. *being aged* 95. *years,* 44. *of which he had been Dean
of St.* Pauls *Church, and that his age had neither impair'd his hearing, nor
dimm'd his eyes, nor weakn'd his memory, nor made any of the faculties of
his mind weak or useless.* 'Tis said that *angling* and *temperance* were
great causes of these blessings, and I wish the like to all that imitate
him, and love the memory of so good a man.

My next and last example shall be that undervaluer of mony, the
late Provost of *Eton* Colledge, Sir *Henry Wotton,** (a man with whom
I have often fish'd and convers'd) a man whose forreign Imployments
in the service of this *Nation,* and whose *experience, learning, wit* and
chearfulness made his company to be esteemed one of the delights of
mankind; this man, whose very approbation of Angling were sufficient to convince any modest censurer of it, this man was also a most
dear lover, and a frequent practiser of the art of angling; of which he
would say, *'Twas an imployment for his idle time, which was then not idly
spent*: for angling was after tedious Study, *a rest to his mind, a chearer
of his spirits, a diverter of sadness, a calmer of unquiet thoughts, a mod-
erator of passions, a procurer of contentedness*: and *that it begat habits
of* peace *and* patience *in those that profess'd and practis'd it.* Indeed,
my friend, you will find angling to be like the vertue of Humility,
which has a calmness of spirit, and a world of other blessings attending upon it.

Sir, This was the saying of that learned man, and I do easily believe
that *peace,* and *patience,* and a calm *content* did cohabit in the chearful
heart of Sir *Henry Wotton,* because I know that when he was beyond
seventy years of age, he made this description of a part of the present
pleasure that possess'd him, as he sate quietly in a Summers evening
on a bank a Fishing; it is a description of the Spring, which, because
it glided as soft and sweetly from his pen, as that river does at this
time by which it was then made, I shall repeat it unto you.

> *This day dame Nature seem'd in love:**
> *The lusty sap began to move;*
> *Fresh juice did stir th' embracing Vines,*
> *And birds had drawn their Valentines,*
> *The jealous* Trout, *that low did lye,*

Rose at a well dissembled flie;*
There stood my friend with patient skill,
Attending of his trembling quill.
Already were the eaves possest
*With the swift Pilgrims dawbed nest:**
The Groves already did rejoyce,
In Philomels *triumphing voice:**
The showers were short, the weather mild,
The morning fresh, the evening smil'd.

    Jone *takes her neat rub'd pail, and now*
She trips to milk the sand-red Cow;
*Where, for some sturdy foot-ball Swain,**
Jone *strokes a* sillibub* *or twain,*
The fields and gardens were beset
With Tulips, Crocus, Violet,
    And now, though late, the modest Rose
    Did more then half a blush disclose.
    Thus all looks gay, and full of chear,
    To welcome the new livery'd year.

These were the thoughts that then possest the undisturbed mind
of Sir *Henry Wotton.* Will you hear the wish of another Angler, and
the commendation of his happy life which he also sings in Verse? *viz.*
Jo. Davors Esq.*

Let me live harmlesly, and near the brink
Of Trent *or* Avon *have a dwelling place;*
Where I may see my quill *or* cork *down sink*
With eager bite of Perch, *or* Bleak, *or* Dace:
And on the world and my Creator think,
Whilst some men strive ill gotten goods t'embrace;
    And others spend their time in base excess
    Of wine, or worse, in war *and* wantonness.

Let them that list, these pastimes still pursue,
And on such pleasing fancies feed their fill,
So I the fields *and* Meadows *green may view,*
And daily by fresh Rivers *walk at will,*
Among the Daisies *and the* Violets *blew,*

Red Hiacynth, *and yellow* Daffadil,
   Purple Narcissus *like the morning rayes,*
   Pale Gandergrasse, *and azure* Culverkeyes.*

I count it higher pleasure to behold
The stately compass of the lofty skie,
And in the midst thereof (like burning gold)
The flaming Chariot of the Worlds great eye,
The watry clouds that in the air up rol'd,
With sundry kinds of painted colours flie;
   And fair Aurora *lifting up her head,*
   Still blushing, rise from old Tithonus *bed.**

The hills *and* mountains *raised from the* plains,
The plains *extended level with the* ground,
The grounds *divided into sundry veins,**
The veins *inclos'd with* rivers *running round;*
These rivers making way through natures chains
With headlong course into the sea profound;
   The raging sea, beneath the vallies low,
   Where lakes *and* rills *and* rivulets *do flow.*

The lofty woods, the forrests wide and long
Adorn'd with leaves and branches fresh and green,
In whose cool bowers the birds with many a song
Do welcome with their Quire the Summers Queen:
The Meadowes fair where Flora's *gifts** *among*
Are intermixt, with verdant grasse between.
   The silver-scaled fish that softly swim
   Within the sweet brooks chrystal, watry stream.

All these, and many more of his Creation
That made the Heavens, the Angler *oft doth see,*
Taking therein no little delectation,
To think how strange, how wonderful they be;
Framing thereof an inward contemplation,
To set his heart from other fancies free;
   And whilst he looks on these with joyful eye,
   His mind is rapt above the starry Skie.

Sir I am glad my memory has not lost these last Verses, because
they are somewhat more pleasant and more sutable to *May-Day,* than

my harsh Discourse, and I am glad your patience hath held out so long, as to hear them and me: for both together have brought us within the sight of the *Thatcht-house*: and I must be your Debtor (if you think it worth your attention) for the rest of my promised discourse, till some other opportunity, and a like time of leisure.

Venat. Sir, you have Angled me on with much pleasure to the *Thatcht-house*: and I now find your words true *That good company makes the way seem short*, for trust me, Sir, I thought we had wanted three miles of this *House* till you shewed it to me: but now we are at it, we'l turn into it, and refresh our selves with a cup of drink and a little rest.

Pisc. Most gladly (Sir) and we'l drink a civil cup to all the *Otter Hunters* that are to meet you to morrow.

Ven. That we will Sir, and to all the lovers of Angling too, of which number, I am now willing to be one my self, for by the help of your good discourse and company, I have put on new thoughts both of the Art of Angling, and of all that professe it: and if you will but meet me to morrow at the time and place appointed, and bestow one day with me and my friends in hunting the *Otter*, I will dedicate the next two dayes to wait upon you, and we two will for that time do nothing but angle, and talk of fish and fishing.

Pisc. 'Tis a match, Sir, I'l not fail you, God willing, to be at *Amwel-hill* to morrow morning before Sun-rising.

CHAP. II.
Observations of the Otter and Chub.

VENAT. My friend *Piscator*, you have kept time with my thoughts, for the Sun is just rising, and I my self just now come to this place, and the dogs have just now put down an *Otter*, look down at the bottom of the hill there in that Meadow, chequered with *water-Lillies*, and *Lady-smocks*,* there you may see what work they make; look, look, you may see all busie, men and dogs, dogs and men, all busie.

Pisc. Sir, I am right glad to meet you, and glad to have so fair an entrance into this dayes sport, and glad to see so many dogs, and more men all in pursuit of the *Otter*;* lets complement* no longer, but joyn unto them; come honest *Venator*, lets be gone, let us make hast; I long to be doing: no reasonable hedg or ditch shall hold me.

Ven. Gentleman Hunts-man, where found you this *Otter*?

Hunt. Marry (Sir) we found her a mile from this place a fishing; she has this morning eaten the greatest part of this *Trout*; she has only left thus much of it as you see, and was fishing for more; when we came we found her just at it: but we were here very early, we were here an hour before Sun-rise, and have given her no rest since we came; sure she will hardly escape all these dogs and men. I am to have the skin if we kill her.

Ven. Why, Sir, what's the skin worth?

Hunt. 'Tis worth ten shillings to make gloves; the gloves of an *Otter* are the best fortification for your hands that can be thought on against wet weather.

Pisc. I pray, honest Huntsman, let me ask you a pleasant question, do you hunt a beast or a fish?*

Hunt. Sir, It is not in my power to resolve you, I leave it to be resolved by the Colledge of *Carthusians*, who have made vows never to eat flesh.* But I have heard, the question hath been debated among many great Clerks, and they seem to differ about it; yet most agree that her tail is Fish: and if her body be Fish too, then I may say, that a Fish will walk upon land, (for an *Otter* does so) sometimes five or six, or ten miles in a night to catch for her young ones, or to glut herself with Fish, and I can tell you that *Pigeons* will fly forty miles for a breakfast, but *Sir*, I am sure the *Otter* devours much Fish, and kills and spoils much more than he eats:* And I can tell you, that this Dog-fisher (for so the Latins call him) can smell a Fish in the water an hundred yards from him (*Gesner** says much farther) and that his stones are good against the Falling-sickness:* and that there is an herb *Benione*,* which being hung in a linnen cloth near a Fish-pond, or any haunt that he uses, makes him to avoid the place; which proves he smells both by water and land; and I can tell you there is brave hunting this Water-dog in *Corn-wall*, where there have been so many, that our learned *Cambden* says, there is a River called *Ottersey*,* which was so named, by reason of the abundance of *Otters* that bred and fed in it.

And thus much for my knowledg of the *Otter*, which you may now see above water at vent, and the dogs close with him; I now see he will not last long, follow therefore my Masters, follow, for *Sweetlips* was like to have him at this last vent.

Ven. Oh me, all the Horse are got over the River, what shall we do now? shall we follow them over the water?

Hunt. No, *Sir*, no, be not so eager, stay a little and follow me, for both they, and the dogs will be suddenly on this side again, I warrant you: and the *Otter* too, it may be: now have at him with *Kilbuck*, for he vents again.

Ven. Marry so he do's, for look he vents in that corner. Now, now *Ringwood** has him: now he's gone again, and has bit the poor dog. Now *Sweetlips* has her; hold her, *Sweetlips*! now all the dogs have her, some above and some under water; but now, now she's tir'd, and past losing: come bring her to me, *Sweetlips*. Look, 'tis a Bitch-*Otter*, and she has lately whelp'd, let's go to the place where she was *put down*, and not far from it you will find all her young ones, I dare warrant you, and kill them all too.

Hunt. Come, Gentlemen, come all, let's go to the place where we *put down* the *Otter*. Look you, hereabout it was that she kennel'd; look you, here it was indeed, for here's her young ones, no less than five; come let's kill them all.

Pisc. No, I pray Sir, save me one, and I'll try if I can make her tame,* as I know an ingenuous Gentleman in *Leicester-shire* (Mr. *Nich. Seagrave*)* has done; who hath not only made her tame, but to catch Fish, and do many other things of much pleasure.

Hunt. Take one with all my heart, but let us kill the rest. And now let's go to an honest Ale-house, where we may have a cup of good *Barley-wine*,* and sing *Old Rose*,* and all of us rejoyce together.

Venat. Come my friend, *Piscator*, let me invite you along with us; I'll bear your charges this night, and you shall bear mine to morrow; for my intention is to accompany you a day or two in Fishing.

Pisc. Sir, your request is granted, and I shall be right glad, both to exchange such a courtesie, and also to enjoy your company.

Venat. Well, now let's go to your sport of Angling.

Pisc. Let's be going with all my heart. God keep you all, Gentlemen, and send you meet this day with another Bitch-Otter, and kill her merrily, and all her young ones too.

Ven. Now, *Piscator*, where will you begin to fish?

Pisc. We are not yet come to a likely place, I must walk a mile further yet, before I begin.

Venat. Well then, I pray, as we walk tell me freely, how do you

like your lodging and mine Hoste and the company? is not mine
Hoste a witty man?

Pisc. Sir, I will tell you presently what I think of your Hoste; but
first I will tell you, I am glad these *Otters* were killed, and I am sorry
there are no more *Otter-killers*: for I know that the want of *Otter-
killers*, & the not keeping the *Fence months** for the preservation of
fish, will in time prove the destruction of all *Rivers*; and those very
few that are left, that make conscience of* the Laws of the Nation,
and of keeping days of abstinence, will be forced to eat flesh, or suffer
more inconveniencies than are yet foreseen.

Venat. Why, Sir, what be those that you call the Fence months?

Pisc. Sir, they be principally three, namely, *March, April,* and
May, for these be the usual months that *Salmon* come out of the Sea
to spawn in most fresh Rivers, and their Fry would about a certain
time return back to the salt water, if they were not hindred by *weires*
and *unlawful gins*, which the greedy Fisher-men set, and so destroy
them by thousands, as they would (being so taught by nature) change
the *fresh* for *salt water*. He that shall view the wise Statutes made
in the 13 of *Edw. the I.* and the like in *Rich. the II.** may see several
provisions made against the destruction of Fish: and though I profess
no knowledg of the Law, yet I am sure the regulation of these defects
might be easily mended. But I remember that a wise friend of mine
did usually say, *That which is every bodies business, is no bodies business.** If it were otherwise, there could not be so many Nets and Fish
that are under the Statute size, sold daily amongst us, and of which
the *conservators** of the waters should be ashamed.

But above all, the taking Fish in Spawning time, may be said to be
against nature; it is like the taking the dam on the nest when she
hatches her young: a sin so against nature, that Almighty God hath in
the Levitical Law* made a Law against it.

But the poor Fish have enemies enough beside such unnatural
Fisher-men, as namely, the *Otters* that I spake of, the *Cormorant*, the
Bittern, the *Osprey*, the *Sea-gull*, the *Hern*, the *Kingfisher*, the
*Gorrara,** the *Puet,** the *Swan, Goose, Ducks*, and the *Craber*, which
some call the Water-rat:* against all which any honest man may make
a just quarrel, but I will not, I will leave them to be quarrelled with,
and kill'd by others; for I am not of a cruel nature, I love to kill nothing but Fish.

And now to your question concerning your Hoste, to speak truly, he is not to me a good companion: for most of his conceits were either Scripture jests, or lascivious jests; for which I count no man witty, for the Devil will help a man that way inclined, to the first; and his own corrupt nature (which he always carries with him) to the latter. But a companion that feasts the company with *wit* and *mirth*, and leaves out the sin (which is usually mixt with them) he is the man; and indeed such a companion should have his charges born: and to such company I hope to bring you this night; for at *Trout-hall,** not far from this place, where I purpose to lodge to night, there is usually an Angler that proves good company: and let me tell you, good company and good discourse are the very sinews of vertue: but for such discourse as we heard last night, it infects others, the very boys will learn to talk and swear as they heard mine Host, and another of the company that shall be nameless; I am sorry the other is a Gentleman, for less Religion will not save their Souls than a beggars; I think more will be required at the last great day. Well, you know what Example is able to do, and I know what the Poet* says in the like case, which is worthy to be noted by all parents and people of civility:

> —— —— *Many a one*
> *Owes to his Country his Religion:*
> *And in another would as strongly grow,*
> *Had but his nurse or mother taught him so.*

This is reason put into Verse, and worthy the consideration of a wise man. But of this no more, for though I love civility, yet I hate severe censures: I'le to my own art, and I doubt not but at yonder tree I shall catch a *Chub*, and then we'l turn to an honest cleanly Hostess, that I know right well; rest our selves there, and dress it for our dinner.

Venat. Oh Sir, a *Chub* is the worst Fish that swims, I hoped for a *Trout* to my dinner.

Pisc. Trust me, *Sir*, there is not a likely place for a *Trout* hereabout, and we staid so long to take our leave of your Huntsmen this morning, that the Sun is got so high, and shines so clear, that I will not undertake the catching of a *Trout* till evening; and though a *Chub* be by you and many others reckoned the worst of *fish*, yet you shall see I'll make it a good Fish, by dressing it.

Ven. Why, how will you dress him?

Pisc. I'll tell you by and by, when I have caught him. Look you here, Sir, do you see? (but you must stand very close) there lye upon the top of the water in this very hole twenty *Chubs*: I'll catch only one, and that shall be the biggest of them all: and that I will do so, I'll hold you* twenty to one, and you shall see it done.

Venat. I marry Sir, now you talk like an Artist, and I'll say you are one, when I shall see you perform what you say you can do; but I yet doubt it.

Pisc. You shall not doubt it long, for you shall see me do it presently: look, the biggest of these *Chubs* has had some bruise upon his tail, by a Pike or some other accident, and that looks like a white spot; that very *Chub* I mean to put into your hands presently; sit you but down in the shade, and stay but a little while, and I'le warrant you I'le bring him to you.

Venat. I'le sit down and hope well, because you seem to be so confident.

Pisc. Look you Sir, there is a tryal of my skill, there he is, that very *Chub* that I shewed you with the white spot on his tail: and I'le be as certain to make him a good dish of meat, as I was to catch him. I'le now lead you to an honest Ale-house where we shall find a cleanly room, *Lavender* in the Windows, and twenty *Ballads* stuck about the wall;* there my Hostess (which I may tell you, is both cleanly and handsome and civil) hath drest many a one for me, and shall now dress it after my fashion, and I warrant it good meat.

Ven. Come Sir, with all my heart, for I begin to be hungry, and long to be at it, and indeed to rest my self too; for though I have walk'd but four miles this morning, yet I begin to be weary; yesterdays hunting hangs still upon me.

Pisc. Well Sir, and you shall quickly be at rest, for yonder is the house I mean to bring you to.

Come Hostess, how do you? Will you first give us a cup of your best drink, and then dress this *Chub*, as you drest my last, when I and my friend were here about eight or ten days ago? but you must do me one courtesie, it must be done instantly.

Host. I will do it, Mr. *Piscator*, and with all the speed I can.

Pisc. Now Sir, has not my Hostess made hast? and does not the fish look lovely?

Ven. Both, upon my word, Sir, and therefore let's say grace and fall to eating of it.

Pisc. Well Sir, how do you like it?

Ven. Trust me, 'tis as good meat as I ever tasted: now let me thank you for it, drink to you, and beg a courtesie of you; but it must not be deny'd me.

Pisc. What is it I pray Sir? you are so modest, that methinks I may promise to grant it before it is asked.

Ven. Why Sir, it is, that from henceforth you would allow me to call you *Master*, and that really I may be your Scholar, for you are such a companion, and have so quickly caught, and so excellently cook'd this fish, as makes me ambitious to be your Scholar.

Pisc. Give me your hand; from this time forward I will be your Master, and teach you as much of this Art as I am able; and will, as you desire me, tell you somewhat of the nature of most of the Fish that we are to angle for, and I am sure I both can and will tell you more than any common *Angler* yet knows.

CHAP. III.

How to fish for, and to dress the Chavender *or* Chub.

PISC. The *Chub*, though he eat well* thus drest, yet as he is usually drest, he does not: he is objected against, not only for being full of small forked bones, disperst through all his body, but that he eats watrish, and that the flesh of him is not firm, but short* and tastless. The *French* esteem him so mean, as to call him *Un Villain*; nevertheless he may be so drest as to make him very good meat; as namely, if he be a large Chub, then dress him thus:

First scale him, and then wash him clean, and then take out his guts; and to that end make the hole as little and near to his gills as you may conveniently, and especially make clean his throat from the grass and weeds that are usually in it (for if that be not very clean, it will make him to taste very sour); having so done, put some sweet herbs into his belly, and then tye him with two or three splinters to a spit, and rost him, basted often with Vinegar, or rather verjuice* and butter, with good store of salt mixt with it.

Being thus drest, you will find him a much better dish of meat than you, or most folk, even than Anglers themselves do imagine; for this dries up the fluid watry humor with which all *Chubs* do abound.

But take this rule with you, That a *Chub* newly taken and newly drest, is so much better than a *Chub* of a days keeping after he is dead, that I can compare him to nothing so fitly as to Cherries newly gathered from a tree, and others that have been bruised and lain a day or two in water. But the *Chub* being thus used and drest presently, and not washed after he is gutted (for note that lying long in water and washing the blood out of any fish after they be gutted, abates much of their sweetness) you will find the Chub being drest in the blood and quickly, to be such meat as will recompence your labour, and disabuse your opinion.

Or you may dress the *Chavender* or *Chub* thus:

When you have scaled him, and cut off his tail and fins, and washed him very clean, then chine or slit him through the middle, as a salt fish is usually cut, then give him three or four cuts or scotches on the back with your knife, and broil him on Char-coal, or Wood-coal that are free from smoke, and all the time he is a broyling baste him with the best sweet Butter, and good store of salt mixt with it; and to this add a little Time cut exceeding small, or bruised into the butter. The Cheven thus drest hath the watry tast taken away, for which so many except against* him. Thus was the Cheven drest that you now liked so well, and commended so much. But note again, that if this Chub that you eat of, had been kept till to morrow, he had not been worth a rush.* And remember that his throat be washt very clean, I say very clean, and his body not washt after he is gutted, as indeed no fish should be.

Well Scholar, you see what pains I have taken to recover the lost credit of the poor despised *Chub*. And now I will give you some rules how to catch him; and I am glad to enter you into the Art of fishing by catching a *Chub*, for there is no Fish better to enter a young Angler, he is so easily caught, but then it must be this particular way.

Go to the same hole in which I caught my *Chub*, where in most hot daies you will find a dozen or twenty *Chevens* floating near the top of the water, get two or three Grashoppers as you go over the meadow, and get secretly behind the tree, and stand as free from motion as is possible, then put a Grashopper on your hook, and let your hook hang a quarter of a yard short of the water, to which end you must rest your rod on some bough of the tree, but it is likely the Chubs will sink down towards the bottom of the water at the first shadow of your Rod (for a Chub is the fearfullest of fishes), and will do so if but a bird flies over him, and makes the least shadow on the water: but they will presently rise up to the top again, and there lie soaring* till some shadow affrights them again: I say when they lie upon the top of the water, look out the best Chub, (which you setting your self in a fit place, may very easily see) and move your Rod as softly as a Snail moves, to that Chub you intend to catch; let your bait fall gently upon the water three or four inches before him, and he will infallibly take the bait, and you will be as sure to catch him; for he is one of the leather-mouth'd* fishes, of which a hook does scarce ever lose its hold; and therefore give him play enough before you offer to take him out of the water. Go your way presently, take my Rod and do as I bid you, and I will sit down and mend my tackling till you return back.

Ven. Truly, my loving Master, you have offered me as fair as I could wish. I'le go and observe your directions.

Look you, Master, what I have done, that which joys my heart, caught just such another *Chub* as yours was.

Pisc. Marry, and I am glad of it: I am like to have a towardly Scholar of you. I now see, that with advice and practice you will make an *Angler* in a short time. Have but a love to it and I'le warrant you.

Venat. But Master, what if I could not have found a *Grashopper*?

Pisc. Then I may tell you, that a *black Snail*, with his belly slit, to shew his white: or a piece of soft *cheese*, will usually do as well: nay, sometimes a *worm*, or any kind of *flie*, as the *Ant-flie*,* the *Flesh-flie*, or *Wall-flie*, or the *Dor* or *Beetle*, (which you may find under a Cow-tird) or a *Bob*,* which you will find in the same place, and in time will be a Beetle; it is a short white worm, like to and bigger than a Gentle, or a *Cod-worm*, or a *Case-worm*,* any of these will do very well to fish in such a manner. And after this manner you may catch a *Trout* in a hot evening: when as you walk by a Brook, and shall see or hear him leap at flies, then if you get a *Grashopper*, put it on your hook, with your line about two yards long, standing behind a bush or tree where his hole is, and make your bait stir up and down on the top of the water: you may if you stand close, be sure of a bite, but not sure to catch him, for he is not a leather mouthed Fish: and after this manner you may fish for him with almost any kind of live flie, but especially with a *Grashopper*.

Venat. But before you go further, I pray good Master, what mean you by a leather-mouthed Fish?

Pisc. By a leather-mouthed Fish, I mean such as have their teeth in their throat, as the *Chub* or *Cheven*, and so the *Barbel*, the *Gudgeon* and *Carp*, and divers others have; and the hook being stuck into the leather or skin of the mouth of such fish does very seldom or never lose its hold: But on the contrary, a *Pike*, a *Pearch*, or *Trout*, and so some other Fish, which have not their teeth in their throats, but in their mouths, (which you shall observe to be very full of bones, and the skin very thin, and little of it): I say, of these fish the hook never takes so sure hold, but you often lose your fish, unless he have gorg'd it.

Ven. I thank you, good Master, for this observation, but now what shall be done with my *Chub* or *Cheven*, that I have caught?

Pisc. Marry Sir, it shall be given away to some poor body, for I'le warrant you I'le give you a *Trout* for your supper: and it is a good beginning of your Art to offer your first fruits to the poor, who will both thank God and you for it, which I see by your silence you seem to consent to. And for your willingness to part with it so charitably, I will also teach more concerning Chub-Fishing: you are to note that in *March* and *April* he is usually taken with wormes; in *May*, *June*, and *July* he will bite at any *fly*, or at *Cherries*, or at *Beetles* with their legs and wings cut off, or at any kind of *Snail*, or at the black *Bee* that breeds in clay walls;* and he never refuses a Grashopper on the top of a swift stream, nor at the bottom the young *humble-bee* that breeds in long grasse,* and is ordinarily found by the Mower of it. In *August*, and in the cooler months a yellow *paste*, made of the strongest cheese, and pounded in a Mortar with a little butter and saffron, (so much of it as being beaten small will turn it to a lemon colour). And some make a paste for the Winter months, at which time the Chub is accounted best, (for then it is observed, that the forked bones are lost, or turned into a kind of gristle, especially if he be baked) of Cheese and Turpentine; he will bite also at a Minnow or Penk, as a Trout will: of which I shall tell you more hereafter, and of divers other baits. But take this for a rule, that in hot weather he is to be fisht for towards the mid-water, or near the top; and in colder weather nearer the bottom. And if you fish for him on the top, with a Beetle or any *fly*, then be sure to let your line be very long, and to keep out of sight. And having told you that his Spawn* is excellent meat and that the head of a large Cheven, the Throat being well washt, is the best part of him, I will say no more of this Fish at the present, but wish you may catch the next you fish for.

But lest you may judg me too nice in urging to have the Chub drest so presently after he is taken, I will commend to your consideration how curious former times have been in the like kind.

You shall read in *Seneca** his natural Questions (*Lib.* 3. *cap.* 17.) that the Ancients were so curious in the newnesse of their Fish, that that seemed not new enough that was not put alive into the guests hand; and he says that to that end they did usually keep them living in glass-bottles in their dining-rooms; and they did glory much in their entertaining of friends to have that Fish taken from under their table alive, that was instantly to be fed upon. And he says, they took great pleasure to see their Mullets change to several colours, when they were dying. But enough of this, for I doubt I have stayed too long from giving you some observations of the *Trout*, and how to fish for him, which shall take up the next of my spare time.

CHAP. IV.

Observations of the nature and breeding of the Trout;
and how to fish for him. And the Milk maids Song.

PISC. The *Trout* is a fish highly valued both in this and forraign *Nations*: he may be justly said, (as the old Poets said of wine, and we English say of Venison) to be a generous* Fish: a Fish that is so like the *Buck* that he also has his seasons, for it is observed, that he comes in and goes out of season with the *Stag* and *Buck. Gesner* says,* his name is of a Germane off-spring, and says he is a fish that feeds clean and purely, in the swiftest streams, and on the hardest gravel; and that he may justly contend with all fresh-water-Fish, as the Mullet may with all Sea-Fish for precedency and daintiness of taste, and that being in right season, the most dainty palats have allowed precedency to him.

And before I go farther in my Discourse, let me tell you, that you are to observe, that as there be some *barren Does*, that are good in Summer, so there be some *barren Trouts* that are good in Winter, but there are not many that are so, for usually they be in their perfection in the month of *May*, and decline with the *Buck*. Now you are to take notice, that in several Countries, as in *Germany* and in other parts, compar'd to ours, Fish do differ much in their bigness, and shape, and other ways, and so do *Trouts*; it is well known that in the Lake *Leman* (the Lake of *Geneva*) there are *Trouts* taken of three Cubits long, as is affirmed by *Gesner*,* a Writer of good credit; and *Mercator** says, the *Trouts* that are taken in the Lake of *Geneva*, are a great part

of the Merchandize of that famous City. And you are further to
know, that there be certain waters that breed *Trouts* remarkable, both
for their number and smallness. I know a little Brook in *Kent*,* that
breeds them to a number incredible, and you may take them twenty
or forty in an hour, but none greater than about the size of a *Gudgion*.*
There are also in divers Rivers, especially that relate to, or be near to
the Sea (as *Winchester*,* or the *Thames* about *Windsor*) a little *Trout*
called a *Samlet* or *Skegger Trout** (in both which places I have caught
twenty or forty at a standing) that will bite as fast and as freely as
Minnows; these be by some taken to be young *Salmons*, but in those
waters they never grow to be bigger than a *Herring*.

There is also in *Kent* near to *Canterbury*, a *Trout* (call'd there a
*Fordidge** *Trout*) a *Trout* (that bears the name of the Town, where it
is usually caught) that is accounted the rarest of Fish; many of them
near the bigness of a *Salmon*, but known by their different colour, and
in their best season they cut very white; and none of these have been
known to be caught with an Angle, unless it were one that was caught
by Sir *George Hastings** (an excellent Angler, and now with God) and
he hath told me, he thought that *Trout* bit not for hunger but wantonness, and it is the rather to be believed, because both he then, and
many others before him, have been curious to search into their bellies, what the food was by which they lived; and have found out nothing by which they might satisfie their curiosity.

Concerning which you are to take notice, that it is reported by
good Authors, that *grasshoppers* and some Fish have no mouths,* but
are nourisht and take breath by the porousness of their Guills, Man
knows not how; And this may be believed, if we consider that when
the *Raven* hath hatcht her eggs, she takes no further care, but, leaves
her young ones, to the care of the God of Nature, who is said in the
Psalms,* *To feed the young Ravens that call upon him*. And they be kept
alive, and fed by a *dew*, or *worms* that breed in their nests, or some
other ways that we Mortals know not, and this may be believed of the
Fordidge Trout, which (as it is said of the *Stork*, that he knows his
season)* so he knows his times (I think almost his day) of coming into
that River out of the Sea, where he lives (and it is like, feeds) nine
months of the Year, and fasts three in the River of *Fordidge*. And you
are to note, that those Townsmen are very punctual in observing the
time of beginning to fish for them; and boast much that their River
affords a Trout, that exceeds all others. And just so does *Sussex* boast

of several Fish; as namely, a *Shelsey* Cockle*, a *Chichester Lobster*, an *Arundel Mullet*, and an *Amerly* Trout*.

And now for some confirmation of the *Fordidge* Trout, you are to know that this Trout is thought to eat nothing in the fresh water; and it may be the better believed, because it is well known, that *Swallows* and *Bats* and *Wagtails*, which are call'd half year birds,* and not seen to flie in *England* for six months in the Year (but about *Michaelmas** leave us for a hotter Climate); yet some of them that have been left behind their fellows, have been found (many thousands *View Sir Fra.* at a time) in hollow trees, or clay-Caves, where they *Bacon, exper. 899.* have been observed, to live and sleep out the whole Winter without meat; and so *Albertus** observes that there is one kind of *See Topsel of* *Frog* that hath her mouth naturally shut up about the *Frogs.* end of *August*, and that she lives so all the Winter: and though it be strange to some, yet it is known to too many among us to be doubted.

And so much for these *Fordidge trouts*, which never afford an *Angler* sport, but either live their time of being in the fresh water, by their meat formerly gotten in the Sea (not unlike the *Swallow* or *Frog*) or by the vertue of the fresh water only; or as the birds of *Paradise*, and the *Camelion** are said to live by the *Sun* and the *Air*.

There is also in *Northumberland* a *Trout* called a *Bull-trout*, of a much greater length and bigness, than any in these Southern parts: and there are in many Rivers that relate to the Sea, *Salmon-trouts*,* as much different from others, both in shape and in their spots, as we see sheep in some Countries differ one from another in their shape and bigness, and in the fineness of their wool: and certainly, as some pastures breed larger sheep, so do some Rivers, by reason of the ground over which they run, breed larger *Trouts*.

Now the next thing that I will commend to your consideration is, that the *Trout* is of a more sudden growth than other Fish: concerning which you are also to take notice, that he lives not so long as the *Pearch* and divers other Fishes do, as Sir *Francis Bacon* hath observed in his History of Life and Death.*

And next you are to take notice, that he is not like the *Crocodile*, which if he lives never so long, yet always thrives till his death: but 'tis not so with the Trout, for after he is come to his full growth, he declines in his body, and keeps his bigness or thrives only in his head till his death. And you are to know, that he will about (especially before) the time of his Spawning, get almost miraculously through

Weires, and *Floud-gates* against the stream; even, through such high and swift places as is almost incredible. Next, that the *Trout* usually Spawns about *October* or *November*, but in some Rivers a little sooner or later: which is the more observable, because most other fish Spawn in the Spring or Summer, when the Sun hath warmed both the earth and water, and made it fit for generation. And you are to note, that he continues many months out of season: for it may be observed of the Trout, that he is like the Buck or the Ox, that will not be fat in many months, though he go in the very same pastures that horses do, which will be fat in one month; and so you may observe, that most other Fishes recover strength, and grow sooner fat, and in season than the Trout doth.

And next, you are to note, that till the Sun gets to such a height as to warm the earth and the water, the Trout is sick and lean, and lowsie, and unwholesom: for you shall in winter find him to have a big head, and then to be lank, and thin, and lean; at which time many of them have sticking on them Sugs, or *Trout lice*,* which is a kind of a worm, in shape like a clove or pin with a big head, and sticks close to him and sucks his moisture; those, I think, the *Trout* breeds himself, and never thrives till he free himself from them, which is when warm weather comes; and then, as he grows stronger, he gets from the dead, still water, into the sharp streams, and the gravel, and there rubs off these worms or lice; and then, as he grows stronger, so he gets him into swifter and swifter streams, and there lies at the watch for any flie or Minnow, that comes near to him; and he especially loves the *May-flie*, which is bred of the *Cod-worm*, or *Caddis*;* and these make the Trout bold and lusty, and he is usually fatter and better meat at the end of that month, than at any time of the year.

Now you are to know, that it is observed, that usually the best *trouts* are either red or yellow, though some (as the *Fordidge trout*) be white and yet good; but that is not usual: and it is a note observable, that the female *Trout* hath usually a less head, and a deeper body than the male *Trout*; and is usually the better meat: and note that a hog-back,* and a little head to either *Trout, Salmon*, or any other fish, is a sign that that fish is in season.

But yet you are to note, that as you see some Willows or palm-trees* bud and blossom sooner than others do, so some Trouts be in Rivers sooner in season; and as some Hollies or Oaks are longer before they cast their leaves, so are some Trouts in Rivers longer before they go out of season.

And you are to note, that there are several kinds of *Trouts*, but these several kinds are not considered but by very few men, for they go under the general name of *Trouts*: just as Pigeons do in most places; though it is certain there are tame, and wild Pigeons: and of the tame, there be *Helmits* and *Runts* and *Carriers*, and *Cropers*,* and indeed too many to name. Nay, the *Royal Society* have found and publisht lately, that there be thirty and three kinds of Spiders:* and yet, all (for ought I know) go under that one general name of *Spider*. And 'tis so with many kinds of Fish, and of *Trouts* especially, which differ in their bigness and shape, and spots, and colour. The great *Kentish Hens** may be an instance, compared to other Hens; And doubtless there is a kind of small Trout, which will never thrive to be big, that breeds very many more than others do, that be of a larger size; which you may rather believe, if you consider, that the little *Wren* and *Titmouse* will have twenty young ones at a time, when usually the noble *Hawk* or the Musical *Thrassal** or *Black-bird* exceed not four or five.

And now you shall see me try my skill to catch a Trout, and at my next walking either this evening, or to morrow morning I will give you direction, how you your self shall fish for him.

Venat. Trust me, Master, I see now it is a harder matter to catch a *Trout* than a *Chub*: for I have put on patience, and followed you these two hours, and not seen a Fish stir, neither at your Minnow nor your Worm.

Pisc. Well Scholar, you must endure worse luck sometime, or you will never make a good Angler. But what say you now? there is a *Trout* now, and a good one too, if I can but hold him, and two or three turns more will tire him: Now you see he lies still, and the sleight* is to land him: Reach me that Landing Net: So (Sir) now he is mine own, what say you now? is not this worth all my labour and your patience?

Venat. On my word Master, this is a gallant *Trout*, what shall we do with him?

Pisc. Marry e'en eat him to supper:* We'l go to my Hostess, from whence we came; she told me, as I was going out of door, that my brother *Peter*, a good Angler and a chearful companion, had sent word he would lodge there to night, and bring a friend with him. My Hostess has two beds, and, I know, you and I may have the best:* we'l rejoice with my brother *Peter* and his friend, tell tales, or sing Ballads, or make a Catch,* or find some harmless sport to content us, and pass away a little time without offence to God or man.

Venat. A match,* good Master, lets go to that house, for the linnen looks white, and smells of Lavender, and I long to lie in a pair of sheets that smell so: lets be going, good Master, for I am hungry again with fishing.

Pisc. Nay, stay a little good Scholar, I caught my last *Trout* with a Worm, now I will put on a Minnow and try a quarter of an hour about yonder trees for another, and so walk towards our Lodging. Look you Scholar, thereabout we shall have a bite presently, or not at all: Have with you* (Sir!) o' my word I have hold of him. Oh it is a great loggerheaded* *Chub*; Come, hang him upon that Willow twig, and lets be going. But turn out of the way a little, good Scholar, towards yonder high *honysuckle hedg*: there we'll sit and sing whilst this showr falls so gently upon the teeming earth, and gives yet a sweeter smell to the lovely flowers that adorn these verdant Meadows.

Look; under that broad *Beech-tree*, I sate down, when I was last this way a fishing, and the birds in the adjoyning Grove seemed to have a friendly contention with an Eccho, whose dead voice seemed to live in a hollow tree, near to the brow of that Primrose-hill; there I sate viewing the silver-streams glide silently towards their center, the tempestuous Sea; yet, sometimes opposed by rugged roots, and pebble stones, which broke their waves, and turned them into foam: and sometimes I beguil'd time by viewing the harmless Lambs, some leaping securely in the cool shade, whilst others sported themselves in the chearful Sun: and saw others craving comfort from the swoln Udders of their bleating Dams. As I thus sate, these and other sights had so fully possest my soul with content, that I thought as the Poet* has happily exprest it:

> *I was for that time lifted above earth;*
> *And possest joys not promis'd in my birth.*

As I left this place, and entred into the next field, a second pleasure entertained me, 'twas a handsom milk-maid that had not yet attain'd so much age and wisdom as to load her mind with any fears of many things that will never be (as too many men too often do) but she cast away all care, and sung like a *Nightingale*: her voice was good, and the Ditty fitted for it; 'twas that smooth song, which was made by *Kit. Marlow*,* now at least fifty years ago: and the Milk-maids Mother sung an answer to it, which was made by Sir *Walter Rawleigh** in his younger days.

They were old fashioned Poetry, but choicely good, I think much better than the strong lines that are now in fashion in this critical age. Look yonder! on my word, yonder they both be a milking again, I will give her the *Chub*, and perswade them to sing those two songs to us.

God speed you good woman, I have been a Fishing, and am going to *Bleak-Hall* to my bed, and having caught more Fish than will sup my self and my friend, I will bestow this upon you and your Daughter, for I use to sell none.

Milk. Marry God requite you Sir, and we'll eat it chearfully: and if you come this way a Fishing two months hence, a grace of God I'le give you a Sillybub of new Verjuice* in a new made Hay-cock, for it, and my *Maudlin* shall sing you one of her best *Ballads*, for she and I both love all *Anglers*, they be such honest, civil, quiet men; in the mean time will you drink a draught of *Red-Cows milk*,* you shall have it freely.

Pisc. No, I thank you, but I pray do us a courtesie that shall stand you and your daughter in nothing, and yet we will think our selves still something in your debt; it is but to sing us a Song, that was sung by your daughter, when I last past over this Meadow, about eight or nine days since.

Milk. What Song was it, I pray? was it, *Come Shepherds deck your herds*, or, *As at noon* Dulcina *rested*, or, Phillida *flouts me*; or, *Chevy Chase*? or, *Jonny Armstrong*? or *Troy Town*?*

Pisc. No, it is none of those: it is a Song that your daughter sung the first part, and you sung the answer to it.

Milk. O, I know it now, I learn'd the first part in my golden age, when I was about the age of my poor daughter; and the latter part, which indeed fits me best now, but two or three years ago, when the cares of the World began to take hold of me: but you shall, God willing, hear them both, and sung as well as we can, for we both love Anglers. Come *Maudlin*, sing the first part to the Gentlemen with a merry heart, and I'le sing the second, when you have done.

The Milk-maids Song.

Come live with me, and be my Love,
And we will all the pleasures prove

That valleys, groves, or hills, or fields,
Or woods, and steepy mountains yeilds.

Where we will sit upon the Rocks,
And see the Shepherds feed our flocks,
By shallow Rivers, *to whose falls,*
Melodious birds sing Madrigals.

And I will make thee beds of Roses,
And then a thousand fragrant Posies,
*A Cap of flowers, and a Kirtle**
Embroidered all with leaves of mirtle.

A Gown made of the finest Wool
Which from our pretty Lambs we pull;
Slippers lin'd choicely for the cold,
With buckles of the purest gold.

A Belt of Straw, and Ivy-buds,
With Coral Clasps and Amber studs:
And if these pleasures may thee move,
Come live with me and be my Love.

Thy silver dishes for thy meat,
As precious as the Gods do eat,
Shall on an Ivory Table be
Prepar'd each day for thee and me.

The Shepherds Swains shall dance and sing
For thy delight each May-morning:
If these delights thy mind may move,
Then live with me, and be my Love.

Venat. Trust me, Master, it is a choice Song, and sweetly sung by honest *Maudlin.* I now see it was not without cause, that our good Queen *Elizabeth* did so often wish her self a Milkmaid* all the month of *May,* because they are not troubled with fears and cares, but sing sweetly all the day, and sleep securely all the night: and without doubt, honest, innocent, pretty *Maudlin* does so. I'le bestow Sir *Thomas Overbury's* Milk-maids wish* upon her, *That she may dye in the Spring, and being dead may have good store of flowers stuck round about her winding sheet.*

The Milk-maids Mothers Answer.

If all the world and Love were young,
And truth in every Shepherds tongue,
These pretty pleasures might me move
To live with thee, and be thy Love.

But time drives flocks from field to fold,
When Rivers rage, and rocks grow cold,
Then Philomel* *becometh dumb,*
And age complains of care to come.

The flowers do fade, and wanton fields
To wayward Winter reckoning yields,
A hony tongue, a heart of gall,
Is fancies spring, but sorrows fall;*

Thy gowns, thy shooes, thy beds of roses,
Thy cap, thy kirtle, and thy posies,
Soon break, soon wither, soon forgotten,
In folly ripe, in reason rotten.

Thy Belt of Straw, and Ivy-buds,
Thy Coral clasps, and Amber-studs,
All these in me no means can move
To come to thee, and be thy Love.

What should we talk of dainties then,
Of better meat than's fit for men?
These are but vain: that's only good
Which God hath blest, and sent for food.

But could Youth last, and love still breed,
Had joys no date, nor age no need;
Then those delights my mind might move,
To live with thee, and be thy Love.

Mother. Well I have done my Song; but stay honest *Anglers*, for I will make *Maudlin* to sing you one short Song more. *Maudlin*; sing that Song that you sung last night, when young *Corydon* the Shepherd plaid so purely* on his *oaten pipe* to you and your Cozen Betty.

Maud. I will Mother.

> *I married a Wife of late,**
> *The more's my unhappy fate:*
> *I married her for love,*
>   *As my fancy did me move,*
> *And not for a worldly estate:*
>
> *But Oh! the* green-sickness*
> *Soon changed her likeness;*
> *And, all her beauty did fail.*
>   *But 'tis not so,*
>   *With those that go,*
>   *Through frost and snow,*
>   *As all men know,*
> *And, carry the Milking-pail.*

Pisc. Well sung good Woman I thank you, I'le give you another dish of fish one of these days; and then, beg another Song of you. Come Scholar, let *Maudlin* alone: do not you offer to spoil her voice. Look, yonder comes mine *Hostess*, to call us to supper. How now? is my Brother *Peter* come?

Hostess. Yes, and a friend with him, they are both glad to hear that you are in these parts, and long to see you, and long to be at supper, for they be very hungry.

CHAP. V.

More Directions how to Fish for, and how to make for the Trout *an* Artificial Minnow, *and* Flies, *with some* Merriment.

PISC. Well met Brother *Peter*, I heard you and a friend would lodge here to night, and that hath made me to bring my Friend to lodge here too. My Friend is one that would fain be *a Brother of the Angle*, he hath been an *Angler* but this day, and I have taught him how to catch a *Chub* by daping with a *Grass-hopper*, and the *Chub* he caught was a lusty one of nineteen inches long. But pray Brother *Peter* who is your companion?

Peter. Brother *Piscator*, my friend is an honest *Country-man*, and his name is *Coridon*, and he is a downright witty companion that met me here purposely to be pleasant and eat a *Trout*, and I have not yet wetted my Line since we met together: but I hope to fit him with a *Trout* for his breakfast, for I'le be early up.

Pisc. Nay Brother you shall not stay so long: for look you here is a Trout

will fill six reasonable bellies. Come Hostess, dress it presently, and get us what other meat the house will afford, and give us some of your best *Barly-wine*,* the good liquor that our honest Fore-fathers did use to drink of; the drink which preserved their health, and made them live so long, and to do so many good deeds.

Peter. O' my word this *Trout* is perfect in season.* Come, I thank you, and here is a hearty draught to you, and to all the brothers of the Angle wheresoever they be, and to my young brothers good fortune to morrow: I will furnish him with a Rod, if you will furnish him with the rest of the Tackling; we will set him up and make him a Fisher.

And I will tell him one thing for his encouragement, that his fortune hath made him happy to be Scholar to such a Master; a Master that knows as much both of the nature and breeding of fish as any man: and can also tell him as well how to catch and cook them, from the *Minnow* to the *Salmon*, as any that I ever met withall.

Pisc. Trust me, brother *Peter*, I find my Scholar to be so sutable to my own humour, which is to be free and pleasant, and civilly merry, that my resolution is to hide nothing that I know from him. Believe me, Scholar, this is my resolution; and so here's to you a hearty draught, and to all that love us, and the honest Art of Angling.

Ven. Trust me, good Master, you shall not sow your seed in barren ground,* for I hope to return you an increase answerable to your hopes; but however you shall find me obedient, and thankful, and serviceable to my best abilitie.

Pisc. 'Tis enough, honest Scholar, come lets to supper. Come my friend *Coridon* this *Trout* looks lovely, it was twentie two inches when it was taken, and the belly of it looked some part of it as yellow as a Marigold, and part of it as white as a lilly, and yet methinks it looks better in this good sawce.

Cor. Indeed honest friend, it looks well, and tastes well, I thank you for it, and so doth my friend *Peter*, or else he is to blame.

Pet. Yes, and so I do, we all thank you, and when we have supt, I will get my friend *Coridon* to sing you a Song for requital.

Cor. I will sing a song, if any body will sing another; else, to be plain with you, *I will sing none*: I am none of those that sing for meat, but for company: I say, *'Tis merry in Hall, when men sing all.**

Pisc. I'l promise you I'l sing a song that was lately made at my request, by Mr. *William Basse,** one that hath made the choice songs of the *Hunter in his cariere*, and of *Tom of Bedlam*, and many others of note; and this that I will sing is in praise of Angling.

Cor. And then mine shall be the praise of a Country mans life: What will the rest sing of?

Pet. I will promise you, I will sing another song in praise of Angling to morrow night, for we will not part till then, but Fish to morrow, and sup together, and the next day every man leave Fishing, and fall to his businesse.

Venat. 'Tis a match, and I will provide you a Song or a Catch against then too, which shall give some addition of mirth to the company; for we will be civil and as merry as beggers.

Pisc. 'Tis a match my Masters, lets ev'n say Grace, and turn to the fire, drink the other cup to wet our whistles, and so sing away all sad thoughts.

Come on my Masters, who begins? I think it is best to draw cuts,* and avoid contention.

Pet. It is a match. Look, the shortest cut falls to *Coridon*.

Cor. Well then, I will begin, for I hate contention.

CORIDONS Song.*

Oh the sweet contentment
The country-man doth find!
high trolollie lollie loe
high trolollie lee,
That quiet contemplation

Possesseth all my mind:
   Then care away,
   And wend along with me.

For Courts are full of flattery,
As hath too oft been tri'd;
   high trolollie lollie loe, &c.
The City full of wantonness,
And both are full of pride:
   Then care away, &c.

But oh the honest Country-man
Speaks truely from his heart,
   high trolollie lollie loe, &c.
His pride is in his tillage,
His horses, and his cart:
   Then care away, &c.

Our cloathing is good sheep skins,
Gray russet for our wives,
   high trolollie lollie loe, &c.
'Tis warmth and not gay cloathing
That doth prolong our lives:
   Then care away, &c.

The plough man, though he labour hard,
Yet on the Holy-Day,
   high trolollie lollie loe, &c.
No Emperour *so merrily*
Does passe his time away:
   Then care away, &c.

To recompence our tillage,
The Heavens *afford us showers;*
   high trolollie lollie loe, &c.
And for our sweet refreshments
The earth affords us bowers:
   Then care away, &c.

The Cuckow *and the* Nightingale
Full merrily do sing,
   high trolollie lollie loe, &c.

And with their pleasant roundelaies*
Bid welcome to the Spring.
　　Then care away, &c.

This is not half the happiness
The country-man enjoyes;
　　high trolollie lollie loe, &c.
Though others think they have as much,
Yet he that says so lies:
　　Then come away, turn
　　Country man with me.
　　　　　　　　　　　　Jo. Chalkhill.

Pisc. Well sung *Coridon*, this song was sung with mettle; and it was choicely fitted to the occasion; I shall love you for it as long as I know you; I would you were a brother of the Angle, for a companion that is chearful, and free from swearing and scurrilous discourse, is worth gold. I love such mirth as does not make friends ashamed to look upon one another next morning; nor men (that cannot well bear it) to repent the money they spend when they be warmed with drink: and take this for a rule, You may pick out such times and such companies, that you may make your selves merrier for a little than a great deal of money; for *'Tis the company and not the charge that makes the feast:** and such a companion you prove, I thank you for it.

But I will not complement you out of the debt that I owe you, and therefore I will begin my Song and wish it may be so well liked.

The Anglers Song.*

As inward love breeds outward talk,
The Hound *some praise, and some the* Hawk:
Some better pleas'd with private sport,
Use Tennis, *some a* Mistress *court:*
　　But these delights I neither wish,
　　Nor envy, while I freely fish.

Who Hunts, *doth oft in danger ride;*
Who Hawks, *lures** oft both far and wide;*
Who uses Games *shall often prove*
A loser; but who falls in love,

Is fettered in fond Cupids *snare:*
My Angle breeds me no such care.

Of Recreation there is none
So free as Fishing is alone;
All other pastimes do no lesse
Than mind and body both possesse:
   My hand alone my work can doe,
   So I can fish and study too.

I care not, I, to fish in seas,
Fresh rivers best my mind do please,
Whose sweet calm course I contemplate,
And seek in life to imitate:
   In civil bounds I fain would keep,
   And for my past offences weep.

And when the timorous Trout *I wait*
To take, and he devours my bait,
How poor a thing sometimes I find
Will captivate a greedy mind:
   And when none bite, I praise the wise,
   Whom vain allurements ne're surprise.

But yet though while I fish I fast;
I make good fortune my repast,
And thereunto my friend invite,
In whom I more than that delight:
   Who is more welcom to my dish,
   Than to my angle was my fish.

As well content no prize to take,
As use of taken prize to make:
For so our Lord was pleased when
He fishers made fishers of men:*
   Where (which is in no other game)
   A man may fish and praise his name.

The first men that our Saviour dear
Did chuse to wait upon him here,
Blest Fishers were, and fish the last
Food was,* that he on earth did taste.

I therefore strive to follow those,
Whom he to follow him hath chose.

Cor. Well sung brother, you have paid your debt in good coin, we
Anglers are all beholding to the good man that made this Song. Come
Hostess, give us more Ale, and lets drink to him.

And now lets every one go to bed that we may rise early; but first
lets pay our reckoning, for I will have nothing to hinder me in the
morning for my purpose is to prevent* the Sun-rising.

Pet. A match; Come *Coridon*, you are to be my Bed-fellow:* I
know, brother, you and your Scholar will lie together; but where shall
we meet to morrow night? for my friend *Coridon* and I will go up the
water towards *Ware*.

Pisc. And my Scholar and I will go down towards *Waltham*.*

Cor. Then lets meet here, for here are fresh sheets that smell of
Lavender, and I am sure we cannot expect better meat, or better usage
in any place.

Pet. 'Tis a match. Good night to every body.

Pisc. And so say I.

Venat. And so say I.

Pisc. Good morrow good Hostess, I see my brother *Peter* is still in
bed: Come give my Scholar and me a Morning-drink, and a bit of
meat to breakfast, and be sure to get a good dish of meat or two
against supper, for we shall come home as hungry as Hawks.* Come
Scholar, lets be going.

Venat. Well now, good Master, as we walk towards the River give
me direction, according to your promise, how I shall fish for a *Trout*.

Pisc. My honest Scholar, I will take this very convenient opportunity to do it.

The Trout is usually caught with a worm or a *Minnow*, (which some
call a *Penk*) or with a *flie, viz.* either a *natural* or an *artificial flie*: concerning which three I will give you some observations and directions.

And first for Worms: Of these there be very many sorts, some
breed only in the earth, as the *Earth-worm*; others of or amongst
Plants, as the *Dug-worm*;* and others breed either out of excrements,
or in the bodies of living creatures, as in the horns of Sheep or Deer;
or some of dead flesh, as the *Maggot* or *gentle*, and others.

Now these be most of them particularly good for particular Fishes:

but for the *Trout* the *dew-worm*, (which some also call the *Lob-worm*) and the *Brandling* are the chief; and especially the first for a great Trout, and the latter for a less. There be also of *Lob-worms* some called *squirrel-tailes*, (a worm that has a red head, a streak down the back and a broad tail) which are noted to be the best, because they are the toughest and most lively, and live longest in the water: for you are to know, that a dead worm is but a dead bait and like to catch nothing, compared to a lively, quick, stirring worm: and for a *Brandling*, he is usually found in an old dunghil, or some very rotten place near to it: but most usually in Cow-dung, or hogs-dung, rather than horse-dung, which is somewhat too hot and dry for that worm. But the best of them are to be found in the bark of the Tanners* which they cast up in heaps after they have used it about their leather.

There are also divers other kinds of worms which for colour and shape alter even as the ground out of which they are got, as the *marsh-worm*, the *tag-tail*, the *stag-worm*, the *dock-worm*, the *oak-worm*, the *gilt-tayle*, the *twachel* or *lob-worm* (which of all others is the most excellent bait for a *Salmon*) and too many to name,* even as many sorts, as some think there be of several hearbs or shrubs, or of several kinds of birds in the air; of which I shall say no more, but tell you, that what worms soever you fish with, are the better for being well scowred,* that is long kept, before they be used; and in case you have not been so provident, then the way to cleanse and scowr them quickly, is to put them all night in water, if they be *Lob-worms*, and then put them into your bag with fennel: but you must not put your Brandlings above an hour in water, and then put them into fennel for suddain use: but if you have time and purpose to keep them long, then they be best preserved in an earthen pot with good store of *Mosse*, which is to be fresh every three or four dayes in Summer, and every week or eight dayes in Winter: or at least the mosse taken from them, and clean washed, and wrung betwixt your hands till it be dry, and then put it to them again. And when your worms, especially the Brandling, begins to be sick, and lose of his bigness, then you may recover him, by putting a little milk or cream (about a spoonful in a day) into them by drops on the mosse; and if there be added to the cream an egge beaten and boiled in it, then it will both fatten and preserve them long. And note, that when the *knot*, which is near to the middle of the *brandling* begins to swell, then he is sick, and, if he be not well look'd to, is near dying. And for mosse, you are to note, that there be divers kinds of it, which I could name to you, but will onely tell you, that that which is likest a *Bucks-Horn* is the best, except it be soft white moss, which grows on some heaths, and is hard to be found. And note, that in a very dry time, when you are put to an extremity for worms, Walnut-tree leaves squeez'd into water, or salt in water, to make it bitter or salt, and then that water poured on the ground, where you shall see worms are used to rise in the night, will make them to appear above ground presently. And you may take notice some say that *Camphire** put into your bag with your mosse and worms, gives them a strong and so tempting a smell, that the fish fare the worse and you the better for it.

And now, I shall shew you how to bait your hook with a worm, so as shall prevent you from much trouble, and the loss of many a hook too; when you Fish for a *Trout* with a running line: that is to say, when you fish for him by hand at the ground, I will direct you in this as plainly as I can, that you may not mistake.

Suppose it be a big Lob-worm, put your hook into him somewhat above the middle, and out again a little below the middle: having so done, draw your worm above the arming of your hook, but note that at the entring of your hook it must not be at the head-end of the worm, but at the tail-end of him, (that the point of your hook may come out toward the head-end) and having drawn him above the arming of your hook, then put the point of your hook again into the very head of the worm, till it come near to the place where the point of the hook first came out: and then draw back that part of the worm that was above the shank or arming of your hook, and so fish with it. And if you mean to fish with two worms, then put the second on before you turn back the hooks-head of the first worm; you cannot lose above two or three worms before you attain to what I direct you; and having attain'd it, you will find it very useful, and thank me for it: For you will run on the ground without tangling.

Now for the *Minnow* or *Penk*, he is not easily found and caught till *March*, or in *April*, for then he appears first in the River, Nature having taught him to shelter and hide himself in the Winter in ditches that be near to the River, and there both to hide and keep himself warm in the mud or in the weeds, which rot not so soon as in a running River, in which place if he were in Winter, the distempered* Floods that are usually in that season, would suffer him to take no rest, but carry him head-long to Mills and Weires to his confusion. And of these *Minnows*, first you are to know, that the biggest size is not the best; and next, that the middle size and the whitest are the best: and then you are to know, that your *Minnow* must be so put on your hook that it must turn round when 'tis drawn against the stream, and that it may turn nimbly, you must put it on a big-sized hook as I shall now direct you, which is thus. Put your hook in at his mouth and out at his gill, then having drawn your hook 2 or 3 inches beyond or through his gill, put it again into his mouth, and the point and beard out at his taile, and then tie the hook and his taile about very neatly with a white thred, which will make it the apter to turn quick in the water: that done, pull back that part of your line which was slack when you did put your hook into the *Minnow* the second time: I say pull that part of your line back so that it shall fasten the head, so that the body of the *Minnow* shall be almost streight on your hook; this done, try how it will turn by drawing it cross the water or against a stream, and if it do not turn nimbly, then turn the tail a little to the right or left hand, and try again, till it turn quick; for if not, you are in danger to catch nothing; for know, that it is impossible that it should turn too quick: And you are yet to know, that in case you want a *Minnow*, then a small *Loch** or a *Stickle-bag,** or any other small fish that will turn quick will serve as well: And you are yet to know, that you may salt them, and by that means keep them ready and fit for use three or four days, or longer, and that of salt, bay-salt* is the best.

And here let me tell you, what many old Anglers know right well, that at some times, and in some waters a *Minnow* is not to be got, and therefore let me tell you, I have (which I will shew to you) an *artificial Minnow*, that will catch a Trout as well as an *artificial Flie*, and it was made by a handsom Woman that had a fine hand, and a live *Minnow* lying by her: *the mould or body of the Minnow was cloth, and wrought upon or over it thus with a needle: the back of it with very sad French green silk, and paler green silk towards the belly, shadowed** as perfectly as you can imagine, just as you see a Minnow; the belly was wrought also with a needle, and it was a part of it white silk, and another part of it with silver thred, the tail and fins were of a quill, which was shaven thin, the eyes were of two little black beads, and the head was so shadowed, and all of it so curiously wrought, and so exactly dissembled, that it would beguile any sharpe sighted Trout in a swift stream. And this Minnow I will now shew you, (look here it is) and if you like it, lend it you, to have two or three made by it, for they be easily carryed about an Angler, and be of excellent use; for note, that a large Trout will come as fiercely at a*

Minnow, as the highest mettled Hawk doth seize on a Partridg, or a
Grey-hound on a Hare*. I have been told, that 160 *Minnows* have been
found in a *Trouts* belly; either the *Trout* had devoured so many; or the
Miller that gave it a friend of mine had forced them down his throat
after he had taken him.

Now for *Flies*, which is the third bait wherewith *Trouts* are usually
taken. You are to know, that there are so many sorts of Flies as there
be of Fruits: I will name you but some of them, as the *dun-flie*, the
stone-flie, the *red-flie*, the *moor-flie*, the *tawny-flie*, the *shell-flie*,
the *cloudy*, or *blackish-flie*, the *flag-flie*, the *vine-flie*: there be of *flies*,
Caterpillars, and *Canker-flies*, and *Bear-flies*, and indeed too many
either for me to name or for you to remember: and their breeding is
so various and wonderful, that I might easily amaze my self, and tire
you in a relation of them.

And yet I will exercise your promised patience by saying a little of
the *Caterpillar* or the *Palmer-flie* or *worm*,* that by them you may guess
what a work it were in a Discourse but to run over those very many
flies, worms and little living creatures with which the Sun and Summer
adorn and beautifie the River banks and Meadows; both for the recreation and contemplation of us Anglers, pleasures which (I think) my
self enjoy more than any other man that is not of my profession.

Pliny holds* an opinion, that many have their birth or being from
a dew that in the Spring falls upon the leaves of trees; and that some
kinds of them are from a dew left upon herbs or flowers; and others
from a dew left upon Coleworts* or Cabbages: All which kinds of
dews being thickned and condensed, are by the Suns generative heat
most of them hatch'd, and in three days made living creatures; and
these of several shapes and colours; some being hard and tough, some
smooth and soft; some are horned in their head, some in their tail,
some have none: some have hair, some none: some have sixteen feet,
*In his history
of Serpents.* some less, and some have none, but (as our *Topsel** hath
with great diligence observed) those which have none,
move upon the earth or upon broad leaves, their motion being not
unlike to the waves of the Sea. Some of them he also observes to be
bred of the Eggs of other Caterpillars, and that those in their time
turn to be *Butter-flies*: and again, that their Eggs turn the following
year to be *Caterpillars*. And some affirm, that every plant has his
particular flie or Caterpillar, which it breeds and feeds. I have seen,
and may therefore affirm it, a green Caterpillar,* or worm, as big as

a small Peascod, which had fourteen legs, eight on the belly, four under the neck, and two near the tail. It was found on a hedge of Privet, and was taken thence, and put into a large Box, and a little branch or two of Privet put to it, on which I saw it feed as sharply as a dog gnaws a bone: it lived thus five or six daies, and thrived, and changed the colour two or three times, but by some neglect in the keeper of it, it then dyed and did not turn to a flie: but if it had lived, it had doubtless turned to one of those flies that some call flies of prey,* which those that walk by the Rivers may in Summer, see fasten on smaller flies, and I think make them their food. And 'tis observable, that as there be these *flies of prey* which be very large, so there be others very little, created, I think, only to feed them, and breed out of I know not what; whose life, they say, Nature intended not to exceed an hour, and yet that life is thus made shorter by other flies, or accident.

'Tis endless to tell you what the curious searchers into Natures productions have observed of these Worms and Flies: But yet I shall tell you what *Aldrovandus*,* our *Topsel*,* and others say of the *Palmer-worm* or *Caterpillar*, That whereas others content themselves to feed on particular herbs or leaves, (for most think those very leaves that gave them life and shape, give them a particular feeding and nourishment, and that upon them they usually abide) yet he observes, that this is called a *pilgrim* or *palmer-worm*, for his very wandring life and various food; not contenting himself (as others do) with any one certain place for his abode, nor any certain kind of herb or flower for his feeding; but will boldly and disorderly wander up and down, and not endure to be kept to a diet, or fixt to a particular place.

Nay, the very colours of *Caterpillars* are, as one has observed, very elegant and beautiful: I shall (for a taste of the rest) describe one of them,* which I will sometime the next month shew you feeding on a Willow-tree, and you shall find him punctually* to answer this very description; *His lips and mouth somewhat yellow, his eyes black as Jet, his forehead purple, his feet and hinder parts green, his tail two forked and black, the whole body stained with a kind of red spots which run along the neck and shoulderblade, not unlike the form of Saint* Andrew's *Cross, or the letter* X, *made thus cross-wise, and a white line drawn down his back to his tail; all which add much beauty to his whole body.* And it is to me observable, that at a fixed age this *Caterpillar* gives over to eat,* and

towards Winter comes to be covered over with a strange shell or
View Sir Fra. Bacon
exper. 728 & 90. in
*his Natural History.** crust called an *Aurelia*,* and so lives a kind of dead
life, without eating all the Winter; and (as others of
several kinds turn to be several kinds of flies and
vermin the Spring following) so this *Caterpillar* then turns to be a
painted Butter-fly.

Come, come my Scholar, you see the River stops our morning
walk, and I will also here stop my discourse, only as we sit down
under this *Honey-suckle* hedg, whilst I look a Line to fit the Rod that
our brother *Peter* hath lent you, I shall for a little confirmation of
what I have said, repeat the observation of *Du Bartas*:*

6. Day of
Du Bartas.
> *God not contented to each kind to give,*
> *And to infuse the vertue generative,*
> *By his wise power made many creatures breed*
> *Of liveless bodies without Venus deed.**
>
> *So the cold humor* breeds the Salamander,*
> *Who (in effect) like to her births commander,*
> *With child with hundred winters, with her touch*
> *Quencheth the fire, though glowing ne'r so much.*
>
> *So in the fire in burning furnace springs*
> *The Fly Perausta* with the flaming wings;*
> *Without the fire it dyes, in it it joyes,*
> *Living in that which all things else destroyes.*

View Gerh.
Herbal and
Cambden.
> *So slow Boötes underneath him sees*
> *In th' Icy Islands goslings hatcht of trees,**
> *Whose fruitful leaves falling into the water,*
> *Are turn'd ('tis known) to living fowls soon after.*
>
> *So rotten planks of broken ships do change*
> *To Barnacles. O transformation strange!*
> *'Twas first a green tree, then a broken hull,*
> *Lately a mushrome, now a flying Gull.*

Venat. O my good Master, this morning-walk has been spent to
my great pleasure and wonder: but I pray, when shall I have your
direction how to make artificial flies, like to those that the *Trout* loves
best? and also how to use them?

Pisc. My honest Scholar, it is now past five of the Clock, we will fish till nine, and then go to breakfast: Go you to yonder *Sycamore-tree*, and hide your Bottle of drink under the hollow root of it; for about that time, and in that place, we will make a brave breakfast with a piece of powdered Beef,* and a Radish or two that I have in my Fish-bag; we shall, I warrant you, make a good, honest, wholsome, hungry breakfast, and I will then give you direction for the making and using of your flies: and in the mean time there is your Rod and Line, and my advice is, that you fish as you see me do, and let's try which can catch the first Fish.

Venat. I thank you Master, I will observe and practice your direction as far as I am able.

Pisc. Look you Scholar, you see I have hold of a good Fish: I now see it is a Trout, I pray, put that Net under him, and touch not my line for if you do, then we break all. Well done Scholar, I thank you.

Now for another. Trust me, I have another bite: come Scholar, come lay down your Rod, and help me to land this as you did the other. So, now we shall be sure to have a good dish of Fish for supper.

Venat. I am glad of that; but I have no fortune: sure, Master, yours is a better Rod, and better tackling.

Pisc. Nay, then take mine, and I will fish with yours. Look you, Scholar, I have another; come, do as you did before. And now I have a bite at another: Oh me! he has broke all; there's half a line and a good hook lost.

Venat. I and a good *Trout* too.

Pisc. Nay, the *Trout* is not lost, for pray take notice no man can lose what he never had.

Venat. Master, I can neither catch with the first nor second Angle: I have no fortune.

Pisc. Look you, Scholar, I have yet another, and now having caught three brace of Trouts, I will tell you a short Tale as we walk towards our breakfast: *A Scholar (a Preacher I should say) that was to preach to procure the approbation of a Parish, that he might be their Lecturer,* had got from his Fellow-pupil the copy of a Sermon that was first preached with great commendation by him that composed it; and though the borrower of it preach'd it word for word, as it was at first, yet it was utterly disliked as it was preached by the second to his Congregation: which the sermon-borrower complained of to the lender of it, and was thus answered; I lent you indeed my* Fiddle, *but not my* Fiddlestick;* *for you* *are to know, that every one cannot make musick with my words, which are fitted for my own mouth.* And so, my Scholar, you are to know, that as the ill pronunciation or ill accenting of words in a Sermon spoils it, so the ill carriage of your line, or not fishing even to a foot in a right place, makes you lose your labour: and you are to know, that though you have my *Fiddle*, that is, my very Rod and Tacklings with which you see I catch Fish; yet you have not my *Fiddlestick*, that is, you yet have not skill to know how to carry your hand and line, nor how to guide it to a right place: and this must be taught you (for you are to remember I told you, Angling is an Art) either by practice, or a long observation or both. But take this for a rule, when you fish for a Trout with a Worm, let your line have so much, and not more Lead than will fit the stream in which you fish; that is to say, more in a great troublesom stream than in a smaller that is quieter; as near as may be, so much as will sink the bait to the bottom, and keep it still in motion, and not more.

But now lets say Grace and fall to breakfast: what say you, Scholar, to the providence of an old Angler? does not this meat taste well? and was not this place well chosen to eat it? for this Sycamore-tree will shade us from the Suns heat.

Venat. All excellent good, and my stomach excellent good too. And I now remember and find that true which devout *Lessius** says, *That poor men, and those that fast often, have much more pleasure in eating than rich men and gluttons, that always feed before their stomachs are empty of their last meat, and call for more: for by that means they rob themselves of that pleasure that hunger brings to poor men.* And I do seriously approve of that saying of yours, *That you had rather be a civil, well govern'd, well grounded, temperate, poor Angler, than a drunken Lord.* But I hope there is none such; however I am certain of this, that I have been at many very costly dinners that have not afforded me half the content that this has done, for which I thank God and you.

And now good Master, proceed to your promised direction for making and ordering my Artificial flie.

Pisc. My honest Scholar, I will do it, for it is a debt due unto you by my promise: and because you shall not think your self more engaged to me than indeed you really are, I will freely give you such directions as were lately given to me by an ingenuous brother of the Angle,* an honest man, and a most excellent *Flie-fisher.*

You are to note, that there are twelve kinds of Artificial made Flies to Angle with upon the top of the water (note by the way, that the fittest season of using these is in a blustering windy day, when the waters are so troubled that the natural flie cannot be seen, or rest upon them). The first is the *dun-flie* in *March*,* the body is made of *dun wool*, the wings of the Partridges feathers. The second is another *dun-Flie*, the body of *Black wool*, and the wings made of the black Drakes feathers, and of the feathers under his tail. The third is the *stone-flie* in *April*, the body is made of *black wool* made yellow under the wings, and under the tail, and so made with wings of the Drake. The fourth is the *ruddy Flie* in the beginning of *May*, the body made of *red wool* wrapt about with black silk, and the feathers are the wings of the Drake, with the feathers of a red Capon also, which hang dangling on his sides next to the tail. The fifth is the *yellow* or *greenish-flie* (in *May* likewise) the body made of *yellow wool*, and the wings made of the red cocks hackle* or tail. The sixth is, the *black Flie* in *May* also, the body made of *black wool* and lapt about with the herl of a Peacocks tail; the wings are made of the wings of a brown Capon with his blew feathers in his head. The seventh is the sad *yellow-flie* in *June*, the body is made of *black wool*, with a yellow list* on either side, and the wings taken off the wings of a Buzzard, bound with black braked* hemp. The eighth is the *moorish flie* made with the body of duskish Wool, and the wings made of the blackish mail* of the Drake. The ninth is the *tawny-flie*, good until the middle of *June*; the body made of *tawny-wool*, the wings made contrary one against the other,* made of the whitish mail of the wild Drake. The tenth is the *Wasp-flie* in *July*, the body made of *black wool*, lapt about with yellow silk, the wings made of the feathers of the Drake, or of the Buzzard. The Eleventh is the *shell-flie*, good in mid *July*, the body made of greenish wool, lapt about with the herle of a Peacocks tail; and the wings made of the wings of the Buzzard. The twelfth is the dark *Drake-flie*, good in *August*, the body made with *black Wool*, lapt about with black silk: his wings are made with the mail of the black Drake, with a black head. Thus have you a Jury of flies likely to betray and condemn all the Trouts in the River.

I shall next give you some other Directions for Flie-fishing, such as are given by Mr. *Thomas Barker*,* a Gentleman that hath spent much time in Fishing: but I shall do it with a little variation.

First, let your Rod be light, and very gentle, I take the best to be of two pieces, and let not your Line exceed (especially for three or four links next to the hook) I say, not exceed three or four hairs* at the

most, though you may Fish a little stronger above in the upper part
of your Line: but if you can attain to Angle with one hair, you shall
have more rises and catch more Fish. Now you must be sure not to
cumber your self with too long a Line, as most do: and before you
begin to Angle, cast* to have the wind on your back, and the Sun (if
it shines) to be before you, and to fish down the stream; and carry the
point or top of your Rod downward, by which means the shadow of
your self, and Rod too will be the least offensive to the Fish, for the
sight of any shade amazes the fish, and spoils your sport, of which you
must take a great care.

In the middle of *March* (till which time a man should not in honesty catch a Trout) or in *April*, if the weather be dark, or a little windy
or cloudy, the best fishing is with the *Palmer-worm*, of which I last
spoke to you, but of these there be divers kinds, or at least of divers
colours; these and the *May-flie* are the ground of all Flie-angling,
which are to be thus made.

First, you must arm your hook* with the line in the inside of it,
then take your Scissars, and cut so much of a brown Mallards feather
as in your own reason* will make the wings of it, you having withal
regard to the bigness or littleness of your hook, then lay the outmost
part of your feather next to your hook, then the point of your feather
next the shank of your hook; and having so done, whip it three or four
times about the hook with the same Silk, with which your hook was
armed, and having made the Silk fast, take the hackle of a *Cock* or
Capons neck, or a *Plovers* top,* which is usually better: take off the
one side of the feather, and then take the hackle, Silk, or Crewel,
Gold or Silver thred, make these fast at the bent of the hook, that is
to say, below your arming; then you must take the hackle, the Silver
or Gold thred, and work it up to the wings, shifting or still removing
your finger, as you turn the Silk about the hook: and still looking at
every stop or turn, that your Gold, or what materials soever you make
your *Flie* of, do lie right and neatly; and if you find they do so, then
when you have made the head, make all fast, and then work your
hackle up to the head, and make that fast: and then with a needle or
pin divide the wing into two, and then with the arming Silk whip it
about cross-waies betwixt the wings; and then with your thumb you
must turn the point of the feather towards the bent of the hook, and
then work three or four times about the shank of the hook, and then
view the proportion, and if all be neat and to your liking fasten.

I confess, no direction can be given to make a man of a dull capacity able to make a Flie well: and yet I know, this with a little practice will help an ingenuous Angler in a good degree: but to see a Flie made by an Artist in that kind, is the best teaching to make it, and then an ingenuous Angler may walk by the River and mark what flies fall on the water that day, and catch one of them, if he see the *Trouts* leap at a fly of that kind: and then having alwaies hooks ready hung with him, and having a bag also always with him, with Bears hair, or the hair of a brown or sad-coloured Heifer, hackles of a Cock or Capon, several coloured Silk and Crewel to make the body of the flie, the feathers of a Drakes head, black or brown Sheeps wool, or Hogs wool, or hair, thred of Gold and of Silver: Silk of several colours (especially sad coloured to make the flies head): and there be also other coloured feathers both of little birds and of peckled foul. I say, having those with him in a bag, and trying to make a flie, though he miss at first, yet shall he at last hit it* better, even to such a perfection, as none can well teach him; and if he hit to make his Flie right, and have the luck to hit also where there is store of *Trouts*, a dark day, and a right wind, he will catch such store of them, as will encourage him to grow more and more in love with the Art of *Fly-making*.

Venat. But my loving master, if any wind will not serve, then I wish I were in *Lapland*, to buy a good wind of one of the honest Witches,* that sell so many winds there, and so cheap.

Pisc. Marry Scholar, but I would not be there, nor indeed from under this tree: for look how it begins to rain, and by the clouds, if I mistake not we shall presently have a smoaking showre,* and therefore sit close, this *Sycamore-tree* will shelter us: and I will tell you, as they shall come into my mind, more observations of flie-fishing for a Trout.

But first for the wind, you are to take notice, that of the winds the *Southwind* is said to be best. One observes, That

> *When the wind is South,*
> *It blows your bait into a fishes mouth.**

Next to that, the *West* wind is believed to be the best: and having told you that the *East* wind is the worst, I need not tell you which wind is the best in the third degree: And yet (as *Solomon* observes*) that *He that considers the wind shall never sow*: so he that busies his head too much about them, (if the weather be not made extream cold by an East wind) shall be a little superstitious: For as it is observed by some, That there is no good Horse of a bad colour;* so I have observed that if it be a cloudy day, and not extream cold, let the Wind sit in what corner it will, and do its worst I heed it not. And yet take this for a rule, that I would willingly fish standing on the Lee-shore: and you are to take notice, that the fish lies or swims nearer the bottom, and in deeper water in Winter than in Summer; and also nearer the bottom in any cold day, and then gets nearest the Lee-side of the water.

But I promised to tell you more of the Flie-fishing for a *Trout*, which I may have time enough to do, for you see it rains *May-butter*:* First for a *May-Flie*, you may make his body with greenish coloured Crewel, or Willowish colour; darkning it in most places with waxed Silk, or rib'd with black hair, or some of them rib'd with silver thred; and such Wings for the colour as you see the flie to have at that season; nay, at that very day on the water. Or you may make the Oak-flie* with an Orange-tawny and black ground, and the brown of a Mallards feather for the Wings; and you are to know, that these two are most excellent flies, that is, the *May-flie* and the *Oak-Flie*. And let me again tell you, that you keep as far from the water as you can possibly, whether you fish with a flie or worm, and fish down the stream;* and when you fish with a flie, if it be possible, let no part of your line touch the water, but your flie only; and be still moving your fly upon the water, or casting it into the water, you your self being also always moving down the stream. Mr. *Barker** commends several sorts of the *Palmer* flies, not only those rib'd with silver and gold, but others that have their bodies all made of black, or some with red, and a red hackle; you may also make the *Hawthorn-flie*,* which is all black, and not big, but very small, the smaller the better; or the *Oak-Flie*, the body of which is Orange-colour and black Crewel, with a brown Wing; or a flie made with a *Peacocks* feather, is excellent in a bright day: You must be sure you want not in your *Magazine-bag** the *Peacocks* feather, and grounds of such wool and Crewel as will make the Grashopper; and note that usually the smallest flies are the best; and note also, that the light flie does usually make most sport in a dark day, and the darkest and least fly in a bright or clear day; and lastly note, that you are to repair upon any occasion to your *Magazine-bag*, and upon any occasion vary and make them lighter or sadder according to your fancy or the day.

And now I shall tell you, that the fishing with a natural flie is excellent, and affords much pleasure; they may be found thus, the *Mayflie* usually in and about that month near to the River side, especially against rain; the *Oak-Flie* on the butt or body of an *Oak* or *Ash* from the beginning of *May* to the end of *August*; it is a brownish flie, and easie to be so found, and stands usually with his head downward, that is to say, towards the root of the tree; the small black flie, or Hawthorn flie, is to be had on any Hawthorn bush after the leaves be come forth: with these and a short Line (as I shewed to Angle for a *Chub*) you may dape or dop, and also with a *Grashopper* behind a tree, or in any deep hole, still making it to move on the top of the water, as if it were alive, and still keeping your self out of sight, you shall certainly have sport if there be *Trouts*; yea, in a hot day, but especially in the evening of a hot day you will have sport.

And now, Scholar, my direction for flie-fishing is ended with this showre, for it has done raining; and now look about you, and see how pleasantly that Meadow looks; nay, and the Earth smells as sweetly too. Come, let me tell you what holy Mr. *Herbert** says of such days and flowers as these, and then we will thank God that we enjoy them, and walk to the River and sit down quietly, and try to catch the other brace of *Trouts*.

> *Sweet day, so cool, so calm, so bright,*
> *The bridal of the earth and skie,*
> *Sweet dews shall weep thy fall to night,*
> > *for thou must die.*

> *Sweet Rose, whose hew angry and brave*
> *Bids the rash gazer wipe his eye,*
> *Thy root is ever in its grave,*
> > *and thou must die.*

> *Sweet Spring, full of sweet days and roses,*
> *A box where sweets compacted lye;*
> *My Musick shews you have your closes,**
> > *and all must dye.*

> *Only a sweet and vertuous soul,*
> *Like seasoned Timber never gives,*
> *But when the whole world turns to coal,*
> > *then chiefly lives.*

Venat. I thank you, good Master, for your good direction for Flie-fishing, and for the sweet enjoyment of the pleasant day, which is so far spent without offence to God or man: and I thank you for the sweet close of your discourse with Mr. *Herberts* Verses, who I have heard loved Angling:* and I do the rather believe it, because he had a spirit suitable to Anglers, and to those primitive Christians, that you love, and have so much commended.

Pisc. Well my loving Scholar, and I am pleased, to know that you are so well pleased with my direction and discourse.

And since you like these Verses of Mr. *Herberts* so well, let me tell you what a reverend and learned Divine that professes to imitate him (and has indeed done so most excellently) hath writ of our *Book* of *Common Prayer*, which I know you will like the better, because he is a friend of mine, and I am sure no enemy to Angling.

> *What? pray'r by th' book? and common? Yes, why not?*
> *The Spirit of grace,*
> *And supplication,*
> *Is not left free alone*
> *For time and place,*
> *But manner too: to read or speak by rote,*
> *Is all alike to him, that prayes*
> *In's heart, what with his mouth he says.*

> *They that in private by themselves alone*
> *Do pray, may take*
> *What liberty they please,*
> *In chusing of the ways*
> *Wherein to make*
> *Their souls most intimate affections known*
> *To him that sees in secret, when*
> *Th' are most conceal'd from other men.*

> *But he, that unto others leads the way*
> *In publick prayer,*
> *Should do it so*
> *As all that hear may know*
> *They need not fear*
> *To tune their hearts unto his tongue, and say,*
> *Amen; not doubt they were betray'd*
> *To blaspheme, when they meant to have pray'd.*

Devotion will add Life unto the Letter,
And why should not
That which Authority
Prescribes, esteemed be
Advantage got?
If th' prayer be good, the commoner the better,
Prayer in the Churches words, as well
*As sense, of all prayers bears the bell.**
                                        Ch. Harvie.*

And now, Scholar, I think it will be time to repair to our Angle-rods, which we left in the water, to fish for themselves, and you shall chuse which shall be yours; and it is an even lay,* one of them catches.

And let me tell you, this kind of fishing with a dead rod, and laying night-hooks, are like putting money to Use,* for they both work for the Owners, when they do nothing but sleep, or eat, or rejoyce; as you know we have done this last hour, and sate as quietly and as free from cares under this *Sycamore*, as *Virgils Tityrus* and his *Melibœus** did under their broad *Beech-tree*: No life, my honest Scholar, no life so happy and so pleasant, as the life of a well governed *Angler*; for when the *Lawyer* is swallowed up with business, and the *States-man* is preventing or contriving plots, then we sit on *Cowslip-banks*, hear the birds sing, and possess our selves in as much quietness as these silent silver streams, which we now see glide so quietly by us. Indeed my good Scholar, we may say of *Angling*, as Dr. *Boteler** said of *Strawberries; Doubtless God could have made a better berry, but doubtless God never did*: And so (if I might be Judge) *God never did make a more calm, quiet, innocent recreation than Angling.*

I'le tell you Scholar, when I sate last on this *Primrose-bank*, and look'd down these Meadows; I thought of them as *Charles* the Emperour* did of the City of *Florence: That they were too pleasant to be look'd on, but only on Holy-days*: as I then sate on this very grass, I turn'd my present thoughts into verse: 'Twas a wish which I'le repeat to you.

The Anglers wish.

I in these flowry Meads wou'd be:
These Chrystal streams should solace me;
To whose harmonious bubling noise,

I with my Angle wo'd rejoice
Sit here and see the Turtle-dove,
Court his chast Mate to acts of love,
Or on that bank, feel the west wind
Breath health and plenty, please my mind
To see sweet dew-drops kiss these flowers,
And then, washt off by April-*showers:*

'Like
Hermit
poor.*

Here hear my Kenna* *sing*¹ *a song,*
There see a Black-*bird feed her young,*
Or a Leverock *build her nest;*
Here, give my weary spirits rest,
And raise my low pitcht thoughts above
Earth, or what poor mortals love:
        Thus free from Law-suits, *and the noise*
        Of Princes Courts I wou'd rejoyce.

Or, with my Bryan,* *and a book,*
Loyter long days near Shawford-brook;*
There sit by him, and eat my meat,
There see the Sun both rise and set:
There bid good morning to next day,
There meditate my time away:
        And angle on, and beg to have
        A quiet passage to a welcome grave.

When I had ended this composure,* I left this place, and saw a Brother of the Angle sit under that *hony-suckle-hedg* (one that will prove worth your acquaintance) I sate down by him, and presently we met with an accidental piece of merriment, which I will relate to you; for it rains still.

On the other side of this very hedge sate a gang of *Gypsies*, and near to them sate a gang of *Beggars*: the *Gypsies* were then to divide all the money that had been got that week, either by stealing linnen or poultrie, or by Fortune-telling, or Legerdemain, or indeed by any other sleights and secrets belonging to their mysterious Government. And the sum that was got that week proved to be but twenty and some odd shillings. The odd money was agreed to be distributed amongst the poor of their own Corporation; and for the remaining twenty shillings, that was to be divided unto four Gentlemen *Gypsies*, according to their several degrees in their Commonwealth.

And the first or chiefest *Gypsie*, was by consent to have a third part of the twenty shillings; which all men know is 6*s*. 8*d*.*

The second was to have a fourth part of the 20*s*. which all men know to be 5*s*.

The third was to have a fifth part of the 20*s*. which all men know to be 4*s*.

The fourth and last *Gypsie*, was to have a sixth part of the 20*s*. which all men know to be 3*s*. 4*d*.

As for example,
3 times 6*s*. 8*d*. is ———————— 20*s*.
And so is 4 times 5*s*. ———————— 20*s*.
And so is 5 times 4*s*. ———————— 20*s*.
And so is 6 times 3*s*. 4*d*. ———————— 20*s*.

And yet he that divided the money was so very a *Gypsie*, that though he gave to every one these said sums, yet he kept one shilling of it for himself.

	s.	*d.*
As for Example,	6	8
	5	0
	4	0
	3	4
make but	19	0

But now you shall know, that when the four *Gypsies* saw that he had got one shilling by dividing the money, though not one of them knew any reason to demand more, yet like Lords and Courtiers every *Gypsie* envied him that was the gainer, and wrangled with him, and every one said the *remaining shilling belonged to him*: and so they fell to so high a contest about it, as none that knows the faithfulness of one *Gypsie* to another, will easily believe; only we that have lived these last twenty years,* are certain that money has been able to do much mischief. However the *Gypsies* were too wise to go to Law, and did therefore chuse their choice friends *Rook* and *Shark*, and our late English *Gusman** to be their Arbitrators and Umpires; and so they left this *Hony-suckle-hedg*, and went to *tell fortunes*, and *cheat*, and get more money and lodging in the next Village.

When these were gone we heard as high a contention amongst the *beggars, Whether it was easiest to rip a Cloak, or to unrip a Cloak?* One *beggar* affirmed it was all one. But that was denied by asking her, *If doing and undoing were all one?* then another said, *'Twas easiest to unrip a Cloak,* for that was to let it alone. But she was answered, by asking her, how she unript it, if she let it alone? And she confest her self mistaken. These and twenty such like questions were proposed, and answered with as much beggarly Logick and earnestness, as was ever heard to proceed from the mouth of the most pertinacious Schismatick;* and sometimes all the Beggars (whose number was neither more nor less than the Poets nine Muses) talk'd all together about this ripping and unripping, and so loud that not one heard what the other said; but at last one beggar crav'd audience, and told them, that old Father *Clause,* whom *Ben Johnson* in his Beggars-bush created King of their Corporation, was that night to lodg at an Ale-house (called *Catch-her-by-the-way*) not far from *Waltham-Cross,* and in the high-road towards *London*; and he therefore desired them to spend no more time about that and such like questions, but refer all to Father *Clause* at night, for he was an upright Judge, and in the mean time draw cuts* what Song should be next sung, and who should sing it; They all agreed to the motion, and the lot fell to her that was the youngest, and veriest Virgin of the Company, and she sung *Frank Davisons* Song,* which he made forty years ago, and all the others of the company joyned to sing the burthen with her: the Ditty was this, but first the burthen.*

> *Bright shines the Sun, play beggars, play,*
> *Here's scraps enough to serve to day.*
>
> *What noise of viols is so sweet*
> *As when our merry clappers* ring?*
> *What mirth doth want when beggars meet?*
> *A beggars life is for a King:*
> *Eat, drink and play, sleep when we list,*
> *Go where we will so stocks* be mist.*
> *Bright shines the Sun, play beggars play,*
> *Here's scraps enough to serve to day.*
>
> *The world is ours and ours alone,*
> *For we alone have world at will;*
> *We purchase not, all is our own,*
> *Both fields and streets we beggars fill:*

> *Play beggars play, play beggars play,*
> *Here's scraps enough to serve to day.*
>
> *A hundred herds of black and white**
> *Upon our Gowns securely feed*
> *And yet if any dare us bite,*
> *He dies therefore as sure as Creed:**
> *Thus beggars Lord it as they please,*
> *And only beggars live at ease:*
>> *Bright shines the sun, play beggars play,*
>> *Here's scraps enough to serve to day.*

Venat. I thank you good Master, for this piece of merriment, and this Song, which was well humoured by the Maker, and well remembered by you.

Pisc. But I pray forget not the Catch which you promised to make against night, for our Country-man, honest *Coridon*, will expect your Catch and my Song, which I must be forced to patch up, for it is so long since I learnt it, that I have forgot a part of it. But come, now it hath done raining, let's stretch our legs a little in a gentle walk to the River, and try what interest our Angles will pay us for lending them so long to be used by the *Trouts*, lent them indeed, like Usurers, for our profit and their destruction.

Venat. Oh me, look you Master, a fish a fish, oh las* Master, I have lost her!

Pisc. I marry Sir, that was a good fish indeed: if I had had the luck to have taken up that Rod, then 'tis twenty to one, he should not have broke my line by running to the rods end as you suffered him: I would have held him within the bent of my Rod* (unless he had been fellow to the great *Trout* that is near an ell long,* which was of such a length and depth, that he had his picture drawn, and now is to be seen at mine Host *Rickabies* at the *George* in *Ware*), and it may be, by giving that very great *Trout* the Rod, that is, by casting it to him into the water,* I might have caught him at the long run, for so I use alwayes to do when I meet with an overgrown fish, and you will learn to do so too hereafter: for I tell you, Scholar, fishing is an Art, or at least, it is an Art to catch fish.

Venat. But Master, I have heard that the great *Trout* you speak of is a *Salmon*.

Pisc. Trust me Scholar, I know not what to say to it. There are many Country people that believe *Hares* change Sexes* every year: And there be very many learned men think so too, for in their dissecting them they find many reasons to incline them to that belief. And to make the wonder seem yet less that Hares change Sexes, note that Doctor *Mer. Casaubon* affirms in his book of credible and incredible things, that *Gasper Peuseus** a learned Physician, tells us of a people that once a year turn wolves, partly in shape, and partly in conditions. And so whether this were a *Salmon* when he came into the fresh water, and his not returning into the Sea hath altered him to another colour or kind, I am not able to say; but I am certain he hath all the signs of being a *Trout* both for his *shape, colour*, and *spots*, and yet many think he is not.

Venat. But Master, will this *Trout* which I had hold of die? for it is like he hath the hook in his belly.

Pisc. I will tell you, Scholar, that unless the hook be fast in his very Gorge, 'tis more than probable he will live, and a little time with the help of the water, will rust the hook, and it will in time wear away: as the gravel doth in the horse hoof, which only leaves a false quarter.*

And now Scholar, lets go to my Rod. Look you Scholar, I have a fish too, but it proves a logger-headed* *Chub*, and this is not much amiss, for this will pleasure some poor body, as we go to our lodging to meet our Brother *Peter* and honest *Coridon*. Come, now bait your hook again, and lay it into the water, for it rains again; and we will ev'n retire to the *Sycamore tree*, and there I will give you more directions concerning Fishing: For I would fain make you an Artist.

Venat. Yes, good Master, I pray let it be so.

Pisc. Well Scholar, now we are sate down and are at ease, I shall tell you a little more of *Trout* fishing, before I speak of the *Salmon* (which I purpose shall be next), and then of the *Pike* or *Luce*. You are to know, there is night as well as day-fishing for a *Trout*, and that in the night the best *Trouts* come out of their holes: and the manner of taking them, is on the top of the water with a great *Lob* or *Garden-worm*, or rather two, which you are to fish with in a place where the waters run somewhat quietly (for in a stream the bait will not be so well discerned). I say in a *quiet* or dead place near to some swift,* there draw your bait over the top of the water to and fro, and if there be a good *Trout* in the hole, he will take it, especially if the night be dark: for then he is bold and lies near the top of the water, watching the motion of any *Frog* or *Water-rat* or *Mouse* that swims betwixt him and the skie; these he hunts after, if he sees the water but wrinkle, or move in one of these dead holes, where these great old *Trouts* usually lie near to their holds; for you are to note, that the great old *Trout* is both subtil and fearful, and lies close all day, and does not usually stir out of his hold, but lies in it as close in the day, as the *timorous Hare* does in her form:* for the chief feeding of either is seldom in the day, but usually in the night, and then the great *Trout* feeds very boldly.

And you must fish for him with a strong Line, and not a little hook, and let him have time to gorge your hook, for he does not usually forsake it, as he oft will in the day-fishing: and if the night be not dark, then Fish so with an *Artificial flie* of a light-colour, and at the snap:* nay, he will sometimes rise at a dead Mouse, or a piece of cloth, or any thing, that seems to swim cross the water, or to be in motion: this is a choice way, but I have not oft used it, because it is void of the pleasures, that such dayes as these, that we two now enjoy, afford an Angler.

And you are to know, that in *Hampshire*, which I think exceeds all *England* for swift, shallow, clear, pleasant Brooks, and store of *Trouts*, they use to catch *Trouts* in the night, by the light of a Torch or straw, which when they have discovered, they strike with a *Trout-spear* or other wayes. This kind of way they catch very many, but I would not believe it till I was an eye-witness of it, nor do I like it now I have seen it.

Venat. But Master, do not *Trouts* see us in the night?

Pisc. Yes, and hear, and smell too, both then and in the day time, for *Gesner* observes,* the *Otter* smells a Fish forty furlongs off him in the water: and that it may be true, seems to be affirmed by Sir *Francis Bacon* (in the eighth Century of his Natural History) who there proves, that waters may be the *Medium* of sounds, by demonstrating it thus, *That if you knock two stones together very deep under the water, those that stand on a bank near to that place may hear the noise without any diminution of it by the water.* He also offers* the like experiment concerning the letting an *Anchor* fall by a very long cable or rope on a rock, or the sand within the Sea: and this being so well observed and demonstrated, as it is by that learned man, has made me to believe that *Eeles* unbed themselves, and stir at the noise of Thunder, and not only, as some think, by the motion or stirring of the earth which is occasioned by that Thunder.

And this reason of Sir *Francis Bacon* (*Exper.* 792.) has made me crave pardon of one that I laught at for affirming, that he knew *Carps* come to a certain place in a Pond, to be fed at the ringing of a Bell, or the beating of a Drum: and however, it shall be a rule for me to make as little noise as I can when I am fishing, untill Sir *Francis Bacon* be confuted, which I shall give any man leave to do.

And, lest you may think him singular in this opinion, I will tell you, this seems to be believed by our learned Doctor *Hackwell*,* who (in his *Apology of Gods Power and Providence*, f. 360) quotes *Pliny* to report, that one of the Emperors had particular Fish-ponds, and in them several Fish, that appeared and came when they were called by their particular names: and St. *James* tells us* (*chap.* 1. *and* 7.) that all things in the Sea have been tamed by Mankind. And *Pliny* tells us (*lib.* 9. 35.) that *Antonia* the Wife of *Drusus* had a *Lamprey*, at whose gils she hung Jewels or Ear-rings; and that others have been so tender-hearted, as to shed tears at the death of Fishes, which they have kept and loved. And these Observations, which will to most hearers seem wonderful, seem to have a further confirmation from *Martial* (*lib.* 4. *epigr.* 30.) who writes thus:

*Piscator fuge ne nocens, &c.**

> Angler, *would'st thou be guiltless? then forbear,*
> *For these are* sacred fishes *that swim here;*
> *Who know their Sovereign, and will lick his hand;*
> *Than which none's greater in the worlds command:*
> *Nay more, th'have names, & when they called are,*
> *Do to their several Owners Call repair.*

All the further use that I shall make of this, shall be, to advise Anglers to be patient, and *forbear swearing, lest they be heard and catch no Fish.**

And so I shall proceed next to tell you, it is certain, that certain fields near *Lemster*,* a Town in *Hereford-shire*, are observed to make the sheep that graze upon them more fat than the next, and also to bear finer wool; that is to say, that, that year in which they feed in such a particular pasture, they shall yield finer wool than they did that year before they came to feed in it, and courser again if they shall return to their former pasture; and again return to a finer wool being fed in the fine-wool-ground. Which I tell you, that you may the better believe that I am certain, if I catch a *Trout* in one Meadow, he shall be *white* and *faint*, and very like to be *lowsie*; and as certainly, if I catch a

Trout in the next Meadow, he shall be *strong*, and *red*, and *lusty*, and much better meat: Trust me, Scholar, I have caught many a *Trout* in a particular Meadow, that the very shape and the enamell'd colour of him hath been such, as hath joyed me to look on him; and I have then with much pleasure concluded with *Solomon*,* *Every thing is beautiful in his season*.

I should by promise speak next of the *Salmon*, but I will by your favour say a little of the *Umber* or *Grayling*; which is so like a *Trout* for his shape and feeding, that I desire I may exercise your patience with a short discourse of him, and then the next shall be of the *Salmon*.

CHAP. VI.

Observations of the Umber *or* Grayling, *and directions how to fish for them.*

PISC. The *Umber* and *Grayling* are thought by some to differ as the *Herring* and *Pilcher** do. But though they may do so in other Nations, I think those in *England* differ nothing but in their names. *Aldrovandus* says,* they be of a Trout kind: and *Gesner* says,* that in his Country (which is *Swisserland*) he is accounted the choicest of all Fish. And in *Italy*, he is in the month of *May* so highly valued, that he is sold then at a much higher rate than any other Fish.* The *French* (which call the *Chub Un Villain*) call the *Umber* of the Lake *Leman, Un Umble Chevalier*; and they value the *Umber* or Grayling so highly, that they say he feeds on Gold,* and say that many have been caught out of their famous River of *Loyre*, out of whose bellies grains of Gold have been often taken. And some think that he feeds on *Water-time*,* and smells of it at his first taking out of the water; and they may think so with as good reason as we do, that our Smelts smell like Violets* at their being first caught; which I think is a truth. *Aldrovandus* says, the *Salmon*, the *Grayling*, and *Trout*, and all Fish that live in clear and sharp streams, are made by their mother *Nature* of such exact shape and pleasant colours, purposely to invite us to a joy and contentedness in feasting with her. Whether this is a truth or not, is not my purpose to dispute; but 'tis certain, all that write of the *Umber* declare him to be very medicinable. And *Gesner* says,* that the fat of an *Umber* or *Grayling* being set with a little Hony a day or two in the Sun in a little glass, is very excellent against redness, or swarthiness, or any thing that breeds in the eyes. *Salvian** takes him to be called *Umber* from his swift swimming or gliding out of sight, more like a shadow or a Ghost than a fish. Much more might be said both of his smell and tast, but I shall only tell you, that St. *Ambrose** the glorious Bishop of *Millan* (who liv'd when the Church kept Fasting-days) calls him the *flower-fish*, or flower of Fishes, and that he was so far in love with him, that he would not let him pass without the honour of a long Discourse; but I must; and pass on to tell you how to take this dainty fish.

First, Note, That he grows not to the bigness of a Trout; for the biggest of them do not usually exceed eighteen inches, he lives in such Rivers as the Trout does, and is usually taken with the same baits as the Trout is, and after the same manner, for he will bite both at the *Minnow*, or *Worm*, or *Fly*, (though he bites not often at the Minnow) and is very gamesome at the *Fly*, and much simpler, and therefore bolder than a *Trout*, for he will rise twenty times at a fly, if you miss him, and yet rise again. He has been taken with a fly made of the red feathers of a *Parakita*,* a strange outlandish bird, and he will rise at a fly not unlike a gnat or a small moth, or indeed, at most flies that are not too big. He is a Fish that lurks close all winter, but is very pleasant and jolly after mid-*April*, and in *May*, and in the hot months: he is of a very fine shape, his flesh is white, his teeth, those little ones that he has, are in his throat, yet he has so tender a mouth, that he is oftner lost after an Angler has hooked him, than any other Fish. Though there be many of these Fishes in the delicate River *Dove*,* and in *Trent*, and some other smaller Rivers, as that which runs by *Salisbury*,* yet he is not so general a Fish as the *Trout*, nor to me so good to eat or to angle for. And so I shall take my leave of him, and now come to some Observations of the *Salmon*, and how to catch him.

CHAP. VII.

Observations of the Salmon, *with directions how to fish for him.*

PISC. The *Salmon* is accounted the King of fresh-water-fish, and is ever bred in Rivers relating to the Sea, yet so high or far from it as admits of no tincture of salt, or brackishness; He is said to breed or cast his spawn in most Rivers in the month of *August*: some say, that then they dig a hole or grave in a safe place in the gravel, and there place their eggs or spawn (after the Melter* has done his natural Office) and then hide it most cunningly, and cover it over with gravel and stones; and then leave it to their Creators protection, who by a gentle heat which he infuses into that cold element makes it brood and beget life in the spawn, and to become *Samlets* early in the spring next following.

The *Salmons* having spent their appointed time, and done this Natural Duty in the fresh waters; they then haste to the Sea before Winter, both the Melter and Spawner:* but, if they be stopt by *Flood-gates* or *Weires*, or lost in the fresh waters, then, those so left behind, by degrees grow *sick*, and *lean*, and *unseasonable*, and *kipper*;* that is to say, have bony gristles grow out of their lower chaps (not unlike a Hawks beak) which hinders their feeding, and in time such Fish so left behind, pine away and dye. 'Tis observed, that he may live thus one year from the Sea; but he then grows insipid, and tasteless, and loses both his blood and strength, and pines and dies the second year. And 'tis noted, that those little *Salmons* called *Skeggers*, which abound in many Rivers relating to the *Sea*, are bred by such sick *Salmons*, that might not go to the Sea, and that though they abound, yet they never thrive to any considerable bigness.

But if the old *Salmon* gets to the Sea, then that gristle which shews him to be *kipper* wears away, or is cast off (as the *Eagle* is said to cast his bill)* and he recovers his strength, and comes next Summer to the same River (if it be possible) to enjoy the former pleasures that there possest him; for (as one has wittily observed) he has (like some persons of Honour and Riches, which have both their Winter and Summer houses)* the fresh Rivers for Summer, and the salt water for Winter to spend his life in; which is not (as Sir *Francis Bacon* hath observed in his *History of Life and Death*)* above ten years: And it is to be observed, that though the *Salmon* does grow big in the Sea, yet he grows not fat but in fresh Rivers; and it is observed, that the farther they get from the Sea, they be both the fatter and better.

Next, I shall tell you, that though they make very hard shift to get out of the fresh Rivers into the Sea: yet they will make harder shift to get out of the salt into the fresh Rivers, to spawn, or possess the pleasures that they have formerly found in them: to which end, they will force themselves through *Flood-gates*, or over *Weires*, or *hedges*, or *stops* in the water, even to a height beyond common belief. *Gesner* speaks* of such places, as are known to be above eight foot high above water. And our *Cambden* mentions* (in his *Britannia*) the like wonder to be in *Pembroke-shire*, where the River *Tivy* falls into the Sea, and that the fall is so down-right, and so high, that the people stand and wonder at the strength and sleight by which they see the *Salmon* use to get out of the Sea into the said River; and the manner and height of the place is so notable, that it is known far by the name of the *Salmon-leap*; concerning which, take this also out of *Michael Draiton,** my honest old friend. As he tells it you in his *Polyalbion.*

> *And when the* Salmon *seeks a fresher stream to find,*
> (*Which hither from the Sea comes yearly by his kind*)
> *As he towards season grows, & stems the watry tract*
> *Where* Tivy *falling down, makes an high cataract,*
> *Forc'd by the rising rocks that there her course oppose*
> *As tho within her bounds they meant her to inclose;*
> *Here, when the labouring fish does at the foot arive,*
> *And finds that by his strength he does but vainly strive,*
> *His tail takes in his mouth,* & bending like a bow*
> *That's to full compass drawn, aloft himself doth throw,*
> *Then springing at his height, as doth a little wand,*
> *That bended end to end, and started from mans hand,*
> *Far off it self doth cast; so does the* Salmon *vault,*
> *And if at first he fail, his second Summer-salt,*
> *He instantly essaies, and from his nimble ring,*
> *Still yerking,* never leaves untill himself he fling*
> *Above the opposing stream.——*

This *Michael Drayton* tells you of this leap or *Summer-salt* of the *Salmon.*

And next I shall tell you, that it is observed by *Gesner* and others,* that there is no better *Salmon* than in *England*: and that though some of our Northern Countries have as fat and as large as the River *Thames*, yet none are of so excellent a tast.

And as I have told you that Sir *Francis Bacon* observes,* the age of a *Salmon* exceeds not ten years, so let me next tell you, that his growth is very sudden: it is said, that after he is got into the Sea, he becomes from a *Samlet*, not so big as a Gudgion, to be a *Salmon*, in as short a time as a Gosling becomes to be a Goose. Much of this has been observed by tying a *Ribband* or some known *tape* or *thred*, in the tail of some young *Salmons*, which have been taken in Weirs as they have swimm'd toward the salt water, and then by taking a part of them again with the known mark at the same place at their return from the Sea, which is usually about six months after; and the like experiment hath been tryed upon young *Swallows*, who have after six months absence, been observed to return to the same chimney, there to make their nests and habitations for the Summer following: which has inclined many to think, that every *Salmon* usually returns to the same River in which it was bred, as young *Pigeons* taken out of the same *Dove-cote*, have also been observed to do.

And you are yet to observe further, that the Hee *Salmon* is usually bigger than the Spawner, and that he is more kipper, and less able to endure a winter in the fresh water, than the She is, yet she is at that time of looking less kipper and better, as watry, and as bad meat.

And yet you are to observe, that as there is no general rule without an exception, so there are some few Rivers in this Nation, that have *Trouts* and *Salmons* in season in winter, as 'tis certain there be in the River *Wy* in *Monmouth-shire*, where they be in season (as *Cambden* observes)* from *September* till *April*. But, my Scholar, the observation of this and many other things, I must in manners omit, because they will prove too large for our narrow compass of time, and therefore I shall next fall upon my direction *how to fish for this Salmon*.

And for that first, you shall observe, that usually he staies not long in a place (as *Trouts* will) but (as I said) covets still to go nearer the Spring head; and that he does not (as the *Trout* and many other fish) lie near the water side or bank or roots of trees, but swims in the deep and broad parts of the water, and usually in the middle, and near the ground; and that there you are to fish for him, and that it is to be caught as the *Trout* is, with a *Worm*, a *Minnow*, (which some call a *Penk*) or with a *Flie*.

And you are to observe, that he is very seldom observed to bite at a *Minnow*, (yet sometimes he will) and not usually at a *flie*, but more usually at a *Worm*, and then most usually at a *Lob* or *Garden-worm*, which should be well scoured that is to say, kept seven or eight daies in Moss before you fish with them: and if you double your time of eight into sixteen, twenty or more daies, it is still the better, for the worms will still be clearer, tougher, and more lively, and continue so longer upon your hook, and they may be kept longer by keeping them cool and in fresh Moss, and some advise to put Camphire* into it.

Note also, that many use to fish for a *Salmon* with a ring of wire on the top of their Rod, through which the Line may run to as great a length as is needful when he is hook'd. And to that end, some use a wheel* about the middle of their Rod, or near their hand, which is to be observed better by seeing one of them, than by a large demonstration of words.

And now I shall tell you, that which may be called a secret: I have been a fishing with old *Oliver Henly*,* (now with God) a noted Fisher, both for *Trout* and *Salmon*, and have observed, that he would usually take three or four worms out of his bag, and put them into a little box in his pocket, where he would usually let them continue half an hour or more, before he would bait his hook with them; I have asked him his reason, and he has replyed, *He did but pick the best out to be in readiness against he baited his hook the next time*: But he has been observed both by others, and my self, to catch more fish than I or any other body, that has ever gone a fishing with him could do; and especially *Salmons*; and I have been told lately by one of his most intimate and secret friends, that the box in which he put those worms, was anointed with a drop, or two or three, of the Oyl of *Ivy berries*, made by expression or infusion; and told that by the worms remaining in that box an hour, or a like time, they had incorporated* a kind of smell that was irresistibly attractive, enough to force any Fish within the smell of them, to bite. This I heard not long since from a friend, but have not tryed it; yet I grant it probable, and refer my Reader to Sir *Francis Bacons* Natural History,* where he proves fishes may hear and doubtless can more probably smell: and I am certain *Gesner* says,* the *Otter* can smell in the water, and I know not but that Fish may do so too: 'tis left for a lover of Angling, or any that desires to improve that Art, to try this conclusion.

I shall also impart two other Experiments (but not tryed by myself) which I will deliver in the same words that they were given me by an excellent Angler and a very friend, in writing; he told me the latter was too good to be told, but in a learned language, lest it should be made common.

Take the stinking oil, drawn out of Polypody *of the Oak* *by a retort,* *mixt with* Turpentine, *and* Hive-honey, *and anoint your bait therewith, and it will doubtless draw the fish to it.*

The other is this: *Vulnera hederae grandissimae inflicta sudant Balsamum oleo gelato, albicantique persimile, odoris vero longe suavissimi.**

'Tis supremely sweet to any fish, and yet *Asa fœtida** may do the like.

But in these things I have no great faith, yet grant it probable, and have had from some chymical men (namely, from Sir *George Hastings** and others) an affirmation of them to be very advantageous: but no more of these, especially not in this place.

I might here, before I take my leave of the *Salmon*, tell you, that there is more than one sort of them, as namely, a *Tecon*,* and another called in some places a *Samlet*, or by some, a *Skegger*: but these (and others which I forbear to name) may be Fish of another kind, (and differ, as we know a *Herring* and a *Pilcher** do), which I think are as different, as the Rivers in which they breed, and must by me be left to the disquisitions of men of more leisure, and of greater abilities, than I profess my self to have.

And lastly, I am to borrow so much of your promised patience, as to tell you that the *Trout* or *Salmon* being in season, have at their first taking out of the water (which continues during life) their bodies adorned, the one with such red spots, and the other with such black or blackish spots, as give them such an addition of natural beauty, as I think, was never given to any woman by the Artificial Paint or Patches* in which they so much pride themselves in this Age. And so I shall leave them both and proceed to some Observations of the *Pike*.

CHAP. VIII.

Observations of the Luce *or* Pike, *with directions how to fish for him.*

PISC. The mighty *Luce* or *Pike* is taken to be the Tyrant (as the *Salmon* is the King) of the fresh waters. 'Tis not to be doubted, but that they are bred, some by generation, and some not: as namely, of a Weed called *Pickerel-weed*, unless learned *Gesner** be much mistaken, for he says, this weed and other glutinous matter, with the help of the Suns heat in some particular Months, and some Ponds apted for it by nature, do become *Pikes*. But doubtless divers *Pikes* are bred after this manner, or are brought into some Ponds some such other wayes as is past mans finding out, of which we have daily testimonies.

Sir *Francis Bacon** in his History of Life and Death, observes the *Pike* to be the longest lived of any fresh-water-fish, and yet he computes it to be not usually above forty years; and others think it to be not above ten years; and yet *Gesner* mentions* a *Pike* taken in *Swedeland* in the Year 1449. with a Ring about his neck, declaring he was put into that Pond by *Frederick* the second,* more than two hundred years before he was last taken, as by the Inscription in that Ring (being Greek) was interpreted by the then Bishop of *Worms*.* But of this no more, but that it is observed, that the old or very great Pikes have in them more of state than goodness; the smaller or middle sized Pikes being by the most and choicest Palates observed to be the best meat; and contrary, the Eel is observed to be the better for age and bigness.

All Pikes that live long prove chargeable to their Keepers, because their life is maintained by the death of so many other Fish, even those of their own kind, which has made him by some Writers to be called the *Tyrant* of the Rivers, or the *Fresh-water-wolf*, by reason of his bold, greedy devouring disposition, which is so keen, as *Gesner* relates, a man going to a Pond (where it seems a *Pike* had devoured all the fish) to water his Mule, had a *Pike* bit his Mule by the lips; to which the *Pike* hung so fast, that the Mule drew him out of the water, and by that accident the owner of the Mule angled out the *Pike*. And the same *Gesner* observes,* that a Maid in *Poland* had a *Pike* bit her by the foot as she was washing clothes in a Pond. And I have heard the like of a woman in *Killingworth** Pond, not far from *Coventry*. But I have been assured by my friend Mr. *Seagrave*,* (of whome I spake to you formerly), that keeps tame *Otters*, that he hath known a *Pike* in extream hunger fight with one of his Otters for a Carp that the Otter had caught and was then bringing out of the water. I have told you who relates these things, and tell you they are persons of credit, and shall conclude this observation, by telling you what a wise man has observed, *It is a hard thing to perswade the belly, because it has no ears.**

But if these relations be disbelieved, it is too evident to be doubted, that a *Pike* will devour a Fish of his own kind, that shall be bigger than his belly or throat will receive, and swallow a part of him, and let the other part remain in his mouth till the swallowed part be digested, and then swallow that other part that was in his mouth, and so put it over by degrees;* which is not unlike the Ox and some other beasts, taking their meat not out of their mouth immediately into their belly, but first into some place betwixt, and then chaw it, or digest it by degrees after, which is called *Chewing the Cud*. And doubtless *Pikes* will bite when they are not hungry, but as some think even for very anger, when a tempting bait comes near to them.

And it is observed, that the *Pike* will eat venemous things (as some kind of *Frogs* are)* and yet live without being harmed by them: for, as some say, he has in him a natural Balsom or Antidote against all poison: and he has a strange heat, that though it appear to us to be cold, can yet digest or put over, any Fish-flesh by degrees without being sick. And others observe, that he never eats the venemous *Frog*, till he have first killed her, and then (as *Ducks* are observed to do to *Frogs* in spawning time, at which time some *Frogs* are observed to be venemous) so throughly washt her, by tumbling her up and down in the water, that he may devour her without danger. And *Gesner* affirms,* that a *Polonian* Gentleman did faithfully assure him, he had seen two young Geese at one time in the belly of a *Pike*. And doubtless a *Pike* in his height of hunger will bite at and devour a dog that swims in a Pond, and there have been examples of it, or the like; for as I told you, *The belly has no ears when hunger comes upon it.*

The *Pike* is also observed to be a solitary, melancholy and a bold Fish: Melancholy, because he always swims or rests himself alone, and never swims in sholes or with company, as *Roach* and *Dace*, and most other Fish do: And bold, because he fears not a shadow, or to see or be seen of any body, as the *Trout* and *Chub*, and all other Fish do.

And it is observed by *Gesner*,* that the Jaw-bones, and Hearts, and Galls of *Pikes* are very medicinable for several diseases, or to stop blood, to abate Fevers, to cure Agues, to oppose or expel the infection of the Plague, and to be many ways medicinable and useful for the good of Mankind; but he observes, that the biting of a *Pike* is venemous and hard to be cured.

And it is observed, that the *Pike* is a fish that breeds but once a year, and that other fish (as namely *Loaches*) do breed oftner: as we are certain tame Pigeons do almost every month, and yet the *Hawk* (a Bird of Prey, as the *Pike* is of Fish) breeds but once in twelve months: and you are to note, that his time of breeding or spawning is usually about the end of *February*, (or somewhat later, in *March*, as the weather proves colder or warmer) and to note, that his manner of breeding is thus, a He and a She *Pike* will usually go together out of a River into some ditch or creek, and that there the Spawner casts her eggs, and the Melter hovers over her all that time that she is casting her spawn, but touches her not.

I might say more of this, but it might be thought curiosity* or worse, and shall therefore forbear it, and take up so much of your attention, as to tell you, that the best of *Pikes* are noted to be in *Rivers*, next those in great *Ponds*, or *Meres*, and the worst in small Ponds.

But before I proceed further, I am to tell you that there is a great antipathy betwixt the *Pike* and some *Frogs*; and this may appear to the Reader of *Dubravius** (a Bishop in *Bohemia*) who in his Book of Fish and Fish-ponds, relates what, he says, he saw with his own eyes, and could not forbear to tell the Reader. Which was:

As he and the Bishop Thurzo were walking by a large Pond in Bohemia, *they saw a Frog, when the Pike lay very sleepily and quiet by the shore side, leap upon his head, and the Frog having exprest malice or anger by his swoln cheeks and staring eyes, did stretch out his legs and embraced the* Pikes *head, and presently reached them to his eyes, tearing with them and his teeth those tender parts; the* Pike *moved with anguish, moves up and down the water, and rubs himself against weeds, and whatever he thought might quit him of his enemy; but all in vain, for the frog did continue to ride triumphantly, and to bite and torment the* Pike, *till his strength failed, and then the frog sunk with the* Pike *to the bottom of the water; then presently the frog appeared again at the top and croaked, and seemed to rejoice like a Conqueror, after which he presently retired to his secret hole. The Bishop, that had beheld the battel, called his fisherman to fetch his nets, and by all means to get the* Pike, *that they might declare what had hapned: and the* Pike *was drawn forth, and both his eyes eaten out, at which when they began to wonder, the Fisherman wished them to forbear, and assured them he was certain that* Pikes *were often so served.*

I told this (which is to be read in the sixth Chapter of the Book of *Dubravius*) unto a friend, who replied, *It was as improbable as to have the mouse scratch out the cats eyes.* But he did not consider, that there be fishing Frogs* (which the *Dalmatians* call the Water-Devil) of which I might tell you as wonderful a story, but I shall tell you, that 'tis not to be doubted, but that there be some Frogs so fearful of the Water-snake, that, when they swim in a place in which they fear to meet with him, they then get a reed across into their mouths, which if they two meet by accident, secures the frog* from the strength and malice of the *Snake*, and note, that the frog usually swims the fastest of the two.

And let me tell you, that as there be *Water* and *Land-frogs,** so there be *Land* and *Water-Snakes.** Concerning which take this observation, that the Land-snake breeds, and hatches her eggs, which become young Snakes, in some old dunghill, or a like hot place; but

the Water-snake, which is not venomous (and as I have been assured
by a great observer of such secrets) does not hatch but breed her
young alive, which she does not then forsake, but bides with them,
and in case of danger will take them all into her mouth and swim away
from any apprehended danger, and then let them out again when she
thinks all danger to be past; These be accidents that we Anglers
sometimes see and often talk of.

But whither am I going? I had almost lost my self by remembring
the Discourse of *Dubravius*. I will therefore stop here, and tell you
according to my promise how to catch this *Pike*.

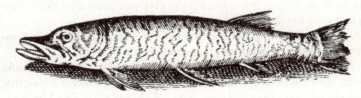

His feeding is usually of *fish* or *frogs*, and sometimes a weed of his
own called *Pickrell-weed*. Of which I told you some think some *Pikes*
are bred;* for they have observed, that where none have been put into
Ponds, yet they have there found many: and that there has been
plenty of that weed in those Ponds, and that that weed both breeds
and feeds them; but whether those *Pikes* so bred will ever breed by
generation as the others do, I shall leave to the disquisitions of men of
more curiosity and leasure than I profess my self to have; and shall
proceed to tell you that you may fish for a *Pike*, either with a *ledger* or
a *walking-bait*; and you are to note, that I call that a Ledger bait,
which is fixed, or made to rest in one certain place when you shall be
absent from it: and I call that a walking bait, which you take with you,
and have ever in motion. Concerning which two, I shall give you this
direction; That your ledger bait is best to be a living bait, though a
dead one may catch, whether it be a fish or a frog; and that you may
make them live the longer, you may or indeed you must take this
course.

First, for your live bait of fish, a *Roach* or *Dace* is (I think) best and
most tempting, and a *Pearch* is the longest lived on a hook, and having
cut off his fin on his back, which may be done without hurting him,
you must take your knife (which cannot be too sharp) and betwixt the
head and the fin on the back, cut or make an incision, or such a scar,

as you may put the arming wire of your hook into it, with as little
bruising or hurting the fish as art and diligence will enable you to do;
and so carrying your arming wire along his back, unto, or near the tail
of your Fish, betwixt the skin and the body of it, draw out that wire
or arming of your hook at another scar near to his tail: then ty him
about it with thred, but no harder than of necessity to prevent hurting the fish; and the better to avoid hurting the fish, some have a kind
of probe* to open the way, for the more easie entrance and passage of
your wire or arming: but as for these, time, and a little experience will
teach you better than I can by words; therefore I will for the present
say no more of this, but come next to give you some directions, how
to bait your hook with a frog.

Ven. But, good Master, did you not say even now, that some *Frogs*
were venemous, and is it not dangerous to touch them?

Pisc. Yes, but I will give you some Rules or Cautions concerning
them: And first, you are to note, that there are two kinds of *Frogs*; that
is to say (if I may so express my self) a *flesh*, and a *fish-frog*:* by *flesh-
frogs*,* I mean *frogs* that breed and live on the land; and of these there
be several sorts also and of several colours, some being peckled, some
greenish, some blackish, or brown: the green *Frog*, which is a small
one, is by *Topsel* taken to be venemous; and so is the *padock* or *Frog-
padock** which usually keeps or breeds on the land, and is very large
and bony, and big, especially the She frog of that kind; yet these will
sometimes come into the water, but it is not often; and the land frogs
are some of them observed by him, to breed by laying eggs: and
others to breed of the slime and dust of the earth, and that in winter
they turn to slime again, and that the next Summer that very slime
returns to be a living creature; this is the opinion of *Pliny*: and
[1] In his 19. Book, *Cardanus*[1] undertakes* to give a reason for the raining
De subtil. ex.   of Frogs: but if it were in my power, it should rain
none but water-Frogs, for those I think are not venemous, especially
the right water-Frog, which about *February* or *March* breeds in
ditches by slime, and blackish eggs in that slime: about which time of
breeding the He and She Frogs are observed to use divers *Simber-
salts** and to croak and make a noise, which the land-frog, or Padock
frog* never does. Now of these water-frogs, if you intend to fish with
a frog for a Pike, you are to chuse the yellowest that you can get, for
that the Pike ever likes best. And thus use your frog, that he may
continue long alive.

Put your hook into his mouth, which you may easily do from the middle of *April* till *August*, and then the frogs mouth grows up,* and he continues so for at least six months without eating, but is sustained, none but he whose name is Wonderful, knows how. I say, put your hook, I mean the arming wire through his mouth, and out at his gills, and then with a fine needle and silk sow the upper part of his leg with only one stitch to the arming wire of your hook, or tie the frogs leg above the upper joynt to the armed wire, and in so doing, use him as though you loved him, that is, harm him as little as you may possibly, that he may live the longer.

And now, having given you this direction for the baiting your ledger hook with a live Fish or frog, my next must be to tell you, how your hook thus baited must or may be used: and it is thus. Having fastened your hook to a line, which if it be not fourteen yards long, should not be less than twelve; you are to fasten that line to any bough near to a hole where a Pike is, or is likely to lie, or to have a haunt, and then wind your line on any forked stick, all your line except half a yard of it or rather more, and split that forked stick with such a nick or notch at one end of it, as may keep the line from any more of it ravelling* from about the stick, than so much of it as you intend; and chuse your forked stick to be of that bigness as may keep the Fish or frog from pulling the forked stick under the water till the Pike bites, and then the Pike having pulled the line forth of the clift* or nick of that stick in which it was gently fastened, he will have line enough to go to his hold and pouch the bait: and if you would have this ledger bait to keep at a fixt place, undisturbed by wind or other accidents which may drive it to the shore side, (for you are to note, that it is likeliest to catch a Pike in the midst of the water) then hang a small Plummet of lead, a stone, or piece of tile, or a turf in a string, and cast it into the water, with the forked stick, to hang upon the ground to be a kind of Anchor to keep the forked stick from moving out of your intended place till the Pike come. This I take to be a very good way, to use so many ledger baits as you intend to make trial of.

Or if you bait your hooks thus with live Fish or Frogs, and in a windy day, fasten them thus to a bough or bundle of straw, and by the help of that wind can get them to move cross a *Pond* or *mere*, you are like to stand still on the shore and see sport presently if there be any store of *Pikes*; or these live baits may make sport, being tied about the body or wings of a *Goose* or *Duck*, and she chased over a *Pond*: and the

like may be done with turning three or four live baits thus fastened to
bladders, or boughs, or bottles* of hay or flags, to swim down a River,
whilst you walk quietly alone on the shore, and are still in expectation
of sport. The rest must be taught you by practice, for time will not
allow me to say more of this kind of fishing with live baits.

And for your dead bait for a *Pike*, for that you may be taught by
one daies going a fishing with me, or any other body that fishes for
him, for the baiting your hook with a dead *Gudgeon* or a *Roach*, and
moving it up and down the water, is too easie a thing to take up any
time to direct you to do it; and yet, because I cut you short in that, I
will commute for it, by telling you that that was told me for a secret:
it is this,

Dissolve Gum *of* Ivy *in* Oyl *of* Spike,* *and therewith anoynt your*
dead bait for a Pike, *and then cast it into a likely place, and when it has*
lain a short time at the bottom, draw it towards the top of the water and so
up the stream, and it is more than likely that you have a Pike *follow with*
more than common eagerness.

And some affirm, that any bait anointed with the marrow of the
Thigh-bone of an *Hern* is a great temptation to any Fish.

These have not been tryed by me, but told me by a friend of note,
that pretended* to do me a courtesie, but if this direction to catch a
Pike thus, do you no good, yet I am certain this direction how to roast
him when he is caught, is choicely good, for I have tryed it; and it is
somewhat the better for not being common, but with my direction
you must take this Caution, that your *Pike* must not be a small one,
that is, it must be more than half a Yard, and should be bigger.

First open your Pike *at the gills, and if need be, cut also a little slit*
towards the belly; out of these take his guts, and keep his liver, which you
are to shred very small with Time, Sweet-marjoram, *and a little* Winter-
savoury; *to these put some pickled* Oysters, *and some* Anchovies, *two or*
three, both these last whole (for the Anchovies *will melt, and the* Oysters
should not) to these you must adde also a pound of sweet butter, which you
are to mix with the herbs that are shred, and let them all be well salted (if
the Pike *be more than a yard long, then you may put into these herbs more*
than a pound, or if he be less, then less Butter will suffice): these being thus
mixt with a blade or two of Mace,* *must be put into the* Pikes *belly, and*
then his belly so sowed up, as to keep all the Butter in his belly if it be pos-
sible, if not, then as much of it as you possibly can, but take not off the
scales; then you are to thrust the spit through his mouth out at his tail, and

then take four, or five, or six split sticks, or very thin lathes, and a convenient quantity of Tape or Filleting,* these lathes are to be tyed round
about the Pikes *body from his head to his tail, and the Tape tyed somewhat
thick to prevent his breaking or falling off from the spit; let him be roasted
very leasurely, and often basted with Claret wine, and Anchovyes, and
Butter mixt together, and also with what moisture falls from him into the
pan: when you have rosted him sufficiently you are to hold under him (when
you unwind or cut the Tape that ties him) such a dish as you purpose to eat
him out of; and let him fall into it with the sawce that is rosted in his belly,
and by this means the* Pike *will be kept unbroken and compleat: then, to the
sawce which was within, and also that sawce in the pan, you are to add a fit
quantity of the best Butter, and to squeeze the juyce of three or four Oranges:
lastly, you may either put into the* Pike *with the* Oysters, *two cloves of*
Garlick, *and take it whole out, when the* Pike *is cut off the spit, or to give
the sawce a* hogo,* let the dish (into which you let the Pike fall) be rubbed
with it: the using or not using of this Garlick is left to your discretion.*

M. B.*

This dish of meat is too good for any but Anglers or very honest
men; and I trust, you will prove both, and therefore I have trusted
you with this secret.

Let me next tell you, that Gesner tells us there are no Pikes in
Spain, and that the largest are in the Lake *Thrasimene* in *Italy*;* and
the next, if not equall to them, are the Pikes of *England*, and that in
England, *Lincolnshire* boasteth to have the biggest. Just so doth *Sussex*
boast of four sorts of fish; namely an *Arundel Mullet*, a *Chichester
Lobster*, a *Shelsey* Cockle*, and an *Amerly* Trout*.

But I will take up no more of your time with this relation, but proceed to give you some observations of the *Carp*, and how to angle for
him, and to dress him, but not till he is caught.

CHAP. IX.

Observations of the Carp, *with Directions how to fish for him.*

PISC. The *Carp* is the Queen of Rivers: a stately, a good, and a very
subtil fish, that was not at first bred, nor hath been long in *England*,
but is now naturalized. It is said, they were brought hither by one

Mr. *Mascal**　a Gentleman, that then lived at *Plumsted* in *Sussex*, a County that abounds more with this fish than any in this Nation.

You may remember that I told you, *Gesner* says,* there are no *Pikes* in *Spain*; and doubtless, there was a time, about a hundred or a few more years ago, when there were no *Carps* in *England*, as may seem to be affirmed by S. *Richard Baker*,* in whose Chronicle you may find these Verses.

> *Hops and Turkies, Carps and Beer*
> *Came into* England *all in a year.*

And doubtless as of Sea-fish the *Herring* dies soonest out of the water, and of fresh-water-fish the *Trout*, so (except the *Eel*) the *Carp* endures most hardness, and lives longest out of his own proper Element. And therefore the report of the Carps being brought out of a forraigne Country into this Nation is the more probable.

Carps and Loaches are observed to Breed several months in one year, which Pikes and most other fish do not. And this is partly proved by tame and wild *Rabbets*, as also by some *Ducks*, which will lay eggs nine of the twelve months, and yet there be other *Ducks* that lay not longer than about one month. And it is the rather to be believed, because you shall scarce or never take a *Male-Carp* without a *Melt*, or a *Female* without a *Roe* or *spawn*, and for the most part very much; and especially all the Summer season; and it is observed, that they breed more naturally in ponds than in running waters, (if they breed there at all); and that those that live in Rivers are taken by men of the best palats to be much the better meat.

And it is observed, that in some ponds *Carps* will not breed, especially in cold ponds; but where they will breed, they breed innumerably; *Aristotle* and *Pliny* say,* six times in a year, if there be no *Pikes* nor *Pearch* to devour their Spawn, when it is cast upon grass, or flags or weeds, where it lies ten or twelve dayes before it be enlivened.*

The *Carp*, if he have water-room and good feed, will grow to a very great bigness and length: I have heard, to be much above a yard long. 'Tis said, (by *Jovius*,* who hath writ of Fishes) that in the Lake *Lurian* in *Italy*, *Carps* have thriven to be more than fifty pound weight, which is the more probable, for as the *Bear* is conceiv'd and born suddenly, and being born is but short-liv'd: So on the contrary, the *Elephant* is said to be two years in his dams belly (some think he is ten years in it) and being born grows in bigness twenty years; and 'tis observ'd too that he lives to the Age of a hundred years. And 'tis also observ'd that the *Crocodile** is very long-liv'd, and more than that, that all that long life he thrives in bigness, and so I think some *Carps* do, especially in some places; though I never saw one above 23. inches, which was a great and a goodly Fish: But have been assured there are of a far greater size, and in *England* too.

Now, as the increase of *Carps* is wonderful for their number, so there is not a reason found out, I think by any, why they should breed in some Ponds, and not in others of the same nature, for soil and all other circumstances: and as their breeding, so are their decays also very mysterious: I have both read it, and been told by a Gentleman of tryed honesty, that he has known sixty or more large *Carps* put into several ponds near to a house, where by reason of the stakes in the ponds, and the Owners constant being near to them, it was impossible they should be stole away from him: and that when he has after three or four years emptied the pond, and expected an increase from them by breeding young ones (for that they might do so, he had, as the rule is, put in three Melters for one Spawner) he has, I say, after three or four years, found neither a young nor old *Carp* remaining. And the like I have known of one that has almost watched the pond, and at a like distance of time, at the fishing of a pond, found of seventy or eighty large *Carps* not above five or six: and that he had forborn longer to fish the said pond, but that he saw in a hot day in Summer, a large *Carp* swim near the top of the water with a Frog upon his head, and that he upon that occasion caused his pond to be let dry: and I say, of seventy or eighty *Carps*, only found five or six in the said pond, and those very sick and lean, and with every one a Frog sticking so fast on the head of the said *Carps*, that the Frog would not be got off without extreme force or killing: and the Gentleman that did affirm this to me, told me he saw it, and did declare his belief to be, (and I also believe the same) that he thought the other *Carps* that were so strangely lost, were so killed by frogs, and then devoured.

And a person of honour* now living in *Worcester shire* assur'd me he had seen a necklace or collar of Tadpoles hang like a chaine or necklace of beads about a *Pikes* neck, and to kill him; whether it were for meat or malice, must be to me a question. *Mr. Fr. Ru.*

But I am faln into this Discourse by accident, of which I might say more, but it has proved longer than I intended, and possibly may not to you be considerable; I shall therefore give you three or four more short observations of the *Carp*, and then fall upon some directions how you shall fish for him.

The age of *Carps* is by Sir *Francis Bacon** (in his History of Life and Death) observed to be but ten years; yet others think they live longer. *Gesner* saies a *Carp** has been known to live in the *Palatinate** above a hundred years: But most conclude, that (contrary to the *Pike* or *Luce*) all *Carps* are the better for age and bigness; the tongues of *Carps* are noted to be choice and costly meat, especially to them that buy them: but *Gesner* saies, *Carps* have no tongue* like other Fish, but a piece of flesh-like-Fish in their mouth like to a tongue, and should be called a palate: But it is certain it is choicely good, and that the *Carp* is to be reckoned amongst those leather-mouthed fish, which I told you have their teeth in their throat, and for that reason he is very seldom lost by breaking his hold, if your hook be once stuck into his chaps.

I told you that Sir *Francis Bacon* thinks that the *Carp* lives but ten years, but *Janus Dubravius** has writ a Book of Fish and Fish-ponds, in which he saies, That *Carps* begin to Spawn at the age of three years, and continue to do so till thirty: he says also,* That in the time of their breeding, which is in Summer, when the Sun hath warmed both the earth and water, and so apted them also for generation; that then three or four Male-*Carps* will follow a Female, and that then she putting on a seeming coyness, they force her through weeds and flags, where she lets fall her Eggs or Spawn, which sticks fast to the weeds, and then they let fall their Melt upon it, and so it becomes in a short time to be a living Fish; and as I told you, it is thought the *Carp* does this several months in the year, and most believe that most fish breed after this manner, except the Eel: and it has been observed, that when the Spawner has weakned her self by doing that natural office, that two or three Melters have helped her from off the weeds, by bearing her up on both sides, and guarding her into the deep. And you may note, that though this may seem a curiosity not worth observing, yet others have judged it worth their time and costs, to make *Glass-hives*,* and order them in such a manner as to see how *Bees* have bred and made their *Honey-combs*, and how they have obeyed their King,* and governed their Common-wealth. But it is thought that all *Carps* are not bred by generation, but that some breed other ways, as some *Pikes* do.*

The Physicians make the *galls* and *stones** in the heads of *Carps* to be very medicinable; but 'tis not to be doubted but that in *Italy* they make great profit of the Spawn of *Carps*, by selling it to the *Jews*, who make it into red *Caviare*, the *Jews* not being by their Law admitted to eat of *Caviare* made of the *Sturgeon*, that being a Fish that wants scales, and (as may appear in *Levit.* 11.)* by them reputed to be unclean.

Much more might be said out of him, and out of *Aristotle*, which *Dubravius* often quotes in his Discourse of Fishes; but it might rather perplex than satisfie you, and therefore I shall rather chuse to direct you how to catch, than spend more time in discoursing either of the nature or the breeding of this *CARP*,

or of any more circumstances concerning him; but yet I shall remember you of what I told you before, that he is a very subtil Fish, and hard to be caught.

And my first direction is, that if you will Fish for a *Carp*, you must put on a very large measure of *patience*; especially to fish for a *River Carp*: I have known a very good Fisher angle diligently four or six hours in a day, for three or four daies together for a *River Carp*, and not have a bite: and you are to note, that in some ponds it is as hard to catch a Carp as in a River; that is to say, where they have store of feed, and the water is of a clayish colour: But you are to remember, that I have told you there is no rule without an exception, and therefore being possest with that hope and patience which I wish to all Fishers, especially to the *Carp-Angler*, I shall tell you with what bait to fish for him. But first you are to know, that it must be either early or late; and let me tell you, that in hot weather (for he will seldom bite in cold) you cannot be too early or too late at it. And some have been so curious as to say, the 10. of *April* is a fatal day for Carps.

The Carp bites either at worms or at paste, and of worms I think the blewish Marsh or Meadow worm* is best; but possibly another worm not too big may do as well, and so may a green Gentle:* And as for pastes, there are almost as many sorts as there are Medicines for the Toothach, but doubtless sweet pastes are best; I mean, pastes made with honey or with sugar: which, that you may the better beguile this crafty Fish, should be thrown into the Pond or place in which you fish for him some hours or longer before you undertake your tryal of skill with the Angle-rod: and doubtless if it be thrown into the water a day or two before, at several times and in small pellets, you are the likelier when you fish for the Carp to obtain your desired sport; or in a large Pond to draw them to any certain place, that they may the better and with more hope be fished for, you are to throw into it in some certain place, either Grains or Blood mixt with Cow dung, or with Bran; or any Garbage, as Chickens guts or the like, and then some of your small sweet pellets with which you purpose to angle: and these small pellets being a few of them also thrown in as you are Angling will be the better.

And your paste must be thus made: Take the flesh of a Rabbet or Cat cut small, and Bean-flowre,* and if that may not be easily got, get other flowre, and then mix these together, and put to them either Sugar, or Honey, which I think better, and then beat these together in a Mortar, or sometimes work them in your hands, (your hands being very clean) and then make it into a Ball, or two, or three, as you like best for your use; but you must work or pound it so long in the Mortar, as to make it so tough as to hang upon your hook without washing from it, yet not too hard; or that you may the better keep it on your hook, you may knead with your paste a little (and not much) white or yellowish wool.

And if you would have this paste keep all the year for any other Fish, then mix with it *Virgin wax** and *clarified honey,** and work them together with your hands before the Fire, then make these into balls, and they will keep all the year.

And if you fish for a Carp with Gentles, then put upon your hook a small piece of Scarlet about this bigness ■, it being soked in, or anointed with *Oyl of Peter,** called by some *Oyl of the Rock,* and if your Gentles be put two or three dayes before into a box or horn anointed with honey, and so put upon your hook as to preserve them to be living, you are as like to kill this crafty fish this way as any other. But still as you are fishing chaw a little white or brown bread in your mouth, and cast it into the pond about the place where your Flote swims. Other baits there be, but these with diligence, and patient watchfulness, will do it better than any that I have ever practised, or heard of: And yet I shall tell you, that the crumbs of white bread and honey made into a paste is a good bait for a *Carp*, and you know it is more easily made. And having said thus much of the *Carp*, my next discourse shall be of the *Bream*, which shall not prove so tedious, and therefore I desire the continuance of your attention.

But first I will tell you how to make this *Carp* that is so curious to be caught, so curious* a dish of meat, as shall make him worth all your labour and patience; and though it is not without some trouble and charges, yet it will recompence both.

Take a Carp (*alive if possible*) *scour him, and rub him clean with water and salt, but scale him not, then open him, and put him with his bloud and his liver* (*which you must save when you open him*) *into a small pot or kettle; then take sweet Marjoram, Time and Parsley, of each half a handful, a sprig of Rosemary, and another of Savoury, bind them into two or three small bundles, and put them to your Carp, with four or five whole Onyons, twenty pickled Oysters, and three Anchovies. Then pour upon your Carp as much Claret wine as will only cover him; and season your Claret well with salt, Cloves and Mace, and the rinds of Oranges and Lemons, that done, cover your pot and set it on a quick-fire, till it be sufficiently boiled; then take out the Carp and lay it with the broth into the dish, and pour upon it a quarter of a pound of the best fresh butter melted and beaten, with half a dozen spoonfuls of the broth, the yolks of two or three eggs, and some of the herbs shred; garnish your dish with Lemons and so serve it up, and much good do you.*

Dr. *T.**

CHAP. X.

Observations of the Bream, *and directions to catch him.*

PISC. The *Bream* being at a full growth is a large and stately Fish: he will breed both in Rivers and Ponds: but loves best to live in ponds, and where, if he likes the water and Air, he will grow not only to be very large, but as fat as a Hog: he is by *Gesner** taken to be more pleasant or sweet than wholsome; this Fish is long in growing, but breeds exceedingly in a water that pleases him; yea, in many Ponds so fast, as to over-store them, and starve the other Fish.

He is very broad with a forked tail, and his scales set in excellent order, he hath large eyes and a narrow sucking mouth; he hath two

sets of teeth, and a lozenge like bone, a bone to help his grinding.*
The Melter is observed to have two large Melts,* and the Female two
large bags of eggs or spawn.

Gesner reports,* that in *Poland* a certain, and a great number of
large Breams were put into a Pond, which in the next following
winter were frozen up into one intire ice, and not one drop of water
remaining, nor one of these fish to be found, though they were diligently searcht for; and yet the next Spring when the ice was thawed,
and the weather warm, and fresh water got into the pond, he affirms
they all appeared again. This *Gesner* affirms, and I quote my Author,
because it seems almost as incredible as the *Resurrection* to an *Atheist*.
But it may win something in point of believing it, to him that considers the breeding or renovation of the Silk-worm and of many insects.
And that is considerable which Sir *Francis Bacon** observes in his
History of Life and Death (*fol.* 20.), that there be some herbs that die
and spring every year, and some endure longer.

But though some do not, yet the *French* esteem this Fish highly,
and to that end have this Proverb,* *He that hath Breams in his pond is
able to bid his friend welcome.* And it is noted, that the best part of a
Bream is his belly and head.

Some say, that *Breams* and *Roaches* will mix their eggs, and melt
together, and so there is in many places a Bastard breed of *Breams*,
that never come to be either large or good, but very numerous.

The Baits good to catch this *BREAM*

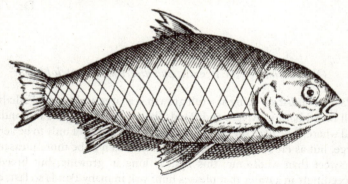

are many. Paste made of brown bread and hony, gentles, or the brood
of wasps that be young, (and then not unlike Gentles) and should be
hardned in an oven, or dried on a tile before the fire to make them

tough; or there is at the root of docks, or flags, or rushes in watry places, a worm not unlike a Maggot, at which Tench* will bite freely. Or he will bite at a Grashopper with his legs nipt off in *June* and *July*, or at several flies under water, which may be found on flags that grow near to the water side. I doubt not but that there be many other baits that are good, but I will turn them all into this most excellent one, either for a *Carp* or *Bream*, in any River or Mere: it was given to me by a most honest and excellent Angler,* and hoping you will prove both, I will impart it to you.

1. Let your bait be as big a *red worm* as you can find, without a knot,* get a pint or quart of them in an evening in garden walks, or Chalky Commons after a showre of rain; and put them with clean Moss well washed and picked, and the water squeezed out of the Moss as dry as you can, into an earthen pot or pipkin set dry, and change the Moss fresh every three or four dayes for three weeks or a month together, then your bait will be at the best, for it will be clear and lively.

2. Having thus prepared your baits, get your tackling ready and fitted for this sport. Take three long Angling Rods, and as many and more silk, or silk and hair lines,* and as many large Swan or Goosequil floats. Then take a piece of Lead made after this manner, and fasten them to the low-ends of your Lines. Then fasten your link-hook also to the lead, and let there be about a foot or ten inches between the lead and the hook; but be sure the lead be heavy enough to sink the float or quil a little under the water, and not the quil to bear up the Lead, for the lead must lie on the ground. Note, that your link next the hook may be smaller than the rest of your line, if you dare adventure for fear of taking the *Pike* or *Pearch*, who will assuredly visit your hooks, till they be taken out (as I will shew you afterwards) before either *Carp* or *Bream* will come near to bite. Note also, that when the worm is well baited, it will crawl up and down, as far as the Lead will give leave, which much enticeth the Fish to bite without suspicion.

3. Having thus prepared your baits, and fitted your tackling, repair to the River, where you have seen them to swim in skuls* or shoals in the Summer time in a hot afternoon, about three or four of the clock, and watch their going forth of their deep holes and returning (which you may well discern) for they return about four of the clock most of them seeking food at the bottom, yet one or two will lie on the top of the water, rolling and tumbling themselves whilst the

rest are under him at the bottom, and so you shall perceive him to keep Sentinel; then mark where he plays most, and stays longest, (which commonly is in the broadest and deepest place of the River) and there, or, near thereabouts, at a clear bottom, and a convenient landing place, take one of your Angles ready fitted as aforesaid, and sound the bottom, which should be about eight or ten foot deep (two yards from the bank is the best). Then consider with your self, whether that water will rise or fall by the next morning by reason of any Water-mills near, and according to your discretion take the depth of the place, where you mean after to cast your ground-bait, and to fish, to half an inch; that the Lead lying on or near the ground-bait, the top of the float may only appear upright half an inch above the water.

Thus you having found and fitted for the place and depth thereof, then go home and prepare your ground-bait, which is next to the fruit of your labours, to be regarded.

The Ground-Bait.

You shall take a peck, or a peck and a half (according to the greatness of the stream, and deepness of the water, where you mean to Angle) of sweet gross-ground barly-malt,* and boil it in a kettle (one or two warms* is enough) then strain it through a Bag into a tub (the liquor whereof hath often done my Horse much good) and when the bag and malt is near cold, take it down to the water-side about eight or nine of the clock in the evening, and not before; cast in two parts of your ground-bait, squeezed hard between both your hands, it will sink presently to the bottom, and be sure it may rest in the very place where you mean to Angle; if the stream run hard or move a little, cast your malt in handfuls a little the higher, upwards the stream. You may between your hands close the Malt so fast in handfuls, that the water will hardly part it with the fall.

Your ground thus baited, and tackling fitted, leave your bag with the rest of your tackling and ground-bait near the sporting-place all night, and in the morning about three or four of the clock visit the water-side (but not too near) for they have a cunning Watch-man, and are watchful themselves too.

Then gently take one of your three rods, and bait your hook, casting it over your ground-bait, and gently and secretly draw it to you till the Lead rests about the middle of the ground-bait.

Then take a second Rod and cast in about a yard above, and your third a yard below the first Rod, and stay the Rods in the ground, but go your self so far from the water-side, that you perceive nothing but the top of the floats, which you must watch most diligently; then when you have a bite, you shall perceive the top of your float to sink suddenly into the water; yet nevertheless be not too hasty to run to your Rods, until you see that the Line goes clear away, then creep to the water-side, and give as much Line as possibly you can: if it be a good *Carp* or *Bream*, they will go to the farther side of the River, then strike gently, and hold your Rod at a bent a little while; but if you both pull together you are sure to lose your Game, for either your line or hook, or hold will break; and after you have overcome them, they will make noble sport, and are very shie to be landed. The *Carp* is far stronger and more mettlesom than the *Bream*.

Much more is to be observed in this kind of Fish and Fishing, but it is far fitter for experience and discourse than paper. Only thus much is necessary for you to know, and, to be mindful and careful of; That if the *Pike* or *Pearch* do breed in that River, they will be sure to bite first, and must first be taken. And for the most part they are very large, and will repair to your ground-bait, not that they will eat of it, but will feed and sport themselves amongst the young Fry, that gather about and hover over the Bait.

The way to discern the *Pike* and to take him, if you mistrust your *Bream*-hook (for I have taken a *Pike* a yard long several times at my *Bream*-hooks, and sometimes he hath had the luck to share my line) may be thus.

Take a small *Bleak*, or *Roach*, or *Gudgion*, and bait it, and set it alive among your Rods two foot deep from the Cork, with a little red worm on the point of the hook, then take a few crums of White-bread, or some of the ground-bait, and sprinkle it gently amongst your Rods. If Mr. *Pike* be there, then the little Fish will skip out of the water at his appearance but the live-set Bait is sure to be taken.

Thus continue your sport from four in the morning till eight, and if it be a gloomy, windy day, they will bite all day long. But this is too long to stand to your rods at one place, and it will spoil your evening sport that day, which is this.

About four of the clock in the Afternoon repair to your baited place, and as soon as you come to the water side, cast in one half of the rest of your ground-bait, and stand off: then whilst the Fish are gathering together (for there they will most certainly come for their supper) you may take a pipe of Tobacco; and then in with your three rods as in the morning: You will find excellent sport that evening till eight of the clock; then cast in the residue of your ground-bait, and next morning by four of the clock visit them again for four hours, which is the best sport of all; and after that let them rest till you and your friends have a mind to more sport.

From St. *James* Tide until *Bartholomew* Tide* is the best, when they have had all the Summers food, they are the fattest.

Observe lastly, That after three or four days fishing together, your Game will be very shie and wary, and you shall hardly get above a bite or two at a baiting; then your only way is to desist from your sport about two or three days; and in the mean time (on the place you late baited, and again intend to bait) you shall take a turf of green, but short grass, as big or bigger than a round Trencher; to the top of this turf, on the green side, you shall with a Needle and green thred fasten one by one as many little red worms as will near cover all the turf: Then take a round board or Trencher, make a hole in the middle thereof, and through the turf placed on the board or Trencher, with a string or cord as long as is fitting, tied to a pole, let it down to the bottom of the water for the Fish to feed upon without disturbance about two or three days; and after that you have drawn it away, you may fall to, and enjoy your former recreation.

*B. A.**

CHAP. XI.

Observations of the Tench, *and advice how to Angle for him.*

PISC. The *Tench*, the Physician of Fishes,* is observed to love Ponds better than Rivers, and to love pits better than either; yet *Cambden** observes there is a River in *Dorset-shire* that abounds with *Tenches*, but doubtless they retire to the most deep and quiet places in it.

This fish hath very large Fins, very small and smooth Scales, a red circle about his Eyes, which are big and of a gold colour, and from either Angle of his mouth there hangs down a little Barb; in every *Tenches* head there are two little stones, which forraign Physicians make great use of, but he is not commended for wholsom meat,* though there be very much use made of them, for outward applications. *Rondelitius* says,* That at his being at *Rome, he saw a great cure done* *by applying a Tench to the feet of a very sick man.* This he says was done after an unusual manner by certain Jews. And it is observed that many of those people have many secrets, yet unknown to Christians; secrets that have never yet been written, but have been since the days of their *Solomon** (who knew the nature of all things, even from the Cedar to the Shrub) delivered by tradition from the Father to the Son, and so from generation to generation without writing, or (unless it were casually) without the least communicating them to any other Nation or Tribe: for to do that they account a prophanation. And yet it is thought that they, or some Spirit worse than they, first told us, that Lice swallowed alive* were a certain cure for the Yellow-Jaundice. This, and many other medicines were discover'd by them or by revelation, for, doubtless we attain'd them not by study.

Well, this fish, besides his eating, is very useful both dead and alive for the good of mankind. But, I will meddle no more with that, my honest humble Art teaches no such boldness; there are too many foolish medlers in Physick and Divinity, that think themselves fit to meddle with hidden secrets, and so bring destruction to their followers. But I'le not meddle with them any farther than to wish them wiser; and shall tell you next (for, I hope, I may be so bold) that the *Tench* is the Physician of fishes, for the *Pike* especially, and that the *Pike*, being either sick or hurt, is cured by the touch of the *Tench*. And it is observed, that the Tyrant *Pike* will not be a Wolf to his Physician, but forbears to devour him though he be never so hungry.

This fish that carries a natural Balsome in him to cure both himself and others, loves yet to feed in very foul water, and amongst weeds. And yet I am sure he eats pleasantly, and doubtless, you will think so too, if you tast him. And I shall therefore proceed to give you some few, and but a few directions how to catch this *Tench*,

of which I have given you these observations.

He will bite at a Paste made of brown bread and honey, or at a marsh worm, or a Lob-worm; he inclines very much to any paste with which Tar is mixt, and he will bite also at a smaller worm, with his head nipp'd off, and a Cod-worm put on the hook before that worm; and I doubt not but that he will also in the three hot months (for in the nine colder he stirs not much) bite at a Flag-worm, or at a green Gentle,* but can positively say no more of the *Tench*, he being a Fish that I have not often Angled for; but I wish my honest Scholar may, and be ever fortunate when he fishes.

CHAP. XII.

Observations of the Pearch, *and directions how to fish for him.*

PISC. The *Pearch* is a very good, and a very bold biting fish; He is one of the Fishes of prey, that like the *Pike* and *Trout*, carries his teeth in his mouth: which is very large, and he dare venture to kill and devour several other kinds of fish: he has a hook't or hog back, which is armed with sharp and stiff bristles, and all his skin armed or covered over with thick, dry, hard scales, and hath (which few other Fish have) two Fins on his back. He is so bold, that he will invade* one of his own kind, which the *Pike* will not do so willingly, and, you may therefore easily believe him to be a bold biter.

The *Pearch* is of great esteem in *Italy* saith *Aldrovandus*,* and especially the least are there esteemed a dainty dish. And *Gesner* prefers* the *Pearch* and *Pike* above the *Trout*, or any fresh-water-Fish: he says the *Germans* have this Proverb, *More wholsom than a Pearch of Rhine*: and he says the River-*Pearch* is so wholsom, that Physicians allow him to be eaten by wounded men or by men in Feavers, or by Women in Child-bed.

He spawns but once a year, and is by Physicians held very nutritive: yet by many to be hard of digestion: They abound more in the River *Poe* and in *England* (says *Rondelitius*)* than other parts, and have in their brain a stone, which is in forraign parts sold by Apothecaries, being there noted to be very medicinable against the stone in the reins:* These be a part of the commendations which some Philosophical brains have bestowed upon the fresh-water *Pearch*: yet they commend the Sea-*Pearch*, which is known by having but one fin on his back* (of which they say, we *English* see but a few) to be a much better fish.

The *Pearch* grows slowly, yet will grow, as I have been credibly informed, to be almost two foot long; for an honest informer told me, such a one was not long since taken by Sir *Abraham Williams*,* a Gentleman of worth, and a Brother of the Angle (that yet lives, and I wish he may): this was a deep bodied Fish: and doubtless durst have devoured a *Pike* of half his own length: for I have told you, he is a bold Fish, such a one as but for extreme hunger, the *Pike* will not devour: for to affright the *Pike* and save himself, the *Pearch* will set up his fins, much like as a *Turkie-Cock* will sometimes set up his tail.

But, my Scholar, the *Pearch* is not only valiant to defend himself, but he is (as I said) a bold biting fish, yet he will not bite at all seasons of the year; he is very abstemious in Winter, yet will bite then in the midst of the day if it be warm: and note that all Fish bite best about the midst of a warm day in Winter, and he hath been observed by some, not usually to bite till the *Mulberry-tree* buds; that is to say, till extreme frosts be past the Spring; for when the *Mulberry-tree* blossoms, many Gardners observe their forward fruit to be past the danger of Frosts, and some have made the like observation of the *Pearches* biting.

But bite the *Pearch* will, and that very boldly: and as one has wittily observed,* if there be twenty or forty in a hole, they may be at one standing all catch'd one after another; they being, as he says, like the wicked of the world, not afraid though their fellows and companions perish in their sight. And you may observe, that they are not like the solitary *Pike*, but love to accompany one another, and march together in troops.

And the baits for this bold Fish

are not many; I mean, he will bite as well at some, or at any of these three, as at any, or all others whatsoever: a *Worm*, a *Minnow*, or a little *Frog* (of which you may find many in hay-time) and of *worms*, the Dunghil-worm called a *Brandling* I take to be best, being well scowred in Moss or Fennel; or he will bite at a worm that lies under a cow-turd with a blewish head. And if you *rove** for a *Pearch* with a *Minnow*, then it is best to be alive, you sticking your hook through his back-fin; or a *Minnow* with the hook in his upper lip, and letting him swim up and down about mid-water, or a little lower, and you still keeping him to about that depth, by a Cork, which ought not to be a very little one: and the like way you are to Fish for the *Pearch*, with a small frog, your hook being fastned through the skin of his leg, towards the upper part of it: And lastly, I will give you but this advice, that you give the *Pearch* time enough when he bites, for there was scarce ever any Angler that has given him too much. And now I think best to rest my self, for I have almost spent my spirits with talking so long.

Venat. Nay, good Master, one fish more, for you see it rains still, and you know our Angles are like mony put to usury; they may thrive though we sit still and do nothing but talk and enjoy one another. Come, come the other fish, good Master.

Pisc. But Scholar, have you nothing to mix with this discourse, which now grows both tedious and tiresom? shall I have nothing from you that seem to have both a good memory, and a chearful Spirit?

Ven. Yes, Master, I will speak you a Copy of Verses that were made by Doctor *Donne*,* and made to shew the world that he could make soft and smooth Verses when he thought smoothness worth his labour; and I love them the better, because they allude to Rivers, and fish and fishing. They be these:

> *Come live with me, and be my Love,*
> *And we will some new pleasures prove,*
> *Of golden sands, and Chrystal brooks,*
> *With silken lines, and silver hooks.*

> *There will the River whispering run,*
> *Warm'd by thy eyes more than the Sun;*
> *And there the enamel'd fish will stay,*
> *Begging themselves they may betray.*

> *When thou wilt swim in that live bath,*
> *Each fish, which every channel hath,*

Most amorously to thee will swim,
Gladder to catch thee, than thou him.

If thou, to be so seen, beest loath
By Sun or Moon, thou darknest both,
And if mine eyes have leave to see,
I need not their light, having thee.

Let others freeze with Angling reeds,
And cut their legs with shels and weeds,
Or treacherously poor fish beset,
With strangling snares, or windowy net.

Let course bold hands, from slimy nest,
The bedded fish in banks outwrest, *
Let curious Traytors sleave silk flies,*
To 'witch poor wandring fishes eyes.

For thee, thou needst no such deceit,
For thou thy self art thine own bait:
That fish that is not catcht thereby,
Is wiser far, alas, than I.

Pisc. Well remembred, honest Scholar, I thank you for these choice Verses, which I have heard formerly, but had quite forgot, till they were recovered by your happy memory. Well, being I have now rested my self a little, I will make you some requital, by telling you some observations of the *Eel*, for it rains still, and because (as you say) our *Angles* are as mony put to Use that thrives when we play, therefore we'l sit still and enjoy our selves a little longer under this *honey-suckle-hedg*.

CHAP. XIII.

Observations of the Eel, *and other fish that want scales,*
and how to fish for them.

PISC. It is agreed by most men, that the *Eel* is a most daintie fish; the Romans have esteemed her the *Helena* of their feasts, and some *The Queen of palat pleasure*. But most men differ about their breeding:

some say they breed by generation as other fish do, and others, that they breed (as some worms do) of mud, as Rats and Mice, and many other living creatures are bred in *Egypt*, by the Suns heat when it shines upon the overflowing of the River *Nilus*: or out of the putrefaction of the earth, and divers other wayes. Those that deny them to breed by generation as other fish do, ask: if any man ever saw an *Eel* to have a Spawn or Melt? and they are answered, that they may be as certain of their breeding as if they had seen Spawn: for they say, that they are certain that *Eels* have all parts fit for generation, like other fish, but so small as not to be easily discerned, by reason of their fatness, but that discerned they may be, and that the He and the She *Eel* may be distinguished by their fins. And *Rondelitius* saies,* he has seen *Eels* cling together like *Dew-worms*.

And others say, that *Eels* growing old breed other *Eels* out of the corruption of their own age,* which Sir *Francis Bacon* sayes,* exceeds not ten years. And others say, that as *Pearls* are made of glutinous dew-drops, which are condensed by the Suns heat in those Countries, so *Eels* are bred of a particular dew falling in the months of *May* or *June* on the banks of some particular Ponds or Rivers (apted by nature for that end) which in a few dayes are by the Suns heat turned into *Eels*, and some of the Ancients* have called the *Eels* that are thus bred, *The Off-spring of Jove*. I have seen in the beginning of *July*, in a River not far from *Canterbury*, some parts of it covered over with young *Eels*, about the thickness of a straw; and these *Eels* did lie on the top of that water, as thick as motes are said to be in the Sun: and I have heard the like of other Rivers, as namely in *Severn*, (where they are called *Yelvers*) and in a *pond* or *mere* near unto *Stafford-shire*, where about a set time in Summer, such small *Eels* abound so much, that many of the poorer sort of people, that inhabit near to it take such *Eels* out of this Mere, with sieves or sheets, and make a kind of Eel-cake of them, and eat it like as Bread. And *Gesner* quotes venerable *Bede** to say, that in *England* there is an Island called *Ely*, by reason of the innumerable number of *Eels* that breed in it. But that *Eels* may be bred as some worms, and some kind of *Bees* and *Wasps* are, either of *dew*, or out of the corruption of the earth, seems to be made probable by the *Barnacles* and young *Goslings* bred by the Suns heat, and the rotten planks of an old Ship, and hatched of trees; both which are related for truths by *Dubartas* and *Lobel*,* and also by our learned *Cambden*, and laborious *Gerard* in his *Herbal*.

It is said by *Rondelitius*,* that those *Eels* that are bred in Rivers that relate to, or be nearer to the Sea, never return to the fresh waters (as the *Salmon* does always desire to do) when they have once tasted the salt water; and I do the more easily believe this, because I am certain that powdered Beef* is a most excellent bait to catch an *Eel*: And though Sir *Francis Bacon* will allow the *Eels* life to be but ten years; yet he in his History of Life and Death,* mentions a *Lamprey* belonging to the *Roman* Emperour to be made tame, and so kept for almost threescore years: and that such useful and pleasant observations were made of this *Lamprey*, that *Crassus* the Orator (who kept her) lamented her Death. And we read (in Doctor *Hackwel*)* that *Hortensius* was seen to weep at the death of a *Lamprey* that he had kept long, and loved exceedingly.

It is granted by all, or most men, that *Eels*, for about six months (that is to say, the six cold months of the year) stir not up and down, neither in the Rivers, nor in the Pools in which they usually are, but get into the soft earth or mud, and there many of them together bed themselves, and live without feeding upon any thing (as I have told you some *Swallows* have been observed to do in hollow trees for those six cold months): and this the *Eel* and *Swallow* do, as not being able to endure winter weather: For *Gesner* quotes *Albertus** to say, that in the year 1125. (that years winter being more cold than usually) *Eels* did by natures instinct get out of the water into a stack of hay in a Meadow upon drie ground, and there bedded themselves, but yet at last a frost kill'd them. And our *Cambden** relates, that in *Lancashire* Fishes were dig'd out of the earth with Spades, where no water was near to the place. I shall say little more of the Eel, but that, as it is observed he is impatient of cold; so it hath been observed, that in warm weather an *Eel* has been known to live five days out of the water.

And lastly, let me tell you that some curious searchers into the natures of Fish, observe that there be several sorts or kinds of *Eels*, as the *silver Eel*,* and green or *greenish Eel* (with which the River of *Thames* abounds, and those are called *Grigs*); and a *blackish Eel*, whose head is more flat and bigger than ordinary *Eels*; and also an *Eel* whose Fins are reddish, and but seldom taken in this Nation, (and yet taken sometimes): These several kinds of *Eels* are (say some) diversly bred, as namely, out of the corruption of the earth, and some by dew, and other ways, (as I have said to you): and yet it is affirmed by some for a certain, that the *silver Eel* is bred by generation, but not by Spawning as other Fish do, but that her brood come alive from her, being then little live Eels no bigger nor longer than a pin; and I have had too many testimonies of this to doubt the truth of it my self, and if I thought it needful I might prove it, but I think it is needless.

And this Eel of which I have said so much to you, may be caught with divers kinds of Baits: as namely with powdered Beef,* with a *Lob* or *Garden-worm*, with a *Minnow*, or gut of a *Hen, Chicken*, or the guts of any Fish, or with almost any thing, for he is a greedy Fish; but the Eel may be caught especially with a little, a very little *Lamprey* which some call a *Pride*, and may in the hot months be found many of them in the River *Thames*, and in many mud-heaps in other Rivers, yea, almost as usually as one finds worms in a dunghill.

Next note, that the Eel seldom stirs in the day, but then hides himself, and therefore he is usually caught by night with one of these baits of which I have spoken, and may be then caught by laying hooks, which you are to fasten to the bank or twigs of a tree; or by throwing a string cross the stream with many hooks at it, and those baited with the aforesaid Baits, and a clod, or plummet, or stone, thrown into the River with this line, that so you may in the morning find it near to some fixt place, and then take it up with a Drag-hook or otherwise: but these things are indeed too common to be spoken of, and an hours fishing with any Angler will teach you better, both for these and many other common things in the practical part of *Angling*, than a weeks discourse. I shall therefore conclude this direction for taking the *Eel*, by telling you, that in a warm day in Summer I have taken many a good Eel by *snigling* and have been much pleased with that sport.

And because you that are but a young Angler know not what snigling is, I will now teach it to you. You remember I told you that Eels do not usually stir in the day time, for then they hide themselves under some covert, or under boards or planks about Flood-gates, or Weires, or Mills, or in holes in the River banks; so that you observing your time in a warm day, when the water is lowest, may take a strong small hook tied to a strong line, or to a string about a yard long, and then into one of these holes, or between any boards about a Mill, or under any great stone or plank, or any place where you think an Eel may hide or shelter her self, you may with the help of a short stick put in your bait, but leasurely, and as far as you may conveniently: and it is scarce to be doubted, but that if there be an Eel within the sight of it, the Eel will bite instantly, and as certainly gorge it: and you need not doubt to have him if you pull him not out of the hole too quickly, but pull him out by degrees, for he lying folded double in his hole, will with the help of his tail break all, unless you give him time to be wearied with pulling, and so get him out by degrees, not pulling too hard.

And to commute for your patient hearing this long Direction I shall next tell you how to make this *EEL*

a most excellent dish of meat:

First, wash him in water and salt, then pull off his skin below his vent or navel, and not much further: having done that, take out his guts as clean as you can, but wash him not: then give him three or four scotches with a knife, and then put into his belly and those scotches, sweet herbs, an Anchovy, and a little Nutmeg grated or cut very small, and your herbs and Anchovis must also be cut very small, and mixt with good butter and salt; having done this, then pull his skin over him all but his head, which you are to cut off, to the end you may tie his skin about that part where his head grew, and it must be so tyed as to keep all his moisture within his skin: and having done this, tie him with Tape or Pack-thred to a spit, and rost him leasurely, and baste him with water and salt till his skin breaks, and then with Butter: and having rosted him enough, let what was put into his belly, and what he drips be his sawce.

S. F.*

When I go to dress an Eel thus, I wish he were as long and big, as that which was caught in *Peterborough* River in the year 1667. which was a yard and three quarters long. If you will not believe me? then go and see at one of the *Coffee-houses* in *King-street* in *Westminster*.

But now let me tell you, that though the Eel thus drest be not only excellent good, but more harmless than any other way, yet it is certain, that Physicians account the Eel dangerous meat;* I will advise you therefore, as *Solomon* says* of Honey, Prov. 25. *Hast thou found it, eat* *no more than is sufficient, lest thou surfeit, for it is not good to eat much honey.* And let me add this that the uncharitable *Italian** bids us, *Give Eels, and no wine to our Enemies.*

And I will beg a little more of your attention to tell you that *Aldrovandus* and divers Physicians* commend the Eel very much for medicine though not for meat. But let me tell you one observation; That the Eel is never out of season,* as *Trouts* and most other fish are at set times, at least most Eels are not.

I might here speak of many other Fish whose shape and nature are much like the Eel, and frequent both the *Sea* and fresh Rivers; as namely the *Lamprel*, the *Lamprey* and the *Lamperne*: as also of the mighty *Conger*,* taken often in *Severn*, about *Glocester*; and might also tell in what high esteem many of them are for the curiosity of their taste; but these are not so proper to be talk'd of by me, because they make us Anglers no sport, therefore I will let them alone as the Jews do,* to whom they are forbidden by their Law.

And Scholar, there is also a Flounder, a Sea-fish, which will wander very far into fresh Rivers, and there lose himself, and dwell and thrive to a hands breadth, and almost twice so long, a fish without scales, and most excellent meat, and a fish that affords much sport to the Angler, with any small worm, but especially a little blewish worm, gotten out of Marsh ground or Meadows, which should be well scowred, but this though it be most excellent meat, yet it wants scales, and is as I told you therefore an abomination to the Jews.

But Scholar, there is a fish that they in *Lancashire* boast very much of, called a *Char*, taken there, (and I think there only) in a Mere called *Winander Mere*; a Mere, says *Cambden*,* that is the largest in this Nation, being ten miles in length, and some say as smooth in the bottom as if it were paved with polisht marble: this fish never exceeds fifteen or sixteen inches in length; and 'tis spotted like a *Trout*, and has scarce a bone but on the back: but this, though I do not know whether it make the Angler sport, yet I would have you take notice of it, because it is a rarity, and of so high esteem with persons of great note.

Nor would I have you ignorant of a rare fish called a *Guiniad*, of which I shall tell you what *Cambden*,* and others speak. The River *Dee* (which runs by *Chester*) springs in *Merionethshire*, and as it runs toward *Chester* it runs through *Pemble-Mere*,* which is a large water: And it is observed, that though the River *Dee* abounds with *Salmon*, and *Pemble-Mere* with the *Guiniad*, yet there is never any *Salmon* caught in the *Mere*, nor a *Guiniad* in the River. And now my next observation shall be of the *Barbel*.

CHAP. XIV.

Observations of the Barbel, *and directions how to fish for him.*

PISC. The *Barbel* is so called (says *Gesner*) by reason of his Barb* or Wattels at his mouth, which are under his nose or chaps. He is one of those leather-mouthed Fishes that I told you of, that does very seldom break his hold if he be once hook'd: but he is so strong, that he will often break both rod or line if he proves to be a big one.

But the *Barbel*, though he be of a fine shape, and looks big, yet he is not accounted the best fish to eat, neither for his wholsomness nor his taste: But the Male is reputed much better than the Female, whose Spawn is very hurtful, as I will presently declare to you.

They flock together like sheep, and are at the worst in *April*, about which time they Spawn, but quickly grow to be in season. He is able to live in the strongest swifts of the Water, and in Summer they love the shallowest and sharpest streams; and love to lurk under weeds, and to feed on gravel against a rising ground, and will root and dig in the sands with his nose like a hog, and there nests himself: yet sometimes he retires to deep and swift Bridges, or Flood-gates, or Weires, where he will nest himself amongst piles, or in hollow places, and take such hold of moss or weeds, that be the water never so swift, it is not able to force him from the place that he contends for. This is his constant custom in Summer, when he and most living creatures sport themselves in the Sun, but at the approach of Winter, then he forsakes the swift streams and shallow waters, and by degrees retires to those parts of the River that are quiet and deeper; in which places (and I think about that time) he Spawns, and as I have formerly told you, with the help of the Melter, hides his Spawn or eggs in holes, which they both dig in the gravel, and then they mutually labour to cover it with the same sand, to prevent it from being devoured by other fish.

There be such store of this fish in the River *Danubie*, that *Rondelitius** says, they may in some places of it, and in some months of the year, be taken by those that dwell near to the River, with their hands, eight or ten load at a time; he says, they begin to be good in

May, and that they cease to be so in *August*, but it is found to be otherwise in this Nation: but thus far we agree with him, that the Spawn of
a *Barbel*, if it be not poison as he says, yet that it is dangerous meat,
and especially in the month of *May*; which is so certain, that *Gesner*
and *Gasius** declare, it had an ill effect upon them even to the endan-
gering of their lives.

This fish is of a fine cast and handsome shape, with small scales,
which are plac'd after a most exact and curious manner,

and, as I told you, may be rather said not to be ill, than to be good
meat; the *Chub* and he have (I think) both lost part of their credit by
ill cookery, they being reputed the worst or coursest of fresh-water-
fish: but the *Barbel* affords an *Angler* choice sport, being a lusty and a
cunning Fish: so lusty and cunning as to endanger the breaking of the
Anglers line, by running his head forcibly towards any covert, or
hole, or bank: and then striking at the line, to break it off with his tail
(as is observed by *Plutarch*,* in his Book *de industria animalium*) and
also so cunning to nibble and suck off your worm close to the hook,
and yet avoid the letting the hook come into his mouth.

The *Barbel* is also curious for his baits, that is to say, that they be
clean and sweet; that is to say, to have your worms well scowred, and
not kept in sowre and musty moss, for he is a curious feeder; but at a
well-scowred Lob-worm, he will bite as boldly as at any bait, and
specially, if the night or two before you fish for him, you shall bait the
places where you intend to fish for him with big worms cut into
pieces: and note, that none did ever over-bait the place, nor fish too
early or too late for a *Barbel*. And the *Barbel* will bite also at Gentles,
which (not being too much scowred, but green) are a choice bait for
him; and so is cheese, which is not to be too hard, but kept a day or
two in a wet linnen cloth to make it tough: with this you may also bait
the water a day or two before you fish for the *Barbel*, and be much the
likelier to catch store: and if the cheese were laid in clarified honey a

short time before (as namely, an hour or two) you were still the likelier to catch Fish: some have directed to cut the cheese into thin pieces, and toast it, and then tie it on the hook with fine silk: and some advise* to fish for the *Barbel* with Sheeps tallow and soft cheese beaten or work'd into a Paste, and that it is choicely good in *August*, and I believe it: but doubtless the Lob-worm well scowred, and the Gentle not too much scowred, and cheese ordered as I have directed, are baits enough, and I think will serve in any month; though I shall commend any Angler that tries conclusions,* and is industrious to improve the Art. And now, my honest Scholar, the long shower,* and my tedious discourse are both ended together: and I shall give you but this Observation, that when you fish for a *Barbel*, your Rod and Line be both long, and of good strength, for (as I told you) you will find him a heavy and a dogged fish to be dealt withall, yet he seldom or never breaks his hold if he be once strucken. And if you would know more of fishing for the *Umber* or *Barbel*, get into favour with Doctor *Sheldon*,* whose skill is above others; and of that the Poor that dwell about him have a comfortable experience.

And now lets go and see what interest the *Trouts* will pay us for letting our *Angle-rods* lie so long, and so quietly in the water for their use. Come, Scholar, which will you take up?

Ven. Which you think fit, Master.

Pisc. Why, you shall take up that; for I am certain by viewing the Line, it has a Fish at it. Look you, Scholar: well done. Come now, take up the other too; well, now you may tell my brother *Peter* at night, that you have caught a leash of *Trouts* this day. And now lets move toward our lodging, and drink a draught of *Red-Cows Milk*, as we go, and give pretty *Maudlin* and her honest mother a brace of *Trouts* for their supper.

Venat. Master, I like your motion very well and I think it is now about milking time, and yonder they be at it.

Pisc. God speed you, good woman, I thank you both for our Songs last night; I and my companion have had such fortune a fishing this day, that we resolve to give you and *Maudlin* a brace of *Trouts* for supper, and we will now taste a draught of your *Red-Cows milk*.

Milkw. Marry, and that you shall with all my heart, and I will be still your debtor when you come this way: if you will but speak the word, I will make you a good *Sillabub*, of new Verjuice,* and then you may sit down in a *hay-cock* and eat it, and *Maudlin* shall sit by and sing you the good old Song of the *Hunting in Chevy Chase*,* or some other good Ballad, for she hath good store of them; *Maudlin*, my honest *Maudlin* hath a notable memory, and she thinks nothing too good for you, because you be such honest men.

Venat. We thank you, and intend once in a month to call upon you again, and give you a little warning, and so good night: good night *Maudlin*. And now, good Master, lets lose no time; but tell me somewhat more of Fishing, and if you please, first something of Fishing for a *Gudgion*.

Pisc. I will, honest Scholar.

CHAP. XV.

Observations of the Gudgion, the Ruffe and the Bleak,
and how to fish for them.

THE *Gudgion* is reputed a Fish of excellent taste, and to be very wholsom: he is of a fine shape, of a silver colour, and beautified with black spots both on his body and tail. He breeds two or three times in the year, and always in Summer. He is commended for a Fish of excellent nourishment: the *Germans* call him *Groundling*, by reason of his feeding on the ground: and he there feasts himself in sharp streams, and on the gravel. He and the *Barbel* both feed so, and do not hunt for flies at any time, as most other Fishes do: he is an excellent fish to enter* a young Angler, being easie to be taken with a small red worm, on or very near to the ground. He is one of those leather-mouthed fish that has his teeth in his throat, and will hardly be lost off from the hook if he be once strucken: they be usually scattered up and down every River in the shallows, in the heat of Summer: but in *Autumn*, when the weeds begin to grow sowr or rot, and the weather colder, then they gather together, and get into the deeper parts of the water: and are to be Fished for there, with your hook always touching the ground, if you Fish for him with a flote, or with a cork: But many will Fish for the *Gudgion* by hand, with a running line upon the ground, without a cork, as a *Trout* is fished for, and it is an excellent way, if you have a gentle rod and as gentle a hand.

There is also another Fish called a *Pope*, and by some a *Ruffe*, a Fish that is not known to be in some Rivers, he is much like the

Pearch for his shape, and taken to be better than the *Pearch*, but will not grow to be bigger than a *Gudgion*; he is an excellent Fish, no Fish that swims is of a pleasanter taste, and he is also excellent to enter a young *Angler*, for he is a greedy biter, and they will usually lie abundance of them together in one reserved* place where the water is deep, and runs quietly; and an easie Angler, if he has found where they lie, may catch forty or fifty, or sometimes twice so many at a standing.

You must Fish for him with a small red-worm, and if you bait the ground with earth, it is excellent.

There is also a *Bleak*, or fresh-water-Sprat, a Fish that is ever in motion, and therefore called by some the *River-Swallow*; for just as you shall observe the *Swallow* to be most evenings in Summer ever in motion, making short and quick turns when he flies to catch Flies in the air (by which he lives) so does the *Bleak* at the top of the water. *Ausonius** would have him called *Bleak* from his whitish colour: his back is of a pleasant sad or Sea-water-green, his belly white and shining as the Mountain-snow: and doubtless though he have the fortune (which vertue has in poor people) to be neglected, yet the *Bleak* ought to be much valued, though we want *Allamot* salt, and the skill that the *Italians* have to turn them into Anchovis.* This fish may be caught with a *Pater-noster* line, that is, six or eight very small hooks tyed along the line one half a foot above the other: I have seen five caught thus at one time, and the bait has been Gentles, than which none is better.

Or this fish may be caught with a fine small artificial flie, which is to be of a very sad, brown colour, and very small, and the hook answerable. There is no better sport than whipping for *Bleaks** in a boat, or on a bank in the swift water in a Summers evening, with a Hazle top about five or six foot long, and a line twice the length of the Rod. I have heard Sir *Henry Wotton** say, that there be many that in *Italy* will catch *Swallows* so, or especially *Martins* (this *Bird-angler* standing on the top of a Steeple to do it, and with a line twice so long as I have spoken of): And let me tell you, Scholar, that both *Martins* and *Bleaks* be most excellent meat.

And let me tell you, that I have known a *Hern* that did constantly frequent one place, caught with a hook baited with a big Minnow or a small *Gudgion*. The line and hook must be strong, and tied to some loose staff so big as she cannot flie away with it, a line not exceeding two Yards.

CHAP. XVI.

Is of nothing, or, that which is nothing worth.

MY purpose was to give you some directions concerning *Roach* and *Dace*, and some other inferiour Fish, which make the Angler excellent sport, for you know there is more pleasure in Hunting the *Hare* than in eating her: but I will forbear at this time to say any more, because you see yonder come our brother *Peter* and honest *Coridon*: but I will promise you, that as you and I fish and walk to morrow towards *London*, if I have now forgotten any thing that I can then remember, I will not keep it from you.

Well met, Gentlemen, this is lucky that we meet so just together at this very door. Come Hostess, where are you? is Supper ready? come, first give us drink, and be as quick as you can, for I believe we are all very hungry. Well, brother *Peter* and *Coridon*, to you both; come drink, and then tell me *what luck of fish*: we two have caught but ten Trouts, of which my Scholar caught three; look here's eight, and a brace we gave away: we have had a most pleasant day for fishing and talking, and are returned home both weary and hungry, and now meat and rest will be pleasant.

Pet. And *Coridon* and I have not had an unpleasant day, and yet I have caught but five Trouts: for indeed we went to a good honest Ale-house, and there we plaid at Shovel-board* half the day; all the time that it rained we were there, and as merry as they that fished, and I am glad we are now with a dry house over our heads, for hark how it rains and blows. Come Hostess, give us more Ale, and our supper with what haste you may; and when we have sup'd let us have your Song, *Piscator*, and the Catch that your Scholar promised us,* or else *Coridon* will be dogged.*

Pisc. Nay, I will not be worse than my word, you shall not want my Song, and I hope I shall be perfect in it.

Venat. And I hope the like for my Catch, which I have ready too, and therefore lets go merrily to supper, and then have a gentle touch at singing and drinking: but the last with moderation.

Cor. Come, now for your Song, for we have fed heartily. Come Hostess, lay a few more sticks on the fire, and now sing when you will.

Pisc. Well then, here's to you *Coridon*; and now for my Song.*

　　　　　Oh the gallant Fishers life,
　　　　　It is the best of any,

Tis full of pleasure, void of strife,
And 'tis belov'd of many:
    Other joys
    are but toys,
    only this
    lawful is,
    for our skill
    breeds no ill,
but content and pleasure.

In a morning up we rise,
Ere Aurora's* *peeping,*
Drink a cup to wash our eyes,
Leave the sluggard sleeping:
    Then we go
    to and fro,
    with our knacks*
    at our backs,
    to such streams
    as the Thames,
if we have the leasure.

When we please to walk abroad
For our recreation,
In the fields is our abode,
Full of delectation.
    Where in a brook
    with a hook,
    or a Lake,
    fish we take,
    there we sit,
    for a bit,
till we fish entangle.

We have Gentles in a horn,
We have paste* and worms too,
We can watch both night and morn,
Suffer rain and storms too:
    None do here
    use to swear,

oaths do fray*
fish away,
we sit still,
and watch our quill;
Fishers must not wrangle.

If the Suns excessive heat
Make our bodies swelter,
To an Osier *hedge we get*
For a friendly shelter,
Where in a dike*
Pearch *or* Pike,
Roach *or* Dace,
we do chase,
Bleak *or* Gudgion
without grudging,
we are still contented.

Or we sometimes pass an hour
Under a green Willow,
That defends us from a showre,
Making earth our pillow,
Where we may
think and pray,
before death
stops our breath:
other joys
are but toys,
and to be lamented.

Jo. Chalkhill.

Venat. Well sung, Master, this days fortune and pleasure, and this nights company and song, do all make me more and more in love with *Angling*. Gentlemen, my Master left me alone for an hour this day, and I verily believe he retired himself from talking with me, that he might be so perfect in this song; was it not Master?

Pisc. Yes indeed, for it is many years since I learn'd it, and having forgotten a part of it, I was forced to patch it up by the help of mine own Invention, who am not excellent at Poetrie, as my part of the song may testifie: But of that I will say no more, lest you should think

I mean by discommending it to beg your commendations of it. And therefore without replications* lets hear your Catch, Scholar, which I hope will be a good one, for you are both Musical, and have a good fancie to boot.

Venat. Marry and that you shall, and as freely as I would have my honest Master tell me some more secrets of fish and Fishing as we walk and fish towards *London* to morrow. But Master, first let me tell you, that, that very hour which you were absent from me, I sate down under a *Willow-tree* by the water side, and considered what you had told me of the Owner of that pleasant Meadow in which you then left me; that he had a plentiful estate, and not a heart to think so; that he had at this time many Law-suits depending,* and that they both damp'd his mirth, and took up so much of his time and thoughts, that he himself had not leisure to take the sweet content that I (who pretended no title to them), took in his fields, for I could there sit quietly, and looking on the water, see some Fishes sport themselves in the silver streams, others, leaping at Flies of several shapes and colours; looking on the Hills, I could behold them spotted with Woods and Groves; looking down the Meadows, could see here a Boy gathering *Lillies* and *Lady-smocks*, and there a Girl cropping *Culverkeyes* and *Cow-slips*, all to make Garlands suitable to this present Month of *May*: these and many other Field-flowers, so perfumed the Air, that I thought that very Meadow like that Field in *Sicily* (of which *Diodorus** speaks) where the perfumes arising from the place, make all Dogs that hunt in it, to fall off, and to lose their hottest sent. I say, as I thus sate joying in my own happy condition, and pitying this poor rich man, that own'd this and many other pleasant Groves and Meadows about me, I did thankfully remember what my Saviour said,* that the *meek possess the Earth*; or rather, they enjoy what the other possess and enjoy not, for Anglers and meek quiet-spirited-men, are free from those high, those restless thoughts which corrode the sweets of life; and they, and they only can say as the Poet* has happily exprest it:

> *Hail blest estate of lowliness!*
> *Happy enjoyments of such minds,*
> *As rich in self-contentedness,*
> *Can, like the reeds in roughest winds*
>   *By yielding make that blow but small*
>   *At which proud Oaks and Cedars fall.*

There came also into my mind at that time, certain Verses in praise of a mean estate, and an humble mind, they were written by *Phineas Fletcher*:* an excellent Divine, and an excellent Angler, and the Author of excellent piscatory Eclogues, in which you shall see the picture of this good mans mind, and I wish mine to be like it.

> *No empty hopes, no Courtly fears him fright,*
> *No begging wants, his middle fortune bite,*
> *But sweet* content *exiles, both* misery *and* spite.

> *His certain* life, that never can deceive him,*
> *Is full of thousand sweets, and rich content;*
> *The smooth-leav'd* beeches *in the field receive him,*
> *With coolest shade, till noon-tides heat be spent:*
> *His life, is neither tost in boisterous Seas,*
> *Or the vexatious world, or lost in slothful ease;*
> *Pleas'd & full blest he lives, when he his God can please.*

> *His bed, more safe than soft, yields quiet sleeps,*
> *While by his side his faithful Spouse hath place,*
> *His little son, into his bosom creeps,*
> *The lively picture of his fathers face.*
> *His humble house, or poor state ne're torment him,*
> *Less he could like, if less his God had lent him,*
> *And when he dies, green turfs do for a tomb content him.*

Gentlemen, these were a part of the thoughts that then possest me, and I there made a conversion of a piece of an old Catch,* and added more to it, fitting them to be sung by us Anglers: come Master, you can sing well, you must sing a part of it as it is in this paper.

> *Mans life, is but vain: for, 'tis subject to pain*
> *And sorrow, and short as a bubble;*
> *'Tis a Hodg-poch* of business, and mony, and care,*
> *And care, and mony, and trouble.*
> *But we'l take no care, when the weather proves fair:*
> *Nor will we vex now tho it rain;*
> *We'l banish all sorrow, and sing till to morrow,*
> *And Angle, and Angle again.*

Pet. I marry Sir, this is Musick indeed, this has cheer'd my heart, and made me to remember six Verses in praise of Musick,* which I will speak to you instantly.

> *Musick, miraculous Rhetorick, that speak'st sense*
> *Without a tongue, excelling eloquence;*
> *With what ease might thy errors be excus'd,*
> *Wert thou as truly lov'd as th'art abus'd?*
> *But though dull souls neglect, & some reprove thee,*
> *I cannot hate thee, 'cause the Angels love thee.*

Ven. And the repetition of these last Verses of musick have call'd to my memory what Mr. *Ed. Waller** (a Lover of the Angle) says of Love and Musick.

> *Whilst I listen to thy voice*
> *(Chloris) I feel my heart decay:*
> > *That powerful voice,*
> > *Calls my fleeting Soul away;*
> > *Oh! suppress that magick sound*
> > *Which destroys without a wound.*

> *Peace* Cloris, *peace, or singing die,*
> > *That together you and I*
> > > *To Heaven may go:*
> > *For all we know*
> *Of what the blessed do above*
> *Is, that they sing, and that they love.*

Pisc. Well remembred brother *Peter*, these Verses came seasonably, and we thank you heartily. Come, we will all joyn together, my Host and all, and sing my Scholars Catch over again, and then each man drink the tother cup* and to bed, and thank God we have a dry house over our heads.

Pisc. Well now, good night to every body.

Pet. And so say I.

Ven. And so say I.

Cor. Good night to you all, and I thank you.

Pisc. Good morrow brother *Peter*, and the like to you honest *Coridon*: come, my Hostess says there is seven shillings to pay, let's each man drink a pot for his mornings draught, and lay down his two

The ANGLERS Song.

CANTUS.

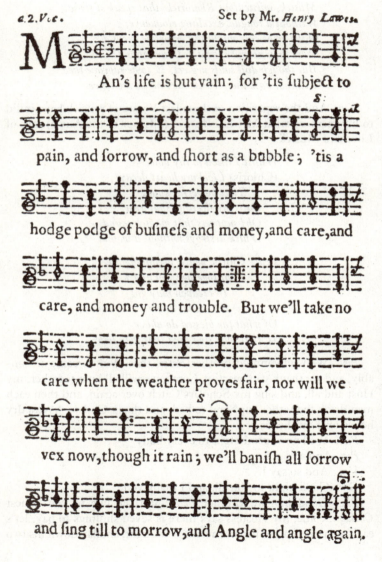

An's life is but vain; for 'tis subject to pain, and sorrow, and short as a bubble; 'tis a hodge podge of business and money, and care, and care, and money and trouble. But we'll take no care when the weather proves fair, nor will we vex now, though it rain; we'll banish all sorrow and sing till to morrow, and Angle and angle again.

The ANGLERS Song.

BASSUS.

a.2.Voc.   Set by Mr. Henry Lawes.

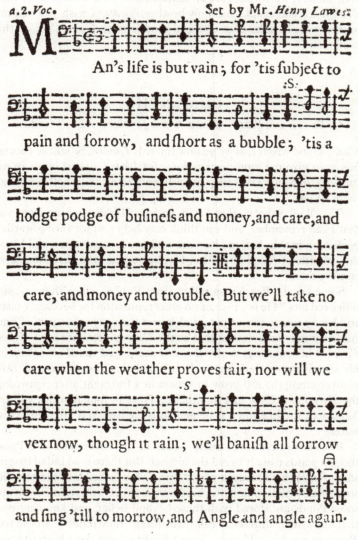

An's life is but vain ; for 'tis subject to

pain and sorrow, and short as a bubble ; 'tis a

hodge podge of business and money, and care, and

care, and money and trouble. But we'll take no

care when the weather proves fair, nor will we

vex now, though it rain ; we'll banish all sorrow

and sing 'till to morrow, and Angle and angle again.

shillings, that so my Hostess may not have occasion to repent her self of being so diligent, and using us* so kindly.

Pet. The motion is liked by every body, and so Hostess, here's your money; we Anglers are all beholding to you, it will not be long e're I'll see you again. And now brother *Piscator* I wish you and my brother your Scholar a fair day, and good fortune. Come *Coridon*, this is our way.

CHAP. XVII.

Of Roach *and* Dace, *& how to fish for them. And of* Caddis.

VEN. Good Master, as we go now towards *London*, be still so courteous as to give me more instructions, for I have several boxes in my memory, in which I will keep them all very safe, there shall not one of them be lost.

Pisc. Well Scholar, that I will, and I will hide nothing from you that I can remember, and can think may help you forward towards a perfection in this Art; and because we have so much time, and I have said so little of *Roach* and *Dace*, I will give you some directions concerning them.

Some say the *Roach* is so called, from *Rutilus*, which they say, signifies red fins.* He is a Fish of no great reputation for his dainty taste, and his Spawn is accounted much better than any other part of him. And you may take notice, that as the *Carp* is accounted the *Water-Fox*, for his cunning; so the *Roach* is accounted the *Water-sheep* for his simplicity or foolishness. It is noted that the *Roach* and *Dace* recover strength, and grow in season in a fortnight after Spawning, the *Barbel* and *Chub* in a month, the *Trout* in four months, and the *Salmon* in the like time, if he gets into the Sea, and after into fresh water.

Roaches be accounted much better in the River than in a Pond, though ponds usually breed the biggest. But there is a kind of bastard small *Roach* that breeds in ponds with a very forked tail, and of a very small size, which some say is bred by the *Bream* and right *Roach*, and some Ponds are stored with these beyond belief; and knowing-men that know their difference call them *Ruds*;* they differ from the true *Roach* as much as a Herring from a Pilchard, and these bastard breed of *Roach* are now scattered in many Rivers, but I think not in *Thames*, which I believe affords the largest and fattest in this Nation, especially below *London-bridg*:* the *Roach* is a leather-mouth'd Fish, and has a kind of saw-like teeth in his throat. And lastly let me tell you, the *Roach* makes an Angler excellent sport, especially the great Roaches about *London*, where I think there be the best Roach-Anglers, and I think the best *Trout-Anglers* be in *Derby-shire*, for the waters there are clear to an extremity.

Next, let me tell you, you shall fish for this *Roach* in Winter with Paste or Gentles, in *April* with worms or Caddis; in the very hot months with little white snails, or with flies under-water, for he seldom takes them at the top, though the Dace will. In many of the hot months, Roaches may also be caught thus: Take a *May-flie* or *Ant-flie*, sink him with a little lead to the bottom near to the Piles or Posts of a Bridg, or near to any posts of a *Weire*, I mean any deep place where Roaches lie quietly, and then pull your flie up very leisurely, and usually a Roach will follow your bait to the very top of the water and gaze on it there, and run at it and take it lest the flie should flie away from him.

I have seen this done at *Windsor* and *Henly-Bridg*,* and great store of *Roach* taken; and sometimes a *Dace* or *Chub*; and in *August* you may fish for them with a Paste made only of the crumbs of Bread, which should be of pure fine Manchet;* and that paste must be so tempered betwixt your hands till it be both soft and tough too; a very little water, and time and labour, and clean hands will make it a most excellent paste: But when you fish with it, you must have a small hook, a quick eye, and a nimble hand, or the bait is lost and the fish too (if one may lose that which he never had). With this paste, you may, as I said, take both the Roach and the Dace or Dare, for they be much of a kind, in matter of feeding, cunning, goodness, and usually in size. And therefore take this general direction for some other baits which may concern you to take notice of. They will bite almost at any flie, but especially at *Antflies*;* concerning which, take this direction, for it is very good.

Take the blackish *Ant-flie* out of the Mole-hill or Ant-hill, in which place you shall find them in the month of *June*, or if that be too early in the year, then doubtless you may find them in *July, August*, and most of *September*; gather them alive with both their wings, and then put them into a Glass that will hold a quart or a pottle; but first

put into the Glass a handful or more of the moist earth, out of which
you gather them, and as much of the roots of the grass of the said
hillock, and then put in the flies gently, that they lose not their wings,
lay a clod of earth over it, and then so many as are put into the glass
without bruising, will live there a month or more, and be always in a
readiness for you to fish with; but if you would have them keep
longer, then get any great earthen pot, or barrel of three or four gal-
lons (which is better) then wash your barrel with water and honey;
and having put into it a quantity of earth and grass roots, then put in
your flies, and cover it, and they will live a quarter of a year; these in
any stream and clear water, are a deadly bait for *Roach* or *Dace*, or for
a *Chub*; and your rule is, to fish not less than a handful* from the
bottom.

I shall next tell you a winter bait for a *Roach*, a *Dace* or *Chub*, and
it is choicely good. About *All-hallantide** (and so till Frost comes)
when you see men ploughing up heath ground, or sandy ground, or
green swards,* then follow the plough, and you shall find a white
worm as big as two Maggots, and it hath a red head, (you may observe
in what ground most are, for there the Crows will be very watchful
and follow the Plough very close) it is all soft, and full of whitish guts;
a worm that is in *Norfolk*, and some other Counties called a *Grub*, and
is bred of the Spawn or Eggs of a Beetle, which she leaves in holes
that she digs in the ground under Cow or Horse dung, and there rests
all Winter, and in *March* or *April* comes to be first a red, and then a
black Beetle: gather a thousand or two of these, and put them with a
peck or two of their own earth into some tub or firkin, and cover and
keep them so warm, that the frost or cold air, or winds kill them not;
these you may keep all winter, and kill fish with them at any time: and
if you put some of them into a little earth and honey a day before you
use them, you will find them an excellent bait for *Bream*, *Carp*, or
indeed for almost any fish.

And after this manner you may also keep Gentles all winter, which
are a good bait then, and much the better for being lively and tough:
or you may breed and keep Gentles thus: Take a piece of Beasts liver,
and with a cross stick, hang it in some corner over a pot or barrel half
full of dry clay, and as the Gentles grow big, they will fall into the
barrel and scowre themselves, and be always ready for use whenso-
ever you incline to fish; and these Gentles may be thus created till
after *Michaelmas.** But if you desire to keep Gentles to fish with all

the year, then get a dead Cat or a Kite and let it be fly-blown, and when the Gentles begin to be alive and to stir, then bury it and them in soft, moist earth, but as free from frost as you can, and these you may dig up at any time when you intend to use them, these will last till *March*, and about that time turn to be Flies.*

But if you be nice to foul your Fingers, (which good Anglers seldom are) then take this Bait: Get a handful of well-made Malt, and put it into a dish of water, and then wash and rub it betwixt your hands till you make it clean, and as free from husks as you can; then put that water from it, and put a small quantity of fresh water to it, and set it in something that is fit for that purpose over the Fire, where it is not to boil apace, but leasurely and very softly, until it become somewhat soft, which you may try by feeling it betwixt your Finger and Thumb, and when it is soft, then put your water from it, and then take a sharp Knife, and turning the sprout end of the Corn* upward, with the point of your Knife take the back part of the husk off from it, and yet leaving a kind of inward husk on the Corn, or else it is marr'd, and then cut off that sprouted end (I mean a little of it) that the white may appear, and so pull off the husk on the cloven side (as I directed you) and then cutting off a very little of the other end, that so your hook may enter; and if your hook be small and good,* you will find this to be a very choice Bait either for Winter or Summer, you sometimes casting a little of it into the place where your float swims.

And to take the *Roach* and *Dace*, a good Bait is the young brood of Wasps or Bees, if you dip their heads in blood; especially good for *Bream*, if they be baked or hardned in their husks in an Oven, after the bread is taken out of it; or hardned on a Fire-shovel; and so also is the thick blood of *Sheep*, being half dried on a Trencher, that so you may cut it into such pieces as may best fit the size of your hook, and a little salt keeps it from growing black, and makes it not the worse but better: This is taken to be a choice Bait if rightly ordered.

There be several Oils of a strong smell that I have been told of, and to be excellent to tempt Fish to bite, of which I could say much, but I remember I once carried a small Bottle from Sir *George Hastings* to Sir *Henry Wotton*, (they were both chymical men)* as a great Present; it was sent, and receiv'd, and us'd with great confidence; and yet upon enquiry I found it did not answer the expectation of Sir *Henry*, which with the help of this and other circumstances, makes me have little belief in such things as many men talk of: not but that I think Fishes both smell and hear (as I have exprest in my former discourse) but there is a mysterious Knack, which (though it be much easier than the Philosophers Stone),* yet is not attainable by common capacities, or else lies locked up in the brain or breast of some chymical man, that like the *Rosi-crucians** will not yet reveal it. But let me nevertheless tell you, that *Camphire** put with moss into your worm-bag with your worms, makes them (if many Anglers be not very much mistaken) a tempting bait, and the Angler more fortunate. But I stepped by chance into this discourse of Oiles and Fishes smelling, and though there might be more said, both of it and of Baits for *Roach* and *Dace*, and other float Fish,* yet I will forbear it at this time, and tell you in the next place how you are to prepare your Tackling: concerning which I will for sport sake give you an old Rhime out of an old Fish-book,* which will prove a part and but a part of what you are to provide.

> *My Rod and my Line, my Float and my Lead,*
> *My Hook & my Plummet, my whetstone and knife,*
> *My Basket, my Baits both living and dead,*
> *My Net and my Meat, for that is the chief:*
> *Then I must have Thred, & Hairs green and small,**
> *With mine Angling purse, and so you have all.*

But you must have all these Tackling, and twice so many more, with which if you mean to be a Fisher, you must store your self; and to that

I have heard, that the tackling hath been prized at fifty pounds in the Inventory of an Angler.

purpose I will go with you either to Mr. *Margrave** who dwells amongst the Book-sellers* in St. *Pauls* Church-Yard, or to M. *John Stubs* near to the *Swan* in *Golding-lane*; they be both honest men, and will fit an *Angler* with what *Tackling* he lacks.

Venat. Then, good Master, let it be at —— —— for he is nearest to my dwelling, and I pray let's meet there the ninth of *May* next, about two of the clock, and I'll want nothing that a Fisher should be furnished with.

Pisc. Well, and I'll not fail you God willing at the time and place appointed.

Venat. I thank you, good Master, and I will not fail you: and, good Master, tell me what Baits more you remember, for it will not now be long ere we shall be at *Tottenham-high-Cross*, and when we come thither I will make you some requital of your pains, by repeating as choice a copy of Verses, as any we have heard since we met together; and that is a proud word for we have heard very good ones.

Pisc. Well, Scholar, and I shall be then right glad to hear them; and I will as we walk tell you whatsoever comes in my mind, that I think may be worth your hearing. You may make another choice Bait thus, Take a handful or two of the best and biggest *Wheat* you can get, boil it in a little milk (like as *Frumity** is boiled) boil it so till it be soft, and then fry it very leasurely with Honey and a little beaten Saffron dissolved in milk, and you will find this a choice Bait, and good I think for any Fish, especially for *Roach, Dace, Chub*, or *Grayling*: I know not but that it may be as good for a River-*carp*, and especially if the ground be a little baited with it.

And you may also note, that the spawn of most Fish is a very tempting bait, being a little hardned on a warm Tile, and cut into fit pieces. Nay, Mulberries and those Black-berries, which grow upon Briers, be good baits for *Chubs* or *Carps*, with these many have been taken in Ponds, and in some Rivers where such Trees have grown near the water and the fruit customarily dropt into it, and there be a hundred other baits more than can be well nam'd, which, by constant baiting the water will become a tempting bait for any Fish in it.

You are also to know, that there be divers kinds of *Caddis*, or *Case-worms*, that are to be found in this Nation in several distinct Counties, and in several little Brooks that relate to bigger Rivers; as namely, one *Cadis* called a *Piper*, whose husk or case is a piece of reed about an inch long or longer, and as big about as the compass of a two pence;* these worms being kept three or four days in a woollen bag with sand at the bottom of it, and the bag wet once a day, will in three or four days turn to be yellow, and these be a choice bait for the *Chub* or *Chavender*, or indeed for any great Fish, for it is a large Bait.

There is also a lesser *Cadis-worm*, called a *Cock-spur*, being in fashion like the spur of a Cock, sharp at one end, and the case or house in which this dwells is made of small husks, and gravel, and slime, most curiously made of these, even so as to be wondred at, but not to be made by man no more than a *King-fishers* nest* can, which is made of little Fishes bones, and have such a Geometrical inter-weaving and connexion, as the like is not to be done by the art of man: This kind of *Cadis* is a choice bait for any float-Fish, it is much less than the *Piper-Cadis*, and to be so ordered, and these may be so preserved ten, fifteen, or twenty days, or it may be longer.

There is also another *Cadis*, called by some a *Straw-worm*, and by some a *Ruff-coat*, whose house or case is made of little pieces of bents,* and rushes, and straws, and water-weeds, and I know not what, which are so knit together with condensed slime, that they stick about her husk or case, not unlike the bristles of a *Hedg-hog*; these three *Cadis's* are commonly taken in the beginning of Summer, and are good indeed to take any kind of fish with float or otherwise. I might tell you of many more, which as these do early, so those have their time also of turning to be flies later in Summer; but I might lose my self, and tire you by such a discourse, I shall therefore but remember you, that to know these, and their several kinds, and to what flies every particular *Cadis* turns, and then how to use them first as they be *Cadis*, and after as they be *flies*, is an art, and an art that every one that professes to be an Angler has not leisure to search after, and if he had is not capable of learning.

I'le tell you, Scholar, several Countries have several kinds of *Caddis's*, that indeed differ as much as dogs do: That is to say, as much as a very *Cur* and a *Greyhound* do. These be usually bred in the very little rills or ditches that run into bigger Rivers, and I think a more proper bait for those very Rivers, than any other. I know not how or of what this *Cadis* receives life, or what coloured flie, it turns to; but doubtless, they are the death of many *Trouts*, and this is one killing way.

Take one (or more if need be) of these large yellow *Cadis*, pull off his head, and with it pull out his black gut, put the body (as little bruised as is possible) on a very little hook, armed on with a Red hair (which will shew like the *Cadis-head*) and a very little thin lead, so put upon the shank of the hook that it may sink presently; throw this bait thus ordered (which will look very yellow) into any great still hole where a Trout is, and he will presently venture his life for it, 'tis not to be doubted if you be not espyed; and that the bait first touch the water, before the line; and this will do best in the deepest stillest water.

Next let me tell you, I have been much pleased to walk quietly by a Brook with a little stick in my hand, with which I might easily take these, and consider the curiosity of their composure; and if you shall ever like to do so, then note, that your stick must be a little Hasel or Willow cleft, or have a nick at one end of it, by which means you may with ease take many of them in that nick out of the water, before you have any occasion to use them. These, my honest Scholar, are some observations told to you as they now come suddenly into my memory, of which you may make some use: but for the practical part, it is that, that makes an Angler: it is diligence, and observation, and practice, and an ambition to be the best in the Art that must do it. I will tell you, Scholar, I once heard one say, *I envy not him that eats better* meat *than I do, nor him that is* richer, *or that wears better* clothes *than I do. I envy no body but him, and him only, that catches more* fish *than I do.* And such a man is like to prove an Angler, and this noble emulation I wish to you and all young Anglers.

CHAP. XVIII.

Of the Minnow *or* Penk, *of the* Loach, *and of the* Bull-head,* *or* Millers-thumb.

PISC. There be also three or four other little fish that I had almost forgot, that are all without scales,* and may for excellency of meat be compared to any fish of greatest value, and largest size. They be usually full of eggs or spawn all the months of Summer; for they breed often, as 'tis observed *mice* and many of the smaller four-footed Creatures of the earth do; and as those, so these come quickly to their full growth and perfection. And it is needful that they breed both often and numerously, for they be (besides other accidents of ruine) both a prey, and baits for other fish. And first, I shall tell you of the *Minnow* or *Penk*.

The *Minnow* hath, when he is in perfect season, and not sick (which is only presently after spawning) a kind of dappled or waved colour, like to a *Panther*, on his sides, inclining to a greenish and skie-colour, his belly being milk-white, and his back almost black or blackish. He is a sharp biter at a small worm, and in hot weather makes excellent sport for young Anglers, or boys, or women that love that Recreation, and in the spring they make of them excellent *Minnow-Tansies*; for being washed well in salt, and their heads and tails cut off, and their guts taken out, and not washt after, they prove excellent for that use, that is, being *fryed with yolks of eggs, the flowers of* Cowslips, *and of* Primroses, *and a little Tansie*, thus us'd they make a dainty dish of meat.

The Loach is, as I told you, a most dainty fish, he breeds and feeds in little and clear swift brooks or rills; and lives there upon the gravel, and in the sharpest* streams: He grows not to be above a finger-long, and no thicker than is suitable to that length. This *LOACH*,

is not unlike the shape of the Eel: He has a beard or wattels like a *Barbel*. He has two fins at his sides, four at his belly and one at his tail; he is dapled with many black or brown spots, his mouth is Barbel-like under his nose. This Fish is usually full of eggs or spawn, and is by *Gesner** and other learned Physicians commended for great nourishment, and to be very grateful both to the palate and stomach of sick persons; he is to be fished for with a very small worm at the bottom, for he very seldom or never rises above the Gravel, on which I told you he usually gets his Living.

The *Millers-thumb* or *Bull-head*, is a Fish of no pleasing shape. He is by *Gesner* compared to the *Sea-toad-fish*,* for his similitude and shape. It has a head big and flat, much greater than sutable to his Body; a mouth very wide and usually gaping. He is without teeth, but his lips are very rough, much like to a File. He hath two Fins near to his gills, which be roundish or crested, two Fins also under the Belly, two on the back, one below the Vent, and the Fin of his tail is round. Nature hath painted the Body of this Fish with *whitish, blackish, brownish* spots. They be usually full of eggs or spawn all the Summer (I mean the Females) and those eggs swell their Vents almost into the form of a dug. They begin to spawn about *April*, and (as I told you) spawn several months in the Summer; and in the winter the Minnow, and Loach and Bull-head dwell in the mud as the Eel doth, or we know not where: no more than we know where the Cuckow and Swallow, and other half year birds (which first appear to us in *April*) spend their six cold winter melancholy months. This *Bull-head* does usually dwell and hide himself in holes or amongst stones in clear water; and in very hot daies will lie a long time very still, and sun himself, and will be easie to be seen upon any flat stone, or any gravel,

at which time, he will suffer an Angler to put a hook baited with a small worm very near unto his very mouth, and he never refuses to bite, nor indeed to be caught with the worst of Anglers. *Matthiolus**
commends him much more for his taste and nourishment, than for his shape or beauty.

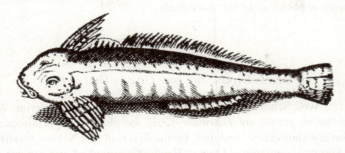

There is also a little Fish called a *Sticklebag*: a Fish without scales, but hath his body fenc'd with several prickles. I know not where he dwells in winter, nor what he is good for in summer, but only to make sport for boys and women-Anglers, and to feed other Fish that be Fish of prey, as Trouts in particular, who will bite at him as at a Penk, and better, if your hook be rightly baited with him, for he may be so baited, as his tail turning like the sail of a wind-mill will make him turn more quick than any *Penk* or *Minnow* can. For note, that the nimble turning of that or the *Minnow* is the perfection of *Minnow-Fishing*. To which end, if you put your hook into his mouth, and out at his tail, and then having first tied him with white thred a little above his tail, and placed him after such a manner on your hook as he is like to turn, then sow up his mouth to your line, and he is like to turn quick, and tempt any *Trout*: but if he do not turn quick, then turn his tail a little more or less towards the inner part; or towards the side of the hook, or put the *Minnow* or *Sticklebag* a little more crooked or more strait on your hook, until it will turn both true and fast; and then doubt not but to tempt any great *Trout* that lies in a swift stream. And the *Loach* that I told you of will do the like: no bait is more tempting, provided the *Loach* be not too big.

And now *Scholar*, with the help of this fine morning, and your patient attention, I have said all that my present memory will afford me concerning most of the several Fish that are usually fisht for in fresh waters.

Venat. But Master, you have by your former civility made me hope that you will make good your promise, and say something of the several Rivers that be of most note in this Nation; and also of *Fish-ponds*, and the ordering of them; and do it I pray good Master, for I love any Discourse of Rivers, and Fish and fishing, the time spent in such discourse passes away very pleasantly.

CHAP. XIX.

Of several Rivers, *and some Observations of Fish.*

PISC. Well Scholar, since the ways and weather do both favour us, and that we yet see not *Tottenham-Cross*, you shall see my willingness to satisfie your desire. And first, for the Rivers of this Nation, there be (as you may note out of Doctor *Heylins* Geography,* and others) in number 325. but those of chiefest note he reckons and describes as followeth.

The chief is *Thamisis*,* compounded of two Rivers, *Thame* and *Isis*; whereof the former rising somewhat beyond *Thame* in *Buckingham-shire*, and the latter in *Cyrencester* in *Glocester-shire* meet together about *Dorcester* in *Oxford-shire*, the issue of which happy conjunction is the *Thamisis* or *Thames*. Hence it flyeth betwixt *Berks*, *Buckingham-shire*, *Middlesex*, *Surry*, *Kent*, and *Essex*, and so weddeth himself to the Kentish *Medway* in the very jaws of the Ocean; this glorious River feeleth the violence and benefit of the Sea more than any River in *Europe*, ebbing and flowing twice a day, more than sixty miles: about whose banks are so many fair Towns, and Princely Palaces that a *German Poet** thus truly spake:

> *Tot Campos,** &c.*

> *We saw so many* Woods *and Princely* bowers,
> *Sweet* Fields, *brave* Palaces, *and* stately Towers,
> *So many* Gardens *drest with curious care*,
> *That* Thames *with* royal Tyber* *may compare.*

2. The second River of note, is *Sabrina* or *Severn*: it hath its beginning in *Plinilimmon-Hill*, in *Montgomery-shire*, and his end seven miles from *Bristol*, washing in the mean space the walls of *Shrewsbury*, *Worcester*, and *Glocester* and divers other places and palaces of note.

3. *Trent*, so called for thirty kind of Fishes that are found in it, or for that it receiveth thirty lesser Rivers,* who having his fountain in *Staffordshire*, and gliding through the Countries of *Nottingham, Lincoln, Leicester*, and *York* augmenteth the turbulent current of *Humber*, the most violent stream of all the Isle. This *Humber* is not, to say truth, a distinct River, having a spring head of his own, but it is rather the mouth or *Eustorium** of divers Rivers here confluent and meeting together; namely, your *Dorwent*,* and especially of *Ouse* and *Trent*; and (as the *Danow*, having received into its *channel*, the River *Dravus, Savus, Tibisnus*,* and divers others) changeth his name into this of *Humberabus*,* as the old Geographers call it.

4. *Medway*, a Kentish River, famous for harbouring the Royal Navy.

5. *Tweed*, the north-east bound of *England*, on whose northern banks is seated the strong and impregnable Town of *Barwick*.*

6. *Tine*, famous for *Newcastle*, and her inexhaustible Coal-pits. These and the rest of principal note, are thus comprehended in one of Mr. *Draytons** Sonnets.

> *The floods queen,* Thames, *for ships and swans is crown'd*
> *And stately* Severn *for her shore is prais'd,*
> *The Chrystal* Trent *for fords and fish renown'd,*
> *And* Avons *fame to* Albions *cliffs is rais'd,*
> Carlegion Chester *vaunts her holy* Dee,*
> York *many wonders of her* Ouse *can tell,*
> The Peak *her* Dove, *whose banks so fertile be,*
> *And* Kent *will say her* Medway *doth excell.*
> Cotswool *commends her* Isis *to the* Tame,*
> *Our Northern borders boast of* Tweeds *fair flood,*
> *Our Western parts extoll their* Willies* *fame,*
> *And the old* Lea *brags of the* Danish *blood.**

These Observations are out of learned Dr. *Heylin*, and my old deceased friend *Michael Drayton*; and because you say, you love such discourses as these of *rivers* and *fish* and *fishing*, I love you the better, and love the more to impart them to you: nevertheless, *Scholar*, if I should begin but to name the several sorts of strange Fish that are usually taken in many of those Rivers that run into the Sea, I might beget wonder in you, or unbelief, or both; and yet I will venture to tell you a real truth concerning one lately dissected by Dr. *Wharton*, a man of great learning and experience, and of equal freedom to communicate it; one that loves me and my Art, one to whom I have been beholding for many of the choicest observations that I have imparted to you. This good man, that dares do any thing rather than tell an untruth, did (I say) tell me, he lately dissected one strange fish and he thus described it to me.

The Fish* was almost a yard broad, and twice that length; his mouth wide enough to receive or take into it the head of a man, his stomach seven or eight inches broad: he is of a slow motion, and usually lyes or lurks close in the mud, and has a moveable string on his head about a span, or near unto a quarter of a yard long, by the moving of which (which is his natural bait) *when he lyes close and unseen in the mud, he draws other smaller fish so close to him that he can suck them into his mouth, and so devours and digests them.*

And, Scholar, do not wonder at this, for besides the credit of the Relator, you are to note, many of these, and Fishes which are of the like and more unusual shapes, are very often taken on the mouths of our Sea-Rivers, and on the Sea-shore; and this will be no wonder to any that have travelled *Egypt*, where 'tis known the famous River *Nilus* does not only breed Fishes that yet want names, but by the overflowing of that River and the help of the Suns heat on the fat slime which that River leaves on the Banks (when it falls back into its natural channel) such strange fish and beasts are also bred, that no man can give a name to, as *Grotius** (in his *Sopham*) and others have observed.

But whither am I straid in this discourse? I will end it by telling you, that at the mouth of some of these Rivers of ours, Herrings are so plentiful, as namely, near to *Yarmouth* in *Norfolk*, and in the West-Country, Pilchers* so very plentiful, as you will wonder to read what our learned *Cambden* relates of them in his *Britannia*,* p. 178, 186.

Well, Scholar, I will stop here, and tell you what by reading and conference I have observed concerning Fish-ponds.

CHAP. XX.

Of fish-ponds, and how to order them.

DOCTOR *Lebault** the learned French man, in his large discourse of *Mason Rustique*, gives this direction for making of *Fish-ponds*, I shall refer you to him to read it at large, but I think I shall contract it, and yet make it as useful.

He adviseth, that when you have dreined the ground, and made the earth firm where the head of the Pond must be, that you must then in that place drive in two or three rows of Oak or Elme Piles, which should be scorcht in the fire, or half burnt before they be driven into the earth, (for being thus used it preserves them much longer from rotting) and having done so, lay Fagots or Bavins* of smaller wood betwixt them, and then earth betwixt and above them, and then having first very well rammed them and the earth, use another pile in like manner as the first were: and note that the second pile is to be of or about the height that you intend to make your Sluce or Flood-gate, or the vent that you intend shall convey the overflowings of your Pond in any flood that shall endanger the breaking of the Pond dam.

Then he advises that you plant Willows or Owlers* about it, or both, and then cast in Bavins in some places not far from the side, and in the most sandy places, for Fish both to spawn upon, and to defend them and the young Frie from the many Fish, and also from Vermin that lie at watch to destroy them, especially the spawn of the *Carp* and *Tench*, when 'tis left to the mercy of ducks or Vermin.

He and *Dubravius** and all others advise, that you make choice of such a place for your Pond, that it may be refresht with a little rill, or with rain water running or falling into it; by which Fish are more inclined both to breed, and are also refresht and fed the better, and do prove to be of a much sweeter and more pleasant taste.

To which end it is observed; that such Pools as be large and have most gravel, and shallows where *fish* may sport themselves, do afford Fish of the purest taste. And note, that in all Pools it is best for fish to have some retiring place, as namely hollow banks, or shelves, or roots of trees to keep them from danger; and when they think fit from the extream heat of Summer; as also, from the extremity of cold in Winter. And note, that if many trees be growing about your Pond, the leaves thereof falling into the water, make it nauseous to the Fish, and the Fish to be so to the eater of it.

'Tis noted that the *Tench* and *Eel* love mud, and the *Carp* loves gravelly ground, and in the hot months to feed on grass: You are to cleanse your Pond, if you intend either profit or pleasure, once every three or four Years, (especially some Ponds) and then let it lye dry six or twelve months, both to kill the water-weeds, as *Water-lillies, Candocks, Reate** and *Bull-rushes* that breed there; and also that as these die for want of water, so grass may grow in the Ponds bottom, which *Carps* will eat greedily in all the hot months if the Pond be clean. The letting your Pond dry and sowing Oats in the bottom is also good, for the fish feed the faster: and being sometime let dry, you may observe what kind of Fish either increases or thrives best in that water; for they differ much both in their breeding and feeding.

Lebault also advises, that if your Ponds be not very large and roomy, that you often feed your fish by throwing into them chippings* of Bread, Curds, Grains, or the entrails of Chickens, or of any fowl or beast that you kill to feed your selves; for these afford Fish a great relief. He says that Frogs and Ducks do much harm, and devour both the Spawn and the young Frie of all Fish, especially of the *Carp*. And I have, besides experience, many testimonies of it. But *Lebault* allows Water-frogs to be good meat, especially in some Months, if they be fat: but you are to note, that he is a *French-man*, and we *English* will hardly believe him, though we know frogs are usually eaten in his Country: however he advises to destroy them and King-fishers out of your ponds; and he advises, not to suffer much shooting at wild fowl, for that (he says) affrightens, and harms, and destroys the Fish.

Note, that Carps and Tench thrive and breed best when no other fish is put with them into the same Pond; for all other fish devour their spawn, or at least the greatest part of it. And note, that clods of grass thrown into any Pond feed any Carps in Summer: and that garden earth and parsley thrown into a Pond, recovers and refreshes the sick fish. And note, that when you store* your pond, you are to put into it two or three Melters for one Spawner,* if you put them into a breeding Pond: but if into a nurse-pond, or feeding pond, in which they will not breed, then no care is to be taken, whether there be most Male or Female Carps.

It is observed, that the best ponds to breed Carps are those that be stony or sandy, and are warm, and free from wind, and that are not deep, but have willow trees and grass on their sides, over which the water does sometimes flow: and note, that Carps do more usually breed in marle pits,* or pits that have clean clay bottoms, or in new ponds, or ponds that lie dry a winter season, than in old ponds, that be full of mud and weeds.

Well *Scholar*, I have told you the substance of all that either *observation* or *discourse*, or a diligent *Survey* of *Dubravius* and *Lebault** hath told me. Not that they in their long discourses have not said more, but the most of the rest are so common observations, as if a man should tell a good Arithmetician, that twice two, is four. I will therefore put an end to this discourse, and we will here sit down and rest us.

CHAP. XXI.

Directions for making of a Line, and for the colouring of both Rod and Line.

PISC. Well, Scholar, I have held you too long about these *Cadis*, and smaller *fish*, and *rivers*, and *Fish-ponds*, and my spirits are almost spent, and so I doubt is your patience; but being we are now almost at *Tottenham*, where I first met you, and where we are to part, I will lose no time, but give you a little direction how to make and order your Lines, and to colour the hair of which you make your Lines, for that is very needful to be known of an Angler; and also how to paint your Rod; especially your top, for a right grown top is a choice Commodity, and should be preserved from the water soaking into it, which makes it in wet weather to be heavy, and fish ill favouredly, and not true, and also it rots quickly for want of painting: and I think a good top is worth preserving, or I had not taken care to keep a top above twenty years.

But first for your line.

First, note, That you are to take care, that your hair be round and clear, and free from galls or scabs, or frets;* for a well-chosen, even, clear, round hair, of a kind of glass-colour, will prove as strong as three uneven, scabby hairs, that are ill chosen, and full of galls or unevenness. You shall seldom find a black hair but it is round, but many white are flat and uneven; therefore if you get a lock of right, round, clear, glass-colour hair make much of it.

And for making your *Line*, observe this rule, First, let your hair be clean washt 'ere you go about to twist it: and then chuse not only the clearest hair for it, but hairs that be of an equal bigness, for such do usually stretch all together, and break altogether, which hairs of an unequal bigness never do, but break singly, and so deceive the Angler that trusts to them.

When you have twisted your links, lay them in water for a quarter of an hour, at least, and then twist them over again before you tie them into a Line: for those that do not so, shall usually find their Line to have a hair or two shrink, and be shorter than the rest at the first fishing with it, which is so much of the strength of the Line lost for want of first watering it, and then re-twisting it; and this is most visible in a seven-hair line, one of those which hath always a black hair in the middle.

And for dying of your hairs do it thus:

Take a pint of strong Ale, half a pound of soot, and a little quantity of the juice of *Walnut*-tree leaves, and an equal quantity of Allom,* put these together into a pot, pan, or pipkin, and boil them half an hour, and having so done, let it cool, and being cold, put your hair into it, and there let it lie; it will turn your hair to be a kind of water or glass colour, or greenish, and the longer you let it lie, the deeper coloured it will be; you might be taught to make many other colours, but it is to little purpose; for doubtless the water-colour, or glass-coloured hair is the most choice and most useful for an *Angler*; but let it not be too green.

But if you desire to colour hair greener, then do it thus: Take a quart of small Ale,* half a pound of Allom, then put these into a pan or pipkin; and your hair into it with them, then put it upon a fire, and let it boil softly for half an hour, and then take out your hair, and let it dry, and having so done, then take a pottle of water, and put into it two handful of Mary-golds,* and cover it with a tile (or what you think fit) and set it again on the Fire, where it is to boil again softly for half an hour, about which time the scum will turn yellow, then put into it half a pound of Copperas* beaten small, and with it the hair that you intend to colour, then let the hair be boiled softly till half the liquor be wasted, and then let it cool three or four hours with your hair in it: and you are to observe, that the more Copperas you put into it, the greener it will be, but doubtless the pale green is best; But if you desire yellow hair, (which is only good when the weeds rot) then put in the more *Mary-golds*, and abate most of the Copperas, or leave it quite out, and take a little Verdigrease* instead of it.

This for colouring your hair. And as for painting your Rod, which must be in Oil, you must first make a size* with glue and water, boiled together, untill the glue be dissolved, and the size of a Lie-colour;* then strike your size upon the wood with a Bristle, or a Brush, or

Pensil, whilst it is hot: that being quite dry, take white Lead, and a little red Lead, and a little cole-black, so much as all together will make an ash-colour; grind these all together with Linseed Oil, let it be thick, and lay it thin upon the wood with a Brush or Pensil, this do for the ground of any colour to lie upon wood.

For a Green.

Take Pink and Verdigreece, and grind them together in Linseed Oil, as thin as you can well grind it, then lay it smoothly on with your Brush, and drive it thin; once doing for the most part will serve, if you lay it well; and if twice be sure your first colour be throughly dry, before you lay on a second.

Well Scholar; having now taught you to paint your Rod: and, we having still a mile to Tottenham High-Cross, *I will, as we walk towards it, in the cool shade of this sweet* Hony-suckle-Hedg, *mention to you some of the thoughts and joys that have possest my Soul since we two met together. And, these thoughts shall be told you, that you also may joyn with me in thankfulness to the giver of every good and perfect gift for our happiness. And, that our present happiness may appear to be the greater, and we the more thankful for it: I will beg you to consider with me, how many do, even at this very time, lie under the torment of the* Stone,* *the* Gout, *and* Tooth-ache; *and, this we are free from. And,* every misery that I miss is a new mercy, *and therefore let us be thankful. There have been since we met, others, that have met disasters of broken Limbs, some have been blasted, others Thunder-strucken; and we have been freed from these, and all those many other miseries that threaten humane nature: let us therefore rejoice and be thankful. Nay, which is a far greater mercy, we are free from the unsupportable burthen of an accusing, tormenting Conscience: a misery that none can bear, and therefore let us praise him for his preventing grace;* *and say,* every misery that I miss, is a new mercy: *Nay, let me tell you there be many that have forty times our Estates, that would give the greatest part of it to be healthful and chearful like us; who with the expence of a little mony have eat,* *and drank, and laught, and Angled, and sung, and slept securely: and rose next day, and cast away care, and sung, and laught, and Angled again: which are blessings, rich men cannot purchase with all their money. Let me tell you Scholar: I have a rich Neighbour, that is always so busie, that he has no leasure to laugh; the whole business of his life, is to get money, and more*

*money, that he may still get more and more money; he is still drudging on,
and says, that* Solomon *says,** the diligent hand maketh rich: *and 'tis
true indeed, but he considers not, that 'tis not in the power of riches to
make a man happy: for, it was wisely said by a man of great observation,*
that there be as many miseries beyond riches, as on this side them:**
and yet God deliver us from pinching poverty; and grant, that having a
competency,** *we may be content and thankful. Let us not repine, or so
much as think the gifts of God unequally dealt, if we see another abound
with riches, when as God knows, the cares that are the keys that keep those
riches, hang often so heavily at the rich mans girdle, that they clog him
with weary days and restless nights, even when others sleep quietly. We see
but the outside of the rich mans happiness: few consider him to be like the*
Silk-worm, *that when she seems to play, is at the very same time spinning
her own bowels, and consuming her self. And this many rich men do; load-
ing themselves with corroding cares, to keep what they have (probably)
unconscionably got. Let us therefore be thankful for health and a competence; and above all, for a quiet Conscience.*

Let me tell you, Scholar, that Diogenes** *walked on a day with his
friend to see a* Country Fair; *where he saw,* Ribbins, *and* Looking-
glasses, *and* Nut-crackers, *and* Fiddles, *and* Hobbyhorses, *and many
other* gim-cracks; *and having observ'd them, and, all the other* finnimbruns** *that make a compleat Country Fair: He said to his friend,* Lord!
How many things are there in this world of which *Diogenes* hath no
need? *And truly, it is so, or might be so, with very many who vex, and toyl
themselves, to get what they have no need of. Can any man charge God,
that he hath not given him enough to make his life happy? no doubtless:
for, nature is content with a little: and yet, you shall hardly meet with a
man, that complains not of some want, though he indeed wants nothing but
his will, it may be, nothing but his will of his poor Neighbour, for not
worshipping, or not flattering him, and thus, when we might be happy and
quiet, we create trouble to our selves. I have heard of a man, that was
angry with himself because he was no taller, and of a Woman, that broke
her* Looking-glass *because it would not shew her face to be as young and
handsom as her next Neighbours was. And, I knew another, to whom God
had given health, and plenty, but, a Wife that nature had made peevish,
and, her Husbands riches had made* Purse-proud, *and must because she
was rich (and for no other vertue) sit in the highest Pew in the Church:
which being denied her, she engag'd her Husband into a contention for it,
and at last, into a Law-suit with a dogged Neighbour, who was as rich as*

he, and, had a Wife as peevish and Purse-proud *as the other: and this Law suit, begot higher oppositions, and actionable words, and more vexations, and Law-suits: for you must remember that both were rich, and must therefore have their wills. Well, this wilful* Purse-proud *Law-suit lasted during the life of the first Husband: after which his wife vext, and chid, and chid and vext, till she also chid and vext herself into her grave, and so the wealth of these poor rich people was curst into a punishment, because they wanted meek and thankful hearts; for those only can make us happy. I knew a man that had health and riches, and several houses all beautiful and ready furnisht, and would often trouble himself and Family to be removing from one house to another; and being ask'd by a friend, why he remov'd so often from one house to another? replyed,* it was to find content in some one of them: *but, his friend knowing his temper, told him, if he would find content in any of his houses, he must leave himself behind him; for, content will never dwell but in a meek and quiet soul. And this may appear if we read and consider what our Saviour says in St.* Matthews *Gospel:* for he there says,* —— Blessed be the merciful for they shall obtain mercy. —— Blessed be the pure in heart; for they shall see God. —— Blessed be the poor in Spirit; for theirs is the Kingdom of Heaven. *And* —— blessed be the meek; for they shall possess the earth.—— *not that the* meek *shall not also obtain mercy, and see God, and be comforted, and at last come to the Kingdom of Heaven; but in the mean time he (and he only) possesses the earth as he goes toward that Kingdom of Heaven, by being humble and cheerful, and content with what his good God has allotted him: he has no turbulent, repining, vexatious thoughts that he deserves better: nor is vext when he sees others possest of more honour or more riches than his wise God has allotted for his share; but he possesses what he has with a meek and contented quietness: such a quietness as makes his very dreams pleasing both to God and himself.*

My honest Scholar, all this is told to incline you to thankfulness; and to incline you the more, let me tell you, that though the Prophet David *was guilty of* Murder *and* Adultery, *and many other of the most deadly sins; yet he was said to be* a man after Gods own heart,* *because he abounded more with thankfulness than any other that is mentioned in holy Scripture, as may appear in his book of Psalms; where there is such a Commixture of his confessing of his sins and unworthiness, and such thankfulness for Gods pardon and mercies, as did make him to be accounted even by God himself, to be* a man after his own heart, *and let us in that, labour to be as like him as we can; let not the blessings we receive daily*

*from God, make us not to value, or not praise him because they be common;
let not us forget to praise him for the innocent mirth and pleasure, we have
met with since we met together, what would a blind man give to see the
pleasant Rivers and meadows and flowers and fountains, that we have met
with since we met together? I have been told, that if a man that was born
blind could obtain to have his sight for but only one hour, during his whole
life, and should at the first opening of his eyes, fix his sight upon the Sun
when it was in his full glory, either at the rising or setting of it; he would
be so transported, and amased, and so admire the glory of it, that he would
not willingly turn his eyes from that first ravishing object, to behold all the
other various beauties this world could present to him. And this, and many
other like blessings we enjoy daily; and for most of them, because they be
so common, most men forget to pay their praises but let not us, because it is
a Sacrifice so pleasing to him that made that Sun, and us, and still protects
us, and gives us flowers and showers and stomachs and meat and content
and leasure to go a fishing.*

*Well Scholar, I have almost tir'd my self, and I fear more than almost
tir'd you: but I now see* Tottenham High-Cross,* *and our short walk
thither shall put a period to my too long discourse, in which, my meaning
was, and is, to plant that in your mind, with which I labour to possess my
own Soul: that is, a meek and thankful heart. And, to that end, I have
shew'd you, that riches without them, do not make any man happy. But
let me tell you, that riches with them remove many fears, and cares, and
therefore my advice is, that you* endeavour to be honestly rich; or, con-
tentedly poor: but, be sure, that your riches be justly got, or you spoil
all. For, *it is well said by* Caussin,* he that loses his Conscience, has
nothing left that is worth keeping. *Therefore be sure you look to that.
And, in the next place, look to your health: and if you have it praise God,
and value it next to a good Conscience; for, health is the second blessing
that we Mortals are capable of: a blessing, that mony cannot buy, and
therefore value it, and be thankful for it. As for money (which may be
said to be the third blessing) neglect it not: but note, that there is no necessity of being rich: for I told you,* there be as many miseries beyond
riches as on this side them: *and, if you have a competence, enjoy it with
a meek, chearful, thankful heart. I will tell you Scholar, I have heard a
grave Divine** say, that* God has two dwellings; one in Heaven; and,
the other in a meek and thankful heart. *Which Almighty God grant to
me, and to my honest Scholar: and so, you are welcom to* Tottenham
High-Cross.

Venat. Well Master, I thank you for all your good directions, but, for none more than this last of thankfulness, which I hope I shall never forget. And pray let's now rest our selves in this sweet shady Arbour, which nature her self has woven with her own fine fingers; 'tis such a contexture of *Woodbines, Sweetbrier, Jessamine*, and *Mirtle*; and so interwoven, as will secure us both from the Suns violent heat; and from the approaching shower, and being sate down I will requite a part of your courtesies with a bottle of *Sack*,* *Milk, Oranges*, and *Sugar*; which all put together, make a drink like *Nectar*,* indeed too good for any body but us *Anglers*: and so Master, here is a full glass to you of that liquor, and when you have pledged me,* I will repeat the Verses* which I promised you; it is a Copy printed amongst some of Sir *Henry Wottons*: and doubtless made either by him, or by a lover of Angling: Come Master, now drink a glass to me, and then I will pledge you, and fall to my repetition; it is a description of such *Country-Recreations* as I have enjoyed since I had the happiness to fall into your company.

> *Quivering* fears, *heart-tearing* cares,
> *Anxious* sighs, *untimely* tears,
>   *Flye, flye to* Courts,
>   *Flye to fond worldlings sports*
> *Where strain'd Sardonick smiles are glosing** still,*
> *And* grief *is forc'd to* laugh *against her will.*
>   *Where mirth's but mummery,**
>   *And sorrows only real be.*
>
> *Fly from our Country*-pastimes, *fly,*
> *Sad troops of humane** misery,*
>   *Come serene looks,*
>   *Clear as the chrystal Brooks,*
> *Or the pure azur'd heaven that smiles to see*
> *The rich attendance on our poverty;*
>   *Peace and a secure mind,*
>   *Which all men seek, we only find.*
>
> *Abused* Mortals, *did you know*
> *Where* joy, hearts-ease *and* comforts *grow?*
>   *You'd scorn proud Towers,*
>   *And seek them in these Bowers,*

Where winds *sometimes our woods perhaps may shake,*
But blustring care *could never tempest make,*
    Nor murmurs ere come nigh us,
    Saving, of fountains that glide by us.

Here's no fantastick Mask* nor Dance,
But of our Kids that frisk and prance;
    Nor wars *are seen,*
    Unless upon the green
Two harmless Lambs *are butting one the other,*
Which done, both bleating run each to his Mother.
    And wounds are never found,
    Save what the plough-share gives the ground.

Here are no entrapping baits
To hasten too, too hasty fates,
    Unless it be
    The fond credulity
Of silly fish, which (worldling like) still look
Upon the bait, but never on the hook:
    Nor envy, 'nless among
    The birds for price of their sweet song.

Go, let the diving Negro *seek*
For Gems hid in some forlorn creek:
    We all pearls scorn,
    Save what the dewy morn
Congeals upon each little spire of grass,
Which careless shepherds beat down as they pass:
    And gold ne're here appears,
    Save what the yellow Ceres* *bears.*

Blest silent groves, oh may you be
For ever mirths best nursery!
    May pure contents
    For ever pitch their tents
Upon these downs, *these* meads, *these* rocks, *these* mountains,
    And Peace still slumber by these purling fountains:
    Which we may every year
    Meet when we come a fishing here.

Pisc. Trust me (Scholar) I thank you heartily for these Verses, they be choicely good, and doubtless made by a lover of Angling: Come, now, drink a glass to me, and I will requite you with another very good Copy: it is a Farewell to the vanities of the World, and some say written by Sir *Harry Wotton,** who I told you was an excellent Angler. But let them be writ by whom they will, he that writ them had a brave soul, and must needs be possest with happy thoughts at the time of their composure:

> *Farewell ye gilded follies, pleasing troubles;*
> *Farewell ye honour'd rags, ye glorious bubbles:*
> *Fame's but a hollow eccho, Gold, pure clay;*
> *Honour the darling but of one short day.*
> *Beauty (th' eyes idol) but a damask'd skin;**
> *State but a golden prison, to live in*
> *And torture free-born minds: embroydred Trains*
> *Meerly but pageants for proud swelling veins:*
> *And Blood Ally'd to Greatness is alone*
> *Inherited, not purchas'd, nor our own.*
> > *Fame, Honour, Beauty, State, Train, Blood and Birth*
> > *Are but the fading Blossoms of the earth.*

> *I would be* great, *but that the Sun doth still*
> *Level his rayes against the rising hill:*
> *I would be* high, *but see the proudest Oak*
> *Most subject to the rending Thunder-stroak:*
> *I would be* rich, *but see men (too unkind)*
> *Dig in the bowels of the richest mind:*
> *I would be* wise, *but that I often see*
> *The Fox suspected, whilst the Ass goes free:*
> *I would be* fair, *but see the fair and proud,*
> *(Like the bright Sun) oft setting in a cloud:*
> *I would be* poor, *but know the humble grass*
> *Still trampled on by each unworthy Ass:*
> Rich *hated:* wise *suspected:* scorn'd if *poor:*
> Great *fear'd:* fair *tempted:* high *still envi'd more:*
> > *I have wish'd all; but now I wish for neither;*
> > *Great, high, rich, wise, nor* fair; *poor Ile be rather.*

> *Would the world now adopt me for her* heir?
> *Would Beauties Queen entitle me the* Fair?

Fame speak me Fortunes Minion? *could I vie*
Angels with India,* *with a speaking eye*
Command bare heads, bow'd knees, strike Justice dumb
As well as blind and lame, or give a tongue
To stones by Epitaphs: be call'd great Master
In the loose Rhimes of every Poetaster?
Could I be more than any man that lives,
Great, fair, rich, wise all in Superlatives:
Yet I more freely would these gifts resign,
Then ever fortune would have made them mine,
   And hold one minute of this holy leasure
   Beyond the riches of this empty pleasure.

Welcome pure thoughts, welcome ye silent Groves,
These guests, these courts my soul most dearly loves:
Now the wing'd people of the skie shall sing
My chearful Anthems to the gladsom Spring:
A Pray'r-Book *now, shall be my looking-glass,*
In which I will adore sweet Vertue's face.
Here dwell no hateful looks, no Palace cares,
No broken Vows dwell here, nor pale-fac'd Fears:
Then here I'le sit, and sigh my hot loves folly,
And learn t'affect an holy melancholy,
   And if Contentment be a stranger then,
   I'le ne're look for it, but in heaven agen.

Venat. Well Master! these Verses be worthy to keep a room in
every mans memory. I thank you for them; and I thank you for your
many instructions, which (God willing) I will not forget: and as St.
*Austin** in his Confessions (*book* 4. *chap.* 3.) commemorates the kindness of his friend *Verecundus*, for lending him and his companion a
Country-house, because there they rested and enjoyed themselves free
from the troubles of the world; so, having had the like advantage,
both by your conversation, and the Art you have taught me, I ought
ever to do the like: for indeed, your company and discourse have been
so useful and pleasant, that I may truly say, *I have only lived since I*
enjoyed them, and turned Angler, and not before. Nevertheless, here I
must part with you, here in this now sad place where I was so happy
as first to meet you: But I shall long for the ninth of *May*, for then I

hope again to enjoy your beloved company at the appointed time and place.* And now I wish for some *somniferous potion*, that might force me to sleep away the intermitted time, which will pass away with me as tediously, as it does with men in sorrow; nevertheless I will make it as short as I can by my *hopes* and *wishes*. And my good Master, I will not forget the doctrine which you told me *Socrates** taught his Scholars, *That they should not think to be honoured so much for being* Philosophers, *as to honour* Philosophy *by their vertuous lives*. You advised me to the like concerning *Angling*, and I will endeavour to do so, and to live like those many *worthy men*, of which you made mention in the former part of your discourse. This is my firm resolution; and as a pious man advised his friend, *That to beget* Mortification *he should frequent* Churches; *and view* Monuments, *and* Charnel-houses, *and then and there consider, how many dead bones time had pil'd up at the gates of death*. So when I would beget *content*, and increase confidence in the *Power*, and *Wisdom*, and *Providence* of Almighty God, I will walk the *Meadows* by some gliding stream, and there contemplate the *Lillies* that take no care,* and those very many other various little living *creatures*, that are not only created but fed (man knows not how) by the goodness of the God of *Nature*, and therefore trust in him. This is my purpose: and so, *Let every thing that hath breath praise the Lord*.* And let the blessing of St. *Peters* Master be with mine.

Pisc. And upon all that are lovers of *Vertue*; and dare trust in his *providence*, and be *quiet*, and go a *Angling*.

Study to be quiet, 1 Thes. 4. 11.

FINIS.

THE
COMPLEAT ANGLER.

Being Instructions how to angle for a
TROUT or GRAYLING in a clear
Stream.

PART. II.

*Qui mihi non credit, faciat licet ipse periclum:
Et fuerit scriptis æquior ille meis.*

LONDON,
Printed for *Richard Marriott*, and *Henry Brome*
in St. *Paul's* Church-yard. MDCLXXVI.

TO
My most Worthy
FATHER* and FRIEND,
MR. IZAAK WALTON
The Elder.

SIR,

Being* you were pleased some years past, to grant me your free leave to do what I have here attempted; and observing, you never retract any promise when made in favour even of your meanest friends; I accordingly expect to see these following particular Directions for the taking of a Trout, *to wait upon your better and more general Rules for all sorts of* Angling: *And, though mine be neither so perfect, so well digested,* nor indeed so handsomely coucht* as they might have been, in so long a time as since your leave was granted; yet, I dare affirm them to be generally true: And they had appeared too in something a neater dress, but that I was surpriz'd with the suddain news of a suddain new Edition* of your* Compleat Angler; *so that, having but a little more than ten days time to turn me in, and rub up my memory (for in truth I have not in all this long time, though I have often thought on't, and almost as often resolv'd to go presently about it) I was forc't upon the instant to scribble what I here present you: which I have also endeavour'd to accommodate to your own Method. And, if mine be clear enough for the honest Brothers of the Angle readily to understand; (which is the only thing I aim at) then I have my end; and shall need to make no further Apology; a writing of this kind, not requiring (if I were Master of any such thing) any Eloquence to set it off, or recommend it; so that if you, in your better Judgment, or kindness rather, can allow it passable for a thing of this nature; You will then do me honour if the* Cypher* *fixt and carv'd in the front of my little fishing-house may be here explained: And, to permit me to attend you in publick, who in private, have ever been, am, and ever resolve to be*

Sir,

Your most affectionate

Son and Servant

Berisford* 10th. of *March* 167⅚.*

Charles Cotton.

THE COMPLEAT ANGLER;

OR,

The Contemplative Man's Recreation.

PART. II.

CHAP. I.

*Piscator Junior & Viator.**

PISCAT. You are happily overtaken Sir; may a man be so bold as to enquire how far you travel this way?

Viator. Yes sure Sir very freely; though it be a question I cannot very well resolve you; as not knowing my self how far it is to *Ashborn,** where I intend to night to take up my Inn.

Piscat. Why then Sir, seeing I perceive you to be a Stranger in these parts; I shall take upon me to inform you, that from the Town you last came through, call'd *Brelsford,** it is five miles, and you are not yet above half a mile on this side.

Viat. So much! I was told it was but ten miles from *Derby,* and methinks I have rode almost so far already.

Piscat. O Sir, find no fault with large measure of good Land, which *Derby-shire* abounds in, as much as most Counties of *England.*

Viat. It may be so, and good Land I confess affords a pleasant prospect: but by your good leave Sir, large measure of foul way is not altogether so acceptable.

Piscat. True Sir, but the foul way serves to justifie the fertility of the soyl; according to the Proverb: *There is good Land, where there is foul way*; and is of good use to inform you of the Riches of the Country you are come into, and of its continual Travel, and Traffick to the Country Town you came from; which is also very observable by the fullness of its Road, and the loaden Horses you meet every where upon the way.

Viat. Well Sir, I will be content to think as well of your Country, as you would desire, and I shall have a great deal of reason both to think, and to speak very well of you, if I may obtain the happiness of your company to the forementioned place, provided your affairs lead you that way, and that they will permit you to slack your pace out of complacency to a Traveller utterly a Stranger in these parts, and who am still to wander further out of my own knowledg.

Piscat. Sir, you invite me to my own advantage, and I am ready to attend you: my way lying through that Town; but my business, that is, my home, some miles beyond it: however I shall have time enough to lodg you in your Quarters, and afterwards to perform my own Journey. In the mean time may I be so bold as to enquire the end of your Journey.

Viat. 'Tis into *Lancashire* Sir, and about some business of concern to a near Relation of mine: for I assure you, I do not use to take so long Journeys, as from *Essex* upon the single account of pleasure.

Piscat. From thence Sir! I do not then wonder you should appear dissatisfied with the length of the Miles, and the foulness of the way: though I am sorry you should begin to quarrel with them so soon; for, believe me Sir, you will find the Miles much longer, and the way much worse before you come to your Journies end.

Viat. Why truly Sir for that, I am prepar'd to expect the worst; but methinks the way is mended since I had the good fortune to fall into your good company.

Piscat. You are not oblig'd to my company for that: but because you are already past the worst, and the greatest part of your way to your Lodging.

Viat. I am very glad to hear it, both for the ease of my self, and my Horse; but especially because I may then expect a freer enjoyment of your conversation; though the shortness of the way will, I fear, make me lose it the sooner.

Piscat. That Sir is not worth your care; and I am sure you deserve much better, for being content with so ill company: but we have already talkt away two Miles of your Journey; for from the Brook before us, that runs at the foot of this Sandy Hill, you have but three Miles to *Ashborn*.

Viat. I meet every where in this Country with these little Brooks, and they look as if they were full of Fish; have they not Trouts in them?

Piscat. That is a question, which is to be excus'd in a Stranger as you are; otherwise, give me leave to tell you, it would seem a kind of affront to our Country, to make a doubt of what we pretend to be famous for, next, if not before, our Malt, Wool, Lead, and Cole; for you are to understand, that we think we have as many fine Rivers, Rivulets, and Brooks, as any Country whatever, and they are all full of Trouts, and some of them the best (it is said) by many degrees in *England*.

Viat. I was first Sir in love with you, and now shall be so enamour'd of your Country by this account you give me of it, as to wish my self a *Derby-shire* Man, or at least that I might live in it: for you must know I am a pretender to the Angle, and doubtless a Trout affords the most pleasure to the Angler, of any sort of Fish whatever; and the best Trouts, must needs make the best sport: But this Brook, and some others I have met with upon this way, are too full of Wood for that recreation.

Piscat. This Sir! why this, and several others like it, which you have past, and some that you are like to pass, have scarce any name amongst us: but we can shew you as fine Rivers, and as clear from wood, or any other encumbrance to hinder an Angler, as any you ever saw; and for clear, beautiful streams, *Hantshire* it self, by Mr. *Izaak Walton's* good leave,* can shew none such; nor I think any Country in *Europe*.

Viat. You go far Sir in the praise of your Country Rivers, and I perceive have read Mr. *Walton's Compleat Angler* by your naming of *Hantshire*, and I pray what is your opinion of that Book?

Piscat. My Opinion of Mr. *Walton's* Book is the same with every Man's, that understands any thing of the Art of Angling, that it is an excellent good one, and that the forementioned Gentleman understands as much of Fish, and Fishing as any Man living: but I must tell you further, that I have the happiness to know his person, and to be intimately acquainted with him, and in him to know the worthiest Man, and to enjoy the best, and the truest Friend any Man ever had: nay, I shall yet acquaint you further, that he gives me leave to call him Father, and I hope is not yet asham'd to own me for his adopted Son.

Viat. In earnest Sir I am ravisht to meet with a friend of Mr. *Izaak Walton's*, and one that does him so much right in so good and true a Character; for I must boast to you, that I have the good fortune to know him too, and came acquainted with him much after the same

manner I do with you; that he was my Master who first taught me to
love Angling, and then to become an Angler; and to be plain with
you, I am the very Man decipher'd in his Book under the name of
Venator, for I was wholly addicted to the Chace; till he taught me as
good, a more quiet, innocent, and less dangerous diversion.

Piscat. Sir, I think my self happy in your acquaintance, and before
we part shall entreat leave to embrace you; you have said enough to
recommend you to my best opinion; for my Father *Walton* will be
seen twice in no Man's company he does not like, and likes none but
such as he believes to be very honest men, which is one of the best
Arguments, or at least of the best Testimonies I have, that I either
am, or that he thinks me one of those, seeing I have not yet found him
weary of me.

Viat. You speak like a true Friend, and in doing so render your self
worthy of his friendship. May I be so bold as to ask your name?

Piscat. Yes surely Sir, and if you please a much nicer* question,
my name is —— and I intend to stay long enough in your company,
if I find you do not dislike mine, to ask yours too. In the mean time,
because we are now almost at *Ashborn*, I shall freely, and bluntly tell
you, that I am a Brother of the Angle too, and peradventure can
give you some instructions how to Angle for a Trout in a clear
River, that my Father *Walton* himself will not disapprove, though
he did either purposely omit, or did not remember them, when you,
and he sate discoursing under the *Sycamore* Tree.* And being you
have already told me whether* your Journey is intended, and that I
am better acquainted with the Country than you are; I will heartily,
and earnestly entreat, you will not think of staying at this Town:
but go on with me six Miles further to my House, where you shall
be extreamly welcom; it is directly in your way, we have day enough
to perform our Journey, & as you like your entertainment, you may
there repose your self a day or two; or as many more as your occa-
sions will permit, to recompence the trouble of so much a longer
Journey.

Viat. Sir, you surprise me with so friendly an invitation upon so
short acquaintance: but how advantagious soever it would be to me,
and that my hast perhaps is not so great, but it might dispense with
such a divertisement* as I promise my self in your Company; yet I
cannot in modesty accept your offer, & must therefore beg your
pardon: I could otherwise, I confess, be glad to wait upon you, if

upon no other account but to talk of Mr. *I. Walton*, and to receive those instructions you say you are able to give me for the deceiving a Trout; in which art I will not deny, but that I have an ambition to be one of the greatest deceivers; though I cannot forbear freely to tell you, that I think it hard to say much more, than has been read to me upon that subject.

Piscat. Well Sir, I grant that too; but you must know that the variety of Rivers, require different ways of Angling: however you shall have the best Rules I am able to give, and I will tell you nothing I have not made my self as certain of, as any Man can be in thirty years experience (for so long I have been a dabler in that art) and that if you please to stay a few days, you shall not in a very great measure see made good to you. But of that hereafter, and now, Sir, if I am not mistaken I have half overcome you; and that I may wholly conquer that modesty of yours, I will take upon me to be so familiar as to say, you must accept my invitation, which that you may the more easily be perswaded to do, I will tell you that my House stands upon the margin of one of the finest Rivers for Trouts, and grayling in *England*; that I have lately built a little Fishing House upon it, dedicated to Anglers, over the door of which you will see the two first Letters of my Father *Walton's* name and mine twisted in *Cypher*;[1]* that you shall lye in the same Bed he has sometimes been con- [1] *as in the* tented with, and have such Country entertainment, as my *Title page.* Friends sometimes accept, and be as welcome too, as the best Friend of them all.

Viat. No doubt Sir, but my Master *Walton* found good reason to be satisfied with his entertainment in your House; for you who are so friendly to a meer Stranger who deserves so little, must needs be exceedingly kind and free to him who deserves so much.

Piscat. Believe me, no! and such as are intimately acquainted with that Gentleman, know him to be a Man, who will not endure to be treated like a Stranger. So that his acceptation of my poor entertainments, has ever been a pure effect of his own humility, and good nature, and nothing else. But Sir, we are now going down the Spittle Hill* into the Town, and therefore let me importune you suddainly to resolve, and most earnestly not to deny me.

Viat. In truth Sir, I am so overcome by your Bounty, that I find I cannot, but must render my self wholly to be dispos'd by you.

Piscat. Why that's heartily, and kindly spoken, and I as heartily thank you; and being you have abandon'd your self to my conduct, we will only call and drink a glass on Horseback at the *Talbot*,* and away.

Viat. I attend you, but what pretty River is this, that runs under this Stone-Bridg? has it a name?

Piscat. Yes, 'Tis call'd *Henmore*, and has in it both Trout, and Grayling; but you will meet with one or two better anon. And so soon as we are past through the Town, I will endeavour by such discourse as best likes you to pass away the time, till you come to your ill Quarters.

Viat. We can talk of nothing with which I shall be more delighted than of Rivers and Angling.

Piscat. Let those be the Subjects then, but we are now come to the *Talbot*, what will you drink Sir, Ale, or Wine?

Viat. Nay, I am for the Country liquor, *Derby-shire* Ale, if you please; for a Man should not methinks come from *London* to drink Wine in the Peak.*

Piscat. You are in the right; and yet let me tell you, you may drink worse *French-wine* in many Taverns in *London*, than they have sometimes at this House. What hoe! bring us a Flaggon of your best Ale, and now Sir my service to you, a good health to the honest Gentleman you know of, and you are welcome into the Peak.

Viat. I thank you Sir, and present you my service again, and to all the honest Brothers of the Angle.

Piscat. I'le pledg you Sir, so, there's for your Ale, and farewell. Come Sir, let us be going; for the sun grows low, and I would have you look about you as you ride; for you will see an odd Country, and sights, that will seem strange to you.

CHAP. II.

PISCAT. So Sir, now we are got to the top of the Hill out of Town, look about you, and tell me how you like the Country.

Viat. Bless me! what Mountains are here! are we not in *Wales*?

Piscat. No, but in almost as Mountainous a Country, and yet these Hills though high, bleak, and craggy, breed and feed good Beef, and Mutton above ground, and afford good store of Lead within.

Viat. They had need of all those commodities to make amends for the ill Land-schape:* But I hope our way does not lye over any of these; for I dread a *precipice*.

Piscat. Believe me but it does, and down one especially, that will appear a little terrible to a Stranger: though the way is passable enough, and so passable, that we who are Natives of these Mountains, and acquainted with them, disdain to alight.

Viat. I hope though that a Forraigner is priviledged to use his own discretion, and that I may have the liberty to entrust my neck to the fidelity of my own feet, rather than to those of my Horse; for I have no more at home.

Piscat. 'Twere hard else. But in the mean time I think 'twere best while this way is pretty even, to mend our pace, that we may be past that Hill I speak of, to the end your apprehension may not be doubled for want of light to discern the easiness of the descent.

Viat. I am willing to put forward* as fast as my Beast will give me leave; though I fear nothing in your Company. But what pretty River is this we are going into?

Piscat. Why this Sir is called *Bently* Brook, and is full of very good Trout, and Grayling; but so encumbred with wood in many places, as is troublesom to an Angler.

Viat. Here are the prettiest Rivers, and the most of them in this Country that ever I saw; do you know how many you have in the Country?

Piscat. I know them all, and they were not hard to reckon, were it worth the trouble; but the most considerable of them I will presently name you. And to begin where we now are (for you must know we are now upon the very skirts of *Derby-shire*) we have first the River *Dove*, that we shall come to by and by, which divides the two Counties of *Derby*, and *Stafford* for many Miles together, and is so call'd from the swiftness of its current,* and that swiftness occasion'd by the declivity of its course, and by being so straitned in that course betwixt the Rocks; by which, and those very high ones, it is hereabout for four, or five Miles confin'd into a very narrow stream. A River that from a contemptible Fountain (which I can cover with my Hat) by the confluence of other Rivers, Rivulets, Brooks, and Rills, is swell'd, (before it fall into *Trent* a little below *Egginton*, where it loses the name), to such a breadth, and depth, as to be in most places navigable, were not the passage frequently interrupted with Fords, and Wires,* and has as fertile Bancks, as any River in *England*, none excepted. And this River from its head for a Mile or two is a black water (as all the rest of the *Derby-shire* Rivers of note, originally are, for they all spring from the Mosses) but is in a few Miles travel so clarified by the addition of several clear, and very great springs (bigger than it self) which gush out of the Lime-stone Rocks, that before it comes to my House, which is but six, or seven Miles from its source, you will find it one of the purest Chrystalline streams you have seen.

Viat. Does *Trent* spring in these parts?

Piscat. Yes in these parts; not in this County, but somewhere towards the upper end of *Stafford-shire*, I think not far from a place call'd *Trentham*,* and thence runs down not far from *Stafford* to *Wolsly* Bridg, and washing the skirts and purlews* of the Forrest of *Needwood** runs down to *Burton* in the same County; thence it comes into this where we now are, and running by *Swarkston*, and *Dunnington*,* receives *Derwent* at *Wildon*,* and so to *Nottingham*, thence to *Newark*, and by *Gainsborough*, to *Kingston* upon *Hull*, where it takes the name of *Humber*, and thence falls into the Sea: but that the Map will best inform you.

Viat. Know you whence this River *Trent* derives its name?*

Piscat. No indeed, and yet I have heard it often discourst upon, when some have given its denomination from the forenamed *Trentham*; though that seems rather a derivative from it; others have said 'tis so call'd from thirty Rivers that fall into it, and there lose their names, which cannot be neither, because it carries that name from its very Fountain, before any other Rivers fall into it; others derive it from thirty several sorts of Fish that breed there, and that is the most likely derivation: But be it how it will, it is doubtless one of the finest Rivers in the World, and the most abounding with excellent Salmon, and all sorts of delicate Fish.

Viat. Pardon me Sir for tempting you into this digression, and then proceed to your other Rivers; for I am mightily delighted with this discourse.

Piscat. It was no interruption, but a very seasonable question; for *Trent* is not only one of our *Derby-shire* Rivers, but the chief of them, and into which all the rest pay the Tribute of their names; which I had perhaps forgot to insist upon, being got to the other end of the County, had you not awoke my memory. But I will now proceed, and the next River of note (for I will take them as they lye Eastward from us) is the River *Wye*; I say of note, for we have two lesser betwixt us and it, namely *Lathkin*, and *Bradford*,* of which *Lathkin* is by many degrees the purest, and most transparent stream, that I ever yet saw either at home or abroad, and breeds 'tis said, the reddest, and the best Trouts in *England*; but neither of these are to be reputed Rivers, being no better than great springs. The River *Wye* then has its source near unto *Buxtons*, a Town some ten Miles from hence, famous for a warm Bath,* and which you are to ride through in your way to *Manchester*, a black water too at the Fountain; but by the same reason with *Dove*, becomes very soon a most delicate clear River, and breeds admirable Trout, and Grayling, reputed by those, who, by living upon its Banks are partial to it, the best of any, and this, running down by *Ashford*, *Bakewell*, and *Haddon*; at a Town a little lower call'd *Rowsly* falls into *Derwent*, and there loses its name. The next in order is *Derwent* a black water too, and that not only from its Fountain, but quite through its progress, not having these Chrystal springs to wash and cleanse it, which the two forementioned have; but abounds with Trout and Grayling (such as they are) towards its source, and with *Salmon* below; and this River from the upper and utmost part of this County, where it springs, taking its course by *Chatsworth*, *Darly*, *Matlock*, *Derby*, *Burrow-Ash*, and *Awberson*,* falls into *Trent* at a place call'd *Wildon*, and there loses its name. The East side of this County of *Derby* is bounded by little inconsiderable Rivers, as *Awber*,* *Eroways*,* and the like, scarce worth naming, but Trouty* too, and further we are not to enquire. But Sir I have carried you, as a Man may say by water,* till we are now come to the descent of the formidable Hill I told you of, at the foot of which runs the River *Dove*, which I cannot but love above all the rest, and therefore prepare your self to be a little frighted.

Viat. Sir, I see you would fortifie me, that I should not shame my self: but I dare follow where you please to lead me, and I see no danger yet; for the descent methinks is thus far green, even, and easy.

Pisc. You will like it worse presently when you come to the brow of the Hill, and now we are there, what think you?

Viat. What do I think? why I think it the strangest place that ever sure Men, and Horses went down, and that (if there be any safety at all) the safest way is to alight.

Pisc. I think so too for you, who are mounted upon a Beast not acquainted with these slippery stones; and though I frequently ride down, I will alight too to bear you company, and to lead you the way, and if you please my Man shall lead your Horse.

Viat. Marry Sir, and thank you too, for I am afraid I shall have enough to do to look to my self; and with my Horse in my hand should be in a double fear, both of breaking my neck, and my Horse's falling on me, for it is as steep as a penthouse.*

Pisc. To look down from hence it appears so, I confess, but the path winds and turns, and will not be found so troublesom.

Viat. Would I were well down though! Hoist thee! there's one fair scape!* these stones are so slippery I cannot stand! yet again! I think I were best lay my heeles in my neck, and tumble down.*

Pisc. If you think your heeles will defend your neck, that is the way to be soon at the bottom; but give me your hand at this broad stone, and then the worst is past.

Viat. I thank you Sir, I am now past it, I can go my self. What's here the sign* of a Bridg? Do you use to Travel with wheel-barrows in this Country?

Pisc. Not that I ever saw Sir, why do you ask that question?

Viat. Because this Bridg certainly was made for nothing else; why a mouse can hardly go over it: 'Tis not two fingers broad.

Pisc. You are pleasant, and I am glad to see you so: but I have rid over the Bridg many a dark night.

Viat. Why according to the *French* proverb, and 'tis a good one among a great many of worse sense and sound that language abounds in, *Ce que Diu garde, est bien gardé.* They, whom God takes care of are in safe protection: but, let me tell you, I would not ride over it for a thousand pounds, nor fall off it for two; and yet I think I dare venture on foot, though if you were not by to laugh at me, I should do it on all four.

Pisc. Well Sir, your mirth becomes you, and I am glad to see you safe over, and now you are welcome into *Stafford-shire.*

Viat. How *Stafford-shire*! what do I there trow!* there is not a word of *Stafford-shire* in all my direction.*

Pisc. You see you are betray'd into it; but it shall be in order to something that will make amends; and 'tis but an ill Mile or two out of your way.

Viat. I believe all things Sir, and doubt nothing. Is this your beloved River *Dove*? 'Tis clear, and swift indeed, but a very little one.

Pisc. You see it here at the worst; we shall come to it anon again after two Miles riding, and so near as to lye upon the very Banks.

Viat. Would we were there once; but I hope we have no more of these Alpes to pass over.

Pisc. No, no Sir, only this ascent before you, which you see is not very uneasy, and then you will no more quarrel with your way.

Viat. Well, if ever I come to *London* (of which many a Man there, if he were in my place would make a question), I will sit down and write my Travels, and like *Tom Coriate** print them at my own charge. Pray what do you call this Hill we come* down?

Pisc. We call it *Hanson Toot*.

Viat. Why farewell *Hanson Toot*, I'le no more on thee; I'le go twenty Miles about first. Puh. I sweat, that my shirt sticks to my back.

Pisc. Come Sir, now we are up the Hill, and now how do you?

Viat. Why very well I humbly thank you Sir, and warm enough I assure you. What have we here, a Church!* As I'm an honest Man a very pretty Church! Have you Churches in this Country Sir?

Pisc. You see we have: but had you seen none, why should you make that doubt Sir?

Viat. Why, if you will not be angry, I'le tell you, I thought my self a Stage,* or two beyond *Christendom*.

Pisc. Come, come, wee'l reconcile you to our Country before we part with you; if shewing you good sport with Angling will do't.

Viat. My respect to you, and that together may do much Sir; otherwise, to be plain with you, I do not find my self much inclin'd that way.

Pisc. Well Sir, your raillery upon our Mountains has brought us almost home; and look you where the same River of *Dove* has again met us to bid you welcome, and to invite you to a dish of Trouts to morrow.

Viat. Is this the same we saw at the foot of *Penmen-Maure*?* It is much a finer River here.

Pisc. It will appear yet much finer to morrow. But look you Sir here appears the House,* that is now like to be your Inn, for want of a better.

Viat. It appears on a suddain, but not before 'twas lookt for, it stands prettily, and here's wood about it too, but so young, as appears to be of your own planting.

Pisc. It is so, will it please you to alight Sir; and now permit me after all your pains and dangers to take you in my arms, and to assure you, that you are infinitely welcome.

Viat. I thank you Sir, and am glad with all my heart I am here, for, in down right truth, I am exceeding weary.

Pisc. You will sleep so much the better; you shall presently have a light supper, and to bed. Come, Sirs, lay the Cloth,* and bring what you have presently, and let the Gentleman's Bed be made ready in the mean time in my Father *Waltons* Chamber; and now Sir here is my service to you, and once more welcome.

Viat. I marry Sir this glass of good Sack* has refresht me, and I'le make as bold with your meat; for the Trot has got me a good stomach.

Pisc. Come Sir fall to then, you see my little supper is always ready when I come home, and I'le make no Stranger of you.

Viat. That your Meal is so soon ready is a sign your Servants know your certain hours, Sir; I confess I did not expect it so soon; but now 'tis here, you shall see I will make my self no Stranger.

Pisc. Much good do your heart, and I thank you for that friendly word: and now Sir my service to you in a Cup of *More-Lands* Ale: for you are now in the *More-Lands*,* but within a spit, and a stride of the peak;* fill my Friend his Glass.

Viat. Believe me you have good Ale in the *More-Lands*; far better than that at *Ashborn*.

Pisc. That it may soon be: for *Ashborn* has (which is a kind of a Riddle) always in it the best Mault, and the worst Ale in *England*. Come take away, and bring us some pipes, and a bottle of Ale, and go to your own Suppers. Are you for this diet Sir?

Viat. Yes Sir, I am for one pipe of Tobacco; and I perceive yours is very good by the smell.

Pisc. The best I can get in *London* I assure you: But Sir, now you have thus far comply'd with my designs, as to take a troublesom Journey into an ill Country, only to satisfie me; how long may I hope to enjoy you?

Viat. Why truly Sir, as long as I conveniently can; and longer I think you would not have me.

Pisc. Not to your inconvenience by any means Sir, but I see you are weary, and therefore I will presently wait on you to your Chamber, where take Counsel of your pillow, and to morrow resolve me.*

Here take the lights, and pray follow them, Sir; Here you are like to lye, and now I have shew'd you your Lodging, I beseech you command any thing you want, and so I wish you good rest.

Viat. Good night *Sir*.

CHAP. III.

PISC. Good morrow *Sir*, what up and drest so early?

Viat. Yes *Sir*, I have been drest this half hour; for I rested so well, and have so great a mind either to take, or to see a Trout taken in your fine River, that I could no longer lye a bed.

Pisc. I am glad to see you so brisk this morning, and so eager of sport; though I must tell you, this day proves so calm, and the Sun rises so bright, as promises no great success to the Angler: but however we'l try, and one way or other we shall sure do something. What will you have to your breakfast, or what will you drink this Morning?

Viat. For Breakfast I never eat any, and for Drink am very indifferent; but if you please to call for a Glass of Ale,* I'm for you; and let it be quickly if you please: for I long to see the little Fishing-house you spoke of, and to be at my Lesson.

Pisc. Well *Sir*, You see the Ale is come without Calling; for though I do not know yours, my people know my diet, which is always one Glass so soon as I am drest, and no more till Dinner,* and so my Servants have served you.

Viat. My thanks, and now if you please let us look out this fine morning.

Pisc. With all my heart, Boy take the Key of my Fishing-house, and carry down those two Angle-Rods in the Hall window thither, with my Fish-pannier, Pouch, and landing Net, and stay you there till we come. Come *Sir* we'l walk after, where by the way I expect you should raise all the exceptions against our Country you can.

Viat. Nay *Sir*, do not think me so ill natur'd, nor so uncivil, I only made a little bold with it last night to divert you, and was only in jest.

Pisc. You were then in as good earnest as I am now with you: but had you been really angry at it, I could not blame you: For, to say the truth, it is not very taking at first sight: But look you, *Sir*, now you are abroad, does not the Sun shine as bright here as in *Essex, Middlesex,* or *Kent,* or any of your Southern Countries?

Viat. 'Tis a delicate Morning indeed, and I now think this a marvellous pretty place.

Pisc. Whether you think so or no, you cannot oblige me more than to say so; and those of my friends who know my humour, and are so kind as to comply with it, usually flatter me that way. But look you *Sir*, now you are at the brink of the Hill, how do you like my River, the Vale it winds through like a Snake, and the scituation* of my little Fishing-house?

Viat. Trust me 'tis all very fine, and the house seems at this distance a neat building.

Pisc. Good enough for that purpose; and here is a bowling Green* too, close by it, so though I am my self no very good bowler, I am not totally devoted to my own pleasure; but that I have also some regard to other men's. And now *Sir* you are come to the door, pray walk in, and there we will sit, and talk as long as you please.

[1] *There is under this Motto, the Cifer mentioned in the Title Page and some part of the Fishing-house has been describ'd; but, the pleasantness of the River, Mountains, and Meadows about it, cannot; unless Sir Philip Sidney, or Mr. Cotton's Father* were again alive to do it.*

Viat. Stay, what's here over the door? *Piscatoribus sacrum.*[1]* Why then I perceive I have some Title here, for I am one of them, though one of the worst, and here below it is the Cifer too you spoke of, and 'tis prettily contriv'd. Has my Master *Walton* ever been here to see it; for it seems new built?

Pisc. Yes he saw it cut in the stone before it was set up; but never in the posture it now stands: for the house was but building when he was last here, and not rais'd so high as the Arch of the dore, and I am afraid he will not see it yet; for he has lately writ me word he doubts his coming down this Summer, which I do assure you was the worst news he could possibly have sent me.

Viat. Men must sometimes mind their affairs to make more room for their pleasures; and 'tis odds he is as much displeas'd with the business, that keeps him from you, as you are that he comes not. But I am the most pleased with this little house of any thing I ever saw: It stands in a kind of *Peninsula* too, with a delicate clear River about it. I dare hardly go in, lest I should not like it so well within as without; but by your leave, I'le try. Why, this is better and better, fine lights, finely wainscoted, and all exceeding neat, with a Marble Table and all in the middle!

Pisc. Enough, *Sir*, enough, I have laid open to you the part where

I can worst defend my self, and now you attaque me there. Come Boy set two Chairs, and whilst I am taking a Pipe of Tobacco, which is alwaies my Breakfast, we will, if you please, talk of some other Subject.

Viat. None fitter then *Sir* for the time and place, than those Instructions you promis'd.

Pisc. I begin to doubt, by something I discover in you, whether I am able to instruct you, or no; though, if you are really a stranger to our clear *Northern* Rivers I still think I can; and therefore, since it is yet too early in the morning at this time of the year, to day being but the Seventh of *March*, to cast a Flie upon the water, if you will direct me what kind of Fishing for a Trout I shall read you a Lecture on, I am willing and ready to obey you.

Viat. Why *Sir*, if you will so far oblige me, and that it may not be too troublesome to you, I would entreat you would run through the whole body of it; and I will not conceal from you, that I am so far in love with you, your courtesie, and pretty Moreland Seat,* as to resolve to stay with you long enough by Intervals (for I will not oppress you) to hear all you can say upon that Subject.

Pisc. You cannot oblige me more than by such a promise, and therefore without more Ceremony I will begin to tell you; that my Father *Walton* having read to you before, it would look like a pre-sumption in me, and peradventure would do so in any other man, to pretend to give Lessons for angling after him, who I do really believe understands as much of it, at least as any man in *England*, did I not pre-acquaint you, that I am not tempted to it by any vain opinion of my self, that I am able to give you better directions; but having from my Childhood pursued the recreation of angling in very clear Rivers (truly I think by much, some of them at least, the clearest in this Kingdom) and the manner of Angling here with us by reason of that exceeding clearness, being something different from the method commonly us'd in others, which by being not near so bright, admit of stronger tackle, and allow a nearer approach to the stream; I may peradventure give you some Instructions, that may be of use even in your own Rivers, and shall bring you acquainted with more Flies, and shew you how to make them, and with what dubbing too, than he has taken notice of in his *Compleat Angler*.*

Viat. I beseech you *Sir* do, and if you will lend me your Steel,*

I will light a Pipe the while, for that is commonly my Breakfast in a morning too.

CHAP. IV.

PISC. Why then *Sir*, to begin methodically, as a Master in any Art should do (and I will not deny, but that I think my self a Master in this) I shall divide Angling for Trout or Grayling into these three ways,

> *At the Top,*
> *At the bottom, and*
> *In the Middle.*

Which three ways, though they are all of them (as I shall hereafter endeavour to make it appear) in some sort common to both those kinds of Fish; yet are they not so generally and absolutely so, but that they will necessarily require a distinction, which in due place I will also give you.

> *That which we call Angling at the top, is with a Flie;*
> *At the bottom with a ground-bait.*
> *In the middle with a Minnow, or Ground-bait.*

Angling at the Top is of two sorts,

> *With a quick Flie:*
> or,
> *With an artificial Flie.*

That we call Angling at the bottom is also of two sorts,

> *By hand:**
> or,
> *With a Cork, or Float.*

That we call Angling in the middle is also of two sorts.

> *With a Minnow for a Trout:*
> or,
> *With a Ground-bait for a Grayling.*

Of all which several sorts of Angling, I will, if you can have the patience to hear me, give you the best account I can.

Viat. The trouble will be yours, and mine the pleasure and the obligation: I beseech you therefore to proceed.

Pisc. Why then first of Flie-Fishing.

CHAP. V.
Of Flie-Fishing.

PISC. Flie-Fishing or Fishing at the top, is, as I said before, of two sorts,

> *With a natural and living Flie*:
> or,
> *With an artificial and made Flie*.

First then of the natural Flie; of which we generally use but two sorts, and those but in the two months of *May* and *June* only, namely the *Green Drake*, and the *Stone-Flie*;* though I have made use of a third that way, called the *Chamblet-Flie** with very good success for *Grayling*, but never saw it angled with by any other after this manner, my Master only excepted, who did many years ago, and was one of the best Anglers, that ever I knew.

These are to be angled with, with a short Line, not much more than half the length of your Rod, if the air be still; or with a longer very near, or all out as long as your Rod, if you have any wind to carry it from you, and this way of Fishing we call *Daping, Dabbing* or *Dibling*, wherein you are always to have your Line flying before you up or down the River as the wind serves, and to angle as near as you can to the bank of the same side whereon you stand, though where you see a Fish rise near you, you may guide your quick Flie over him, whether in the middle, or on the contrary side, and if you are pretty well out of sight, either by kneeling, or the Interposition of a bank, or bush, you may almost be sure to raise, and take him too, if it be presently done; the Fish will otherwise peradventure be remov'd to some other place, if it be in the still deeps, where he is always in motion, and roving up and down to look for prey, though in a stream, you may alwaies almost, especially if there be a good stone near, find him in the same place. Your Line ought in this Case to be three good hairs next the hook, both by reason you are in this kind of angling, to expect the biggest Fish, and also that wanting length to give him Line after he is struck, you must be forc't to tugg for't; to which I will also add, that not an Inch of your Line being to be suffered to touch the water in dibbling; it may be allow'd to be the stronger. I should now give you a Description of those Flies, their shape and colour, and then give you an account of their breeding, and withal shew you how to keep and use them; but shall defer that to their proper place and season.

Viat. In earnest, Sir, you discourse very rationally of this affair, and I am glad to find my self mistaken in you; for in plain truth I did not expect so much from you.

Pisc. Nay Sir, I can tell you a great deal more than this, and will conceal nothing from you. But I must now come to the second way of angling at the top, which is with an artificial Flie, which also I will shew you how to make before I have done, but first shall acquaint you, that with this you are to angle with a Line longer by a yard and a half, or sometimes two yards than your Rod, and with both this, and the other in a still day in the streams, in a breeze, that curles the water in the still deeps, where (excepting in *May* and *June*, that the best Trouts will lye in shallow streams to watch for prey, and even then too) you are like to hit the best Fish.

For the length of your Rod you are always to be govern'd by the breadth of the River you shall chuse to angle at; and for a Trout River, one of five or six yards long is commonly enough, and longer (though never so neatly and artificially made) it ought not to be, if you intend to Fish at ease, and if otherwise, where lies the sport?

Of these, the best that ever I saw are made in *York-shire*, which are all of one piece; that is to say, of several, six, eight, ten or twelve pieces, so neatly piec't, and ty'd together with fine thred below, and Silk above, as to make it taper, like a switch,* and to ply with a true bent to your hand; and these are too light, being made of Fir wood, for two or three lengths, nearest to the hand, and of other wood nearer to the top, that a Man might very easily manage the longest of them that ever I saw, with one hand; and these when you have given over Angling for a season, being taken to pieces, and laid up in some dry place, may afterwards be set together again in their former postures, and will be as strait, sound, and good as the first hour they were made, and being laid in* Oyl and colour according to your Master *Waltons* direction,* will last many years.

The length of your line, to a Man that knows how to handle his Rod, and to cast it, is no manner of encumbrance, excepting in woody places, and in landing of a Fish, which every one that can afford to Angle for pleasure, has some body to do for him, and the length of line is a mighty advantage to the fishing at distance; and to fish *fine,** and far off* is the first and principal Rule for Trout Angling.

Your Line in this case should never be less, nor ever exceed two hairs next to the hook, for one (though some I know will pretend to more Art, than their fellows) is indeed too few, the least accident, with the finest hand being sufficient to break it: but he that cannot kill a Trout of twenty inches long with two, in a River clear of wood and weeds, as this and some others of ours are, deserves not the name of an Angler.

Now to have your whole line as it ought to be, two of the first lengths, nearest the hook, should be of two hairs a piece, the next three lengths above them of three, the next three above them of four, and so of five, and six, and seven, to the very top: by which means your Rod and tackle will in a manner be taper* from your very hand to your hook; your line will fall much better and straiter, and cast your Flie to any certain place to which the hand and eye shall direct it, with less weight and violence, that would otherwise circle the water, and fright away the fish.

In casting your line, do it always before you, and so that your flie may first fall upon the water, and as little of your line with it as is possible, though if the wind be stiff, you will then of necessity be compell'd to drown a good part of your line to keep your flie in the water: and in casting your flie, you must aim at the further, or nearer Bank, as the wind serves your turn, which also will be with, and against you on the same side several times in an hour, as the River winds in its course, and you will be forc't to Angle up and down by turns accordingly; but are to endeavour, as much as you can, to have the wind evermore on your back, and always be sure to stand as far off the Bank as your length will give you leave when you throw to the contrary side, though when the wind will not permit you so to do, and that you are constrain'd to Angle on the same side whereon you stand, you must then stand on the very brink of the River, and cast your Flie at the utmost length of your Rod and Line, up or down the River as the gale serves.

It only remains, touching your Line, to enquire whether your two hairs next to the hook, are better twisted, or open; and for that, I should declare that I think the open way the better, because it makes less shew in the water, but that I have found an inconvenience, or two, or three, that have made me almost weary of that way; of which one is, that without dispute they are not so strong open, as twisted;* another, that they are not easily to be fastned of so exact an equal length in the arming, that the one will not cause the other to bagge, by which means a Man has but one hair, upon the matter, to trust to; and the last is, that these loose flying hairs are not only more apt to catch upon every twig, or bent* they meet with; but moreover the hook, in falling upon the water, will very often rebound, and fly back betwixt the hairs, and there stick (which in a rough water especially, is not presently to be discern'd by the Angler) so as the point of the hook shall stand revers't, by which means your Flie swims backward, makes a much greater circle in the water, and till taken home to you, and set right, will never raise any Fish, or if it should, I am sure, but by a very extraordinary chance, can hit none.

Having done with both these ways of fishing at the top, the length of your Rod, and Line and all: I am next to teach you how to make a Flie; and afterwards of what dubbing you are to make the several Flies I shall hereafter name to you.

In making a Flie then (which is not a Hackle* or Palmer Flie for of those, and their several kinds we shall have occasion to speak every Month in the Year) you are first to hold your hook fast betwixt the fore finger and thumb of your left hand, with the back of the shanck upwards, and the point towards your fingers end; then take a strong small silk* of the colour of the Flie you intend to make, wax it well with wax of the same colour too (to which end you are always, by the way, to have wax of all colours about you) and draw it betwixt your finger and thumb, to the head of the shanck, and then whip it twice or thrice about the bare hook, which, you must know, is done, both to prevent slipping, and also that the shanck of the hook may not cut the hairs of your Towght, (which sometimes it will otherwise do) which being done, take your Line, and draw it likewise betwixt your finger and thumb, holding the Hook so fast, as only to suffer it to pass by, untill you have the knot of your Towght almost to the middle of the shanck of your hook, on the inside of it, then whip your silk twice or thrice about both hook and Line, as hard as the strength of the silk will permit, which being done, strip the feather for the wings proportionable to the bigness of your Flie, placing that side downwards, which grew uppermost before, upon the back of the hook, leaving so much only as to serve for the length of the wing of the point of the plume, lying revers't from the end of the shanck upwards, then whip your silk twice, or thrice about the root end of the feather, hook, and towght, which being done clip off the root end of the feather close by the arming, and then whip the silk fast and firm about the hook, and towght untill you come to the bend of the hook: but not further (as you do at *London*; and so make a very unhandsom, and, in plain *English*, a very unnatural and shapeless Flie) which being done, cut away the end of your towght, and fasten it, and then take your dubbing which is to make the body of your Flie, as much as you think convenient, and holding it lightly, with your hook, betwixt the finger, and thumb of your left hand, take your silk with the right, and twisting it betwixt the finger and thumb of that hand, the dubbing will spin it self about the silk, which when it has done, whip it about the arm'd hook* backward, till you come to the setting on of the wings; and then take the feather for the wings, and divide it equally into two parts, and turn them back towards the bend of the Hook, the one on the one side, and the other on the other of the shanck, holding them fast in that posture betwixt the fore finger, and thumb of your left hand, which done, warp them so down, as to stand, and slope towards the bend of the hook, and having warpt up to the end of the shanck, hold the Flie fast betwixt the finger and thumb of your left hand, and then take the silk betwixt the finger, and thumb of your right hand, and where the warping* ends, pinch or nip it with your thumb nail against your finger, and strip away the remainder of your dubbing from the silk, and then with the bare silk whip it once or twice about, make the wings to stand in due order, fasten, and cut it off; after which with the point of a needle raise up the dubbing gently from the warp, twitch off the superfluous hairs of your dubbing, leave the wings of an equal length (your Flie will never else swim true) and the work is done. And this way of making a Flie (which is certainly the best of all other) was taught me by a Kinsman of mine, one Captain *Henry Jackson*,* a near neighbour, an admirable Flie Angler, by many degrees the best Flie maker, that ever I yet met with. And now that I have told you how a Flie is to be made, you shall presently see me make one, with which you may peradventure take a Trout this morning, notwithstanding the unlikeliness of the day; for it is now nine of the Clock, and Fish will begin to rise, if they will rise to day; I will walk along by you, and look on, and after dinner I will proceed in my lecture of Flie-Fishing.

Viat. I confess I long to be at the River, and yet I could sit here all day to hear you: but some of the one, and some of the other will do well: and I have a mighty ambition to take a Trout in your River *Dove*.

Pisc. I warrant you shall: I would not for more, than I will speak of but you should, seeing I have so extoll'd my River to you: nay I will keep you here a Month, but you shall have one good day of sport before you go.

Viat. You will find me I doubt too tractable that way; for in good earnest, if business would give me leave, and that if it were fit, I could find in my heart to stay with you for ever.

Pisc. I thank you *Sir*, for that kind expression, and now let me look out my things to make this flie.

CHAP. VI.

PISC. Boy, come give me my dubbing bagg here presently; and now Sir, since I find you so honest a man, I will make no scruple to lay open my Treasure before you.

Viat. Did ever any one see the like! What a heap of Trumpery is here! certainly never an Angler in *Europe* has his shop half so well furnisht, as you have.

Pisc. You perhaps may think now, that I rake together this Trumpery, as you call it, for shew only, to the end that such as see it (which are not many I assure you) may think me a great Master in the Art of angling: but let me tell you here are some colours (as contemptible as they seem here) that are very hard to be got, and scarce any one of them, which if it should be lost, I should not miss, and be concern'd about the loss of it too, once in the year; but look you, Sir, amongst all these I will chuse out these two colours only, of which this is Bears-hair, this darker no great matter what; but I am sure I have kill'd a great deal of Fish with it; and with one or both of these you shall take Trout or Grayling this very day, notwithstanding all disadvantages, or my Art shall fail me.

Viat. You promise comfortably, and I have a great deal of reason to believe every thing you say; but I wish the Flie were made, that we were at it.

Pisc. That will not be long in doing: and pray observe then. You see first how I hold my hook, and thus I begin. Look you here are my first two or three whips about the bare hook, thus I joyn hook and line, thus I put on my wings, thus I twirle and lap on* my dubbing, thus I work it up towards the head, thus I part my wings, thus I nip my superfluous dubbing from my silk, thus fasten, thus trim and adjust my Flie, and there's a Flie made, and now how do you like it?

Viat. In earnest, admirably well, and it perfectly resembles a Flie; but we about *London* make the bodies of our Flies both much bigger and longer, so long as even almost to the very beard of the Hook.

Pisc. I know it very well, and had one of those Flies given me by an honest Gentleman, who came with my Father *Walton* to give me a Visit, which (to tell you the truth) I hung in my parlour Window to laugh at: but *Sir*, you know the Proverb, *They who go to* Rome, *must do as they at* Rome *do*; and believe me you must here make your Flies after this fashion, or you will take no Fish. Come I will look you out a Line, and you shall put it on, and try it. There *Sir*, now I think you are fitted, and now beyond the farther end of the walk you shall begin, I see at that bend of the water above, the air crisps the water a little, knit your Line first here, and then go up thither, and see what you can do.

Viat. Did you see that *Sir*?

Pisc. Yes, I saw the Fish, and he saw you too, which made him turn short, you must fish further off, if you intend to have any sport here, this is no *New-River** let me tell you. That was a good Trout believe me, did you touch him?

Viat. No, I would I had, we would not have parted so. Look you there was another; this is an excellent Flie.

Pisc. That Flie I am sure would kill Fish, if the day were right; but they only chew at it I see, and will not take it. Come *Sir*, let us return back to the Fishing-house; this still water I see will not do our business to day; you shall now, if you please, make a Flie your self, and try what you can do in the streams with that, and I know a Trout taken with a Flie of your own making will please you better than twenty with one of mine. Give me that Bag again, *Sirrah*; look you *Sir*, there is a hook, towght, silk, and a feather for the wings, be doing with those, and I will look you out a Dubbing, that I think will do.

Viat. This is a very little hook.

Pisc. That may serve to inform you, that it is for a very little Flie, and you must make your wings accordingly; for as the case stands it must be a little Flie, and a very little one too, that must do your business. Well said! believe me you shift your fingers very handsomely; I doubt I have taken upon me to teach my Master. So here's your dubbing now.

Viat. This dubbing is very black.

Pisc. It appears so in hand; but step to the doors and hold it up betwixt your eye and the Sun, and it will appear a shining red; let me tell you never a man in *England* can discern the true colour of a dubbing any way but that, and therefore chuse always to make your Flies on such a bright Sun-shine day as this, which also you may the better do, because it is worth nothing to fish in, here put it on, and be sure to make the body of your Flie as slender as you can. Very good! Upon my word you have made a marvellous handsom Flie.

Viat. I am very glad to hear it; 'tis the first that ever I made of this kind in my life.

Pisc. Away, away! You are a Doctor* at it! but I will not commend you too much, lest I make you proud. Come put it on, and you shall now go downward to some streams betwixt the rocks below the little foot bridg you see there, and try your Fortune. Take heed of slipping into the water as you follow me under this rock: So now you are over, and now throw in.

Viat. This is a fine stream indeed: There's one! I have him!

Pisc. And a precious catch you have of him; pull him out! I see you have a tender hand: This is a diminutive Gentleman, e'en throw him in again, and let him grow till he be more worthy your anger.

Viat. Pardon me, *Sir*, all's Fish that comes to'th' hook with me now. Another!

Pisc. And of the same standing.

Viat. I see I shall have good sport now: Another! and a Grayling. Why you have Fish here at will.

Pisc. Come, come, cross the Bridge, and go down the other side lower, where you will find finer streams, and better sport I hope than this. Look you *Sir*, here is a fine stream now, you have length enough, stand a little further off, let me entreat you, and do but Fish this stream like an Artist, and peradventure a good Fish may fall to your share. How now! what is all gone?

Viat. No, I but touch't him; but that was a Fish worth taking.

Pisc. Why now let me tell you, you lost that Fish by your own fault, and through your own eagerness and haste; for you are never to offer to strike* a good Fish, if he do not strike himself, till first you see him turn his head after he has taken your Flie, and then you can never strain your tackle in the striking, if you strike with any manner of moderation. Come throw in one again, and fish me this stream by inches; for I assure you here are very good Fish, both Trout and Grayling, lie here; and at that great stone on the other side, 'tis ten to one a good Trout gives you the meeting.

Viat. I have him now, but he is gone down towards the bottom, I cannot see what he is; yet he should be a good Fish by his weight; but he makes no great stir.

Pisc. Why then, by what you say, I dare venture to assure you, 'tis a Grayling, who is one of the deadest hearted Fishes in the world, and the bigger he is the more easily taken. Look you, now you see him plain; I told you what he was, bring hither that landing net, Boy, and now *Sir*, he is your own; and believe me a good one, sixteen Inches long I warrant him, I have taken none such this year.

Viat. I never saw a Grayling before look so black.

Pisc. Did you not? Why then let me tell you, that you never saw one before in right season: for then a Grayling is very black about his head, guills, and down his back, and has his Belly of a dark grey, dappled with black spots, as you see this is, and I am apt to conclude, that from thence he derives his name of *Umber*. Though I must tell you this Fish is past his prime, and begins to decline, and was in better season at Christmas than he is now. But move on, for it grows towards dinner-time, and there is a very great and fine stream below, under that Rock, that fills the deepest pool in all the River, where you are almost sure of a good Fish.

Viat. Let him come, I'le try a fall with him; but I had thought, that the Grayling had been always in season with the Trout, and had come in, and gone out with him.

Pisc. Oh no! assure your self a Grayling is a winter-fish*: but such a one as would deceive any but such as know him very well indeed, for his flesh, even in his worst season, is so firm, and will so easily calver,* that in plain truth he is very good meat at all times; but in his perfect season (which, by the way, none but an overgrown Grayling will ever be) I think him so good a fish, as to be little inferiour to the best Trout that ever I tasted in my life.

Viat. Here's another skip-jack,* and I have rais'd five or six more at least whilst you were speaking: Well, go thy way little *Dove!* thou art the finest River, that ever I saw, and the fullest of fish. Indeed, *Sir*, I like it so well, that I am afraid you will be troubled with me once a year, so long as we two live.

Pisc. I am afraid I shall not *Sir*; but were you once here a *May* or a *June*, if good sport would tempt you, I should then expect you would sometimes see me; for you would then say it were a fine River indeed, if you had once seen the sport at the height.

Viat. Which I will do, if I live, and that you please to give me leave; there was one, and there another.

Pisc. And all this in a strange River, and with a Flie of your own making! why what a dangerous man are you!

Viat. I, *Sir*, but who taught me? and as *Dametas* says* by his man *Dorus*, so you may say by me,

> *If my man such praises have,*
> *What then have I, that taught the Knave?*

But what have we got here? A Rock springing up in the middle of the River! this is one of the oddest sights, that ever I saw.

Pisc. Why, *Sir*, from that *Pike*[1],* that you see standing up there distant from the rock, this is call'd *Pike-Pool*: and young Mr. *Izaac Walton**

[1] *'Tis a Rock, in the fashion of a Spire-Steeple; and, almost as big. It stands in the midst of the River* Dove; *and not far from Mr.* Cotton's *house, below which place this delicate River takes a swift Carere betwixt many mighty Rocks, much higher and bigger than St.* Pauls Church,* *before 'twas burnt. And this* Dove *being oppos'd by one of the highest of them, has at last, forc't it self away through it; and after a miles concealment, appears again with more glory and beauty than before that opposition; running through the most pleasant Valleys and most fruitful Meadows, that this Nation can justly boast of.*

was so pleas'd with it, as to draw it in Landscape* in black and white in a blank Book I have at home, as he has done several prospects of my house also, which I keep for a memorial of his favour, and will shew you, when we come up to dinner.

Viat. Has young Master *Izaak Walton* been here too?

Pisc. Yes marry has he Sir, and that again, and again too, and in *France* since, and at *Rome*, and at *Venice*,* and I can't tell where: but I intend to ask him a great many hard questions so soon as

I can see him, which will be, God willing, next Month. In the mean time, Sir, to come to this fine stream at the head of this great Pool, you must venture over these slippery cobling stones;* believe me, Sir, there you were nimble or else you had been down; but now you are got over, look to your self; for on my word if a Fish rise here, he is like to be such a one, as will endanger your tackle: How now!

Viat. I think you have such command here over the Fishes, that you can raise them by your word, as they say Conjurers can do Spirits, and afterward make them do what you bid them: for here's a Trout has taken my Flie, I had rather have lost a Crown.* What luck's this! He was a lovely Fish, and turn'd up a side like a Salmon.

Pisc. O Sir, this is a War where you sometimes win, and must sometimes expect to loose. Never concern your self for the loss of your Flie; for ten to one I teach you to make a better. Who's that calls?

Serv. Sir, Will it please you to come to dinner?

Pisc. We come. You hear Sir we are call'd, and now take your choice, whether you will climb this steep Hill before you, from the top of which you will go directly into the House, or back again over these stepping stones, and about by the Bridg.

Viat. Nay, sure the nearest way is best; at least my stomach tells me so; and I am now so well acquainted with your Rocks, that I fear them not.

Pisc. Come then, follow me, and so soon as we have din'd, we will down again to the little House; where I will begin at the place I left off about Flie-Fishing, and read you another Lecture; for I have a great deal more to say upon that Subject.

Viat. The more the better; I could never have met with a more obliging Master, my first excepted; nor such sport can all the Rivers about *London* ever afford, as is to be found in this pretty River.

Pisc. You deserve to have better, both because I see you are willing to take pains, and for liking this little so well; and better I hope to shew you before we part.

CHAP. VII.

VIAT. Come Sir, having now well din'd, and being again set in your little House; I will now challenge your promise, and entreat you to proceed in your instruction for Flie-fishing, which, that you may be the better encourag'd to do, I will assure you, that I have not lost, I think, one syllable of what you have told me; but very well retain all your directions both for the Rod, Line, and making a Flie, and now desire an account of the Flies themselves.

Pisc. Why Sir, I am ready to give it you, and shall have the whole afternoon to do it in, if no body come in to interrupt us; for you must know (besides the unfitness of the day) that the afternoons so early in *March* signifie very little to Angling with a Flie, though with a Minnow, or a Worm something might (I confess) be done.

To begin then where I left off, my Father *Walton** tells us but of 12 Artificial flies only, to Angle with at the top, and gives their names; of which some are common with us here; and I think I guess at most of them by his description, and I believe they all breed, and are taken in our Rivers, though we do not make them either of the same Dubbing, or fashion. And it may be in the Rivers about *London*, which I presume he has most frequented, and where 'tis likely he has done most execution, there is not much notice taken of many more: but we are acquainted with several others here (though perhaps I may reckon some of his by other names too) but if I do, I shall make you amends by an addition to his Catalogue. And although the forenamed great Master in the Art of Angling (for so in truth he is) tells you that no man should in honesty catch a Trout till the middle of *March*, yet I hope he will give a Man leave sooner to take a Grayling, which, as I told you, is in the dead Months in his best season; and do assure you (which I remember by a very remarkable token) I did once take upon the sixt day of December one, and only one, of the biggest Graylings and the best in season, that ever I yet saw, or tasted; and do usually take Trouts too, and with a Flie, not only before the middle of this Month, but almost every year in *February*, unless it be a very ill spring indeed, and have sometimes in *January*, so early as New-years-tide, and in frost and snow taken Grayling in a warm sunshine day for an hour or two about Noon; and to fish for him with a Grub it is then the best time of all.

I shall therefore begin my Flie-fishing with that Month (though I confess very few begin so soon, and that such as are so fond of the sport as to embrace all opportunities, can rarely in that Month find a day fit for their purpose) and tell you, that upon my knowledg these Flies in a warm sun, for an hour or two in the day, are certainly taken.

January.

1. A red brown with wings of the Male of a Malard almost white: the dubbing of the tail of a black long coated Cur, such as they commonly make muffs of; for the hair on the tail of such a Dog dyes, and turns to a red Brown, but the hair of a smoth coated Dog of the same colour will not do, because it will not dye, but retains its natural colour, and this flie is taken in a warm sun, this whole Month thorough.

2. There is also a very little bright Dun Gnat, as little as can possibly be made, so little as never to be fisht with, with above one hair next the hook, and this is to be made of a mixt dubbing of Martins fur,* and the white of a Hares scut; with a very white, and small wing; and 'tis no great matter how fine you fish, for nothing will rise in this Month but a Grayling, and of them I never at this season saw any taken with a Flie, of above a foot long in my life: but of little ones about the bigness of a smelt in a warm day, and a glowing Sun, you may take enough with these two Flies, and they are both taken the whole Month through.

February.

1. Where the Red-brown of the last Month ends, another almost of the same colour begins with this, saving that the dubbing of this must be of something a blacker colour, and both of them warpt on with red silk; the dubbing that should make this Flie, and that is the truest colour, is to be got of the black spot of a Hogs ear: not that a black spot in any part of the Hog will not afford the same colour; but that the hair in that place is by many degrees softer, and more fit for the purpose: his wing must be as the other, and this kills all this Month, and is call'd the lesser Red-brown.

2. This Month also a plain Hackle, or palmer-Flie made with a rough black body, either of black Spaniels furr, or the whirl of an *Estridg* feather,* and the red Hackle of a Capon over all, will kill, and if the weather be right make very good sport.

3. Also a lesser Hackle with a black body also, silver twist over that, and a red feather over all, will fill your pannier if the Month be open, and not bound up in Ice, and snow, with very good Fish; but in case of a frost and snow, you are to Angle only with the smallest Gnats, Browns and Duns* you can make, and with those are only to expect Graylings no bigger than sprats.

4. In this Month, upon a whirling round water, we have a great Hackle, the body black, and wrapped with a red feather of a Capon untrim'd; that is, the whole length of the Hackle staring out* (for we sometimes barb* the Hackle feather short all over; sometimes barb it only a little, and sometimes barb it close underneath), leaving the whole length of the feather on the top, or back of the Flie which makes it swim better, and as occasion serves kills very great Fish.

5. We make use also in this Month of another great Hackle the body black, and rib'd over with Gold twist,* and a red feather over all, which also does great execution.

6. Also a great Dun, made with Dun Bears Hair, and the wings of the grey feather of a Mallard near unto his tail, which is absolutely the best Flie can be thrown upon a River this Month, and with which an Angler shall have admirable sport.

7. We have also this Month the great blew Dun, the dubbing of the bottom of Bears hair next to the roots, mixt with a little blew Camlet, the wings of the dark grey feather of a Mallard.

8. We have also this Month a Dark-Brown, the dubbing of the brown hair of the Flanck of a brended* Cow, and the wings of the grey-Drakes feather.

And note, that these several Hackels, or Palmer Flies, are some for one Water, and one Skye, and some for another, and according to the change of those, we alter their size, and colour, and note also, that both in this, and all other Months of the Year, when you do not certainly know what Flie is taken; or cannot see any Fish to rise, you are then to put on a small Hackle, if the Water be clear, or a bigger if something dark, untill you have taken one, and then thrusting your finger thorough his Guils, to pull out his Gorge, which being open'd with your knife, you will then discover what Flie is taken, and may fit your self accordingly.

For the making of a Hackle, or Palmer Flie my Father *Walton** has already given you sufficient direction.

March.

For this Month you are to use all the same Hackels, and Flies* with the other, but you are to make them less.

1. We have besides for this Month a little Dun call'd a whirling Dun (though it is not the whirling Dun indeed,* which is one of the

best Flies we have) and for this the dubbing must be of the bottom fur of a Squirrels tail and the wing of the grey feather of a Drake.

2. Also a bright brown, the dubbing either of the brown of a Spaniel, or that of a Cows flanck, with a grey wing.*

3. Also a whitish Dun made of the roots of Camels hair, and the wings of the grey feather of a Mallard.

4. There is also for this Month a Flie, call'd the Thorn Tree Flie;* the dubbing an absolute black mixt with eight or ten hairs of *Isabella* colour'd Mohair, the body as little as can be made, and the wings of a bright Malards feather, an admirable Flie, and in great repute amongst us for a killer.

5. There is besides this another blew Dun, the dubbing of which it is made being thus to be got. Take a small tooth comb, and with it comb the neck of a black Grey hound, and the down that sticks in the teeth, will be the finest blew, that ever you saw. The wings of this Flie can hardly be too white, and he is taken about the tenth of this Month, and lasteth till the four and twentieth.

6. From the tenth of this Month* also till towards the end, is taken a little black Gnat; the dubbing either of the fur of a black water-Dog, or the down of a young black water-Coot,* the wings of the Male of a Mallard as white as may be, the body as little as you can possibly make it, and the wings as short as his body.

7. From the Sixteenth of this Month also to the end of it, we use a bright brown, the dubbing for which, is to be had out of a Skinners Lime-pits,* and of the hair of an abortive Calf, which the lime will turn to be so bright, as to shine like Gold, for the wings of this Flie, the feather of a brown Hen is best; which Flie is also taken till the tenth of *April*.

April.

All the same Hackles, and Flies that were taken in *March* will be taken in this Month also, with this distinction only concerning the Flies, that all the browns be lapt with red silk, and the Duns with yellow.

1. To these a small bright brown, made of Spaniels fur, with a light grey wing; in a bright day, and a clear water is very well taken.

2. We have too a little dark brown, the dubbing of that colour, and some violet Camlet mixt, and the wing of the grey feather of a Mallard.

3. From the sixth of this Month to the tenth, we have also a Flie call'd the violet Flie, made of a dark violet stuff, with the wings of the grey feather of a Mallard.

4. About the twelfth of this Month comes in the Flie call'd the whirling Dun,* which is taken every day about the mid time of day all this Month through, and by fits from thence to the end of *June*, and is commonly made of the down of a Fox Cub, which is of an Ash colour at the roots, next the skin, and ribb'd about with yellow silk, the wings of the pale grey feather of a Mallard.

5. There is also a yellow Dun, the dubbing of Camels hair, and yellow Camlet, or wool mixt, and a white grey wing.

6. There is also this Month another little brown, besides that mention'd before, made with a very slender body, the dubbing of dark brown, and violet Camlet mixt, and a grey wing; which though the direction for the making be near the other, is yet another Flie, and will take when the other will not, especially in a bright day, and a clear water.

7. About the twentieth of this Month comes in a Flie call'd the Horse-flesh Flie,* the dubbing of which is a blew Mohair, with pink colour'd, and red Tammy* mixt, a light colour'd wing, and a dark brown head. This flie is taken best in an Evening, and kills from two hours before Sun set till twilight, and is taken the Month thorough.

May.

And now Sir, that we are entring into the Month of *May*, I think it requisite to beg not only your attention, but also your best patience; for I must now be a little tedious with you, and dwell upon this Month longer than ordinary; which that you may the better endure, I must tell you, this Month deserves, and requires to be insisted on, for as much as it alone, and the next following afford more pleasure to the Flie-Angler, than all the rest; and here it is that you are to expect an account of the Green Drake, and stone-flie, promis'd you so long ago,* and some others that are peculiar to this Month, and part of the Month following, and that (though not so great either in bulk, or name) do yet stand in competition with the two before named, and so, that it is yet undecided amongst the Anglers to which of the pretenders to the Title of the May-flie,* it does properly, and duly belong, neither dare I (where so many of the learned in this Art of Angling are got in dispute about the controversie) take upon me to determine; but I think I ought to have a vote amongst them, and according to that priviledg, shall give you my free opinion, and per-adventure when I have told you all, you may incline to think me in the right.

Viat. I have so great a deference to your judgment in these mat-ters, that I must always be of your opinion; and the more you speak, the faster I grow to my attention, for I can never be weary of hearing you upon this Subject.

Pisc. Why that's encouragement enough; and now prepare your self for a tedious Lecture; but I will first begin with the flies of less esteem (though almost any thing will take a Trout in *May*) that I may afterwards insist the longer upon those of greater note, and reputa-tion; know therefore that the first flie we take notice of in this Month, is call'd the Turky-flie.*

1. The dubbing ravell'd out of some blew stuff, and lapt about with yellow silk, the wings of a grey Mallards feather.

2. Next a great Hackle, or Palmer-flie, with a yellow body ribb'd with Gold twist, and large wings of a Mallards feather dyed yellow, with a red Capons Hackle over all,

3. Then a black flie, the dubbing of a black Spaniels fur, and the wings of a grey Mallards feather.

4. After that a light brown with a slender body, the dubbing twirl'd upon small* red silk, and rais'd with the point of a needle, that the ribs or rows of silk may appear through the wings of the grey feather of a Mallard.

5. Next a little Dun, the dubbing of a Bears dun whirl'd upon yellow silk, the wings of the grey feather of a Mallard.

6. Then a white Gnat, with a pale wing, and a black head.

7. There is also this Month a flie call'd the Peacock-flie, the body made of a whirl of a Peacocks feather, with a red head, and wings of a Mallards feather.

8. We have then another very killing flie, known by the name of the Dun-Cut, the dubbing of which is a Bears dun, with a little blew, and yellow mixt with it, a large dun wing, and two horns at the head, made of the hairs of a Squirrels tail.

9. The next is the Cow-Lady,* a little flie, the body of a Peacocks feather, the wing of a red feather, or strips of the red hackle of a Cock.

10. We have then the Cow-turd flie;* the dubbing light brown, and

yellow mixt, the wing the dark grey feather of a Mallard. And note
that besides these abovementioned, all the same Hackles and Flies,
the Hackles only brighter, and the Flies smaller, that are taken in
April, will also be taken this Month, as also all Browns, and Duns:
and now I come to my Stone-Flie, and Green-Drake, which are the
Matadores for Trout and Grayling, and in their season kill more Fish
in our *Derbyshire* Rivers, than all the rest past, and to come, in the
whole Year besides.

But first I am to tell you, that we have four several flies which contend for the Title of the May-Flie, namely,

> *The Green-Drake,*
> *The Stone-Flie,*
> *The Black Flie,* and*
> *The little yellow May-Flie.**

And all these have their Champions and Advocates to dispute,
and plead their priority; though I do not understand why the two
last named should; the first two having so manifestly the advantage,
both in their beauty, and the wonderful execution they do in their
season.

11. Of these the Green-Drake comes in about the twentieth of this
Month, or betwixt that, and the latter end (for they are sometimes
sooner, and sometimes later according to the quality of the Year) but
never well taken till towards the end of this Month, and the beginning
of *June*. The Stone-Flie comes much sooner, so early as the middle of
April; but is never well taken till towards the middle of *May*, and
continues to kill much longer than the Green-Drake stays with us, so
long as to the end almost of *June*; and indeed, so long as there are any
of them to be seen upon the water; and sometimes in an Artificial Flie,
and late at night, or before Sun rise in a morning, longer.

Now both these Flies (and I believe many others, though I think
not all) are certainly, and demonstratively bred in the very Rivers
where they are taken, our Caddis or Cod-bait which lye under stones
in the bottom of the water, most of them turning into those two
Flies,* and being gather'd in the husk, or crust, near the time of their
maturity, are very easily known, and distinguisht, and are of all other
the most remarkable, both for their size, as being of all other the biggest (the shortest of them being a full inch long, or more) and for the
execution they do, the Trout, and Grayling being much more greedy

of them, than of any others; and indeed the Trout never feeds fat, nor comes into his perfect season, till these Flies come in.

Of these the Green-Drake never discloses* from his husk, till he be first there grown to full maturity, body, wings, and all, and then he creeps out of his cell, but with his wings so crimpt, and ruffled, by being prest together in that narrow room, that they are for some hours totally useless to him, by which means he is compelled either to creep upon the flags, sedges, and blades of grass (if his first rising from the bottom of the water be near the banks of the River) till the Air, and Sun, stiffen and smooth them! or if his first appearance above water happen to be in the middle, he then lies upon the surface of the water like a Ship at Hull* (for his feet are totally useless to him there, and he cannot creep upon the water as the Stone-Flie can) untill his wings have got stiffness to fly with, if by some Trout, or Grayling he be not taken in the interim (which ten to one he is) and then his wings stand high, and clos'd exact upon his back, like the Butterfly, and his motion in flying is the same. His Body is in some of a paler, in others of a darker yellow (for they are not all exactly of a colour) rib'd with rows of green, long, slender, and growing sharp towards the tail, at the end of which he has three long small whisks* of a very dark colour, almost black, and his tail turns up towards his back like a Mallard, from whence questionless he has his name of the green-Drake. These (as I think I told you before) we commonly dape, or dibble with, and having gather'd great store of them into a long draw box,* with holes in the Cover to give them Air (where also they will continue fresh, and vigorous a night or more) we take them out thence by the wings, and bait them thus upon the Hook. We first take one (for we commonly Fish with two of them at a time) and putting the point of the Hook into the thickest part of his Body under one of his wings, run it directly through and out at the other side, leaving him spitted cross* upon the Hook, and then taking the other, put him on after the same manner, but with his head the contrary way, in which posture they will live upon the Hook, and play with their wings for a quarter of an hour, or more: but you must have a care to keep their wings dry, both from the water, and also that your fingers be not wet when you take them out to bait them; for then your bait is spoil'd.

Having now told you how to Angle with this Flie alive, I am now to tell you next, how to make an Artificial Flie, that will so perfectly resemble him, as to be taken in a rough windy day, when no Flies can lye upon the water; nor are to be found about the Banks and sides of the River, to a wonder, and with which you shall certainly kill the best Trout, and Grayling in the River.

The Artificial Green-Drake then is made upon a large Hook, the Dubbing, Camels hair, bright Bears hair, the soft down that is comb'd from a Hogs bristles, and yellow Camlet well mixt together, the body long, and ribb'd about with green silk, or rather yellow waxt with green-wax, the whisks of the tail of the long hairs of sables, or fitchet,* and the wings of the white grey feather of a Mallard dyed yellow, which also is to be dyed thus.

Take the root of a Barbary Tree,* and shave it, and put to it Woody viss,* with as much Alum as a Walnut, and boyl your feathers in it with Rain water; and they will be of a very fine yellow.

I have now done with the Green-drake excepting to tell you, that he is taken at all hours during his season, whilst there is any day upon the Sky; and with a made Flie, I once took, ten days after he was absolutely gone,* in a Cloudy day, after a showr, and in a whistling wind, five and thirty very great Trouts, and Graylings betwixt five, and eight of the Clock in the Evening, and had no less than five, or six Flies with three good hairs a piece taken from me in despite of my heart, besides.

12. I should now come next to the Stone-Flie, but there is another Gentleman in my way: that must of necessity come in between, and that is the Grey-Drake,* which in all shapes, and dimensions is perfectly the same with the other, but quite almost of another colour, being of a paler, and more livid yellow, and green, and ribb'd with black quite down his body, with black shining wings, and so diaphanous and tender, cob-web like, that they are of no manner of use for Daping; but come in, and are taken after the Green-Drake, and in an Artificial Flie kill very well, which Flie is thus made, the Dubbing of the down of a Hogs bristles, and black Spaniels fur mixt, and ribb'd down the body with black silk, the whisks of the hairs of the beard of a black Cat, and the wings of the black grey feather of a Mallard.

And now I come to the Stone-Flie, but am afraid I have already wearied your patience, which if I have, I beseech you freely tell me so, and I will defer the remaining instructions for Flie-Angling till some other time.

Viat. No truly Sir, I can never be weary of hearing you: but if you think fit, because I am afraid I am too troublesom, to refresh your self with a glass, and a pipe; you may afterwards proceed, and I shall be exceedingly pleas'd to hear you.

Pisc. I thank you *Sir* for that motion; for believe me I am dry with talking. Here Boy, give us here a Bottle, and a Glass; and *Sir*, my service to you, and to all our Friends in the South.

Viat. Your Servant *Sir*, and I'le pledg you as heartily; for the good powder'd beef* I eat* at Dinner, or something else, has made me thirsty.

CHAP. VIII.

VIAT. So, *Sir*, I am now ready for another Lesson so soon as you please to give it me.

Pisc. And I, *Sir*, as ready to give you the best I can. Having told you the time of the Stone-Flie's coming in, and that he is bred of a Caddis* in the very River where he is taken, I am next to tell you, that

13. This same Stone-Flie has not the patience to continue in his Crust, or Husk till his wings be full grown; but so soon as ever they begin to put out, that he feels himself strong (at which time we call him a Jack), squeezes himself out of Prison, and crawls to the top of some stone, where if he can find a chink that will receive him, or can creep betwixt two stones, the one lying hollow upon the other (which, by the way, we also lay so purposely to find them) he there lurks till his wings be full grown, and there is your only place to find him (and from thence doubtless he derives his name) though, for want of such convenience, he will make shift with the hollow of a Bank, or any other place where the wind cannot come to fetch him off. His body is long, and pretty thick, and as broad at the tail almost, as in the middle; his colour a very fine brown, ribb'd with yellow, and much yellower on the belly than the back, he has two or three whisks* also at the tag of his tail, and two little horns upon his head, his wings, when full grown, are double, and flat down his back of the same colour, but rather darker than his body, and longer than it; though he makes but little use of them, for you shall rarely see him flying, though often swimming, and padling with several feet he has under his belly upon the water, without stirring a wing: but the Drake* will

mount Steeple height into the Air, though he is to be found upon flags and grass too, and indeed every where high and low, near the River; there being so many of them in their season, as were they not a very inoffensive insect, would look like a Plague; and these Drakes (since I forgot to tell you before, I will tell you here) are taken by the Fish to that incredible degree, that upon a calm day you shall see the still deeps continually all over circles by the Fishes rising, who will gorge themselves with those Flies, till they purge again out of their Guills; and the Trouts are at that time so lusty and strong, that one of eight, or ten inches long, will then more struggle, and tug, and more endanger your Tackle, than one twice as big in winter: but pardon this digression.

This Stone-flie then we dape or dibble with as with the Drake, but with this difference, that whereas the green-Drake* is common both to stream and still,* and to all hours of the day, we seldom dape with this but in the streams, for in a whistling wind a made Flie in the deep is better, and rarely, but early and late, it not being so proper for the mid-time of the day; though a great *Grayling* will then take it very well in a sharp stream, and here and there a Trout too: but much better toward 8, 9, 10. or eleven of the clock at night, at which time also the best Fish rise, and the later the better, provided you can see your Flie, and when you cannot, a made Flie will murder, which is to be made thus: The dubbing of bears dun with a little brown and yellow Camlet very well mixt; but so plac'd that your Flie may be more yellow on the belly and towards the tail underneath than in any other part, and you are to place two or three hairs of a black Cats beard on the top of the hook in your arming, so as to be turn'd up, when you warp on your dubbing, and to stand almost upright, and staring one from another, and note that your Flie is to be ribb'd with yellow silk, and the wings long, and very large, of the dark grey feather of a Mallard.

14. The next *May-Flie* is the black Flie, made with a black body of the whirle of an Ostridg-feather, rib'd with silver twist, and the black hackle of a Cock over all; and is a killing Flie, but not to be nam'd with either of the other.

15. The last *May-Flie* (that is of the four pretenders) is the little yellow *May-Flie*, in shape exactly the same with the green Drake, but a very little one, and of as bright a yellow as can be seen; which is

made of a bright yellow Camlet, and the wings of a white grey feather died yellow.

16. The last Flie for this month (and which continues all *June*, though it comes in the middle of *May*) is the Flie called the Camlet-Flie, in shape like a moth with fine diapred, or water-wings,* and with which (as I told you before) I sometimes used to dibble; and Grayling will rise mightily at it. But the artificial Flie (which is only in use amongst our Anglers) is made of a dark brown shining Camlet, rib'd over with a very small light green silk, the wings of the double grey feather of a Mallard; and 'tis a killing Flie for small Fish, and so much for *May*.

June.

From the first to the four and twentieth, the green-Drake and Stone-Flie* are taken (as I told you before).

1. From the twelfth to the four and twentieth late at night is taken a Flie, called the Owl-Flie;* the dubbing of a white Weesel's tail,* and a white Grey wing.

2. We have then another *Dunne*, call'd the *Barm-flie*,* from it's yesty* colour, the dubbing of the fur of a yellow dun Cat, and a grey wing of a Mallards feather.

3. We have also a hackle with a purple body, whipt about with a red Capons feather.

4. As also a gold twist Hackle with a purple body, whipt about with a red Capons feather.

5. To these we have this month a Flesh-flie,* the dubbing of a black Spaniels furre, and blew wool mixt, and a grey wing.

6. Also another little flesh-flie,* the body made of the whirle of a Peacocks feather, and the wings of the grey feather of a Drake.

7. We have then the Peacock-flie, the body and wing both made of the feather of that bird.

8. There is also the flying Ant, or Ant-flie,* the dubbing of brown and red Camlet mixt, with a light grey wing.

9. We have likewise a brown Gnat, with a very slender body of brown and violet Camlet well mixt, and a light grey wing.

10. And another little black Gnat,* the dubbing of black mohair, and a white Grey wing.

11. As also a green Grashopper, the dubbing of green and yellow

Wool mixed, rib'd over with green Silk, and a red Capons feather over all.

12. And lastly a little dun Grashopper, the body slender made of a dun Camlet, and a dun hackle at the top.

July.

First all the small flies that were taken in *June*, are also taken in this month.

1. We have then the Orange Flie, the dubbing of Orange Wool, and the wing of a black feather.

2. Also a little white dun, the body made of white Mohair, and the wings blew of a Herons feather.

3. We have likewise this month a Wasp-flie,* made either of a dark brown dubbing, or else the furre of a black Cats tail, ribb'd about with yellow silk, and the wing of the grey feather of a Mallard.

4. Another flie taken this month is a black Hackle, the body made of the whirle of a Peacock's feather, and a black hackle feather on the top.

5. We have also another made of a Peacocks whirle without wings.

6. Another flie also is taken this month call'd the shel-flie, the dubbing of yellow-green Jersey Wool,* and a little white Hoggs hair mixt, which I call the Palm-flie, and do believe it is taken for a Palm,* that drops off the willows into the water; for this flie I have seen Trouts take little pieces of moss, as they have swam down the River, by which I conclude that the best way to hit the right colour is to compare your dubbing with the Moss, and mix the colours as near as you can.

7. There is also taken this month a black blew Dun, the dubbing of the furre of a black Rabbet mixt with a little yellow, the wings of the Feather of a blew Pigeons wing.

August.

The same Flies with *July*.

1. Then another Ant-flie, the dubbing of the black brown hair of a Cow, some red warpt in for the Tagg of his tail, and a dark wing, a killing flie.

2. Next a flie call'd the Fern-flie, the dubbing of the fur of a Hares neck, that is of the colour of Fearn, or Brackin,* with a darkish grey wing of a Mallards feather, a killer too.

3. Besides these we have a white Hackle, the body of white Mo-hair, and wrapped about with a white Hackle Feather, and this is assuredly taken for Thistle-down.

4. We have also this month a Harry-long-leggs,* the body made of Bears dun, and blew Wool mixt, and a brown hackle Feather over all.

Lastly in this month all the same browns and duns are taken, that were taken in *May*.

September.

This month the same Flies are taken, that are taken in *April*.

1. To which I shall only add a Camel-brown Flie, the dubbing pull'd out of the lime of a Wall* whipt about with red Silk, and a darkish grey Mallards feather for the wing.

2. And one other for which we have no name; but it is made of the black hair of a Badgers skin mixt with the yellow softest down of a sanded* Hog.

October.

The same Flies are taken this month, that were taken in *March*.

November.

The same Flies that were taken in *February*, are taken this month also.

December.

Few men angle with the Flie this month, no more than they do in *January*: but yet if the weather be warm (as I have known it some-times in my life to be, even in this cold Country where it is least expected) then a brown that looks red in the hand, and yellowish betwixt your eye and the Sun, will both raise and kill in a clear water, and free from snow-broth:* but at the best 'tis hardly worth a man's labour.

And now *Sir*, I have done with Flie-fishing, or angling at the top, excepting once more to tell you, that of all these (and I have named you a great many very killing flies) none are fit to be compared with the Drake and Stone-flie, both for many and very great fish; and yet there are some daies, that are by no means proper for the sport, and in a calm you shall not have near so much sport even with daping, as in a whistling gale of wind, for two reasons, both because you are not then so easily discovered by the fish, and also because there are then but few flies can lye upon the water; for where they have so much choice, you may easily imagine they will not be so eager and forward to rise at a bait, that both the shadow of your body, and that of your Rod, nay of your very line, in a hot calm day will, in spite of your best caution, render suspected to them: but even then, in swift streams, or by sitting down patiently behind a willow bush, you shall do more execution than at almost any other time of the year with any other flie, though one may sometimes hit of a day, when he shall come home very well satisfied with sport with several other Flies: but with these two, the green Drake and the Stone-flie,* I do verily believe I could some daies in my life, had I not been weary of slaughter, have loaden a lusty boy, and have sometimes, I do honestly assure you, given over upon the meer account of satiety of sport; which will be no hard matter to believe, when I likewise assure you, that with this very flie, I have in this very River that runs by us in three or four hours taken thirty, five and thirty, and forty of the best Trouts in the River. What shame and pity is it then, that such a River should be destroyed by the basest sort of people, by those unlawful ways of fire and netting in the night, and of damming, groping, spearing, hanging and hooking by day, which are now grown so common, that, though we have very good Laws to punish such Offenders, every Rascal does it, for ought I see, *impunè*.*

To conclude, I cannot now in honesty but frankly tell you, that many of these flies I have nam'd, at least so made as we make them here, will peradventure do you no great service in your Southern Rivers, and will not conceal from you, but that I have sent flies to several friends in *London*, that for ought I could ever hear, never did any great feats with them, and therefore if you intend to profit by my instructions, you must come to angle with me here in the Peak; and so, if you please, let us walk up to Supper, and to morrow, if the day be windy, as our daies here commonly are, 'tis ten to one but we shall take a good dish of fish for dinner.

CHAP. IX.

Pisc. A good day to you, *Sir*; I see you will alwaies be stirring before me.

Viat. Why, to tell you the truth, I am so allur'd with the sport I had yesterday, that I long to be at the River again, and when I heard the wind sing in my Chamber window, could forbear no longer, but leap out of bed, and had just made an end of dressing my self, as you came in.

Pisc. Well, I am both glad you are so ready for the day, and that the day is so fit for you, and look you I have made you three or four flies this morning, this silver twist hackle, this bears dun, this light brown and this dark brown, any of which I dare say will do; but you may try them all, and see which does best, only I must ask your pardon that I cannot wait upon you this Morning, a little business being fal'n out, that for two or three hours, will deprive me of your Company: but I'le come call you home to dinner, and my man shall attend you.

Viat. Oh *Sir*, mind your affairs by all means, do but lend me a little of your skill to these fine flies, and, unless it have forsaken me since yesterday, I shall find luck of my own I hope to do something.

Pisc. The best Instruction I can give you, is, that, seeing the wind curles the water, and blows the right way, you would now angle up the still deep to day; for betwixt the Rocks where the streams are, you would find it now too brisk, and besides I would have you take fish in both Waters.

Viat. I'le obey your Direction, and so a good morning to you. Come young man, let you and I walk together. But heark you, *Sir*, I have not done with you yet; I expect another Lesson for angling at the bottom, in the afternoon.

Pisc. Well, Sir, I'le be ready for you.

CHAP. X.

Pisc. Oh *Sir*, are you return'd? you have but just prevented* me. I was coming to call you.

Viat. I am glad then I have sav'd you the labour.

Pisc. And how have you sped?

Viat. You shall see that, *Sir*, presently, look you *Sir*, here are three

[1] *Spoke like a South-Country man.*
brace[1] of Trouts, one of them the biggest but one, that ever I kill'd with a flie in my life, and yet I lost a bigger than that, with my Flie to boot, and here are three Graylings, and one of them longer by some inches than that I took yesterday, and yet I thought that a good one too.

Pisc. Why you have made a pretty good mornings work on't, and now *Sir*, what think you of our River *Dove*?

Viat. I think it to be the best Trout River in *England*; and am so far in love with it, that if it were mine, and that I could keep it to my self, I would not exchange that water, for all the Land it runs over; to be totally debarr'd from't.

Pisc. That Complement to the River, speaks you a true lover of the Art of angling: And now, *Sir*, to make part of amends for sending you so uncivilly out alone this Morning, I will my self dress you this dish of fish for your dinner, walk but into the parlour, you will find one Book or other in the window to entertain you the while, and you shall have it presently.

Viat. Well *Sir*, I obey you.

Pisc. Look you *Sir*, have I not made haste?

Viat. Believe me *Sir*, that you have, and it looks so well, I long to be at it.

Pisc. Fall to then; now *Sir* what say you! am I a tolerable Cook or no?

Viat. So good a one, that I did never eat so good Fish in my life. This Fish is infinitely better, than any I ever tasted of the kind in my life. 'Tis quite another thing, than our Trouts about *London*.

Pisc. You would say so, if that Trout you eat of were in right season: but pray eat of the Grayling, which upon my word at this time, is by much the better Fish.

Viat. In earnest, and so it is: and I have one request to make to you, which is, that as you have taught me to catch Trout and Grayling, you will now teach me how to dress them as these are drest, which questionless is of all other the best way.

Pisc. That I will *Sir*, with all my heart, and am glad you like them so well, as to make that request, and they are drest thus.

Take your Trout, wash, and dry him with a clean Napkin; then open him, and having taken out his guts, and all the blood, wipe him very

clean within, but wash him not, and give him three scotches with a Knife to the bone on one side only. *After which take a clean Kettle, and put in as much hard stale Beer (but it must not be dead),* Vinegar, and a little Whitewine, and Water, as will cover the Fish you intend to boyl; then throw into the Liquor a good quantity of Salt, the Rind of a Lemon, a handful of slic't Horse-Radish root, with a handsom little fagot of Rosemary, Time, and Winter-Savory. Then set your Kettle upon a quick fire of wood, and let your Liquor boyl up to the height before you put in your Fish, and then, if there be many, put them in one by one, that they may not so cool the Liquor, as to make it fall; and whilst your Fish is boyling, beat up the Butter for your Sawce with a Ladle full or two of the Liquor it is boyling in, and being boyld enough, immediately pour the Liquor from the Fish, and being laid in a Dish, pour your Butter upon it, and strewing it plentifully over with shav'd Horse-Raddish, and a little pounded Ginger, garnish your sides of your Dish, and the Fish it self with a slic't Lemon, or two, and serve it up.* A Grayling is also to be drest exactly after the same manner, saving that he is to be scal'd, which a Trout never is: and that must be done either with ones nails, or very lightly and carefully with a Knife for [fear of] bruising the Fish. And note, that these kinds of Fish, a Trout especially, if he is not eaten within four, or five hours after he be taken, is worth nothing.

But come *Sir*, I see you have din'd, and therefore if you please we will walk down again to the little House, and there I will read you a Lecture of Angling at the bottom.

CHAP. XI.

VIAT. So *Sir*, Now we are here, and set: let me have my instructions for Angling for Trout, and Grayling at the bottom; which though not so easy, so cleanly, nor (as 'tis said) so Gentile* a way of Fishing, as with a Flie; is yet (if I mistake not) a good holding* way and takes Fish when nothing else will.

Pisc. You are in the right, it does so: and a worm is so sure a bait at all times, that, excepting in a Flood, I would I had laid a thousand pounds that I kill'd Fish more, or less with it, Winter or Summer every day throughout the Year; those days always excepted, that, upon a more serious account always ought so to be. But not longer to delay you, I will begin, and tell you, that Angling at the bottom is also

commonly of two sorts (and yet there is a third way of Angling with
a Ground-bait, and to very great effect too, as shall be said hereafter)
namely,

> *By Hand*:
> > or,
> *With a Cork, or Float.*

That we call Angling by hand is of three sorts.

The first with a line about half the length of the Rod, a good
weighty plum, and three hairs next the Hook, which we call a running
Line, and with one large Brandling, or a dew-worm of a moderate
size, or two small ones of the first, or any other sort, proper for a
Trout, of which my Father *Walton* has already given you the names,
and sav'd me a labour; or indeed almost any worm whatever; for if a
Trout be in the humour to bite, it must be such a worm as I never yet
saw, that he will refuse; and if you Fish with two, you are then to bait
your hook thus. You are first to run the point of your hook in at the
very head of your first worm, and so down through his body till it be
past the knot,* and then let it out, and strip the worm above the
arming (that you may not bruise it with your fingers) till you have
put on the other by running the point of the Hook in below the knot,
and upwards through his body towards his head till it be but just
cover'd with the head, which being done, you are then to slip the first
worm down over the arming again, till the knots of both worms meet
together.

The second way of Angling by hand, and with a running Line, is
with a Line something longer than the former, and with Tackle made
after this same manner. At the utmost extremity of your Line, where
the Hook is always plac'd in all other ways of Angling, you are to have
a large Pistol, or Carabine* Bullet, into which the end of your Line is
to be fastned with a Peg, or Pin even and close with the Bullet, and
about half a foot above that, a branch of Line, of two, or three handfuls* long; or more, for a swift stream, with a Hook at the end thereof
baited with some of the forenamed worms, and another half foot
above that another arm'd, and baited after the same manner; but with
another sort of worm, without any lead at all above: by which means
you will always certainly find the true bottom in all depths, which
with the Plums upon your Line above you can never do, but that your
bait must always drag whilst you are sounding (which in this way of

Angling must be continually) by which means you are like to have more trouble, and peradventure worse success. And both these ways of Angling at the bottom are most proper for a dark, and muddy water, by reason that in such a condition of the stream, a Man may stand as near as he will, and neither his own shadow, nor the roundness of his Tackle will hinder his sport.

The third way of Angling by hand with a Ground-bait, and by much the best of all other, is, with a Line full as long, or a yard and half longer than your Rod, with no more than one hair next the hook, and for two or three lengths above it, and no more than one small pellet of shot for your plum, your Hook little, your worms of the smaller Brandlings very well scour'd, and only one upon your hook at a time, which is thus to be baited. The point of your hook is to be put in at the very tagg of his tail, and run up his body quite over all the arming, and still stript on an inch at least upon the hair, the head and remaining part hanging downward; and with this line and hook thus baited you are evermore to angle in the streams, always in a clear rather than a troubled water, and always up the River, still casting out your worm before you with a light one-handed Rod, like an artificial Flie, where it will be taken, sometimes at the top, or within a very little of the *Superficies* of the water, and almost always before that light plumb can sink it to the bottom, both by reason of the stream, and also that you must always keep your worm in motion by drawing still back towards you, as if you were angling with a flie; and believe me, whoever will try it, shall find this the best way of all other to angle with a worm, in a bright water especially; but then his rod must be very light and pliant, and very true and finely made, which with a skilful hand will do wonders, and in a clear stream is undoubtedly the best way of angling for a Trout, or Grayling with a worm, by many degrees, that any man can make choice of, and of most ease and delight to the Angler. To which let me add, that if the Angler be of a constitution that will suffer him to wade, and will slip into the tail of a shallow stream,* to the Calf of the leg or the knee, and so keep off the bank, he shall almost take what fish he pleases.

The second way of angling at the bottom is with a Cork or float; and that is also of two sorts.

With a worm:

or,

With a Grub or Caddis.

With a worm you are to have your line within a foot, or a foot and half
as long as your rod, in a dark water with two, or if you will with three;
but in a clear water never with above one hair next the hook, and two or
three for four or five lengths above it, and a worm of what size you
please, your plums fitted to your Cork, your Cork to the condition of
the River (that is to the swiftness or slowness of it) and both, when the
water is very clear, as fine as you can, and then you are never to bait with
above one of the lesser sort of Brandlings; or, if they are very little ones
indeed, you may then bait with two after the manner before directed.

When you angle for a Trout, you are to do it as deep, that is, as
near the bottom as you can, provided your bait do not drag, or if it do,
a Trout will sometimes take it in that posture: if for a Grayling, you
are then to fish further from the bottom, he being a fish that usually
swims nearer to the middle of the water, and lyes alwaies loose:* or
however is more apt to rise than a Trout, and more inclin'd to rise
than to descend even to a Ground-bait.

With a Grub or Caddis, you are to angle with the same length of
Line; or if it be all out as long as your Rod, 'tis not the worse, with
never above one hair for two or three lengths next the hook, and with
the smallest Cork, or float, and the least weight of plumb you can
that will but sink, and that the swiftness of your stream will allow;
which also you may help, and avoid the violence of the Current, by
angling in the returnes* of a stream, or the Eddies betwixt two
streams, which also are the most likely places wherein to kill a Fish in
a stream, either at the top or bottom.

Of Grubs for a Grayling, the Ash-Grub, which is plump, milk-
white, bent round from head to tail, and exceeding tender with a red
head; or the Dock worm,* or Grub of a pale yellow, longer, lanker,
and tougher than the other, with rows of feet all down his belly, and
a red head also are the best, I say for a Grayling, because, although a
Trout will take both these (the Ash-Grub especially) yet he does not
do it so freely as the other, and I have usually taken ten Graylings for
one Trout with that bait, though if a Trout come, I have observed,
that he is commonly a very good one.

These baits we usually keep in Bran, in which an Ash-Grub commonly grows tougher, and will better endure baiting, though he is yet
so tender, that it will be necessary to warp in a piece of a stiff hair with
your arming, leaving it standing out about a straw breadth at the head
of your hook, so as to keep the Grub either from slipping totally off

when baited, or at least down to the point of the hook, by which means your arming will be left wholly naked and bare, which is neither so sightly, nor so likely to be taken; though to help that (which will however very oft fall out) I always arm the hook* I design for this Bait with the whitest horse-hair I can chuse, which it self will resemble, and shine like that bait, and consequently will do more good, or less harm than an arming of any other colour. These Grubs are to be baited thus, the hook is to be put in under the head or Chaps* of the bait, and guided down the middle of the belly without suffering it to peep out by the way (for then, the Ash-Grub especially, will issue out water and milk, till nothing but the skin shall remain, and the bend of the hook will appear black through it) till the point of your hook come so low, that the head of your bait may rest, and stick upon the hair that stands out to hold it, by which means it can neither slip of it self; neither will the force of the stream, nor quick pulling out, upon any mistake, strip it off.

Now the Caddis, or Cod-bait (which is a sure killing bait, and for the most part, by much, surer, than either of the other) may be put upon the Hook, two or three together, and is sometimes (to very great effect) joyn'd to a worm, and sometimes to an Artificial Flie to cover the point of the Hook; but is always to be Angled with at the bottom (when by it self especially) with the finest Tackle; and is for all times of the year, the most holding bait of all other whatever, both for Trout, and Grayling.

There are several other baits besides these few I have nam'd you, which also do very great execution at the bottom, and some that are peculiar to certain Countries, and Rivers, of which every Angler may in his own place, make his own observation: and some others that I do not think fit to put you in mind of, because I would not corrupt you, and would have you, as in all things else I observe you to be a very honest Gentleman, a fair Angler. And so much for the second sort of Angling for a Trout at the bottom.

Viat. But Sir, I beseech you give me leave to ask you one question, Is there no art to be us'd to worms, to make them allure the Fish, and in a manner compel them to bite at the bait?

Pisc. Not that I know of; or did I know any such secret, I would not use it my self, and therefore would not teach it you. Though I will not deny to you, that in my younger days, I have made tryal of Oyl of Ospray,* Oyl of Ivy, Camphire,* Assa-faetida, juice of Nettles, and several other devices that I was taught by several Anglers I met with, but could never find any advantage by them; and can scarce believe there is any thing to be done that way, though I must tell you I have seen some men, who I thought went to work no more artificially* than I, and have yet with the same kind of worms I had, in my own sight taken five, and sometimes ten for one. But we'l let that business alone if you please; and because we have time enough, and that I would deliver you from the trouble of any more Lectures, I will, if you please, proceed to the last way of angling for a Trout or Grayling, which is in the middle; after which I shall have no more to trouble you with.

Viat. 'Tis no trouble, *Sir*, but the greatest satisfaction that can be, and I attend you.

CHAP. XII.

PISC. Angling in the middle then for a Trout or Grayling is of two sorts.

With a Pink or Minnow for a Trout:
or,
With a Worm, Grub or Caddis for a Grayling.

For the first, it is with a Minnow half a foot, or a foot within the *Superficies* of the water, and as to the rest that concerns this sort of angling, I shall wholly refer you to Mr. *Walton*'s direction, who is undoubtedly the best Angler with a Minnow in *England*; only in plain truth I do not approve of those baits he keeps in salt,* unless where the Living ones are not possibly to be had (though I know he frequently kills with them, and peradventure more, than with any other, nay I have seen him refuse a living one for one of them) and much less of his artificial one;* for though we do it with a counterfeit flie, me thinks it should hardly be expected, that a man should deceive a fish with a counterfeit fish. Which having said, I shall only add, and that out of my own experience, that I do believe a Bull-head, with his Guill-fins cut off (at some times of the year especially) to be a much better bait for a Trout, than a Minnow, and a Loach much better than that, to prove which I shall only tell you that I have much oftner taken Trouts with a Bull-head or a Loach in their Throats (for there a Trout has questionless his first digestion) than a Minnow; and that one day especially, having Angled a good part of the day with a Minnow, and that in as hopeful a day, and as fit a water, as could be wisht for that purpose, without raising any one Fish; I at last fell to 't with the worm, and with that took fourteen in a very short space, amongst all which, there was not to my remembrance, so much as one, that had not a Loach or two, and some of them three, four, five, and six Loaches, in his throat and stomach; from whence I concluded, that had I Angled with that bait, I had made a notable days work of 't.

But after all, there is a better way of Angling with a Minnow, than perhaps is fit either to teach or to practice; to which I shall only add, that a Grayling will certainly rise at, and sometimes take a Minnow, though it will be hard to be believ'd by any one, who shall consider the littleness of that Fishes mouth, very unfit to take so great a bait: but is affirm'd by many, that he will sometimes do it, and I my self know it to be true, for though I never took a Grayling so, yet a Man of mine once did, and within so few paces of me, that I am as certain of it, as I can be of any thing I did not see, and (which made it appear the more strange) the Grayling was not above eleven inches long.

I must here also beg leave of your Master, and mine, not to controvert, but to tell him, that I cannot consent to his way of throwing in his Rod* to an overgrown Trout, and afterwards recovering his Fish with his Tackle. For though I am satisfied he has sometimes done it, because he says so; yet I have found it quite otherwise, and though I have taken with the Angle, I may safely say, some thousands of Trouts in my life, my top never snapt, though my Line still continued fast to the remaining part of my Rod (by some lengths of Line curl'd round about my top, and there fastned with waxt silk, against such an accident) nor my hand never slackt, or slipt by any other chance, but I almost always infallibly lost my Fish, whether great, or little, though my Hook came home again. And I have often wondred how a Trout should so suddainly disengage himself from so great a Hook, as that we bait with a Minnow, and so deep bearded, as those Hooks commonly are, when I have seen by the forenam'd accidents, or the slipping of a knot in the upper part of the Line, by suddain, and hard striking, that though the Line has immediately been recover'd, almost before it could be all drawn into the water, the Fish clear'd, and gone in a moment. And yet to justifie what he says, I have sometimes known a Trout, having carried away a whole Line, found dead three, or four days after with the Hook fast sticking in him: but then it is to be suppos'd he had gorg'd it, which a Trout will do, if you be not too quick with him when he comes at a Minnow, as sure and much sooner than a Pike; and I my self have also, once or twice in my life, taken the same Fish with my own Flie sticking in his Chaps,* that he had taken from me the day before, by the slipping of a Hook in the arming: but I am very confident a Trout will not be troubled two hours with any Hook, that has so much as one handful* of Line left behind with it, or that is not struck through a bone, if it be in any part of his mouth only; nay, I do certainly know, that a Trout so soon as ever he feels himself prickt, if he carries away the Hook, goes immediately to the bottom, and will there root like a Hog upon the Gravel, till he either rub out, or break the Hook in the middle. And so much for this first sort of Angling in the middle for a Trout.

The second way of Angling in the middle, is with a Worm, Grub, Caddis, or any other Ground-bait for a Grayling, and that is with a Cork, and a foot from the bottom, a Grayling taking it much better there, than at the bottom, as has been said before; and this always in a clear water, and with the finest Tackle.

To which we may also, and with very good reason, add the third way of Angling by hand with a Ground-bait, as a third way of Fishing in the middle, which is common to both Trout, and Grayling, and (as I said before) the best way of Angling with a Worm, of all other I ever try'd whatever.

And now Sir, I have said all I can at present think of concerning Angling for a Trout and Grayling; and I doubt not, have tir'd you sufficiently: but I will give you no more trouble of this kind, whilst you stay; which I hope will be a good while longer.

Viat. That will not be above a day longer; but if I live till *May* come twelve Month, you are sure of me again, either with my Master *Walton*, or without him, and in the mean time shall acquaint him how much you have made of me for his sake, and I hope he loves me well enough, to thank you for it.

Pisc. I shall be glad *Sir*, of your good Company at the time you speak of and shall be loath to part with you now; but when you tell me you must go, I will then wait upon you more Miles on your way, than I have tempted you out of it, and heartily wish you a good Journey.

FINIS.

To my most Honoured Friend,
Charles Cotton, *Esq*;

Sir,

You now see, I have return'd you, your very pleasant, and useful discourse of the Art of *Flie-Fishing*, Printed, just as 'twas sent me: for I have been so obedient to your desires, as to endure all the praises you have ventur'd to fix upon me in it. And, when I have thankt you for them, as the effects of an undissembled love: then, let me tell you *Sir*, that I will really endeavour to live up to the Character you have given of me, if there were no other reason; yet for this alone, that you, that love me so well; and always think what you speak, may not, for my sake, suffer by a mistake in your Judgment.

And *Sir*, I have ventur'd to fill a part of your Margin,* by way of Paraphrase, for the Readers clearer understanding the situation both of your *Fishing-House*, and the pleasantness of that you dwell in. And I have ventur'd also to give him a Copy of Verses, that, you were pleas'd to send me, now some Years past; in which, he may see a good Picture of both; and, so much of your own mind too, as will make any Reader that is blest with a Generous Soul, to love you the better. I confess, that for doing this, you may justly Judg me too bold: if you do, I will say so too: and so far commute for my offence, that, though I be more than a hundred Miles from you, and in the eighty third Year of my Age, yet I will forget both, and next Month begin a Pilgrimage to beg your pardon, for, I would dye in your favour: and till then will live.

Sir,
Your most affectionate
Father and Friend,
Izaak Walton.

London, *April.*
29th. 1676.

THE
RETIREMENT.

Stanzes Irreguliers

TO

Mr. *IZAAK WALTON*.

Farewell thou busie World, and, may
  We never meet again:
 Here I can eat, and sleep, and pray,
 And do more good in one short day,
 Than he, who his whole Age out wears
Upon the most conspicuous Theaters,
Where nought, but vanity and vice appears.

2.

 Good God! how sweet are all things here!
 How beautiful the Fields appear!
 How cleanly, do we feed and lye!
 Lord! what good hours do we keep!
    How quietly we sleep!
 What peace, what unanimity!
 How innocent from the lewd fashion,
Is all our business, all our recreation!

3.

 Oh, how happy here's our leasure!
 Oh, how innocent our pleasure!
 Oh, ye Valleys, Oh ye Mountains!
 Oh, ye Groves, and Chrystal Fountains,
    How I love at liberty,
 By turns, to come and visit ye!

4.

 Dear solitude, the Souls best friend,
That Man, acquainted with himself dost make,
*And, all his makers wonders to intend,**

With thee, I here converse at will,
And would be glad to do so still,
For, it is thou alone, that keep'st the Soul awake.

5.

How Calm, and quiet a delight,
Is it, alone
To read, and meditate, and write;
By none offended, and, offending none?
To walk, ride, sit, or sleep at ones own ease!
And, pleasing a Mans self, none other to displease.

6.

Oh my beloved Nymph fair Dove;
Princess of rivers, how I love
Upon thy flowry Banks to lye,
And view thy silver stream,
When guilded by a Summers beam!
And in it, all thy wanton fry
Playing at liberty:
And, with my Angle upon them
The all of treachery
I ever learnt industriously to try.

7.

Such streams, Romes *yellow* Tyber *cannot show,*
The Iberian Tagus *or Ligurian* Po;
The Mause,* the Danube, *and the* Rhine
Are puddle water all, compar'd with thine:
And Loyres *pure streams yet too polluted are*
With thine much purer to compare;
The rapid Garonne, *and the winding* Seine,
Are both too mean
Beloved Dove, *with thee*
To vie priority;
Nay, Tame *and* Isis, *when conjoyn'd* submit,*
And lay their Trophies at thy silver feet.

8.

Oh my beloved Rocks *that rise*
To awe the Earth, and brave the Skies:
From some aspiring Mountains crown,
How dearly do I love,
Giddy with pleasure, to look down,
And from the vales, to view the noble heights above!

9.

Oh my beloved Caves!* from dog-stars heat,*
And all anxieties, my safe retreat:
What safety, privacy, what true delight,
In th' artificial night,
Your gloomy entrals make,
Have I taken, do I take!
How oft when grief has made me fly
To hide me from society,
Even, of my dearest friends, have I
In your recesses friendly shade,
All my sorrows open laid,
And, my most secret woes, entrusted to your privacy!

10.

Lord! would men let me alone;
What an over happy one
Should I think my self to be!
Might I in this desart place
(Which most Men in discourse disgrace)*
Live but undisturb'd and free!
Here, in this despis'd recess
Would I, maugre Winters cold,
And the Summers worst excess,
Try, to live out to sixty full years old!*
And, all the while
Without an envious eye,
On any thriving under fortunes smile,
Contented live, and then, contented dye.

C. C.

FINIS.

Courteous Reader.

YOU may be pleas'd to take notice, that at the Sign of the Three Trouts in St. *Paul's* Church-Yard, on the North side, you may be fitted with all sorts of the best Fishing Tackle, by

John Margrave.

EXPLANATORY NOTES

ABBREVIATIONS

Aldrovandi	Ulisse Aldrovandi, *De Piscibus* (Bologna, 1613)
Bacon	Sir Francis Bacon, *Historie of Life and Death* (London, 1638)
Barker	Thomas Barker, *The Art of Angling* (London, 1651)
Camden	William Camden, *Britain, or a Chorographicall Description*, trans. Philemon Holland (London, 1637)
Du Bartas	Guillaume de Saluste, Sieur Du Bartas, *The Divine Weeks and Works*, trans. Josuah Sylvester, ed. Susan Snyder (Oxford, 1979)
Gesner	Conrad Gesner, *Historiae Animalium*, bk. 4, *Qui est de Piscium . . . Natura* (Frankfurt, 1604)
Hakewill	George Hakewill, *An Apologie of the Power and Providence of God in the Government of the World* (Oxford, 1627)
Heywood	Gerald G. P. Heywood, *Charles Cotton and His River* (Manchester, 1928)
Pliny	Pliny, *The Naturall Historie*, trans. Philemon Holland (London, 1634)
Samuel	William Samuel, *The Arte of Angling*, ed. Gerald Eades Bentley, introd. Carl Otto V. Kienbusch, notes by Henry L. Savage (Princeton, 1956)
Topsell, *Beastes*	Edward Topsell, *The Historie of Foure-Footed Beastes* (London, 1607)
Topsell, *Serpents*	Edward Topsell, *The Historie of Serpents* (London, 1608)

In these notes, I have occasionally drawn on the editions of *The Compleat Angler* cited in the Bibliography, as well as the previous Oxford World's Classics edition (1982) edited by John Buxton and introduced by John Buchan. I wish to thank Richard F. Hardin for his helpful suggestions about my translations of the Latin dedicatory poems. Quotations from the Bible are from the Authorized Version, first published in 1611.

PART I

3 *JOHN OFFLEY OF Madely Manor . . . Stafford*: the grandson of Sir Thomas Offley, Lord Mayor of London (1556–7), he died in 1658. Although Walton spent much of his life in London, he was born and raised in Staffordshire.

curiosity: hobby.

Sir Henry Wotton: (1568–1639), ambassador, writer, connoisseur of art and architecture, and provost of Eton College. Walton edited Wotton's collected works, *Reliquiae Wottonianae* (1651), for which he also wrote a prefatory biography.

5 *sowre-complexion'd*: complexion here means temperament.

Nat. and R. Roe: probably relatives of Walton through his sister, Anne Grinsell.

the excellent picture: six pictures of fish—including the trout—appeared in the first edition of *The Compleat Angler*; Walton added four additional images to the second edition of 1655. It is not known by whom the illustrations were drawn or engraved.

6 *Cambden*: William Camden (1551–1623), historian and headmaster of Westminster School, published his *Britannia* (in Latin) in 1586; an English translation by Philemon Holland appeared in 1610.

Mr. Hales . . . School of Defence: George Hale, *The Private Schoole of Defence* (London, 1614).

7 *this fifth Impression*: *The Compleat Angler* was first published in 1653; the fifth edition, the last published during Walton's lifetime, was issued in 1676 and is the basis of the present edition. See the Note on the Text.

9 *Erasmus in his learned Colloquies*: Desiderius Erasmus (1469–1536), Dutch scholar. Erasmus's *Colloquia* (Colloquies), first published in 1518, is a collection of dialogues in Latin designed for students.

Jo. Floud: John Floud, Walton's brother-in-law by his first wife, Rachel Floud. This poem first appears in the second edition of 1655, where it is entitled 'To my dear Brother-in-law, Mʳ. IZ Walton, upon his *Complete Angler*'.

10 *Et piscatorem piscis amare potest*: from Martial's *Epigrams*, 6.63, l. 6, about a legacy-hunter: '"Munera magna tamen misit". sed misit in hamo; | et piscatorem piscis amare potest?' ('Yet he sent me great gifts'. But he sent them on a hook; and can a fish love the fisherman?')

Ch. Harvie: Christopher Harvey (1597–1663), Church of England clergyman and poet. Harvey wrote his collection of devotional poems, *The Synagogue*, in imitation of George Herbert's *The Temple*; beginning with the second edition (1655), Walton included a poem from Harvey's collection in *The Compleat Angler* (see pp. 82–3 and note to p. 83).

Flora: goddess of flowering plants.

11 *Snig*: a young or small eel.

Gotham: a village proverbial for its inhabitants' foolishness.

The Tench (Physician of the Brook): see p. 117.

12 *Hydrophobie*: hydrophobia is an aversion to water or other liquids symptomatic of rabies when transmitted to humans.

Actaeon: in mythology, Actaeon was a hunter who accidentally saw the goddess Diana while she was bathing; to punish him, Diana turned Actaeon into a stag, and he was pursued and killed by his pack of hounds.

Tho. Weaver: Thomas Weaver (1616–62), clergyman and poet. Chaplain or petty canon at Christ Church Cathedral, Oxford, in the 1640s; as a staunch royalist, Weaver was ejected from this position and perhaps imprisoned in 1648. Because of the politics of his *Songs and Poems of Love and Drollery* (1654), Weaver was arrested, imprisoned, and tried for treason, but the judge argued in favour of Weaver and he was acquitted. At the Restoration, Weaver was appointed the customs collector for Liverpool.

13 *his matchless Donne and Wotton*: refers to Walton's biographies of John Donne (first published in 1640) and Sir Henry Wotton (first published in 1651).

Ouldsworth and Featly: Ouldsworth is Dr Richard Holdsworth (1590–1649), Church of England clergyman and master of Emmanuel College, Cambridge; arrested and imprisoned in 1643 for royalism, appointed dean of Worcester by Charles I in 1647. 'Featly' may be Daniel Featley (1582–1645), Church of England clergyman, controversialist, and author of a popular collection of prayers, *Ancilla Pietatis: or, The Handmaid to Private Devotion* (London, 1626 and many later editions). Featley, who had been a royal chaplain to Charles I, was targeted with vandalism and violence by parliamentary soldiers in the early 1640s and was removed from his livings and imprisoned in 1643.

Morley: despite the past tense, probably George Morley (1598?–1684), later bishop of Winchester. During the 1640s, Morley was a royal chaplain and a canon of Christ Church in Oxford; after he was ejected from his canonry in 1648, Morley went into exile on the Continent, where he served Charles II and prominent royalists. At the Restoration, Morley became bishop of Worcester; in 1662, he became bishop of Winchester. Walton, who had been a friend of Morley since the 1630s, served briefly as Morley's steward at Worcester and then apparently lived as a member of Morley's household for much of the rest of his life. Walton wrote his biographies of both Richard Hooker (1665) and Robert Sanderson (1678) at the urging of Morley, and he dedicated the 1670 collected edition of his *Lives* to Morley.

some vex they from their lands are thrown: beginning in 1643, ordinances were passed which allowed Parliament to seize and dispose of the estates of royalists.

13 *like the Dutch . . . live at peace now*: perhaps a reference to the Peace of Münster (1648), which ended eighty years of war between the Netherlands and Spain.

Edv. Powel, Mr. of Arts: an Edward Powel (or 'Powell'), 'Master in Arts and chief School-Master in *Stafford*', preached a sermon in 1661 'at the Assizes for *Staffordshire* held at *Wolver-hampton*' which he subsequently published as *The Danger of the Errors of the Rulers* (London, 1662, A^v and title page). Someone of the same name provided commendatory verses for James Shirley's *Poems* (1646) and the Beaumont and Fletcher folio of 1647.

14 *Rob. Floud*: Robert Floud, Walton's brother-in-law by his first wife, Rachel Floud. 'C.' perhaps stands for 'Cambridge'; Robert Floud proceeded BA at St John's College, Cambridge, in 1627. Floud's poem first appeared in the second edition of 1655, where it was entitled 'To my dear Brother in law, Mr. *Is. Walton* on his *Complete Angler*'.

Clarissimo . . . velit: 'To my most distinguished and dearest Brother, Master Izaak Walton, the most expert in the Art of Angling. Only one fish is the Doctor of the rest, and health is assured to those for whom it is lawful to touch the Doctor. Here is a wonderful figure of our Saviour Jesus, where every letter holds his mystery [in Greek, the first letters of the phrase 'Jesus Christ, Son of God, Saviour' form the word *ichthus* (fish); this ancient Christian acrostic is translated into Latin on p. 14]. I desire this fish; may you capture this fish, good brother of the fishing rod: he would pay off here both my debts and yours to God. He is the fish and the fisherman; believe me, a fish would want to love such an one even though he were an angler.' The final line of the poem plays on the quotation from Martial that concludes Harvey's poem on p. 10.

Henry Bayley: this poem first appeared in the 1655 edition of the *Angler*, where the author's surname was given as 'Bagley'. A Henry Bagley was minister of the Chapel Royal, Savoy (in central London), from 1619 to 1625.

16 *Ad Virum optimum . . . piscandum studes*: 'To the best of men and most expert fisherman, Izaak Walton. Hail, Walton, learned master of the art of angling! Great champion of the fishing rod, happy are you, whether you traverse alone a secluded valley, meanwhile watching the waters flowing past, or perhaps standing on the margin of a pure river or sitting on the firm and grassy bank, you deceive the scaly herd with your skilled hand. O happy are you, who—far from business, free from the dust and noise of the marketplace and city and far from the crowd, near the gently flowing waters—deceive the roving fish with honest fraud. Therefore while nearly all the rest of the race of mortals by turns either spread nets for themselves and bait traps with gifts as with a hook, or try to catch wealthy old men, you, meanwhile, weave snares for the swimming flock: you entice that greedy foreigner, the pike, with a hook; or you capture the insatiable perch with a very small bleak, or a trout with a red worm or smooth mussel, or the wary

carp that is hardly ever caught with a rod and line (but your art overcomes him); or with bait you draw in the healing tench or the little palate-pleasing gudgeon; or your prey is the barbel, less wholesome albeit larger and distinguished by its weighty moustache. These are your arts while the season and time permit, and no day passes without a line. Not only the practice, but also the theory of this art is well known to you, whence you are at once a good angler and also a good writer: you are the master who understands the strokes of both the fishing rod and the pen. How you truly instruct the novice fisherman! Behold, you, the second Oppian, write the Halieutica ['On Fishing'] with an elegant pen, and you duly set forth your angling precepts, arts, and methods, and the diverse baits, and the character and variety of fish. Nor do you think it is enough to hand down the art of angling (notwithstanding that it is a kind of school of virtue and teaches patience and self-control), but you give greater lessons and proofs of loftier art: the everlasting monuments of character and the noblest patterns of life. For as long as you write of profound Hooker, and the devout and eloquent Donne, and of divine Herbert, the holy poet, we see these worthies painted skilfully by your brush and expert hand, Izaak. By you these Heroes live again after death. O what pleasure it is to read your books! Thus you catch us with books as you catch fish with lines; although intent on the hook, yet you pursue the Muses and literature while you strive after fish.'

Aliud . . . en orbis fuit!. 'Another to Izaak Walton, the best man and angler.

Izaak, congratulations on this art of angling! With this art, Peter gave testimony to the Prince [Jesus; see Matthew 16:15–18]. With this art, not long before Peter (that well-known Suetonius testifies [*The Lives of the Twelve Caesars*, bk. 2, ch. 83]) the father of his country, Caesar Augustus—a learned angler—was wont to refresh himself with a hook and a fishing rod. Now you, my friend, are, after Caesar, the greatest glory of the famous hook and the angling tribe. Well done, O professor of an art that is by no means undistinguished, learned doctor surveying the fish-market! You the master and I your disciple (for they speak of me as an aspiring angler), truly we have found a noble comrade in this art. What more, Walton, remains to be said? Lo, our Lord Himself on earth was an angler!'

Jaco. Dup. D.D.: James Duport (1606–79), dean of Peterborough and master of Magdalene College, Cambridge. Earlier in his career, Duport was an influential tutor at Trinity College, Cambridge, as well as Regius professor of Greek; at the Restoration, he was made a Doctor of Divinity at Cambridge and a royal chaplain. Duport published George Herbert's Latin epigrams in his *Ecclesiastes Solomonis* (1662) and contributed a commendatory poem to Walton's biography of Herbert in the edition of Walton's *Lives* published in 1675.

17 *PISCATOR. VENATOR. AUCEPS.*: Latin for Fisherman, Hunter, Falconer.

whether: whither, to which place.

17 *Thatcht House in Hodsden*: Piscator and his companions are walking north from Tottenham toward Ware along a road that follows the course of the River Lea (see Maps 1 and 2). The town of Hoddesden is located about 15 miles from Tottenham; the Thatched House was an inn on the High Street.

Theobalds: a magnificent country house built in the 1560s by William Cecil, Lord Burghley, which became a royal palace in 1607; James I died there in 1625. During the Commonwealth, much of Theobalds was dismantled by Parliament and its materials were sold to benefit the army. Theobalds was located about 9 miles from Tottenham.

mews a Hawk: to 'mew' is to confine and care for a hawk, as at moulting time.

18 *Good company . . . shorter*: proverbial.

Otter dogs: otter hounds, large dogs with shaggy coats and webbed feet. Huntsmen would use small packs of eight 'couples' of otter hounds (that is, sixteen dogs) to hunt otters.

noble Mr Sadlers: Ralph Sadler (*d.* 1660), whose estate was at Standon, Hertfordshire, about 7 miles NE of Ware. Walton knew Sadler's family, which had Staffordshire connections. Sadler 'delighted much in hawking and hunting, and the Pleasures of a Country Life; was famous for his noble Table, his great Hospitality to his Neighbours, and his abundant Charity to the Poor'; he also successfully brought an action of trespass against a man 'for fishing in the River *Standon* leading thro' his own Land, and for erecting a Weer there' (Sir Henry Chauncy, *The Historical Antiquities of Hertfordshire*, i (1700; Dorking, 1975), 430).

Amwell hill: located NW of the village of Amwell in Hertfordshire, about 1.5 miles south of Ware and 17 miles north of Tottenham.

prevent: arrive before.

vermin: otters had been officially classified as 'vermin' by an Act of Parliament in 1566, and parishes would pay between sixpence and one shilling for each dead otter.

19 *Lucian*: (*c.* AD 120–80), ancient Greek rhetorician and satirist. Walton adapts, with significant alteration, an epigram by 'T. H.' (Thomas Hickes) which prefaces *Certaine Select Dialogues of Lucian*, trans. Francis Hickes (Oxford, 1634), A4^r.

what Solomon says of Scoffers: Proverbs 24:9.

Mountange: Michel de Montaigne (1533–92), French philosophical writer. Montaigne's 'Apologie de Raymond Sebond' (Apology for Raymond Sebond) appears in his *Essais* (Essays); Sebond (*d.* 1436) was a Catalan theologian. Walton here adapts John Florio's English translation of the *Essais* (Montaigne, *Essayes*, trans. Florio (2nd edn., London, 1613), 250).

21 *testifie*: prove.

use: am accustomed.

Joves servant in Ordinary: in classical mythology, the eagle was associated with Zeus, the supreme god; Juvenal calls the eagle 'famulae Iovis' (the attendant of Jove) in Satire 14, l. 81. The expression 'in ordinary' means 'in an official capacity'.

the son of Daedalus: Icarus escaped from Crete with his father by flying with wings made of feathers and wax. But Icarus disregarded Daedalus' advice and flew too close to the sun, whereupon the wax of his wings melted and Icarus fell into the sea and drowned.

carere: career; in falconry, a flight of the bird, about 120 yards.

witness the not breaking of Ice: i.e. as can be seen if solid ice is not broken.

Air or breath of life . . . dies presently: see Genesis 2:7 and Psalm 104:29.

22 *excrements*: outgrowths, here referring to feathers.

curious: ingenious.

Lark: skylark (*Alauda arvensis*).

Thrassel: song thrush (*Turdus philomelos*).

the honest Robin, that loves mankind both alive and dead: 'The Robin-red-brest if he find a man or woman dead, will cover all his face with mosse, and some thinke that if the body should remaine unburied, that hee woulde cover the whole body also' (Thomas Johnson, *Cornucopiae* (London, 1596), F1ᵛ).

Varro his Aviarie: Marcus Terentius Varro (116–27 BC), Roman scholar and satirist. Varro discusses his aviary in his agricultural manual, *De Re Rustica* (On Farming), bk. 3, ch. 4.

when the Turks besieged Malta or Rhodes: in 1480–1, the Ottomans unsuccessfully besieged the Knights Hospitaller of St John of Jerusalem (a Roman Catholic military order) in Rhodes. In 1522 the Ottomans captured Rhodes, and the Knights eventually moved to Malta. The Ottomans followed and in 1565, after one of the greatest sieges in history, were repulsed with heavy losses.

Mr. G. Sandis in his Travels: in *A Relation of a Journey* (1615), 209, the English traveller and writer George Sandys (1578–1644) describes the use of doves to carry messages in the Middle East.

23 *the Dove was sent out of the Ark by Noah*: Genesis 8:8–12.

for the Sacrifices of the Law: Leviticus 12:6, 8; Luke 2:24.

when God would feed the Prophet Elijah: 1 Kings 17:4–6.

the shape of a Dove: Luke 3:22.

the laborious Bee . . . their own Commonwealth: bees were understood to exemplify industrious personal behaviour, as well as rational political organization.

the long-winged and the short-winged Hawk: Falconidae and Accipitridae.

The Gerfalcon and Jerkin: gyrfalcon (*Falco rusticolus*) and male gyrfalcon.

The six following couples likewise name the female and then the male of the same species:

> *Falcon and Tassel-gentel*: female and male peregrine falcons (*Falco peregrinus*);
>
> *Laner and Laneret*: lanner and lanneret, female and male of the lanner falcon (*Falco biarmicus*);
>
> *Bockerel and Bockeret*: the female and male of an unidentified species of long-winged hawk;
>
> *Saker and Sacaret*: the female and male of the saker falcon (*Falco cherrug*);
>
> *Marlin and Jack Marlin*: female and male of the merlin (*Falco columbarius*);
>
> *Hobby and Jack*: the female and male hobby (*Falco subbuteo*).

23   *Stelletto*: unidentified.

Bloud red Rook from Turky: the roc, a huge mythical bird of prey.

Waskite from Virginia: perhaps the swallow-tailed kite (*Elanoides forficatus*).

Iron: i.e. *erne*, a male eagle. The next two couples also name the female and then the male of the same species:

> *Goshawk and Tarcel*: the female and male goshawk (*Accipiter gentilis*);
>
> *Sparhawk and Musket:* the female and male sparrowhawk (*Accipiter nisus*).

French Pye of two sorts: the great grey shrike (*Lanius excubitor*) and the lesser grey shrike (*Lanius minor*).

24   *Stanyel, the Ringtail*: stanyel, the kestrel (*Falco tinnunculus*); the ringtail is any of several very similar female and juvenile harriers, esp. the hen harrier (*Circus cyaneus*) and Montagu's harrier (*Circus pygargus*).

The forked Kite, the bald Buzzard: the red kite *(Milvus milvus)* and the osprey (*Pandion haliaetus*).

Hen-driver: the hen harrier (*Circus cyaneus*).

the Eires, the Brancher, the Ramish Hawk, the Haggard, and the two sorts of Lentners: eires, eyas (?), a young hawk whose training is incomplete; brancher, a young hawk when it first leaves the nest; ramish, ramage (?), a young, untamed hawk; haggard, a wild female hawk caught when in her adult plumage; lentner, a hawk taken in Lent.

Ayries, their Mewings, rare order of casting: aeries are nesting places; mewings, moultings. Hawks *cast* (vomit up) indigestible substances.

reclaiming: in falconry, the recalling of a hawk.

Stag ... Buck: stag, male of the red deer; buck, male of the fallow deer.

the Fichat, the Fulimart, the Ferret, the Pole-cat, the Mould-warp: the members of the weasel family (Mustelidae) were not clearly distinguished from each other in the seventeenth century. The term 'fichat' (fitchet) was a name for the polecat (*Mustela putorius*), but it was also used to refer to the weasel (*Mustela nivalis*). 'Fulimart' (foumart) was another name for the polecat. Ferret is a domesticated descendant of the polecat; mould-warp is the European mole (*Talpa europaea*).

How could Cleopatra . . . at one Supper: Plutarch reports that Antony (not Cleopatra) served eight wild boars at a 'supper' (*Lives of the Noble Grecians and Romaines*, trans. Sir Thomas North (London, 1603), 923).

25 *the little Pismire*: ant. Walton alludes to Aesop's fable of the Ant and the Grasshopper (see e.g. *Aesops Fables, With Their Morals* (London, 1651), 124–6).

Xenophon: see Xenophon, *Cyrupaedia: The Institution and Life of Cyrus*, trans. Philemon Holland (London, 1632), 12–15, 4–5.

Rascal game: the young, lean, or inferior deer of a herd.

Moses in the Law permitted to the Jews: Leviticus 11:3, Deuteronomy 14:6.

26 *it is neither our fault nor our custom*: Piscator evokes the proverb, 'If you swear you shall catch no fish.'

the Element upon which the Spirit of God did first move: Genesis 1:2.

the Element which God commanded to bring forth living creatures abundantly: Genesis 1:21.

skilled in all the learning of the Egyptians: Acts 7:22.

the friend of God: Abraham is called 'the Friend of God' in James 2:23; in Exodus 33:11, 'the Lord spake unto Moses face to face, as a man speaketh unto his friend'.

many Philosophers: the Greek philosopher Thales of Miletus (early sixth century BC) taught that water is the origin of all matter.

27 *they affirm, they can reduce this wood back again to water*: Walton's source for this experiment is unknown.

increase: offspring.

the casting off of Lent: from the Tudor period until the Interregnum, the English government had mandated the observation of several meatless 'fish days' each week, in addition to periods of fasting prescribed by the Church, to promote ocean fisheries and thus strengthen the navy.

in Story: in historical writings.

the chief diet: Leviticus 11:9 and Deuteronomy 14:9 say that the Israelites may eat water creatures that have fins and scales but do not suggest that the Israelites' diet should primarily consist of fish.

the Whale: the whale is a mammal, not a fish.

The Romans: Macrobius (Ambrosius Theodosius Macrobius, *fl.* AD 400) and Varro (Marcus Terentius Varro, 116–27 BC) were Roman writers; Walton's comments about fish in Roman culture derive from Hakewill, 356–61.

Dr. Wharton: Dr Thomas Wharton (1614–73) served in the royalist garrison at Bolton from 1642 to 1645. He practised medicine in London from 1648 and became a fellow of the College of Physicians in 1650. Wharton was one of the few physicians to remain in London during the outbreak of plague in 1665.

28 *St. Jerome*: St Jerome (*c.*347–420), Christian scholar best known for his Latin translation of the Bible, the Vulgate.

Tully: Cicero.

in and near to Rome: Walton draws these descriptions, with a few errors, from John Raymond, *An Itinerary Contayning a Voyage, Made Through Italy* (London, 1648). The sites associated with Livy are in Padua, and Virgil's tomb is located at Naples.

God is said to have spoken to a Fish: Jonah 2:10.

made a Whale a Ship: Jonah 1–2. The creature that swallows Jonah is called 'a great fish', not a whale.

Theobalds house: see note to p. 17.

except against: object to.

29 *this Park-wall*: the park at Theobalds (see note to p. 17) had been enlarged by James I and enclosed by a brick wall that stretched for 10 miles; in 1650, the park contained more than 2,500 acres.

any Hawk you have nam'd: Auceps, not Venator, gave a list of hawks.

like Poetry, men are to be born so: proverbial.

wit: intellect.

like Vertue, a reward to it self: proverbial.

30 *the antiquity of Angling*: this paragraph draws from Gervase Markham's *The Pleasures of Princes, or, Good Mens Recreations*, p. 3, which was appended to the second part of Markham's *The English Husbandman* (London, 1614). Markham's treatise was a prose version of John Dennys's poem *The Secrets of Angling* (1613); in that work, Dennys describes how Deucalion and his wife, Pyrrha, repeopled the earth after the great flood by throwing stones over their shoulders which immediately became adult humans, and how Deucalion invented angling to feed everyone (B8ʳ–C1ᵛ). On Dennys and his poem, see note to p. 41.

Belus: son of the sea god Poseidon.

Seth: one of Adam's children born after the murder of Abel. Josephus, *Antiquities of the Jews*, 1.2.3, says that the descendants of Seth inscribed their discoveries on two pillars, one made of brick and the other of stone.

in the Prophet Amos . . . in the Book of Job . . . mention is made also of fish-hooks: Amos 4:2, Job 41:1. The author of the Book of Job is unknown.

communicable: talkative.

31 *Pet. du Moulin*: Pierre du Moulin (1568–1658), French Protestant divine who received a prebend at Canterbury Cathedral after writing works of religious controversy in support of James I. Walton essentially quotes from

the preface to one of these works, *The Accomplishment of the Prophecies*, trans. J. Heath (Oxford, 1613), A3ʳ.

an ingenuous Spaniard: unidentified.

32 *Aristotle*: (384–322 BC), ancient Greek philosopher and scientist. Walton draws on the description of the '*Eleusinian* Spring' in Sylvester's translation of Du Bartas (3rd Day of 1st Week, ll. 247–50), but Du Bartas does not mention Aristotle.

a River in Epirus . . . it is called Mole: Walton draws on Du Bartas's *Divine Weeks and Works*, trans. Josuah Sylvester, for most of his accounts of rivers in this paragraph (3rd Day of 1st Week, ll. 235–72). For British rivers, with some muddled references and alterations, Walton draws on Camden, 762, 297 (the well that ebbs and flows, the River Mole); Drayton, *Poly-Olbion*, Song 22, ll. 11–14 (petrifying stream-bank in England); and Gerardus Mercator, *Historia Mundi: or Mercators Atlas*, trans. W[ye]. S[altonstall]. (London, 1635), 46 (petrifying Irish lake).

Anus: Anas, the Guadiana River.

Josephus: Flavius Josephus (AD 37/8–*c*.100), Jewish historian. In *The Jewish War*, bk. 7, ch. 5, Josephus describes the Sabbatic River, but (reversing Walton's account) says that it is dry for six days and flows only on the seventh; Du Bartas also refers to this river (3rd Day of 1st Week, ll. 243–6), and his account of the river's behaviour accords with Walton's.

Pliny the Philosopher: Pliny the Elder (23–79), Roman scholar and author of the encyclopaedic *Natural History*. Walton refers to bk. 9, chs. 3, 8, and 22.

Balaena or Whirle-Pool: Pliny says that 'the Whales and Whirlepooles called Balaenae, take up in length as much as foure acres . . . of land' (bk. 9, ch. 3); Walton gives the figure as 2 acres.

33 *Cadara (an Island near this place)*: Pliny says, 'In the red sea there lies a great demie Island [peninsula] named Cadara' (bk. 9, ch. 3); in Walton's paraphrase, 'this place' is the Indian Sea.

Dr. Casaubons Discourse of Credulity, and Incredulity: Meric Casaubon (1599–1671), scholar and divine. In the 1640s, Casaubon—who had been made Doctor of Divinity at Oxford by Charles I—was imprisoned, fined, and deprived of his livings in Kent and his prebendal stall at Christ Church, Canterbury. He later rejected Cromwell's lucrative commission to write a history of the civil wars. Casaubon discusses dolphins in his treatise *Of Credulity and Incredulity in Things Natural, Civil, and Divine* (London, 1668), 235–51.

John Tredescant . . . Elias Ashmole: John Tradescant the elder (*d*. 1638), a gardener employed by the Stuart elite, created a famous collection of rare plants and curiosities at his home in Lambeth. His namesake son (*bap*. 1608, *d*. 1662), also a gardener, travelled to Virginia multiple times and brought back plants and other objects to add to the family's museum. The younger John Tradescant published a catalogue of the collection, *Musaeum Tradescantianum*, in 1656; Walton's list of specimens draws on pp. 8, 6, and 4. Elias Ashmole (1617–92), a lawyer, astrologer, and antiquarian, helped the younger Tradescant to compile and publish the catalogue. Thanks to some sharp practice and sustained legal action against the younger Tradescant's widow, Ashmole eventually gained possession of the Tradescant curiosities, which he subsequently donated to Oxford University as the founding collection of the Ashmolean Museum.

33 *Hog-fish . . . Cony-Fish*: hog-fish is perhaps the red scorpionfish (*Scorpaena scrofa*); cony-fish is a burbot (*Lota lota*).

the Poyson-fish: unidentified.

Solan Geese: gannets (*Morus bassanus*), large white seabirds.

Mr. George Herbert: George Herbert (1593–1633), Church of England clergyman and poet. Herbert's collection of devotional poems, *The Temple*, was published after his death and quickly became very popular and influential; Walton quotes, with slight alterations, from 'Providence', stanzas 36, 8, and 7. Walton published his *Life* of Herbert in 1670.

ows: owns.

34 *Pliny says*: Pliny, bk. 9, ch. 2.

Gesner: Conrad Gesner (1516–65), Swiss physician and naturalist. Gesner's *Historiae Animalium* (Studies of Animals), first published in Zurich from 1551 to 1587, was a compendium of information about animals; the fourth book of this work, about fish, is frequently used by Walton, and Walton's references to other authors often derive from Gesner.

Rondeletius: Guillaume Rondelet (1507–66), French physician and naturalist. Rondelet's *Libri de Piscibus Marinis* (Books of Marine Fish), published in 1554–5, describes aquatic mammals and invertebrates as well as fish.

Ausonius: Decimus Magnus Ausonius (*c*.310–*c*.395), Latin poet from Gaul. *Mosella*, his poem about the Moselle River, includes a catalogue of fish.

Divine Dubartas: Guillaume de Salluste, sieur Du Bartas (1544–90), French Protestant poet. Author of *La Semaine* (The Week), about the creation of the world, and its sequel, *La Seconde Semaine* (The Second Week), about biblical history. The merchant and poet Josuah Sylvester (1562/3–1618) translated these works into English as *Bartas his Devine Weekes and Workes* (London, 1608); with some alterations, Walton here draws on the 5th Day of the 1st Week, ll. 29–48.

Stares: starlings.

Urchins: hedgehogs.

The mitred Bishop, and the cowled Fryer: Rondeletius, *De Piscibus Marinis* (Lyons, 1554), provides descriptions and images of both a fish that looks like a bishop (bk. 16, ch. 21) and a fish that looks like a monk (bk. 16, ch. 20).

Polonian: Polish.

35 *Cuttle-fish . . . Sea-Angler*: Walton cites Montaigne's 'An Apologie of Raymond Sebond', in his *Essayes*, trans. John Florio (London, 1613), 256.

Montaigne ascribes to the cuttlefish the behaviour of the angler fish (*Lophius piscatorius*), a bottom-dwelling fish that attracts its prey by twitching a fleshy flap on its dorsal ray.

a Hermit: Walton draws on Du Bartas's description of the '*Hermite-Fish*', that is, the hermit crab (5th Day of 1st Week, ll. 389–408).

Ælian . . . Adonis: Claudius Aelianus (*c.*170–*c.*235), Roman writer. Aelian's *De Animalium Natura* (On the Nature of Animals), originally written in Greek, is a compilation of lore about animals; his account of the Adonis (a mythical fish) is in bk. 9, ch. 36.

the Sargus: a sea bream (family Sparidae); Du Bartas, 5th Day, 1st Week, ll. 195–200.

Horning their husbands: a man with an adulterous wife was said to wear horns.

Cantharus: black sea bream (*Spondyliosoma cantharus*); Du Bartas, 5th Day, 1st Week, ll. 201–4.

36 *the Thracian women*: Walton draws on the wording of Du Bartas's description of the behaviour of mullets (5th Day, 1st Week, 209–12).

But for chast love . . . life and death: Du Bartas, 5th Day, 1st Week, ll. 205–8; pheer (fere) means mate; prest means ready.

House-Cock: male of the domestic chicken.

Job for a pattern of patience: St James, not God, names Job as an exemplar of patience (James 5:11).

the Spawner and the Melter: the female and male fish.

37 *They that occupy themselves in deep waters see the wonderful works of God*: Psalm 107:23–4.

a power to speak all languages: Acts 2:1–4.

the Scribes and the Mony-changers: Luke 11:44; Matthew 21:12–13.

the Catalogue of his twelve Apostles: Matthew 10:2–4.

three to bear him company at his Transfiguration: the three fishermen-disciples at the Transfiguration were Peter, James, and John; see e.g. Matthew 17:1–8.

38 *an ingenuous and learned man*: John Donne; in this paragraph, Walton draws from 'A Sermon Preached to Queen Anne, at Denmarke-house' (14 December 1617), *Sermons of John Donne*, ed. George R. Potter and Evelyn M. Simpson, i (Berkeley, 1953), Sermon 5, pp. 236–7.

Eyes like the fish-pools of Heshbon: Song of Solomon 7:4.

Amos, who was a Shepherd: Amos 1:1.

Fish-hooks: see note to p. 30.

meek Moses the friend of God: for 'meek Moses', see Numbers 12:3; for 'friend of God', see note to p. 26.

our Saviours bidding: Matthew 17:24–7.

38 *Ferdinand Mendez Pinto . . . a Fishing*: Fernão Mendes Pinto (*c*.1510–83), Portuguese adventurer. His *Peregrinação* (Peregrination), first published in 1614, recounts Pinto's experiences in Asia; an English translation by Henry Cogan was published in 1653 (*The Voyages and Adventures, of Ferdinand Mendez Pinto, a Portugal*). Walton seems to refer to Pinto's account of the King of Bungo and his men (not 'Priests') catching a whale (p. 319).

used Angling as a principal recreation: Plutarch recounts that to impress Cleopatra, Antony commanded fishermen to dive into the water and surreptitiously attach fish to his hook while he was angling. The next day, Cleopatra ensured that one of her servants reached Antony's hook first and put a salted fish on it (*The Lives of the Noble Grecians and Romaines*, trans. Sir Thomas North (London, 1603), 924).

39 *Ecclesiastical Canons*: the laws of the Church. A canon dating from the fourth century, 'De Clerico Venatore' (About a Clergyman as a Hunter), prohibited clerics from hunting 'voluptatis causa' (for pleasure).

Perkins: William Perkins (1558–1602), Church of England clergyman and theologian. Perkins defines 'Recreation' as 'an exercise joyned with the feare of God'; although he does not specifically mention angling, he includes 'shooting', 'hunting of wilde beasts', and 'the searching out, or the contemplation of the workes of God' in his list of allowed activities (*Workes*, i (London, 1612), 57–8).

Doctor Whitaker: William Whitaker (1547/8–95), theologian and master of St John's College, Cambridge. Whitaker was the nephew of Alexander Nowell (see next note). Thomas Fuller observed, 'Fishing with an angle is to some rather a torture th[a]n a pleasure, to stand an houre as mute as the fish they mean to take: yet herewithall Doctour Whitaker was much delighted' (*The Holy State* (Cambridge, 1648), 184).

Doctor Nowel: Alexander Nowell (*c*.1516/17–1602), dean of St Paul's, London. Nowell had been an undergraduate and then fellow of Brasenose College, Oxford, and he later gave financial support to the college. Nowell, who had fled abroad during the reign of Mary I, wrote several versions of the catechism for the Church of England that were frequently republished.

his Monument stands yet undefaced: during the civil wars, parliamentarian troops used St Paul's Cathedral as a barracks and stable and vandalized the building's fabric. Alexander Nowell's monument was not destroyed until 1666, however, when the cathedral burned in the Great Fire of London.

Convocation: an assembly of clergy in the Church of England that deliberates on ecclesiastical matters.

Catechism . . . Service Book: Alexander Nowell (see note above) wrote and published several versions of the catechism, but not the brief form included in the Book of Common Prayer ('our good old Service Book').

40 *Sir Henry Wotton*: see note to p. 3.

This day dame Nature seem'd in love: slightly adapted from the poem 'On a Banck as I sate a Fishing, A Description of the Spring', in *Reliquiae Wottonianae*, 524 (see note to p. 3).

41 *well dissembled flie*: an artificial fly.

swift Pilgrims dawbed nest: the house martin, a migratory bird, often builds its mud nest under the eaves of buildings.

Philomels triumphing voice: song of the nightingale. In classical mythology, Philomela was eventually turned into a nightingale after she had been attacked by her brother-in-law, Tereus, who first raped Philomela and then cut out her tongue to prevent her from speaking of his crime.

foot-ball Swain: football was very popular in rural England during Walton's lifetime, and games frequently took the form of 'more or less ritualized combat between communities, often represented by virtually the entire young male population of whole parishes' (David Underdown, *Revel, Riot, and Rebellion* (Oxford, 1985), 75).

strokes a sillibub: 'stroke' could mean 'to whip', but could also mean 'to milk a cow'; 'sillibub' is syllabub. In Walton's time, syllabub 'was a confection of white wine, cider, or fruit juice, well sweetened with sugar and flavoured with lemon or nutmeg, to which cream or milk was added with considerable force', sometimes by 'milking the cow directly on to the liquor in the syllabub pot' (C. Anne Wilson, *Food and Drink in Britain: From the Stone Age to the 19th Century* (Chicago, 1991), 170).

Jo. Davors, Esq.: John Dennys (*d.* 1609) lived near Pucklechurch, Gloucestershire. Dennys's fishing poem, *The Secrets of Angling*, first appeared in 1613, with three subsequent editions published by 1652; Walton quotes, with some alterations, from B4ᵛ–B5ᵛ (1652 edn.). The author of *The Secrets of Angling* was identified on the title page only as 'J.D. Esquire', and Walton was not alone in misattributing the poem. On Walton's use of *The Secrets of Angling*, see also the note to p. 30.

42 *Gandergrasse . . . Culverkeyes*: gandergrasse (gandergoose), early purple orchid (*Orchis mascula*); culverkeyes, English bluebells (*Hyacinthoides non-scripta*).

Aurora . . . Tithonus bed: Aurora, goddess of the dawn, left her aged lover Tithonus every morning to drive her chariot across the sky.

veins: watersheds.

Flora's gifts: flowers; see note to p. 10.

43 *Lady-smocks*: cuckoo flowers (*Cardamine pratensis*).

all in pursuit of the Otter: on the practice of otter-hunting, see note to p. 18.

complement: exchange compliments.

44 *a beast or a fish*: Walton draws much of his material about otters from Topsell, *Beastes*, 572–4.

Carthusians . . . never to eat flesh: 'I hear that the *Carthusian* Fryers or Monkes . . . which are forbidden to touch al manner of flesh, of other foure-footed-beasts, yet they are not prohibited the eating of Otters' (Topsell, *Beastes*, 574).

44 *spoils much more than he eats*: Walton refers inconsistently to the sex of the otter in this passage; the adult otter that is hunted and killed is female.

Gesner: see note to p. 34. Topsell's *Historie of Foure-Footed Beastes*, from which Walton derives much of this paragraph, is essentially a translation of Gesner's *Historiae Animalium*, bk. 1, *De Quadrupedibus viviparis* (About Viviparous Mammals); comments about the otter's olfactory abilities are found on p. 685 of the 1620 edition of Gesner.

Falling-sickness: epilepsy.

Benione: gum benzoin, a fragrant resin obtained from the *Styrax benzoin* tree native to Indonesia.

Cambden says . . . Ottersey: Camden, 206; Ottersey, the River Ottery.

45 *Sweetlips . . . Kilbuck . . . Ringwood*: Nicholas Cox includes these names in his catalogue of 'some general Names of Hounds and Beagles' (*The Gentleman's Recreation* (London, 1686), 19–20).

I'll try if I can make her tame: otters were 'sometimes tamed, and used in the northern parts of the world, especially in *Scandinavia* to drive the fishes into the fishermens nets' (Topsell, *Beastes*, 573), and James I used tame otters to catch salmon.

Mr. Nich. Seagrave: nothing else is known of Nicholas Seagrave; he was probably related to James Duport, who wrote commendatory verses for *The Compleat Angler* (see note to p. 16).

Barley-wine: beer.

Old Rose: a popular song.

46 *the Fence months*: the breeding season when fishing is prohibited.

make conscience of: keep as a matter of conscience.

13 of Edw. the I. and the like in Rich. the II.: statutes (13th Edw. I, stat. 1, cap. 47 and 13 Rich. II, stat. 1, cap. 19) that prohibit the catching of salmon between 15 April and 24 June.

That which is every bodies business, is no bodies business: proverbial.

conservators: persons in charge of a river who supervise all the activities that occur on or along it.

the Levitical Law: Deuteronomy 22:6–7.

Gorrara: probably a loon or diver (family Gaviidae). Naturalists formerly used the term *Colymbus* to refer to a loon, and the catalogue of the famous Tradescant collection of curiosities (which Walton, as he recounts on p. 33, had visited) contains this entry: 'The Gorara or Colymbus from *Muscovy*: And another taken upon the *Thames* and given by *Elias Ashmole*, Esq.' (John Tradescant, *Musaeum Tradescantianum* (London, 1656), 4).

the Puet: the black-headed gull, formerly known as the pewit or peewit gull (*Chroicocephalus ridibundus*).

the Craber, which some call the Water-rat: the European water vole (*Arvicola amphibius*).

47 *Trout-hall*: the anglers do not stay at Trout Hall, but instead return to the alehouse (named Bleak Hall—see p. 59) where they had dined. Piscator changes plans when he learns that Peter and his friend will be lodging at Bleak Hall that evening (pp. 57–8).

the Poet: Lucius Cary, second Viscount Falkland (1609/10–43). Piscator quotes, with one very slight change, from Cary's 'An Elegie on Dr. Donne', which was published in *Poems, by J.D. With elegies on the authors death* (London, 1633); the lines quoted appear on p. 390. Walton also contributed a poem to this volume.

48 *I'll hold you*: I'll wager you.

an honest Ale-house . . . twenty Ballads stuck about the wall: seventeenth-century alehouses provided inexpensive food and lodging, as well as ale and beer. A broadside ballad consisted of rhymed lyrics, often about current events, that were written to be sung to a well-known tune; the ballad was printed on one side of a single sheet of paper and usually featured woodcut illustrations and a decorative border as well. Ballads were a very popular, cheap form of entertainment, and they were often pasted onto the walls of private homes, inns, and alehouses.

49 *eat well*: has good texture and flavour.

short: crumbling.

verjuice: a kind of strong vinegar made from fermented unripe grapes or crab apples.

50 *except against*: object to.

had not been worth a rush: would have been worthless (proverbial).

soaring: staying at the surface of the water.

51 *leather-mouth'd*: explained on pp. 51–2.

Ant-flie: one of the winged ants, or perfect males and females, of an ant's nest.

Bob: the grub or larva of a beetle.

Cod-worm, or a Case-worm: both names for the caddis worm, the larva of the caddis fly (order Trichoptera). Many caddis worms make portable cases from sand, twigs, and other debris.

52 *the black Bee that breeds in clay walls*: perhaps the female hairy-footed flower bee (*Anthophora plumipes*), which is 'jet black apart from her orange pollen brushes' and often nests 'in the mortar of old walls' (Michael Chinery, *Complete British Insects* (London, 2005), 350).

the young humble-bee that breeds in long grasse: the bumblebee. Several species of bumblebees nest in grass tussocks, but Walton may be referring specifically to the common carder bumblebee or brown bumblebee (*Bombus pascuorum*), which persists late into the autumn.

his Spawn: the soft roe of the male.

53 *Seneca*: Walton has obtained his reference to Seneca's *Natural Questions* from Hakewill (pp. 358–9).

generous: of good stock.

Gesner says: Gesner, p. 1002, l. 70 and p. 1011, ll. 11–12.

three Cubits long, as is affirmed by Gesner: Gesner says 4 feet (p. 1012, ll. 44–5); a cubit was 18–22 inches.

Mercator: Gerardus Mercator (1512–94), Flemish cartographer who developed a system for creating maps structured by what became known as the Mercator projection. Walton found Mercator's comments about the trout of Lake Léman (Lake Geneva) in *Historia Mundi*, 413.

54 *a little Brook in Kent*: perhaps the River Cray.

about the size of a Gudgion: the gudgeon grows at most to 8 inches but is usually less than 6 inches long.

as Winchester: as the River Itchen at Winchester.

a Samlet or Skegger Trout: a young salmon.

Fordidge: Fordwich, a village in Kent upon the River Stour, located about 3 miles NE of Canterbury.

Sir George Hastings: perhaps Sir George Hastings (*d.* 1641) of Ashby-de-la-Zouch, Leicestershire. Hastings was admitted to Sidney Sussex College, Cambridge, in 1605 and to Gray's Inn in 1611; he served as an MP in the 1620s. Walton later refers to Hastings as a 'chymical man' (someone interested in chemistry or alchemy) and an associate of Sir Henry Wotton (see pp. 97 and 143).

grasshoppers and some Fish have no mouths: the idea that grasshoppers do not have mouths is discussed in Thomas Moffet's *Theater of Insects*, appended to Edward Topsell's *History of Four-Footed Beasts and Serpents* (London, 1658), 990.

in the Psalms: Psalm 147:9.

the Stork . . . knows his season: Jeremiah 8:7.

55 *Shelsey*: Selsey.

Amerly: Amberley.

half year birds: the passage in Sir Francis Bacon's *Sylva Sylvarum, or A Naturall History* (London, 1651) to which Walton refers discusses the hibernation of animals, including bats (p. 194).

Michaelmas: 29 September.

Albertus: Albertus Magnus (*c.*1200–80), Dominican bishop and philosopher. Topsell, *Serpents*, quotes Albertus on p. 180.

birds of Paradise, and the Camelion: Du Bartas suggests that birds of paradise feed only on air (5th Day of the 1st Week, ll. 791–8); Topsell refutes the belief that chameleons are 'nourished with the winde' (*The History of Four-Footed Beasts and Serpents* (London, 1658), 672).

Bull-trout . . . Salmon-trouts: brown trout or sea trout (*Salmo trutta*).

Sir Francis Bacon... History of Life and Death: Francis Bacon, Viscount St Alban (1561–1626), Lord Chancellor, politician, and philosopher who sought to reform the study of nature. He discusses the lifespan of trout in *The Historie of Life and Death*, 59–60.

56 *Sugs, or Trout lice*: a species of fish lice—which are crustaceans, not insects—parasitic on trout.

the May-flie, which is bred of the Cod-worm, or Caddis: caddis flies (order Trichoptera) are the adult form of what Walton calls 'the *Cod-worm*' (see note to p. 51). On the use of the term 'mayfly', see note to p. 202.

hogback: an arched back resembling that of a pig.

Willows or palm-trees: William Coles remarks of the willow, 'The Blossoms come forth before any Leaves appear, and are in their most flourishing estate, usually before *Easter*, divers gathering them to deck up their houses on Palm Sunday, and therefore the said Flowers are called *Palme*' (*Adam in Eden: Or, Natures Paradise* (London, 1657), 73).

57 *Helmits and Runts and Carriers, and Cropers*: helmits = helmets, pigeons with plumage on the head of a different colour from that of the body. Runts = breeds of large, stout pigeons. Carriers = a breed of pigeons with a strong instinct for finding their way home. Cropers = croppers, a breed of pigeons that puff out their crops; pouter pigeons.

the Royal Society . . . kinds of Spiders: the Royal Society of London for Improving Natural Knowledge was founded in 1660. Martin Lister's 'Table of 33 Sorts of Spiders to be Found in England' was published in the Society's *Philosophical Transactions*, vi (London, 1671), 2170–5.

great Kentish Hens: probably a breed of poultry similar to the Dorking, a five-toed chicken raised in south-east England since Roman times. An ancient breed known as the Kent or Old Sussex Fowl was recognized at the first poultry show held in England in 1845.

the Musical Thrassal: the song thrush (*Turdus philomelos*).

the sleight: feat of skill.

eat him to supper: eat him for supper.

My Hostess has two beds . . . you and I may have the best: travellers in seventeenth-century England were often expected to share beds with other guests; the Saracen's Head Inn in Ware contained a huge bed that could accommodate twelve people.

58 *a Catch*: a musical round.

A match: agreed.

Have with you: 'Done!'

loggerheaded: having a disproportionately large head.

the Poet: unidentified.

that smooth song, which was made by Kit. Marlow: Christopher Marlowe (*bap.* 1564, *d.* 1593), playwright and poet. Stanzas 1–5 and 7 of 'Come live with me' are attributed to Marlowe in the poetry collection *Englands*

Helicon (1600), where the poem is entitled 'The passionate Sheepheard to his love'. Walton added the sixth stanza—which otherwise survives only in the Thornborough Commonplace Book and a broadside in the Roxburghe Collection—to the second edition of *The Compleat Angler* in 1655.

59 *an answer to it, which was made by Sir Walter Rawleigh*: Sir Walter Ralegh (1554–1618), courtier, explorer, and author. Versions of 'If all the world', paired with versions of 'Come live with me' (see previous note), had been published earlier with no author given; Walton is largely responsible for the attribution of the poem to Ralegh. Both songs were sung to the same popular tune.

a Sillybub of new Verjuice: see notes to pp. 41 and 49.

Red-Cows milk: 'The red Cow giveth the best milke' (Gervase Markham, *Cheape and Good Husbandry* (London, 1614), 43).

Come Shepherds . . . Troy Town: all six titles refer to popular songs: see Claude M. Simpson, *The British Broadside Ballad and Its Music* (New Brunswick, 1966), 126–7, 201–5, 576–8, 96–101, 401–3, 587–90. Walton has altered the title of the first song from 'Come, Shepherds, deck your heads' to '*Come Shepherds deck your herds*'.

60 *Kirtle*: outer petticoat.

Queen Elizabeth . . . wish her self a Milkmaid: according to Holinshed, when Elizabeth was held at Woodstock during the reign of her half-sister, Mary, she 'wished hir selfe to be a milkemaid . . . saieng that hir case was better, and life more merier than was hirs in that state as she was' (*The Third Volume of Chronicles* (London, 1586), 1158).

Sir Thomas Overbury's Milk-maids wish: Sir Thomas Overbury (*bap.* 1581, *d.* 1613), courtier and author. Overbury was a close friend and associate of James I's favourite, Robert Carr, later earl of Somerset. The two men became estranged when Overbury opposed Carr's marriage to Frances Howard, the countess of Essex; Overbury was imprisoned and died in the Tower of London, perhaps poisoned at the behest of Frances Howard. Overbury's poem 'A Wife' was published after his death, along with a series of 'characters'—brief, stereotyped prose descriptions of different categories of people—that Overbury did not write. The description of 'A fayre and happy Milke-mayd' concludes with the sentiment that is slightly misquoted by Walton (Sir Thomas Overbury, *New and Choise Characters* (London, 1615), K5ᵛ).

61 *Philomel*: see note to p. 41.

fall: autumn.

purely: excellently.

62 *I married a Wife of late*: Walton created these stanzas from two different songs written by the royalist ballad-writer Martin Parker (*fl.* 1624–7). The first stanza, slightly altered, is from 'Keep a good tongue in your head', ll. 1–5, and the second stanza, with several alterations, is from 'The Milke-maids life', ll. 57–64. Both songs were sung to the same tune. See the

website of the English Broadside Ballad Archive (EBBA) at the University of California at Santa Barbara—<http://ebba.english.ucsb.edu>—for complete texts of both ballads (EBBA ID: 30344 and EBBA ID: 30170) and a recording of 'Keep a good tongue in your head'.

the green-sickness: a condition believed to afflict young virginal women, the symptoms of which included amenorrhoea, lassitude, dietary problems, and changes in skin colour.

63   *Barly-wine*: beer.

perfect in season: in the best condition for eating.

sow your seed in barren ground: Venator evokes the parable of the sower and the seed from Matthew 13:3–9.

64   *'Tis merry in Hall, when men sing all*: proverbial.

William Basse: (*c*.1583–1653?), servant of Sir Richard Wenman of Oxfordshire and poet. Basse published several volumes of poetry, as well as songs and commendatory verses. Walton refers to 'Maister Basse his Careere, or, The New Hunting of the Hare' (printed as a broadside *c*.1620); Basse's 'Tom of Bedlam' may be the song published, without authorial attribution, in John Playford's *Choice Ayres, Songs, & Dialogues* (London, 1676), 94.

draw cuts: draw lots by drawing sticks or straws of unequal length.

CORIDONS Song: written by John Chalkhill (*c*.1595–1642). Chalkhill was admitted to Trinity College, Cambridge, in 1610; his sister, Martha, was the stepmother of Anne Ken, Walton's second wife, whom Walton married more than five years after Chalkhill's death. Walton published Chalkhill's pastoral narrative poem *Thealma and Clearchus* in 1683. Another poem by Chalkhill appears on pp. 132–4.

66   *roundelaies*: songs in which a refrain is continually repeated.

'Tis the company and not the charge that makes the feast: proverbial.

The Anglers Song: written by William Basse (see note to p. 64).

lures: in falconry, to recall a hawk with a lure (a device made of leather and feathers, to which is attached a long cord, from which the hawk is fed during training).

67   *fishers of men*: Matthew 4:18-19; Mark 1:16-17.

fish the last | *Food was*: Luke 24:41–3.

68   *prevent*: act in advance of.

you are to be my Bed-fellow: see note to p. 57.

my Scholar and I will go down towards Waltham: see Maps 1 and 2.

as hungry as Hawks: proverbial.

Dug-worm: a kind of red worm.

69   *the bark of the Tanners*: the bark of the oak, willow, chestnut, etc., contains tannin or tannic acid, which is used for turning skins into leather.

69 *divers other kinds of worms ... too many to name*: Sir John Hawkins writes of this passage:

> To avoid confusion, it may be necessary to remark, that the same kind of worm is, in different places, known by different names: thus the Marsh and the Meadow-Worm, are the same; and the Lob-Worm, or Twachel, is also called the Dew-Worm, and the Garden-Worm, and the Dock-Worm, is, in some places, called the Flag-Worm.
> The *Tag-Tail* is found in *March* and *April*, in marled lands, or meadows, after a shower of rain, or in a morning, when the weather is calm, and not cold.
> To find the *Oak-Worm*, beat on an Oak-Tree, that grows over a highway or bare place, and they will fall for you to gather.
> To find the *Dock-Worm*, go to an old pond, or pit, and pull up some of the flags; shake the roots in the water, and amongst the fibres that grow from the roots you will find little husks, or cases, of a reddish or yellowish colour; open these carefully with a pin, and take from thence a little worm, pale and yellow, or white, like a Gentle, but longer and slenderer, with rows of feet down his belly, and a red head: this is the Dock or Flag-Worm (Izaak Walton, *The Complete Angler*, ed. Hawkins (London, 1760), 90).

scowred: scoured, that is, cleansed by purging.

70 *Camphire*: camphor, a whitish translucent crystalline volatile substance, belonging chemically to the vegetable oils and having a bitter aromatic taste and a strong characteristic smell.

distempered: stormy.

71 *Loch*: loach.

Stickle-bag: stickleback (family Gasterosteidae).

bay-salt: salt obtained in large crystals by the slow evaporation of seawater.

shadowed: having colours or tints gradually passing one into another.

72 *highest mettled*: highest-spirited.

the Palmer-flie or worm: one of various species of hairy caterpillars; the name refers to 'palmers', nomadic pilgrims who carried palm-leaves after making journeys to the Holy Land.

Pliny holds: Pliny, bk. 11, ch. 32; cited by Topsell, *Serpents*, 107. The theory of spontaneous generation, which posited that animals could come into existence through natural but non-sexual processes, likewise appears in the poem by Du Bartas that Piscator quotes on p. 74.

Coleworts: plants of the cabbage kind (genus *Brassica*).

Topsel: Edward Topsell (*bap.* 1572, *d.* 1625), Church of England clergyman and author. Topsell's compilations about natural history—*The Historie of Foure-Footed Beastes* (London, 1607) and *The Historie of Serpents* (London,

1608)—rely heavily on Gesner's *Historiae Animalium*. In this paragraph, Walton draws on Topsell's discussion of caterpillars in *Serpents*, 103.

a green Caterpillar: James Rennie identifies this caterpillar as that of the privet hawkmoth (*Sphinx ligustri*) (*The Complete Angler*, by Izaak Walton, ed. Rennie (London, 1835), 101). Dragonflies, which Walton calls 'flies of prey', are not related to this caterpillar.

73 *flies of prey*: dragonflies.

Aldrovandus: Ulisse Aldrovandi (1522–1605), Italian physician and naturalist.

Topsel: Topsell, *Serpents*, 105.

one of them: Walton relies here on Topsell, *Serpents*, 104. The caterpillar described seems to be that of the puss moth (*Cerura vinula*) (*The Complete Angler*, by Izaak Walton and Charles Cotton, ed. J. E. Harting, i (London, 1893), 148 n.).

punctually: precisely.

gives over to eat: stops eating.

74 *Aurelia*: chrysalis.

Bacon . . . his Natural History: the passages cited by Walton in Sir Francis Bacon's *Sylva Sylvarum, or, A Naturall History* (London, 1651) discuss the generation and feeding of caterpillars (p. 153) and the nourishment of trees and other living creatures (p. 24).

Du Bartas: see note to p. 34. Walton quotes, with several minor changes, from Du Bartas, 6th Day of 1st Week, ll. 1101–20.

without Venus deed: see note to p. 72.

So the cold humor: moisture. It was believed that the salamander was so cold that it could endure and extinguish fire.

The Fly Perausta: pyrausta, a mythical insect supposed to live in fire.

So slow Boötes . . . goslings hatcht of trees: Boötes, a northern constellation, the Wagoner, situated at the tail of the Great Bear. John Gerard writes, 'There are founde in the north parts of Scotland, & the Ilands adjacent, called Orchades, certaine trees, whereon doe growe certaine shell fishes, of a white colour tending to russet; wherein are conteined little living creatures: which shels in time of maturitie doe open, and out of them grow those little living things; which falling into the water, doe become foules, whom we call Barnakles, in the north of England Brant Geese, and in Lancashire tree Geese: but the other that do fall upon the land, perish and come to nothing' (*The Herball or Generall Historie of Plantes* (London, 1597), 1391). For Camden's remarks on the belief that geese grow from trees, see Camden, 48.

75 *powdered Beef*: beef that has been sprinkled with dry salt to preserve it.

Lecturer: one of a class of preachers in the Church of England, usually chosen by the parish and supported by voluntary contributions, whose duty consists mainly in delivering afternoon or evening 'lectures'.

75 *my Fiddle, but not my Fiddlestick*: proverbial.

76 *devout Lessius*: Leonard Lessius (1554–1623), Flemish Jesuit theologian. Walton here develops ideas he found in the English translation of Lessius's *Hygiasticon: Or, The Right Course of Preserving Life and Health unto Extream Old Age* (Cambridge, 1634), 148–9.

an ingenuous brother of the Angle: Walton draws this paragraph from Leonard Mascall's *A Booke of Fishing with Hooke & Line* (London, 1590), 16–18. The list of twelve flies first appeared in the *Treatyse of Fysshynge wyth an Angle* that was published in the second edition of *The Boke of St Albans* (Westminster, 1496).

77 *in March*: until the middle of the eighteenth century, the English used the Julian ('Old Style') calendar rather than the more accurate Gregorian ('New Style') calendar, which is now generally used in non-Islamic countries. Walton's Old Style dates are thus ten or eleven days earlier than ours.

hackle: the long, shining feathers on the cock's neck.

list: border.

braked: beaten and crushed.

mail: breast-feathers.

one against the other: on opposite sides of the body.

Thomas Barker: author of *The Art of Angling*, first published in 1651, in which he says that he has 'Angled these fourty years' (p. 2). Barker, originally from Shropshire, lived in Westminster.

three or four hairs: see headnote to Glossary.

78 *cast*: contrive.

arm your hook: bind the arming (see Glossary) tightly on to the shank of the hook.

in your own reason: in your own judgement.

a Plovers top: the crest of a lapwing (*Vanellus vanellus*).

79 *hit it*: succeed.

in Lapland, to buy a good wind of one of the honest Witches: Lapland was renowned for its witches, and witches in general were thought to sell winds.

a smoaking showre: a pelting downpour of rain. This term is not defined in the *Oxford English Dictionary*; I have derived my definition from John Tillinghast, *Saint Paul's Ship-wrack in his Voyage to Rome* (London, 1637): 'It is called in the originall . . . a forcing raine, *imbrem urgentem*, a smoaking shower, which mightily fell upon them' (p. 99).

When the wind is South, | *It blows your bait into a fishes mouth*: this statement became proverbial, but Walton probably draws on Thomas Barker's observation that 'with the Winde in the South, then that blows the Flie in the Trouts mouth' (Barker, 2).

Solomon observes: Ecclesiastes 11:4.

80 *there is no good Horse of a bad colour*: proverbial.

rains May-butter: rains cats and dogs (Otto Jespersen, *A Modern English Grammar on Historical Principles*, iii (Heidelberg, 1927), 237). May-butter is unsalted butter, bleached in the sun for two weeks during early summer, which was used as a children's medicine.

Oak-flie: the snipe-fly (*Rhagio scolopaceus*).

fish down the stream: Walton paraphrases this advice from Thomas Barker: 'You must Angle alwaies with the poynt of your Rod down the stream' (Barker, p. 3).

Mr. Barker: Barker, 6–7. Walton derives much of the next paragraph—on fishing with natural flies—from Barker as well (Barker, 7–8). On Barker, see note to p. 77.

Hawthorn-flie: modelled after the St Mark's-fly (also known as the hawthorn fly), *Bibio marci*.

Magazine-bag: portable receptacle for materials.

81 *holy Mr. Herbert*: see note to p. 33. This poem, entitled 'Vertue', first appeared in 1633 in Herbert's *The Temple* (p. 80); Walton has made several slight changes in wording.

closes: cadences.

82 *who I have heard loved Angling*: in his *Life* of George Herbert, Walton observes that Herbert's 'chiefest recreation was Musick' (*The Lives of John Donne, Sir Henry Wotton, Richard Hooker, George Herbert, and Robert Sanderson*, introd. George Saintsbury (1927; London, 1973), 303).

83 *bears the bell*: takes the first place.

Ch. Harvie.: see note to p. 10. Christopher Harvey's collection of religious verse, *The Synagogue*, was first published, anonymously, in 1640. In 1647 Harvey published an enlarged, highly politicized edition of *The Synagogue* with new poems—like this one, 'The Book of Common Prayer'—which defended Church practices opposed by Puritans. (The Book of Common Prayer had been outlawed in 1645.) Walton first included Harvey's poem in the second edition of *The Compleat Angler* (1655), to which Harvey also contributed a commendatory poem (see pp. 9–10); Walton reciprocated with a commendatory poem for the 1657 edition of *The Synagogue*.

an even lay: a wager in which the chances are equal on either side.

putting money to Use: practising usury, that is, lending money at interest.

Virgils Tityrus and his Meliboeus: in Virgil's first Eclogue, the pastoral dialogue between Tityrus and Meliboeus occurs beneath the canopy of a large beech tree.

Dr. Boteler: perhaps the well-known and eccentric Cambridge physician William Butler (1535–1618).

83 *Charles the Emperour*: Charles V (1500–58), Holy Roman Emperor, captured Florence in 1530. Walton, however, quotes from John Raymond, *An Itinerary Contayning a Voyage, Made Through Italy* (London, 1648): 'A *Flandrian* Embassadour leaving *Florence*, told the Great Duke his City deserv'd to bee seen never but on Holy-dayes' (A1ʳ).

84 *my Kenna*: Walton's second wife, Anne Ken (1610–62), whom he married in 1647.

Like Hermit poor: Walton's reference to this song is closest to the version of the lyrics found in John Playford's *Select Ayres and Dialogues* (London, 1659), which begins, 'Like Hermit poor in pensive place obscure, | I mean to spend my days of endless doubt' (p. 1). The poem had appeared in anthologies since the 16th century; in Playford's collection, the song is entitled 'A Lovers Melancholy Repose' and is set to music by Nicholas Lanier.

my Bryan: unidentified; some editors have suggested that Walton refers to his dog.

Shawford-brook: probably the name of the River Sow as it flows through Shallowford, a hamlet located about 5.5 miles NW of Stafford. Walton bought property in this area in the 1650s, and a cottage at Shallowford now houses a museum devoted to Walton.

composure: composition.

85 *6s. 8d.*: six shillings (denoted by *s.*) and eight pennies (denoted by *d.*, for Latin *denarius, denarii*). A penny was equal to one-twelfth of a shilling; a shilling was equal to one-twentieth of a pound sterling.

these last twenty years: Charles I had raised revenues by a series of unpopular measures, including the nationwide extension of a tax called 'Ship Money'.

our late English Gusman: *The English Gusman; or the History of that Unparallel'd Thief James Hind*, by George Fidge, was published in 1652. James Hind (*bap*. 1616, *d*. 1652) was a highwayman and royalist soldier from Chipping Norton, Oxfordshire, who, after fighting for Charles II at the battle of Worcester in 1651, was executed for treason. The original, Spanish 'Gusman' was the hero of Mateo Alemán's picaresque novel *Guzmán de Alfarache* (1599; a second part, 1604); an English translation, *The Rogue: or The Life of Guzman de Alfarache*, was published in 1622.

86 *Schismatick*: one who separates from an existing church on account of a difference of opinion; in this context, a Puritan.

Father Clause: Walton refers to the Jacobean play *The Beggars' Bush*, which was written not by Ben Jonson but by John Fletcher (1579–1625), perhaps in collaboration with Francis Beaumont (1584/5–1616) and/or Philip Massinger (1583–1640). Gerrard, the father of Florez, the rightful earl of Flanders, disguises himself as a beggar named Clause and is elected king of the beggars near Bruges. 'Beggar's-bush' was a proverbial term meaning 'penury'.

Waltham-Cross: Waltham Cross, a small village in Hertfordshire on the road to Ware, 11 miles from London; see Map 1.

draw cuts: see note to p. 64.

Frank Davisons Song: Francis Davison (*b.* 1573/4, *d.* 1613–1619), writer and anthologist. Distantly related to Walton's first wife, Rachel Floud; matriculated at Emmanuel College, Cambridge (1586); admitted to Gray's Inn (1593). In 1602, Davison published *A Poetical Rapsody*, a collection of poems by Davison and others; given his replication of a later variant, Walton apparently knew the poem from one of three subsequent editions of the collection (1608, 1611, or 1621). The author of the poem, however, was not Davison: see *A Poetical Rhapsody, 1602–1621*, ed. Hyder Edward Rollins, ii (Cambridge, MA, 1931), 170–1.

burthen: burden, or refrain.

clappers: rattles used by beggars to attract attention.

stocks: vagrants and 'sturdy beggars'—people who were physically able to work but refused to do so—were punished by being confined in the parish stocks. Stocks consisted of two notched planks set edgewise one over the other, with the upper plank capable of being raised. The person to be punished was placed in a sitting posture with his ankles confined in the notches. Some stocks were structured to confine the offender's wrists and neck as well.

87 *A hundred herds of black and white*: cattle; here used metaphorically for verminous insects.

as sure as Creed: proverbial.

las: alas.

within the bent of my Rod: i.e. I would not have let him get away so far that the rod was pulled down into a straight line with the fishing line.

an ell long: an English ell is 45 inches.

by casting it to him into the water: Charles Cotton disapproved of this practice: see p. 221.

88 *Hares change Sexes*: this belief was often outlined only to be debunked; see e.g. Topsell, *Beastes*, 266.

Casaubon . . . Peuseus: on Meric Casaubon, see note to p. 33. Peuseus is Kaspar Peucer (1525–1602), German scholar and physician. Casaubon rejects Peucer's statement (*Of Credulity and Incredulity in Things Natural, Civil, and Divine* (London, 1668), 252).

a false quarter: a defect in a horse's hoof, each side of which is called a 'quarter'.

logger-headed: see note to p. 58.

some swift: a rapid current.

89 *form*: the nest in which a hare crouches.

at the snap: that is, (strike) at the first touch of the fish.

89 *Gesner observes*: see note to p. 44.

    Sir Francis Bacon . . . He also offers: Sir Francis Bacon, *Sylva Sylvarum, or, A Naturall History* (London, 1651), 167, Experiment 792.

90 *Doctor Hackwell*: George Hakewill (*bap.* 1578, *d.* 1649), Church of England clergyman and author; Doctor of Divinity; rector of Heanton Punchardon, Devon; chaplain to Prince Charles; rector of Exeter College, Oxford. In *An Apologie of the Power and Providence of God in the Government of the World* (London, 1627), Hakewill attempts to refute the widespread idea that the natural order inevitably deteriorates; the references to Pliny are found on p. 360.

    St. James tells us: James 3:7.

    Piscator fuge ne nocens, &c.: the title is a shortened version of the first line of Martial's epigram, 'Piscator fuge ne nocens recedas'. Both Martial's Latin original and the English translation given by Walton are found in Hakewill, 360.

    forbear swearing . . . catch no Fish: proverbial; see note to p. 26.

    Lemster: Leominster was proverbially famous for its high-quality wool.

91 *Solomon*: Ecclesiastes 3:11.

    differ as the Herring and Pilcher: Pilcher is pilchard (*Sardina pilchardus*). The herring is similar to the pilchard, but larger.

    Aldrovandus says: Aldrovandi, 593. On Aldrovandus, see note to p. 73.

    Gesner says: Gesner, p. 1033, ll. 20–2.

    any other Fish: Gesner, p. 982, ll. 27–8.

    Un Umble Chevalier . . . feeds on Gold: Gesner, p. 1004, l. 63 and p. 981, ll. 41–50.

    Water-time: water-thyme; unidentified.

    Smelts smell like Violets: 'Smellts are so called, because they smell so sweet; yea if you draw them, and then dry them in a shadowy place (being seasonably taken), they still retain a smell as it were of violets' (Thomas Moffet, *Healths Improvement* (London, 1655), 187–8).

    Gesner says: Gesner, p. 983, ll. 4–14.

92 *Salvian*: Ippolito Salviani (1514–72), Italian physician and author of *Aquatilium Animalium Historiae* (1554); cited in Aldrovandi, 79.

    St. Ambrose: (339–97), bishop of Milan; Ambrose's *Hexaemeron* (On the Six Days of Creation) cited in Gesner, p. 980, ll. 18–24.

    Parakita: parakeet.

    delicate River Dove: see Charles Cotton's description of the River Dove on pp. 177–8. It seems that Walton often visited Cotton to go angling in the Dove.

    which runs by Salisbury: five rivers—the Nadder, Ebble, Wylye, Bourne, and Avon—meet at Salisbury.

93 *Melter*: milter, that is, a spawning male fish.

Spawner: a spawning female fish.

unseasonable, and kipper: unseasonable, not in the best state for eating. A male salmon is called a 'kipper' during the spawning season, at which time its lower jaw becomes hooked upward with a sharp cartilaginous beak.

as the Eagle is said to cast his bill: eagles do not shed their beaks. Sir Francis Bacon writes, 'The Eagle casting her Bill, and so becomming young, is the *Embleme* of *long life*' (Bacon, 53).

both their Winter and Summer houses: Du Bartas, 5th Day of 1st Week, ll. 119–24.

History of Life and Death: Bacon, 60.

94 *Gesner speaks*: Gesner, p. 828, ll. 64–8. Gesner gives the height as 8 cubits, not 8 feet; a cubit was 18–22 inches.

Cambden mentions: Camden, 654–5.

Michael Draiton: Michael Drayton (1563–1631), poet. His *Poly-Olbion* (1612–22) is a long topographical description of England. This passage, with several minor alterations, is from Song 6, ll. 39–55 (*The Works of Michael Drayton*, ed. J. W. Hebel et al., iv (Oxford, 1961), 112).

His tail takes in his mouth: a myth.

yerking: springing.

Gesner and others: Gesner, p. 826, ll. 25–6.

Sir Francis Bacon observes: Bacon, 60.

95 *as Cambden observes*: Camden, 633.

Camphire: see note to p. 70.

96 *wheel*: a reel, which neither Walton nor Charles Cotton used.

Oliver Henly: records of the High Court of Admiralty from 1633–4 mention 'Oliver Henly of St Mary Woolchurch, London, haberdasher aged 61'. (Peter Wilson Coldham, *English Adventurers and Emigrants, 1609–1660* (Baltimore, 1984), 41).

incorporated: absorbed into their bodies.

Sir Francis Bacons Natural History: Bacon asserts 'that *Water* may be the *Medium* of *Sounds*', but he does not discuss whether fish can hear or smell (*Sylva Sylvarum, or, A Naturall History* (London, 1651), 167, Experiment 792).

Gesner says: see note to p. 44.

Polypody of the Oak: the fern *Polypodium vulgare*.

retort: container used for distilling liquids.

Vulnera . . . suavissimi: 'Wounds made in a large branch of ivy exude a balsam congealed from the plant's oil that is very similar to whitewash and truly smells very sweet for a long time.'

97 *Asa fœtida*: asafoetida, a solidified resinous gum with a strong odour, obtained from a plant native to central Asia.

chymical men . . . Sir George Hastings: see note to p. 54.

a Tecon: an immature salmon. Richard Franck remarks of the names given to young salmon, 'in the South they call him *Samlet*; but if you step to the West, he is better known there by the name of *Skeggar*; when in the East they avow him *Penk*; but to the Northward, *Brood* and *Locksper*, so from thence to a *Tecon*; then to a *Salmon*' (*Northern Memoirs* (London, 1694), 255).

Pilcher: pilchard (*Sardina pilchardus*).

Artificial Paint or Patches: artificial paint = make-up. Patches were small pieces of black silk cut into decorative shapes and worn on the face, either for adornment or to conceal blemishes.

Pickerel-weed . . . learned Gesner: Gesner, p. 503, ll. 49–51. Walton apparently conflates this passage with William Samuel's remark that the pike 'hath a weede of his owne, which also hee will feede on, called Pickrell weede' (Samuel, C_{viii}^{v}). Pickerel weed = pondweed (*Potamogeton natans*). William Samuel was a Huntingdonshire vicar whose book *The Arte of Angling* (1577) greatly influenced Walton. On the theory of spontaneous generation to which Walton subscribes, see note to p. 72.

Sir Francis Bacon: Bacon, 59–60.

98 *Gesner mentions*: Gesner, $a3^{v}$.

Frederick the second: Frederick II (1194–1250), Holy Roman emperor.

Worms: a city in south-western Germany.

Gesner relates . . . Gesner observes: Gesner, p. 503, ll. 11–14, 15–17.

Killingworth: Kenilworth.

Mr. Seagrave: see note to p. 45.

It is a hard thing . . . no ears: proverbial.

so put it over by degrees: Walton follows Gesner, p. 503, ll. 7–9. 'Put over' refers to the passing of food from a hawk's crop to its stomach.

99 *venemous . . . as some kind of Frogs are*: many frogs produce toxins from glands in their skin.

Gesner affirms: Gesner, p. 503, ll. 15–16.

Polonian: Polish.

observed by Gesner: Gesner, p. 505, ll. 18–21, 46.

curiosity: undue inquisitiveness.

100 *Dubravius*: Jan Dubravius (*d.* 1553), Bishop of Olmütz in Moravia. The English translation of Dubravius's *De Piscinis* (1559) was published as *A New Booke of Good Husbandry* (London, 1599); the story Walton recounts is found on pp. 5^{v}–6^{r}.

fishing Frogs: angler fish (*Lophius piscatorius*); see note to p. 35.

secures the frog: the reed sticking out on either side of the frog's mouth prevents the snake from swallowing him.

Water and Land-frogs: all frogs are amphibious. Although some species of frogs live less in the water than others, there is no species which does not resort to the water during the breeding season.

Land and Water-Snakes: there are no British water snakes, but the grass snake (*Natrix natrix*) swims well; the grass snake lays eggs, whereas the adder (*Vipera berus*) produces live young.

101 *I told you some think some Pikes are bred*: see note to p. 97.

102 *probe*: a baiting-needle.

a fish-frog: see note to p. 100.

flesh-frogs: see note to p. 100. Walton derives most of the information in this paragraph, including the references to Pliny and Cardanus, from Topsell, *Serpents*, 177–9, 185–7.

the padock or Frog-padock: a toad.

Cardanus undertakes: Girolamo Cardano (1501–76), Italian physician, natural philosopher, and mathematician. His book *De Subtilitate Rerum* (The Subtlety of Things, 1550) was an encyclopaedic collection of experiments, inventions, and anecdotes. Walton draws his comments about Cardano from Topsell, *Serpents*: see note above.

Simber-salts: somersaults.

the land-frog, or Padock frog: the toad.

103 *the frogs mouth grows up*: see p. 55.

ravelling: unwinding.

clift: cleft.

104 *bottles*: bundles.

Gum of Ivy in Oyl of Spike: gum of ivy is the thickened juice of the stem of the ivy; 'Oyl of Spike' is an essential oil distilled from lavender.

pretended: intended.

a blade or two of Mace: mace is the net-like web covering a nutmeg that has been dried and flattened for use as an aromatic spice.

105 *Filleting*: woven material used for binding.

hogo: French *haut gout*, a high flavour.

M. B.: unidentified.

Gesner tells us . . . in Italy: Gesner, p. 502, ll. 31–2. Lake Thrasimene is Lake Trasimeno.

Shelsey: Selsey.

Amerly: Amberley.

106 *Mr. Mascal*: Leonard Mascall reports, 'The Carpe hath not long beene in this realme. The first bringer of them into England (as I have beene credibly enformed) was maister Mascoll of Plumsted in Sussex' (*A Booke of Fishing*

with Hooke and Line (London, 1590), 7). Mascall (*d.* 1589) was a translator, author, and clerk of the kitchen to Matthew Parker, archbishop of Canterbury; he was not related to the 'Mascoll' responsible for introducing carp to England. Mascall published how-to manuals and books of recipes on such topics as arboriculture, stain-removal, and animal husbandry. His work on fishing, based on the fifteenth-century *Treatyse of Fysshynge wyth an Angle*, was published posthumously.

106 *I told you, Gesner says*: see p. 105.

S. Richard Baker: Sir Richard Baker (*c.*1568–1645), religious writer and historian. Matriculated at Oxford from Hart Hall and shared lodgings with Sir Henry Wotton; lost his fortune and lands by standing security for his father-in-law's debts and lived the last decade of his life in the Fleet prison in London, where he began to write. Baker's most influential work, *A Chronicle of the Kings of England* (London, 1643), was dedicated to the prince of Wales; in his account of the reign of Henry VIII, Baker states, 'About his fifteenth yeere, it happened that divers things were newly brought into *England*, whereupon this Rime was made: "*Turkes, Carps, Hoppes, Piccarell and Beere,* | *Came into ENGLAND all in one yeere*"' (iii. 66).

Aristotle and Pliny say: cited in Gesner, p. 312, ll. 46–8.

be enlivened: receive life.

Jovius: Paulus Jovius or Paolo Giovio (1483–1552), bishop of Nocera and historian. In his treatise *De Romanis Piscibus* (On Roman Fish), first published in 1524, Giovio mentions large fish, but he does not refer specifically to carp. Lake Lurian is Lake Como.

107 *Bear . . . Elephant . . . Crocodile*: Bacon, 45–6, 60.

a person of honour: despite the incorrect title 'Mr.', probably Sir Francis Russell of Strensham, Worcestershire, whose sister, Mary, became Charles Cotton's second wife in 1674.

108 *Sir Francis Bacon*: Bacon, 60.

Gesner saies a Carp: Gesner, p. 312, ll. 69–71.

the Palatinate: a state of the Holy Roman Empire under the count palatine, now part of Germany.

Gesner saies, Carps have no tongue: Gesner, p. 310, ll. 20–34.

Janus Dubravius: Jan Dubravius, *A New Booke of Good Husbandry* (London, 1599), 19ᵛ–20; see note to p. 100.

he says also: this passage is adapted not from Dubravius, but from John Taverner, *Certaine Experiments Concerning Fish and Fruite* (London, 1600), 18.

Glass-hives: a Gloucestershire clergyman named William Mews (or Mewe) constructed a tiered octagonal glass beehive in 1649, the design of which was later modified by Christopher Wren and published by Samuel Hartlib.

their King: bees have a queen, not a king.

all Carps are not bred by generation . . . as some Pikes do: see p. 97.

the galls and stones: Gesner, p. 313, ll. 57–65.

109 *in Levit. 11.*: Leviticus 11:9–12.

Meadow worm: the common earthworm (*Lumbricus terrestris*).

110 *a green Gentle*: a maggot or larva of the flesh-fly or bluebottle that has not been purged; see Walton's instructions on p. 128.

Bean-flowre: bean flour, normally used for making coarse breads.

Virgin wax: pure, high-quality beeswax.

clarified honey: honey melted and purified in a waterbath.

Oyl of Peter: petroleum, crude oil.

111 *curious . . . curious*: requires great skill . . . delicate.

Dr. T.: unidentified.

Gesner: Gesner, p. 316, l. 43.

112 *help his grinding*: fish generally swallow their food whole.

Melts: milts or testes.

Gesner reports: Gesner, p. 317, ll. 19–32.

Sir Francis Bacon: Bacon, 59–60.

this Proverb: Gesner, p. 317, ll. 61–3.

113 *Tench*: an error for 'Bream'.

a most honest and excellent Angler: the identity of this angler, whose initials Walton gives as 'B. A.' (see p. 116), is unknown.

a knot: the clitellum, the raised band encircling the middle of an earthworm's body.

silk, or silk and hair lines: see headnote to Glossary.

skuls: schools.

114 *gross-ground barly-malt*: coarsely ground barley that has been 'malted'—steeped, germinated, and kiln-dried—in preparation for brewing, distilling, or vinegar-making.

warms: walms, spells of boiling.

116 *St. James Tide until Bartholomew Tide*: 25 July to 24 August.

B. A.: see note to p. 113.

the Physician of Fishes: see p. 117.

Cambden: Camden writes of 'the most famous river *Stoure* passing full of tenches and Eeles especially' (p. 214).

he is not commended for wholsom meat: Robert Lovell reports that Dr John Caius (1510–73) called tenches 'good plaisters; but bad nourishment' (*Panzooryktologia . . . Or A Compleat History of Animals and Minerals* (Oxford, 1661), 227).

Rondelitius says: Rondeletius cited in Gesner, p. 985, ll. 3–6. On Rondeletius, see note to p. 34.

117 *Solomon*: 1 Kings 4:29–33.

 Lice swallowed alive: the consumption of lice was understood in Walton's time as a remedy for jaundice, but this belief was not usually ascribed to the Jews.

118 *green Gentle*: see note to p. 109.

 invade: attack.

 Aldrovandus: Aldrovandi, 624. On Aldrovandus, see note to p. 73.

 Gesner prefers: Gesner, p. 701, ll. 4–5, 14–16.

 Rondelitius: rather than Rondeletius, Gesner cites Platina on perch in the River Po and Cardanus on perch in England (p. 700, l. 9 and p. 701, l. 69).

 reins: kidneys.

119 *the Sea-Pearch . . . having but one fin on his back*: the two dorsal fins of sea perch (family Serranidae) are usually connected.

 Sir Abraham Williams: Williams served Princess Elizabeth, queen of Bohemia (Elizabeth Stuart, daughter of James I), as an agent in England; Sir Henry Wotton knew him.

 one has wittily observed: Walton echoes William Samuel's description of the behaviour of the ruffe (C_{vi}–$C_{vi}{}^v$).

120 *rove*: to troll using live bait, allowing the bait to swim in a natural manner at a depth regularly adjusted by the angler.

 Doctor Donne: John Donne (1572–1631), poet and Church of England clergyman. Doctor of divinity; vicar of St Dunstan-in-the-West (where Walton was a parishioner); dean of St Paul's; and influential preacher. Walton wrote a biography of Donne, the first edition of which was published in 1640. This poem, which parodies that of Marlowe found on pp. 59–60, was first published in Donne's *Poems* in 1633 and was later given the title 'The Baite'; Walton has made several changes in his version of the text.

121 *Let course bold hands . . . outwrest*: a reference to 'tickling' or 'guddling' fish, that is, groping for them under stones or along banks, a technique used especially to catch trout.

 sleave: to divide silk thread into filaments. Walton has changed Donne's text, which reads, 'Or curious traitors, sleave silke flies | Bewitch poore fishes wandring eyes' (Donne, *Poems* (London, 1650), 38).

122 *Rondelitius saies*: Rondeletius cited in Gesner, p. 42, ll. 16–17; Walton has added the simile about worms.

 others say . . . corruption of their own age: Gesner, p. 40, ll. 65–6.

 Sir Francis Bacon sayes: Bacon, 60.

 some of the Ancients: Gesner, p. 44, ll. 58–9. On the theory of spontaneous generation, see note to p. 72.

 Gesner quotes venerable Bede: Gesner, p. 43, ll. 59–60.

 Lobel: Matthias de L'Obel (1538–1616), French physician and botanist who spent much of his career in England. L'Obel includes pictures of geese ostensibly generated from trees and barnacles in his *Icones Stirpium* (Images of Plants, 1581), ii. 259. For Du Bartas, Camden, and Gerard on goose-bearing trees and barnacles, see p. 74 and notes.

123 *Rondelitius*: Rondeletius cited in Gesner, p. 40, ll. 53–4.

powdered Beef: see note to p. 75.

Bacon . . . in his History of Life and Death: Bacon, 60, 59.

Doctor Hackwel: see note to p. 90; the passage cited here is found in Hakewill, 360. Quintus Hortensius Hortalus (114–50 BC) was a Roman orator and politician.

Gesner quotes Albertus: Gesner, p. 45, ll. 36–9; Gesner cites the *Annales Augustae Vindelicae* (Annals of Augsburg), not Albertus.

Cambden: Camden reports that under the turf near the River Alt, 'there is a certaine dead and blackish water . . . and in it swimme little fishes that are caught by the diggers of turfe' (p. 748).

silver Eel: many names have been applied to the different developmental stages of eels. As eels migrate from fresh water to the sea, their sides and bellies become silver.

124 *powdered Beef*: see note to p. 75.

125 *S. F.*: unidentified.

Physicians account the Eel dangerous meat: Thomas Moffet observes, '*Eeles* have so sweet a flesh, that they and Lampreyes were dedicated to that filthy Goddess *Gula* or gluttony; yet withall it is so unwholesome, that some *Zoilus* or *Momus* would have accused nature, for putting so sweet a taste into so dangerous a meat' (*Healths Improvement* (London, 1655), 178).

Solomon says: Proverbs 25:16 and 27.

126 *the uncharitable Italian*: the humanist Bartolomeo Platina (1421–81), author of *De Honesta Voluptate et Valetudine* (On Right Pleasure and Good Health). In book 8, chapter 42, Platina concludes his discussion of eel pie by recommending, 'Coctam demum hostibus appones; nihil enim boni in se habet' (When it is finally cooked, serve it to your enemies, for it has nothing good in it) (*Platina: On Right Pleasure and Good Health*, ed. Mary Ella Milham (Tempe, AZ, 1998), 372–3). Platina is quoted in Gesner, p. 47, l. 26.

Aldrovandus and divers Physicians: Aldrovandi, 551–2. On Aldrovandus, see note to p. 73.

out of season: not in prime condition for eating.

Lamprel . . . Lamperne . . . Conger: lamprel, a lamprey (an eel-like fish of the family Petromyzonidae) that is not fully grown; lamperne, river lamprey (*Lampetra fluviatilis*); conger, conger eel (*Conger conger*).

as the Jews do: Leviticus 11:9–12.

Winander Mere . . . says Cambden: Windermere; Camden, 755.

Guiniad . . . Cambden: Guiniad, the freshwater houting (*Coregonus lavaretus*); Camden, 666.

126 *Pemble-Mere*: Bala Lake.

127 *Gesner . . . Barb*: Gesner, p. 123, ll. 20–1. The 'barb' is a slender fleshy appendage hanging from the corner of the mouth of some fish.

Rondelitius: Gesner, p. 124, l. 66 to p. 125, l. 2; Gesner cites Albertus, not Rondeletius.

128 *Gesner and Gasius*: Gesner, p. 125, ll. 17–26. Gesner cites the treatise *De Conservatione Sanitatis* (Venice, 1491) by the Italian physician Antonio Gazio (1449–1528). Both Gazio ('Gasius') and Gesner describe their personal experiences of the dire consequences of eating barbel eggs.

Plutarch: Plutarch discusses the methods by which hooked fish try to escape in *De Sollertia Animalium* (On the Intelligence of Animals), ch. 24.

129 *some have directed . . . some advise*: Leonard Mascall provides instructions for preparing cheese in these ways as bait for barbel in *A Booke of Fishing with Hooke & Line* (London, 1590), 7, 16.

tries conclusions: tries experiments.

the long shower: it began on p. 79.

Doctor Sheldon: Gilbert Sheldon (1598–1677), Church of England clergyman. Born in Staffordshire. Doctor of Divinity; warden of All Souls, Oxford (ejected and imprisoned, 1648); chaplain to Charles I. After the Restoration, dean of the Chapel Royal, bishop of London, and archbishop of Canterbury. Sheldon was part of a group of ejected clergymen who corresponded about their shared love of angling during the Interregnum (B. D. Greenslade, '*The Compleat Angler* and the Sequestered Clergy', *Review of English Studies*, NS 5/20 (1954), 361–6). In concert with George Morley (see note to p. 13), Sheldon persuaded Walton to write his biography of Richard Hooker (1665).

Sillabub, of new Verjuice: on syllabub, see note to p. 41; on verjuice, see note to p. 49.

130 *Hunting in Chevy Chase*: a ballad entitled 'A memorable song upon the unhappy hunting in Chevy Chase' was first published about 1630. This ballad is also mentioned on p. 59. See the website of the English Broadside Ballad Archive (EBBA) at the University of California at Santa Barbara—<http://ebba.english.ucsb.edu>—for the text and a recording of the song (EBBA ID: 20279).

enter: initiate.

131 *reserved*: secluded.

Ausonius: see note to p. 34.

Allamot salt . . . Anchovis: the meaning of the term '*Allamot*' is unclear. It may refer to Altomonte in Calabria, where a salt mine was located, or it may be a corruption of *A la mode*; John Collins, in *Salt and Fishery* (London, 1682), describes a way of preparing brined beef as '*A-La-mode (or Larded) Beef*' (p. 132). Regardless, no method of preparation can transform bleaks into anchovies, as they are different species of fish.

whipping for Bleaks: casting the line upon the water with whip-like strokes.

Sir Henry Wotton: see note to p. 3.

132 *Shovel-board*: a game in which players propel disks along a highly polished surface marked with transverse lines.

your Song, Piscator, and the Catch that your Scholar promised us: see p. 64.

dogged: surly.

my Song: on the song's author, John Chalkhill, see note to p. 64. This poem appears only in *The Compleat Angler* and, it seems, in altered form (see p. 134).

133 *Aurora*: see note to p. 42.

knacks: ingenious contrivances; here, refers to angling equipment, perhaps with a pun on another meaning of 'knacks' as clever literary compositions.

paste: dough-like mixture used as bait.

134 *fray*: frighten; Chalkhill evokes the proverb, 'If you swear, you'll catch no fish.'

dike: channel of water.

135 *without replications*: without answers or protests.

depending: waiting for settlement.

that Field in Sicily . . . Diodorus: 'The rape of *Proserpina* (they say) was in the fields near *Ætna* hard by the City, which are garnished with Lilies and severall kinds of flowers meet for a Godesse; insomuch that hounds there through the fragrancy of the smell lose their sents, the sweetnesse of the flowers overcoming their sense' (Diodorus Siculus, *The History of Diodorus Siculus*, trans. H. C. [Henry Cogan] (London, 1653), 226).

my Saviour said: Matthew 5:5.

the Poet: unidentified.

136 *Phineas Fletcher*: Phineas Fletcher (1582–1650), Church of England clergyman and poet. Educated at King's College, Cambridge, where he wrote most of his poetry; rector of Hilgay, Norfolk. Author of *Sicelides* (a piscatory pastoral drama), *Piscatorie Eclogs*, and *The Purple Island, or, The Isle of Man*. Walton quotes, with slight alterations, not from the *Piscatorie Eclogs* but from *The Purple Island* (1633), Canto 12, st. 3, 5, 6.

certain: unvarying.

a conversion of a piece of an old Catch: Venator has transformed a 'catch' (a round) into a song with parts in harmony. In the first four editions of *The Compleat Angler*, the treble (*cantus*) and bass (*bassus*) parts appeared on facing pages with the bass printed upside down, thus allowing two people to perform the song in harmony with the book open between them. 'The Anglers Song' appears, with both parts integrated into one piece of music, in John Playford's *Select Ayres and Dialogues* (London, 1659), 62.

136 *Hodg-poch*: hotchpotch, a confused mixture.

137 *six Verses in praise of Musick*: slightly different versions of this poem appear in John Hilton's *Catch that Catch Can* (London, 1652), A2^v, and John Playford's *Select Ayres and Dialogues* (London, 1659), 114. In Hilton, the author of the poem is identified as 'W. D.' and in Playford as 'W. D. Kn[ight]'; previous editors of Walton have suggested that 'W. D.' may be the poet and dramatist Sir William Davenant (1606–68).

Waller: Edmund Waller (1606–87), poet and politician. These verses, the wording of which Walton has altered slightly, first appeared in Waller's *Poems* (London, 1645), 135.

the tother cup: the second cup.

140 *using us*: behaving towards us.

Some say . . . red fins: *rutilus* (Latin) means red, golden red, or reddish yellow. The fins of the roach (*Rutilus rutilus*) are various shades of red; the iris of the roach's eye is also red.

Ruds: rudd (*Scardinius erythrophthalmus*), a separate species of fish, not the product of cross-breeding between roach and bream.

141 *London-bridg*: Old London Bridge, a stone structure that was demolished in the nineteenth century, was the only bridge over the Thames at London in Walton's day.

Henly-Bridg: the present stone bridge at Henley-on-Thames, Oxfordshire, replaced the old wooden one in 1786.

Manchet: the finest quality of wheaten bread.

Antflies: see note to p. 51.

142 *a handful*: a linear measure of 4 inches.

All-hallantide: Allhallowtide, the season of All Saints; All Saints' or All Hallows' Day is 1 November.

green swards: grass-covered areas.

Michaelmas: 29 September.

143 *But if you desire to keep Gentles . . . turn to be Flies*: Walton follows, with a few minor changes, Samuel's *Arte of Angling*, E$_{viii}$–E$_{viii}$^{v}.

Corn: a seed of grain.

Get a handful . . . if your hook be small and good: Walton follows Samuel, E$_{vi}$^{v}–E$_{vii}$.

Sir George Hastings to Sir Henry Wotton . . . chymical men: see notes to pp. 54 and 3.

144 *Philosophers Stone*: a mythical solid substance believed capable of changing any metal into gold or silver.

the Rosi-crucians: members of a fictitious secret society, supposedly founded by a figure named Christian Rosenkreutz who reputedly studied various forms of secret and magic knowledge.

Camphire: see note to p. 70.

float Fish: presumably fish that can be taken with a baited line supported by a float.

an old Rhime out of an old Fish-book: the source is unidentified.

Hairs green and small: fine horsehair twisted into fishing line and dyed; Walton describes this process on p. 156.

Mr. Margrave: see p. 229 for the advertisement for John Margrave's tackle shop as it appeared after Cotton's text in the 1676 edition. Nothing else is known of John Stubs.

amongst the Book-sellers: many booksellers were located in the area around St Paul's Cathedral in London.

145 *Frumity*: frumenty, a dish made of hulled wheat boiled in milk and seasoned with cinnamon, sugar, etc.

a two pence: a small silver coin (also called a half-groat) of the value of two pennies, which was about 17 mm in diameter.

King-fishers nest: the common kingfisher (*Alcedo atthis*) nests near water in a chamber at the end of a 2-foot tunnel dug into a bank; as the parent birds feed their offspring, fish-bones pile up in the nest.

146 *bents*: grass-like reeds, sedges, and other plants.

147 *Bull-head*: *Cottus gobio*. The European bullhead is not the same species called a 'bullhead' in North America.

all without scales: minnows have minute scales.

148 *sharpest*: most rapid.

Gesner: Gesner, p. 406, ll. 12–13.

by Gesner compared to the Sea-toad-fish: Gesner, p. 401, ll. 5–6. Sea-toad-fish = the European toadfish (*Batrachoides didactylus*).

149 *Matthiolus*: Pietro Andrea Mattioli (1501–77), Italian physician and botanist. Walton's source for this comment is unidentified.

150 *Doctor Heylins Geography*: Peter Heylyn (1599–1662), Church of England clergyman, polemicist, and historian. Chaplain to Charles I and canon of Westminster before the civil wars; ejected from his benefices by Parliament; subdean of Westminster at the Restoration. Heylyn's work of historical geography, *Microcosmos: A Little Description of the Great World*, first published in 1621, was very popular and went through many editions; on pp. 150–1, including the two quotations from Drayton, Walton quotes nearly verbatim from a later version of Heylyn's text (pp. 461–3 in the 1625 edition).

Thamisis: the River Thame is a tributary of the River Thames; 'Isis' is an alternative name for the River Thames used especially in Oxford. A common but false etymology interpreted a Latin form of the name of the Thames, *Tamesis*, to mean *Thame + Isis*.

150 *a German Poet*: the poet is unidentified, but Heylyn gives the Latin original of the lines as well as the English translation.

Tot Campos: Latin for 'so many fields'.

royal Tyber: the Tiber River, which flows through Rome.

151 *Trent, so called . . . thirty lesser Rivers*: 'Trent', derived from the ancient British language, may mean 'great wanderer'.

Eustorium: for Latin *aestuarium*, 'estuary'.

Dorwent: River Derwent.

the Danow . . . Tibisnus: the Danube River in Europe and its tributaries the Drava, the Sava, and the Tisza.

changeth his name into this of Humberabus: Walton misquotes Heylyn's text, which reads 'changeth his name into *Ister*: so also the *Trent* receaving and meeting the waters abovenamed, changeth his name into this of *Humber*; *Abios* the old Geographers call it' (Peter Heylyn, *Microcosmos* (Oxford, 1625), 462).

Barwick: Berwick; despite its fortifications, the town was not impregnable and frequently shifted back and forth between English and Scottish control until 1482, when it was finally surrendered to England.

Drayton: see note to p. 94. These lines, with slight changes, are from Amour 24 in Drayton's *Ideas Mirrour* (London, 1594).

Carlegion Chester . . . holy Dee: the Welsh name for Chester was *Caerlleon*, meaning 'the fortress-city of the legions'; the city is located on the River Dee.

Cotswool . . . Isis to the Tame: Cotswool = Cotswold Hills; for Isis/Tame, see note to p. 150.

Willies: the River Wylye in Wiltshire.

the old Lea brags of the Danish blood: 'In 896 the Danish fleet proceeded up the Lea as far as Hertford, when Alfred ordered the dykes of the river to be cut at a shallow part near Waltham, so that there was not sufficient water for their vessels, and the Danes had to fight their way across the country to the west of England' (William Page (ed.), *Victoria County History of Hertfordshire*, ii (London, 1908; repr. 1971), 2).

152 *dissected by Dr. Wharton . . . The Fish*: on Wharton, see note to p. 27; the specimen dissected may have been an angler fish (*Lophius piscatorius*).

Grotius: Hugo Grotius (1583–1645), Dutch jurist and scholar. Grotius's Latin tragedy, entitled *Sophompaneas, or Joseph*, was published in an English translation by Francis Goldsmith in 1652; the chorus at the end of Act 3, which Goldsmith annotated at length, describes the Nile.

Pilchers: pilchards (*Sardina pilchardus*).

Cambden . . . in his Britannia: Camden, 478, 186.

Doctor Lebault: Jean Liébault (1535–96), physician, who expanded Charles Estienne's Latin husbandry manual for a French edition, *L'Agriculture et maison rustique* (Paris, 1570). Walton uses the 1616 English edition of this treatise, *Maison Rustique, Or, The Countrey Farme*, translated by Richard Surflet and revised and augmented by Gervase Markham, pp. 505–9, as well as several passages from other authors.

153 *Fagots or Bavins*: bundles of brushwood or light underwood; faggots are bound together with two bands, bavins with only one band.

Owlers: alders.

Dubravius: see note to p. 100; the reference is to Dubravius, *A New Booke of Good Husbandry* (London, 1599), 8ʳ.

Candocks, Reate: candocks are yellow water lilies (*Nuphar lutea*); reate is water crowfoot (*Ranunculus aquatilis*).

154 *chippings*: parings of the crust of a loaf.

store: stock (with fish).

Melters . . . Spawner: male fish . . . female fish.

marle pits: marl—a mixture of clay and calcium carbonate formed in prehistoric bodies of water—was used as a fertilizer.

Dubravius and Lebault: on Dubravius, see note to p. 100. Lebault is Jean Liébault, on whom see note to p. 152.

155 *galls . . . frets*: unsound places . . . decayed spots.

156 *Allom*: alum, an astringent mineral salt used in dyeing.

small Ale: weak ale.

Mary-golds: marigolds.

Copperas: protosulphate of iron, also called 'green vitriol'.

Verdigrease: verdigris, a green or greenish blue substance, much used as a pigment, obtained by the action of dilute acetic acid on thin plates of copper or as a green rust naturally forming on copper and brass.

size: a glutinous wash that can be applied to a surface to provide a suitable ground for painting.

a Lie-colour: lye—alkalized water used as a detergent—is nearly colourless.

157 *the Stone*: kidney or bladder stones.

his preventing grace: God's provision of spiritual guidance and help in anticipation of human action or need.

eat: eaten.

158 *Solomon says*: Proverbs 10:4.

it was wisely said . . . as on this side them: a commonplace book associated with Sir Henry Wotton (see note to p. 3) contains the saying, 'Many think there are as many miseries beyond happiness, as on this side of it' (*The Life and Letters of Sir Henry Wotton*, ed. Logan Pearsall Smith, ii (1907; Oxford, 1966), 491).

158 *competency*: a sufficient means of life.

Diogenes: Diogenes Laertius (*c.*200 BC), Greek author of *The Lives, Opinions, and Sayings of Famous Philosophers*. In Diogenes' work, it is Socrates who expresses his disregard for consumer goods (*De Vitis Dogmatis et Apophthegmatis Eorum qui in Philosophia Clarverunt* (London, 1664), 39).

finnimbruns: trifles.

159 *in St. Matthews Gospel*: Matthew 5:7, 8, 3, and 5.

a man after Gods own heart: Acts 13:22.

160 *Tottenham High-Cross*: an ancient wooden cross stood on the east side of the high road in the centre of Tottenham; an octagonal brick column, erected early in the seventeenth century and Gothicized two centuries later, still marks its site.

Caussin: Nicholas Caussin (1583–1651), French Jesuit, royal confessor, and author of devotional works. Walton draws on Sir Thomas Hawkins's English translation of Caussin's *The Holy Court* (3rd edn., London, 1663), a3^r.

a grave Divine: Thomas Washbourne, Church of England clergyman, *Divine Poems* (London, 1654), 31:

> Lord, thou hast told us that there be
> Two dwellings which belong to thee,
> And those two (that's the wonder)
> Are far asunder.
>
> The one the highest heaven is,
> The mansions of eternal bliss;
> The other's the contrite
> And humble sprite.

161 *Sack*: a class of white wines formerly imported from Spain and the Canary Islands.

Nectar: in classical mythology, the drink of the gods.

when you have pledged me: to pledge is to drink to a person as a gesture of friendship.

the Verses: this poem appears in *Reliquiae Wottonianae* (London, 1651), 531–3, under the title 'A Description of the Countrey's Recreations', with the author designated as unknown. Walton edited the *Reliquiae*: see the note to p. 3.

glosing: flattering.

mummery: ridiculous ceremony.

humane: human.

162 *Mask*: masque, that is, an entertainment in which masked participants dance.

Ceres: the Roman goddess of agriculture.

163 *another very good Copy . . . some say written by Sir Harry Wotton*: Walton did not include this poem in *Reliquiae Wottonianae* (see note to p. 3); it was elsewhere ascribed to Sir Kenelm Digby.

damask'd skin: blush-coloured like a damask rose (*Rosa gallica* var. *damascena*).

164 *vie | Angels with India*: rival India for wealth. An angel was an English gold coin, bearing a figure of the Archangel Michael defeating the dragon.

St. Austin: St Augustine (354–430), Christian bishop and theologian. The passage in Augustine's autobiographical *Confessions* to which Walton refers is found in bk. 9, ch. 3.

165 *at the appointed time and place*: Venator and Piscator have agreed to meet at the shop of a London tackle vendor at two o'clock on 9 May: see p. 144.

Socrates: (*c*.470–399 BC), Greek philosopher. Walton's source for this statement is unknown.

Lillies that take no care: Matthew 6:28 and Luke 12:27.

Let every thing that hath breath praise the Lord: Psalm 150: 6.

PART II

167 *Qui mihi non credit . . . meis*: 'He who does not believe me, let him make the attempt himself, and he will be fairer to my writings.' This motto quotes part of an epigram by Erasmus that was first published in his *Adagiorum Opus* (Work of Proverbs) (Basel, 1533), verso of title page; on Erasmus, see note to p. 9.

169 *FATHER*: see p. 173.

Being: it being the case that.

digested: reduced to order.

coucht: couched, expressed in words.

a suddain new Edition: see the Note on the Text.

the Cypher: a monogram composed of Walton's and Cotton's initials. Walton, who oversaw the details of publication, had this cipher engraved for the title page of Cotton's part (see p. 167).

Berisford: Beresford Hall and its grounds stood on the west (Staffordshire) side of the River Dove in Beresford Dale, a continuation to the north of Dove Dale. Beresford Hall passed from the Beresfords early in the seventeenth century to the Stanhopes of Elvaston, whose heiress, Olive Stanhope, eloped with Cotton's father. In Cotton's time Beresford Hall was 'a three storied, stone-built, gabled house of the characteristic Elizabethan type, at right angles to which a rectangular two storied wing had apparently been added at a rather later date' (Heywood, 45); the house was demolished in 1856.

169 *167⅚*: under the Julian ('Old Style') calendar used in England until the middle of the eighteenth century, the year began on 25 March.

171 *Piscator . . . Viator*: Fisherman . . . Traveller.

Ashborn: Ashbourne, in Derbyshire (see Map 3).

Brelsford: the Derbyshire village of Brailsford is about 6 miles from Ashbourne (see Map 3).

173 *Hantshire it self, by Mr. Izaak Walton's good leave*: see p. 89.

174 *nicer*: more intimate or familiar.

when you, and he sate discoursing under the Sycamore Tree: see pp. 76, 88.

whether: whither, the place to which.

dispense with such a divertisement: allow such a diversion.

175 *Cypher*: initials intertwined to form a monogram.

the Spittle Hill: 'Spital Hill, above Ashbourne, marks the site of a hospital for the sick. . . . In the Hundred Rolls (Edw. I.) mention is made of "a Sick Hospital at the head of the town of Ashbourn, named after St John the Baptist"' (John Ward, *Pleasant Rambles Around Derby* (2nd edn., Derby, 1895), 119).

176 *the Talbot*: The Talbot, located 'in the market-place', was Ashbourne's first inn; it was demolished in 1786 (*The Complete Angler*, by Izaak Walton, ed. Sir Nicholas Harris Nicolas (London, 1875), 227n.).

the Peak: a hilly region in Derbyshire and Staffordshire, situated at the southern end of the Pennines, now known as the Peak District.

177 *Land-schape*: landscape, a prospect of country scenery.

to put forward: to press forward, advance.

so call'd from the swiftness of its current: the name 'Dove' derives from Celtic and means 'the dark river'.

Wires: weirs.

178 *not far from a place call'd Trentham*: the Trent rises near Biddulph Moor in north Staffordshire, which is about 15 miles from Trentham.

skirts and purlews: boundary and purlieus, tracts of land on the border of a forest that were formerly included within the forest boundaries and are still partly subject to the forest laws, especially those relating to the hunting or killing of game.

Forrest of Needwood: an ancient royal forest—that is, a woodland district set apart for hunting wild beasts and game, etc., with special laws and officers of its own—in Staffordshire. Cotton was the king's lieutenant of Needwood Forest.

Dunnington: Donington Park, about 2 miles from the village of Castle Donington in Leicestershire.

Wildon: Wilne, Derbyshire.

Trent derives its name: see note to p. 151. 'Trentham' is a derivative of 'Trent', meaning 'the homestead or estate on the river Trent'.

179 *Lathkin, and Bradford*: the River Lathkill and the River Bradford unite at the village of Alport and run into the Wye below Haddon Hall.

famous for a warm Bath: a thermal spring, known since Roman times, rises in the town of Buxton, Derbyshire.

Awberson: probably Alvaston.

Awber: probably a misprint for the Amber, a Derbyshire river that flows into the Derwent.

Eroways: the River Erewash.

Trouty: full of, abounding in, or containing trout. According to the *Oxford English Dictionary*, this is the first appearance of the word 'trouty'.

I have carried you, as a Man may say by water: Piscator Junior plays on the idiom 'by water', which normally refers to the navigation of a ship or boat on a sea, lake, river, etc.

180 *penthouse*: a structure with a sloping roof.

scape: escape.

lay my heeles in my neck, and tumble down: 'curl myself up and roll down the hill'.

the sign: the mere semblance.

I there trow: I suppose.

direction: instructions how to go to a place.

181 *Tom Coriate*: Thomas Coryate (1577?–1617), traveller and writer, began his career as the de facto court jester for Henry, Prince of Wales. Coryate travelled extensively—often on foot—in Europe, the Middle East, and India and published accounts of his journeys, the first of which was entitled *Coryats Crudities* (London, 1611).

come: came.

a Church: St Peter's church in Alstonefield, Staffordshire, was Cotton's parish church; it contains a pew that belonged to the Cotton family.

Stage: the distance travelled between two places of rest on a road.

Penmen-Maure: Viator thinks Hanson Toot is as terrifying as Penmaenmawr, a steep mountain on the coast of northern Wales. Because of quarrying, Penmaenmawr now stands hundreds of feet shorter than it did in the seventeenth century.

the House: Beresford Hall, Cotton's family seat; see note to p. 169.

182 *Cloth*: tablecloth.

glass of good Sack: see note to p. 161.

More-Lands: 'The northern portion of the county of Stafford forms a broad angle, of which the eastern side joins to Derbyshire, and the western to Cheshire. The greater part of it consists of a tract called the *Moorlands*, a region in general hilly, sterile, and open' (J. Aikin, *A Description of the Country from Thirty to Forty Miles Round Manchester* (London, 1795), 98).

182   *the peak*: see note to p. 176.

resolve me: answer my question.

183   *Breakfast . . . a Glass of Ale*: Piscator's consumption of some food for breakfast in Part I (see pp. 68 and 75) was more typical of seventeenth-century practice, but it was always customary to drink ale or beer at this meal.

Dinner: the main meal, eaten about the middle of the day; see p. 197.

184   *scituation*: situation, site.

bowling Green: a smooth lawn used for playing the game 'bowls', in which a ball that is biased (flattened on one side) is rolled towards a smaller stationary ball (a 'jack').

Piscatoribus sacrum: 'Dedicated to fishermen'.

Mr. Cotton's Father: as a young man, Charles Cotton the elder (*d.* 1658) was socially and culturally well connected, a friend of Walton and other such notable figures as John Fletcher, Ben Jonson, Sir Henry Wotton, John Donne, Robert Herrick, Richard Lovelace, Sir William Davenant, and Edward Hyde, first Earl of Clarendon. But in later life, Clarendon reports, the elder Cotton's financially ruinous lawsuits, marital discord, and self-indulgence 'rendered his age less reverenced than his youth had been; and gave his best friends cause to have wished that he had not lived so long' (*Life of Edward, Earl of Clarendon* (Oxford, 1857), i. 30).

185   *Seat*: residence of a country gentleman.

in his Compleat Angler: see pp. 76–7.

Steel: a piece of steel shaped for the purpose of striking sparks with a flint.

186   *By hand*: see pp. 216–17. In 1750, Moses Browne described how to angle 'By *Hand*, or with the *Running-line, viz.* with so many Shot on it as will sink it to the Bottom, and suffer the Bait to be carried with the Stream; . . . In this you use no Float, but the Bite is easily seen by the Top of the Rod, or felt from the Hand' (*The Compleat Angler*, by Izaak Walton, ed. Browne (London, 1750), p. 310).

187   *the Green Drake, and the Stone-Flie*: green drake, the sub-imago or dun (that is, the stage between the nymph and the adult) of the mayfly (*Ephemera danica* and *E. vulgata*). Cotton did not understand that a dun is a sub-adult version of a mayfly (which he believed to develop from a caddis worm), and thus he regarded the green drake as a separate species. Cotton describes the emergence of the green drake on p. 205. Stonefly is one of the species of the order Plecoptera. Cotton also refers to artificial flies made in imitation of these insects by the same names.

Chamblet-Flie: see note to p. 209.

188   *switch*: a slender tapering riding whip.

laid in: painted with.

your Master Waltons direction: see pp. 156–7.

189 *to fish fine*: delicately.

taper: tapering.

190 *open, as twisted*: the original text reads 'twisted, as open', but the context makes it clear that Cotton meant the reverse.

bent: see note to p. 146.

a Hackle: the making of a hackle fly is described on p. 78.

small silk: fine silk thread.

191 *the arm'd hook*: see note to p. 78.

warping: the wound thread which attaches the artificial fly to the hook.

Captain Henry Jackson: Henry Jackson of Stanshope, who died in 1702, is commemorated in the church in Alstonefield as a benefactor of the poor.

193 *lap on*: attach.

New-River: the New River, which begins near Ware and runs roughly parallel to the western bank of the River Lea, is an artificial river that was created in the early seventeenth century to bring water to London.

194 *a Doctor*: very skilled.

195 *strike*: i.e., by a turn of the wrist to hook a fish that has failed to hook itself.

a Grayling is a winter-fish: Cotton contradicts Walton's assessment as to when the grayling is in season: see p. 92.

196 *calver*: the mode of fish preparation designated by the term 'calver' is obscure; one writer states that a 'calver' fish 'is to be boiled in Wine, Vinegar, and all sorts of Spices' (Randle Holme, *The Academy of Armory* (London, 1688), 82).

skip-jack: a small fish that leaps out of the water.

as Dametas says: Sir Philip Sidney, *The Countesse of Pembrokes Arcadia* (London, 1590), bk. 1, p. 83; Dametas sings, 'For if my man must praises have, | What then must I that keepe the knave?'

Pike: peak. This rock still stands in the River Dove.

young Mr. Izaac Walton: Walton's only surviving son, Izaak Walton (1651–1719), who became a Church of England clergyman and died unmarried.

Landschape: see note to p. 177.

St. Pauls Church: St Paul's Cathedral, which was destroyed in the Great Fire of London in 1666.

and in France since, and at Rome, and at Venice: Izaak Walton the younger, accompanied by his uncle, Thomas Ken, toured the Continent in 1675.

197 *cobling stones*: cobblestones, rounded stones suitable for paving.

Crown: a coin of the value of five shillings. (A shilling was equal to twelve pennies or one-twentieth of a pound sterling.)

198 *my Father Walton*: see pp. 76–7.

199 *Martins fur*: marten's fur. Cotton wrote a delightful poem about his beloved pet marten, Matty, whose fur was 'soft as down' ('On My Pretty Marten', in *Poems of Charles Cotton, 1630–1687*, ed. John Beresford (New York, 1923), 107).

the whirl of an Estridg feather: whirl, see the Glossary; Estridg is an ostrich.

Browns and Duns: artificial flies that are, respectively, brown and dusky-coloured. On the latter, see the Glossary.

200 *staring out*: standing on end.

barb: clip.

twist: thread.

brended: brindled.

my Father Walton: see p. 78.

all the same Hackels, and Flies: 'Cotton's artificial flies are divided into two main categories, namely, "Flies" (that is, winged flies) and "Hackles". The former are dressed with dubbing bodies and without hackles, the dubbing at the shoulder being relied on to represent the legs; the latter palmerwise, with cock hackles and bodies either of herl or dubbing with or without gold or silver ribbing' (Heywood, 97).

the whirling Dun indeed: Heywood (p. 104) suggests this is the spinner (adult) of the *Ephemeridae* (mayflies).

201 *grey wing*: the original text mistakenly reads 'Grayling'.

the Thorn Tree Flie: Heywood (p. 113) identifies this insect as the hawthorn fly (*Bibio marci*).

Isabella: greyish yellow.

the tenth of this Month: Cotton, like Walton, uses the Old Style calendar (see note to p. 77). To change one of Cotton's dates to the New Style calendar, add ten or eleven days to it.

water-Coot: the coot (*Fulica atra*).

Skinners Lime-pits: pits in which tanners dress skins with lime to remove the hair, etc.

202 *the whirling Dun*: see note to p. 200.

Horse-flesh Flie: a horsefly (family Tabanidae).

Tammy: a fine worsted woollen cloth, often glazed.

the Green Drake . . . promis'd you so long ago: see p. 187 and note.

the Title of the May-flie: the name 'mayfly' was used broadly and inconsistently in the seventeenth century. 'Mayfly' could refer to a caddis or sedge fly (order Trichoptera), a stonefly (order Plecoptera), or any insect of the order Ephemeroptera; the term could also refer specifically to the adult of *Ephemera danica* and *Ephemera vulgata*. For a detailed discussion of the history of the word 'mayfly', see C. B. McCully, *Fly-Fishing: A Book of Words* (Manchester, 1992), 128–31.

203 *the Turky-flie*: Heywood (p. 115) suggests this is the turkey brown (*Paraleptophlebia submarginata*).

small: fine-textured.

the Cow-Lady: a ladybird beetle (family Coccinellidae).

Cow-turd flie: yellow dung fly (*Scathophaga stercoraria*).

204 *Black Flie*: Heywood (pp. 117–18) suggests this is the hawthorn fly (*Bibio marci*).

little yellow May-Flie: perhaps the yellow may dun (*Heptagenia sulphurea*).

Caddis or Cod-bait . . . turning into those two Flies: see the notes to pp. 51 and 187. Neither the stonefly nor the green drake is an adult version of a caddis worm.

205 *discloses*: hatches.

at Hull: drifting with sails furled.

whisks: slender hair-like appendages.

draw box: drawer.

cross: across.

206 *sables, or fitchet*: sable, a weasel-like mammal (*Mustela zibellina*); fitchet, the polecat (*Mustela putorius*).

Barbary Tree: barberry bush.

viss: wiss, a Scottish term for the moisture that exudes from bark as it is prepared for use in tanning.

after he was absolutely gone: i.e., after the last living fly of the species had disappeared.

Grey-Drake: the female adult (or 'spinner') of the mayfly, *Ephemera danica* and *Ephemera vulgata*. Cotton does not seem to recognize that the grey drake is the adult version of the green drake (see note to p. 187).

207 *powder'd beef*: see note to p. 75.

eat: ate.

that he is bred of a Caddis: stoneflies do not develop from caddis worms.

whisks: see note to p. 205.

Drake: mayfly (*Ephemera danica* and *Ephemera vulgata*).

208 *the green-Drake*: see note to p. 187.

stream and still: flowing and still water.

209 *the Camlet-Flie . . . with fine diapred, or water-wings*: the fly has wings that are variegated or have a wavy surface. Heywood (p. 118) identifies this insect as the alderfly (family Sialidae).

the green-Drake and Stone-Flie: see note to p. 187.

Owl-Flie: the alderfly (*Sialis lutaria*).

a white Weesel's tail: the fur of the stoat (*Mustela erminea*) turns white in the winter.

209 *Barm-flie*: 'may represent the summer appearance of the Yellow Dun. . . . On the other hand the name Barm-fly has come down to us as denoting, not a Dun, but one of the yellower tinted Phryganidæ' (Heywood, 119).

yesty: yeasty, that is, yellowish.

Flesh-flie: Heywood identifies this insect as the bluebottle (p. 119).

another little flesh-flie: 'a representative of those lesser flies of the House-fly tribe [family Muscidae]' (Heywood, 119).

the flying Ant, or Ant-flie: see note to p. 51.

little black Gnat: 'perhaps . . . a true Black Gnat, *Bibio johannis*' (C. B. McCully, *Fly-Fishing: A Book of Words* (Manchester, 1992), 85).

210 *Wasp-flie*: a hover-fly (family Syrphidae).

Jersey Wool: wool that has been combed in preparation for spinning.

Palm: see note to p. 56.

211 *Brackin*: bracken, that is, a large fern, especially *Pteridium aquilinum*.

Harry-long-leggs: a large crane-fly (a two-winged fly of the family Tipulidae).

dubbing pull'd out of the lime of a Wall: animal hair—ox, cow, or goat—was mixed into plaster to give it strength; such hair became distinctively coloured and waterproof.

sanded: of a sandy colour.

snow-broth: melted snow.

212 *the green Drake and the Stone-flie*: see note to p. 187.

impunè: unpunished.

213 *prevented*: anticipated.

215 *hard stale Beer (but it must not be dead)*: beer that is stale and thus 'hard' (acidic), but not so stale that it has become completely flat ('dead').

Gentile: genteel.

holding: tenacious, retentive.

216 *the knot*: see note to p. 113.

Carabine: carbine, a kind of firearm shorter than a musket, used by the cavalry and other troops.

handfuls: see note to p. 142.

217 *the tail of a shallow stream*: the lower end of a stream, where smooth water succeeds a swift or turbulent flow.

218 *lyes alwaies loose*: i.e., not among weeds, or in holes.

returnes: returns, i.e. bends.

Ash-Grub . . . Dock worm: beetle larvae. Dock = a coarse weedy herb of the genus *Rumex*; here, probably refers to *R. obtusifolius* (broad-leaved dock).

219 *arm the hook*: see note to p. 78.

Chaps: the jaws forming the mouth.

Oyl of Ospray: 'the oyl or fat which this bird hath in her rump, and which hanging in the air, she lets fall drop by drop into the water; by the force wherof the Fishes being stupefied, and as it were Planet-strucken, become destitute of all motion, and so suffer themselves without difficulty to be taken; though some are so vain as to put Oyl of *Osprey* into their receipts or prescriptions for taking Fishes, by the smell whereof the Fishes being allured, . . . yield themselves to be handled and taken out of the water by such as have their hands anointed with it' (John Ray, *The Ornithology of Francis Willughby* (London, 1678), 61).

Camphire: see note to p. 70.

220 *artificially*: ingeniously.

those baits he keeps in salt: see p. 71.

his artificial one: see p. 71.

221 *his way of throwing in his Rod*: see p. 87.

222 *Chaps*: see note to p. 219.

one handful: see note to p. 142.

223 *a part of your Margin*: the marginal notes on pp. 184 and 196 are by Walton.

225 *intend*: pay attention to.

226 *Mause*: the River Meuse.

Tame and Isis, when conjoyn'd: see note to p. 150.

227 *my beloved Caves*: Cotton reputedly would hide from his creditors in a cave on the grounds of Beresford Hall.

dog-stars heat: Sirius, in the constellation of the Greater Dog, was believed to cause excessive heat when it rose just before sunrise.

disgrace: disparage.

Try, to live out to sixty full years old: Cotton died a couple of months short of his fifty-seventh birthday.

GLOSSARY OF ANGLING TERMS

WALTON and Cotton used typical seventeenth-century English fishing tackle. Their rods—each of which could be disassembled into six or more separate pieces—would have been 15 to 18 feet long. A line about 20 feet long was attached to the tip of each rod: the line was made from lengths of twisted horsehair knotted together every 2 feet or so, and it gradually tapered from a thickness of up to forty hairs at the rod's tip to just one or two hairs next to the hook; as Walton mentions on p. 113, silk or a mixture of silk and horsehair might also be used to fashion the line. The line could be dyed to camouflage it according to different conditions. Floats were made from cork or the quills of the feathers of swans and geese. Although the reel had been invented, neither Walton nor Cotton used one. For more information about seventeenth-century English angling practices, see the sources in the Select Bibliography.[1]

angle a fish hook

arming, arming-wire the link of wire or horsehair that was attached to a hook so that it could in turn be attached to the line

bear's dun the dull brown fur of a bear, used in making artificial flies

beard the barb of a fish hook

camlet the pile of velvet,[2] used in making artificial flies

cork a piece of cork used as a float for a fishing line

dab, dape, dibble, dop to fish by letting the bait dip and bob lightly on the water

drag-hook a hook used for dragging

dubbing the materials used in the dressing of an artificial fly

dun 1) a dusky-coloured artificial fly that imitates the almost-adult (sub-imago) stage of the life cycle of upwinged flies (Ephemeroptera); 2) the grey-brown colour of these insects

float, flote the cork or quill used to support a baited line

ground-bait 1) a bait thrown to the bottom of the water in which it is intended to fish, in order to lure the fish thither; 2) a bait used in bottom-fishing

hackle an artificial fly, dressed wholly or principally with hackle feathers (that is, the long shining feathers from the neck of certain domestic fowl)

---

[1] I wish to thank Andrew Herd for his helpful suggestions about the material in this Glossary.

[2] Andrew Herd, *The History of Fly Fishing*, i (Ellesmere, 2011), 429 n. 25.

hair horsehair

herl *see* whirl

lead weight made from lead used to sink a fishing line in the water

link one of the segments of a horsehair fishing line

link-hook the link that holds the hook

palmer an artificial fly covered with bristling hairs or fibres, esp. from a hackle wound in an open spiral along the length of the shank, intended to represent fuzzy caterpillars

pater-noster line a fishing line with a weight at the end, to which hooks are attached at intervals

plum, plummet a weight attached to a fishing line

quick fly a living insect attached to a hook and used as a lure

quill a narrow tubular float made from the quill of a feather

running line a line not tied to the top of the rod but instead passing to the butt through a ring at the tip

top the terminal section of a fishing rod

towght a link, that is, one section of a horsehair fishing line

warp to fasten the materials of an artificial fly onto the hook

whirl also **herl**, a barb or fibre of the shaft of a tail feather of an ostrich or peacock used in making artificial flies

American Literature

British and Irish Literature

Children's Literature

Classics and Ancient Literature

Colonial Literature

Eastern Literature

European Literature

Gothic Literature

History

Medieval Literature

Oxford English Drama

Philosophy

Poetry

Politics

Religion

The Oxford Shakespeare

A complete list of Oxford World's Classics, including Authors in Context, Oxford English Drama, and the Oxford Shakespeare, is available in the UK from the Marketing Services Department, Oxford University Press, Great Clarendon Street, Oxford OX2 6DP, or visit the website at www.oup.com/uk/worldsclassics.

In the USA, visit www.oup.com/us/owc for a complete title list.

Oxford World's Classics are available from all good bookshops. In case of difficulty, customers in the UK should contact Oxford University Press Bookshop, 116 High Street, Oxford OX1 4BR.

	An Anthology of Elizabethan Prose Fiction
	Early Modern Women's Writing
	Three Early Modern Utopias (Utopia; New Atlantis; The Isle of Pines)
FRANCIS BACON	**Essays**
	The Major Works
APHRA BEHN	**Oroonoko and Other Writings**
	The Rover and Other Plays
JOHN BUNYAN	**Grace Abounding**
	The Pilgrim's Progress
JOHN DONNE	**The Major Works**
	Selected Poetry
JOHN FOXE	**Book of Martyrs**
BEN JONSON	**The Alchemist and Other Plays**
	The Devil is an Ass and Other Plays
	Five Plays
JOHN MILTON	**The Major Works**
	Paradise Lost
	Selected Poetry
EARL OF ROCHESTER	**Selected Poems**
SIR PHILIP SIDNEY	**The Old Arcadia**
	The Major Works
SIR PHILIP and MARY SIDNEY	**The Sidney Psalter**
IZAAK WALTON	**The Compleat Angler**

NICCOLÒ MACHIAVELLI	**The Prince**
THOMAS MALTHUS	**An Essay on the Principle of Population**
KARL MARX	**Capital** **The Communist Manifesto**
J. S. MILL	**On Liberty and Other Essays** **Principles of Political Economy and** **Chapters on Socialism**
FRIEDRICH NIETZSCHE	**Beyond Good and Evil** **The Birth of Tragedy** **On the Genealogy of Morals** **Thus Spoke Zarathustra** **Twilight of the Idols**
THOMAS PAINE	**Rights of Man, Common Sense, and** **Other Political Writings**
JEAN-JACQUES ROUSSEAU	**The Social Contract** **Discourse on the Origin of Inequality**
ARTHUR SCHOPENHAUER	**The Two Fundamental Problems of** **Ethics**
ADAM SMITH	**An Inquiry into the Nature and Causes** **of the Wealth of Nations**
MARY WOLLSTONECRAFT	**A Vindication of the Rights of Woman**